Harriet Hudson was born in Kent. After taking a degree in English literature, she was director of a London publishing company and is now a freelance editor and writer. She is married to an American, and they live in a Kentish village on the North Downs. She is the author of *Look for me by Moonlight* and *When Nightingales Sang* and also writes crime novels under her real name, Amy Myers.

# The Sun in Glory

Harriet Hudson

KNIGHT

First published in 1991
by HEADLINE BOOK PUBLISHING PLC

First published in paperback in 1992
by HEADLINE BOOK PUBLISHING PLC

This edition published 1997 by
Knight an imprint of Brockhampton Press

10 9 8 7 6 5 4 3 2 1

ISBN 1 86019 6349

Typeset by St George Typesetting, Redruth, Cornwall

Printed and bound in Great Britain by
Mackays of Chatham PLC, Chatham, Kent

Brockhampton Press
20 Bloomsbury Street
London
WC1B 3QA

For Sally
with love

# Acknowledgements

I owe a great debt to two 'magnificent men' in the world of flying machines, the aviation historians Norman L.R. Franks and Chaz Bowyer. The latter generously let me loose with his archive on pre-World-War-I aviation, and the former read and criticised my text; any errors that might still lurk within it would have crept in during amendments made at later stages in my efforts to meet his points.

To my agent, Dot Lumley, and editor, Jane Morpeth, I owe much as it was only with their unstinted and sensitive help that the project was wheeled on to the airfield, let alone got airborne. My thanks also to my mother for her help on costume, and to Martin French, Carol Tyler and Henry Green.

Among the more recent publications I consulted are *British Aviation: The Pioneer Years* by Harald Penrose (Putman, 1967), *The Flying Cathedral* by Arthur Gould Lee (Methuen, 1965), *The Invention of the Aeroplane* by Charles Gibbs Smith (Faber, 1966), *The Water Closet* by Roy Palmer (David & Charles, 1973), *Edwardian Inventions* by Rodney Dale and Joan Grey (Star Books, 1979) and articles by Arthur H. Joyce, Philip Banbury and David G. Collyer in the magazine *Bygone Kent* (Meresborough Books). No amount of reading, however, can substitute for gazing at the machines themselves, still to be seen in museums such as the Shuttleworth Collection, and the Power-House Museum, Sydney.

Finally, I should make it clear that the story of this novel is fictitious and credit for the first British person to fly, after Colonel Cody, should go to J.T.C. Moore-Brabazon (later Lord Brabazon of Tara) and for the first British woman to gain her pilot's certificate, to Mrs Maurice Hewlett in August 1911.

# Prologue

William Potts eyed with distaste the accumulated cigar butts on the floor of the first-class compartment of the London, Chatham and Dover railway. Surely there was a way to combat man's less attractive characteristics? His fertile mind began to dream . . .

'It wouldn't work, William,' said his wife calmly, following his train of thought with the ease of long experience.

He presented a face of bland inquiry towards her, to hide his guilt. Had he not promised to devote more time to the factory, and less to his workshop, or 'shed' as Mildred persisted in calling it?

'But if the spittoon had a hole at the bottom covered with a lid, and a light spring which was connected by a rod to a button, so that with the touch of a finger it might empty itself on to the permanent way, surely—'

The words ceased abruptly as the carriage lurched screeching into the air, and William was flung across the carriage, amid tumbling luggage, on top of his wife. A moment's eerie silence then, replacing the hiss of steam and steady rhythm of the wheels, there came shrieking and noise of breaking glass, indistinct cries for help. A last puff of steam drifted by the crazily angled window, and still the screaming, children's cries of terror. With a lurch of fear, as his senses reasserted themselves, William saw a black leg-of-mutton sleeve splayed out and realised that his wife must be pinioned beneath him by splintered wood, fallen luggage and the rack itself which had been dislodged and was lying under him.

'Mildred,' he said sharply, at the same time trying to ease himself from the debris without further harm to her. The

1

second that it took her to answer was frightening, never-ending. Then her voice, comforting, strong, reassuring: 'I'm all right, William.'

'Don't move. Not till I tell you.' Time to take stock of the situation. Thank God Pollykins hadn't been with them. He cautiously flexed all his muscles; he was all right. Speedily now, he tore the debris from his wife with one hand, clinging to the door jamb with the other, helping her into a sitting position. Her blouse, where her coat had ripped open, was splashed with blood and she was still dazed. Then he realised the blood was coming from himself not her, and his panic subsided. Without wasting effort on more words he wedged her into a corner of the seat, her feet suspended in space, and wiped the blood from the cut on his chin caused by the shattered glass of a gas lamp.

'Are you *sure* you're not hurt?' he asked anxiously.

'No, but—'

'Then stay there, my love, while I see what's happening.' Taking off his frock coat he manoeuvred himself nimbly, despite his middle-aged girth, through the door now hanging off at an angle, and down on to the embankment by the side of the permanent way.

His plump face paled at what he saw ahead where the third-class carriages had been. Now they were only a tangled heap of wood, metal and glass spilling down the steep embankment. Only five minutes earlier he had seen crowds of laughing, swearing, singing hoppers clambering into the railway train at Sittingbourne Station to return to the East End after their six-week holiday, surrounded by pots, pans, children, perambulators and battered boxes. Now those same belongings lay spilled like their owners over the green grass: a bright red skirt, a child's windmill still turning in the breeze, caught in a wheel spoke. And the hoppers themselves were silenced into mangled flesh and blood.

Bewildered, shocked groups of survivors huddled silently together or numbly clawed at unrelenting metal, tearing at wreckage. Overhead the telegraph wires chattered their message of disaster; porters and

2

guards from Newington Station were already running up to help with rescue.

'What can I do?' Potts hurled at the train's guard. With glazed eyes, the guard shook his head impotently. What could anyone do? Impatiently, Potts took charge himself, seizing the guard's whistle and blowing it hard. 'Here,' he yelled. 'You, you, you,' he commanded in his factory-floor tones.

Glad of the easing of responsibility, men pulled themselves together to form groups, and Potts set off down the embankment, detailing some men to shore up wreckage so that no further damage might occur to the injured, others to search for survivors still buried. The front carriage was the worst hit, a mass of twisted wreckage. William Potts took a look inside what had been one compartment and retched. An arm flung out from the bottom of the pile of jagged wood, metal and heavy luggage, no longer attached to a body; a man, dead, hung draped over the heap, pierced through by a deadly sliver of wood from the roof, his shabby boots at a sharp angle to his body. A baby lay dead outside, thrown clean through what had been the window.

'Nothing to do here,' said the guard hurriedly, choking. 'Nothing could survive that lot. Better move on, there's more we can do at the back.'

'There's a movement,' William said sharply. But the guard, galvanised now with the urgency of the situation, was already moving on.

William couldn't help, he'd only make things worse. But he was sure, almost sure, that slowly, incredibly, the heap was moving. Wriggling, burrowing, a pair of bootless feet emerged soles upwards, scratched and bleeding, then a tiny bottom hunched in the air, then the remains of a grimy torn yellow frock.

'William, come—' Mildred Potts, in defiance of orders, her black-braided coat torn and muddy, had come to assist her husband, and wondered at his still absorption. She followed his gaze to what appeared to be a bundle of rags in the midst of horrific carnage. Then she saw the

3

bundle was moving. It clambered to its feet and glared at them out of dark, angry, lost eyes.

'I'm Rosie,' it said defiantly. 'I want to go home.'

# Chapter One

*Where had it all begun, the quest, the passion? Sometimes it seemed it had been born in her, yet she knew this could not have been so. It had played no part in that other life, the life that had changed so radically when she was six years old, a life of dirt and laughter, of hunger, and close family togetherness, of two dim figures she knew must have been her parents, and other smaller figures further off in that distant landscape. So if not then, when had it begun?*

*Not the day William and Mildred Potts had taken her into their home, nor for some time after as, pitchforked into a new world, she wept inside for the old.*

*Where had it all begun? It had exploded into being on a hillside, long before the twentieth century had dawned with its radiant promise, long before the shadows of war had crossed the serene and confident Edwardian skies, long before he had come . . .*

'You help me hold the string now, Rosie,' said William kindly.

High, high in the sky. It was a bird, like the bird she'd seen on the privy roof at the dark place one day and tried to capture, only it flew away, right up into the sky where she couldn't reach it. This one couldn't fly away. It had a long cord, held firmly by that man – any time he wanted he could pull the bird back to earth. She'd like to be a bird flying away for ever. High, high – what was up there, behind those clouds? Was it her Ma and Pa just like Polly said? No, she wasn't going to think of them, just like she hadn't since it happened. They were waiting for her – at home perhaps. What was home? She didn't quite know, but she had heard Uncle William and Auntie Mildred talking about how much she was missing home, so she knew it was important. Surely home could not be in that dark place she couldn't remember very clearly, but which filled her with a strange fear when she thought of it?

'Run, Rosie, let's run.'

'Shan't.' She stood mutinously, trying to pull away while William insisted, enclosing her tiny hand in his large one. The cord was pulling at her, hurting. She hated it.

William sighed as he pulled the kite in. It had been nearly six months now since Rosie had come to live with them in the October of 1893, and they were near to giving up. It seemed a good idea at first, company for their little Pollykins who was clearly going to be an only child, and who, at six, was exactly Rosie's own age, since both had been born in July. But they had lived to rue the day.

The Fisherbutts, shaken for the first time from their usual placid tolerance of the eccentricities of life at Brynbourne Place, had given notice twice. Horrified, William had appealed man-to-man to Horace Fisherbutt, who had reluctantly agreed to speak to the missis. Mrs Maud Fisherbutt, housekeeper and head cook, had twice been persuaded to change her mind. But on the second occasion a firm probationary period had been set. Yet Rosie still refused to obey anybody, wet the bed nearly every night and despite all Mildred's efforts refused to speak to anybody save Polly. Her rough accent made it difficult even for Polly to understand sometimes. She had never seen a bath, daily washing was a strange and unwelcome idea and she had little idea of the purpose of a Potts Pedestal Water Closet. Once she had got over her initial awe, she'd been the very devil, William gloomily reflected. She'd run away twice. Goodness knows where she thought she was going. Home, she said. Anyone would think they ill-treated her, William thought irritably. They'd tracked her down once at Manning's hop farm, and once at the carrier's in Bredhill trying to stow away in the hope of reaching London. Never at a railway station, he noticed. How to explain to a six-year-old that there was no home

6

to run away to? They'd discussed finding an orphanage for her, but without enthusiasm. William Potts believed in going on, not back. Yet Rosie was upsetting the whole household. Mildred was at her wits' end. Polly, an enigma to William at the best of times, now flatly refused to accompany him on kite-flying days, preferring as usual to play with her painting box. She took after her mother, and Mildred took her side. Suddenly every woman in his life seemed bent on defying him. Especially this one.

'Try again, Rosie,' said William, with sudden resolution, grasping her hand again, and firmly putting the string in it. 'Make it go up. *Run*!'

Whether it was the sudden sharpness in his voice, or the urge to feel the turf under her feet, or the feel of the kite cord in her hand, but, casting one scared look behind her, Rosie obeyed, running, running, spinning out the cord, feeling the wind grasp it and take it for its own, spinning round to look at it. There it was now, fluttering, dancing, and she had done it; she was part of it.

'That's right, now play out the string,' came William's encouraging shout.

But she didn't hear him. It was alive, this magic thing of wood and paper, and wanting to be free, free. The breeze was pulling and the kite dived and rose again; she looked up to see it soaring and sweeping, making faces down at her, calling to her. 'Come up, Rosie,' it was saying, 'come up here. It's so easy.'

She stood on tiptoe, stretched her arms as high as she could. It wanted to go higher, it must go higher . . .

'Up,' she shouted, perhaps to the kite, perhaps to William, perhaps to herself. 'Up, up, up.' She jumped up and down in her excitement, her brown curls bobbing, and the kite dancing and jerking on the end of the cord.

William panted up to her.

'I want to be with it,' she shouted at him, her eyes bright. 'Oh, I want to go up with it. Come on, let's fly—'

At the very end of its cord now, the kite weaved and danced, then suddenly, caught by an air current, spiralled and fell to earth.

Rosie screamed, and buried her head in Potts's

waistcoat. He felt her thin body heaving, the dampness of her tears. 'There,' he said, understanding. 'Let's pick it up together. Poor kite.'

'Don't want to.' That thing on the ground, so still, so dead, was that the magic that had soared above?

But William pulled her after him, picked up the kite and placed it once more in her unwilling hands. When she threw it from her, he replaced it. 'Fly it,' he ordered sternly. Unwillingly, disbelievingly, Rosie obeyed. The kite failed to rise twice, then on the third time hesitantly it lifted in the breeze, almost fell, then caught the current again, soaring triumphantly upwards.

A happy smile crossed Rosie's face. 'I want to go too,' she announced, jumping up and down. 'Why can't I?'

William shook his head and laughed. 'Man has been trying to fly for centuries, Rosie, and very soon he'll do it. But not quite yet.' There'd been so many attempts, so many broken dreams, but one day . . .

'Want to. I want to go higher and higher and higher and higher.'

'Man mustn't go too high, Rosie. He'll end up like Icarus,' said Potts absently. He was thinking about kites. If one added several together to share the load, with a tail of course for directional stability . . .

'What's Icarus?' Rosie inquired with interest.

'He was a young man in an old story who wanted to escape from an island. His father built wings for them both and flew upwards and escaped. But Icarus flew too near the sun and the wax that held the wings together melted, and down he came, just like your kite.'

Rosie thought this over. 'But my kite went up again,' she pointed out.

'So it did, Rosie, so it did,' he said kindly. Perhaps these kites, if big enough, could carry a load, perhaps even a man . . .

Brynbourne Place stood proudly on the top of the North Kentish downs looking towards Sittingbourne and the Swale in the distance. An old mediaeval hall-house, it had been added to haphazardly over the generations, until it was firmly taken in hand by the Georgians and encased into well-proportioned, red-brick elegance. Shielded by its guardian oaks and with exceptionally large grounds and farmland, it had remained in the hands of one family for generations. When the last of the family, an old lady, died in 1890, the house was found to have been unaltered in a hundred years.

It was promptly acquired by William Potts, to the great perturbation of local society who regarded the industrialist and his wife as vulgar by definition. They were ambitious traders, bringing the unwelcome tang of commerce into the midst of their civilised circle – this without having met them. There was anxious consultation as to whether or not the Potts should be called upon. It was unanimously decided in the end, not. There was, by their standards, a large element of truth in their judgements. What confounded them was the Potts appeared not only not to mind one jot, but not even to notice they were being ostracised. If the artistocracy, and in particular the Bellowes of neighbouring Court Manor, did not call, there were plenty of people in the village of Bredhill for Mrs Potts to befriend, and William Potts, living in a dream world of his own, did not care one way or the other. He spent much of his time at the Sittingbourne factory of Potts Pedestal Water Closets and most of the rest in his workshop at Brynbourne, erected behind the stables, and when the noise grew too great, in a barn further afield.

Potts Pedestal WCs had originally been simply Potts Plumbing, started by William's father in a modest way to take advantage of the growing public awareness after the Chadwick Report on the Sanitary Conditions of the Labouring Classes, and became firmly established after the 1875 Act making sanitary facilities obligatory in all new houses.

Algernon Potts had branched into valve closets, calling his model the Rose after the old custom of going into the garden 'to pluck a rose', and then into fulfilling a steady market with the cheap Hopper Closet for servants. However, it had taken young William, as he was known in the firm although he was already nearly thirty, and impatient with the limiting demands of the life to which he was consigned, to pioneer the new wash-out closet in the late 'seventies. By 1890, the year his father died, Potts Ltd had soared into untold realms of success with over 100,000 sold of the Potts Albion Closet. Having then acquired Brynbourne, his quick mind remained at work, and in the following year the Potts Marigold Pedestal Closet had stormed into being. Wash-down closets with the flush directly aimed at the water in the basin were clearly the path to the future. Business boomed. Thus in 1894 William Potts found himself with more money than he knew what to do with, but a sense that life held more for him than bigger and better water closets. They were necessary, they could even be beautiful, but, frustrated, he knew he had more to offer mankind.

Having driven his staff half mad with persistent inventions, an effective ball valve to replace the Croyden vertical, a low-level cistern to increase pressure on the discharge, and by campaigning for the repeal of the Act limiting the flush to two gallons, finally baulked of inspiration he invented a seat that played 'The Lost Chord' when sat upon. Mildred, like her monarch, had not been amused and the offending article had been consigned to the Fisherbutts' quarters and then vanished completely. He then dabbled in his workshop, deflected to new fields of endeavour.

'Why can't someone invent expanding waistcoat buttons?' he muttered after a particularly important and lavish luncheon. He promptly did so, and from there he went on to invent a dozen ideas for the easing of life's little problems. But this too he found dissatisfying after a while.

'It's all very well, Mildred, but I still can't help feeling I'm not contributing to life,' he pointed out.

Mildred was contributing quite sufficiently to life herself at the time, by running the new household, Mr Potts and the then four-year-old Polly, and had grown to rely on the times William spent in the shed for the organisation of the domestic affairs.

'Then invent something to help others, William,' she suggested practically.

She was to rue the day. Fired with missionary zeal, William Potts studied the needs of others with anxious, loving concern. Spying the sufferings of a mouse caught in a trap, he promptly invented a non-harmful mousetrap, whereby the mouse would step on a seesaw which would precipitate it into a closed box beneath.

Seeing old Jobbins working with increasingly arthritic joints in the gardens, and too kindhearted to turn him away, he invented a weeding tool that required no bending. But it was Albert Cobham the postman who paved the path to the future. He had been far from well, and seeing him puffing up the slight incline of their drive one day, William set his prodigious mind to thinking. Mildred saw little of him, but heard much of the sound of saws and drills from the shed, until one day she spied William seated precariously upon a strange velocipede riding in triumph up their drive.

'Why,' he asked Mildred rhetorically, resting a hand on the governess cart in which she sat ready to set off for the village, 'do I have to push to cycle forward, and harder going up an incline? It's because of the resistance,' he answered himself, 'resistance from the air in front.'

'If,' he continued eagerly, 'we multiply the surface presented to the wind by the square of the speed and multiply that by the coefficient we then have the measure of the resistance. Now if I pedalled twice as hard, the resistance is quadrupled, and if three times the speed nine times greater. But what if I use this resistance to help me go forward, eh?' He waved a lordly hand.

Mildred Potts regarded the contraption in silence. The bicycle was flanked on each side by what appeared to be two thin, angled wooden planks, a foot apart, rounded at the ends and braced together for support each with a wire attached to the handlebars for control.

'You see,' he said confidently, 'it will catch the wind as I angle each one. Watch.'

It did indeed catch the wind. He bowled off down the drive, followed by an apprehensive Mildred in the governess cart; as he yanked on the wire, the wooden wings caught the wind and bowled him along in fine style,

11

finally depositing him with great loss of dignity into old Jobbins's mulch placed ready to assist the rhododendrons. Not a whit dismayed he climbed out, brushed a hand absentmindedly over the sticky mess on his trousers, and admired his invention.

'You see?' he said. 'It works.'

'I doubt whether Mr Cobham will be so impressed,' commented Mildred drily.

'All inventions grow from little ideas,' said William, hurt. And he remounted and bowled back to the shed with some difficulty, going in the opposite direction, to resume thought.

It had been at this point that Rosie had erupted into their lives.

'Uncle William, there's no wind today,' Rosie cried, staring out of the huge bay window of Brynbourne's drawing room, willing the breeze to stir the leaves of the huge oaks. Today was the experiment with the big kite that would lift Papa up in the air to go sailing with the birds. Papa? It had come quite naturally to her thoughts. Papa, like Polly called him.

'We'll make our own wind,' William replied confidently, putting his finger to his lips conspiratorially. Mildred knew nothing of today's adventure. Intent on his own concerns, he overlooked the fact that Rosie should be in the schoolroom with Polly, and Rosie had no intention of reminding him. A figure of awe though Auntie Mildred was, the temptations of kites outweighed all such considerations – even if it led to yet another stormy clash of wills.

Soon William, Rosie, Harris the coachman and Mr Fisherbutt were assembled round the thirty-foot kite. Mr Fisherbutt, a man of fifty, as long and lean as his wife was short and plump, wore his habitual long-suffering look, which he had less opportunity to practise, as he spent more and more time in the workshop and less and less at Mrs Fisherbutt's beck and call. He remained half fearful, half fascinated by the Master's odd ways, developing decidedly firm views of his own on scientific progress, and the sounds of altercation could often be heard emanating from the workshop.

Potts had an instinct he was barking up the wrong tree with this hexagonal approach in this all-important kite, but he was too much the novice to take great risk at this stage and Major Baden-Powell who had lifted himself off the ground in January had championed hexagonal kites, he'd heard.

Rosie danced round the winch while Harris and Mr Fisherbutt sent one kite after another up the cable in their allotted positions. Harris held the control wires as Potts clambered into the precarious basket seat, surrounded by his own controls. He checked the wind speed on his anemometer.

'Go, go,' shouted Rosie, dancing perilously near the kite and having to be restrained by Mr Fisherbutt.

William signalled. The kites billowed above him, straining on their cable, but William did not budge from the ground.

'What,' said a stentorian voice, 'do you think you are doing?' Mildred had arrived unexpectedly and unnoticed and far from pleased.

'An experiment, my dear,' said William happily. 'Another try, if you please, Mr Fisherbutt.'

'Stand away, Mr Fisherbutt,' said Mildred grimly. 'That's enough of this nonsense. Do you want to break your neck, William?'

'I could go up,' interjected Rosie hopefully. 'Papa's too heavy. I'm light enough.'

'That you will not, young lady,' said Mildred, rounding on her. 'You're supposed to be at your lessons and you're coming with me. Now.'

Miss the kite? Miss the great moment when this beautiful dancing contraption would rise in the air and take Papa with it? Her eyes were horrorstricken.

'I won't, I won't,' she shouted more in terror than temper. 'I want to fly with Papa.'

'Flying's not for little girls,' said Mildred, trying to keep her voice reasonable. 'Come along now.' She laid her hand on Rosie's arm.

13

Seeing her as the enemy now, Rosie screamed, and screamed again. 'I'll go home. This isn't home. I hate lessons. My ma and pa'll take me home.'

'Rosie!' Papa's voice made her suddenly quiet. 'This is your home now. Do you understand?'

Rosie blinked through tears. Home? With Auntie Mildred, so unlike her ma with her hugs and thumps. This wasn't home any more than was the dark place. But it *was* where kites were – and that was where she wanted to be for the moment. She nodded doubtfully.

'I won't fly any more today,' said William reassuringly, as Mildred took Rosie's hand to take her back to Brynbourne.

'I'm not surprised,' said Mildred scathingly. 'Talk about "Down will come baby, cradle and—" '

'That's it,' cried William suddenly, dancing up and down with excitement. 'My love, you have given me the answer,' he announced grandly. 'Of course it won't lift me, with the basket slung between *two* cables. No stability. A *single* cable is what we want. And steeper dihedral – the angle's wrong! My love, pray accompany us to the workshop. Forward, Mr Fisherbutt, if you please!'

'I have no doubt you are right, William,' said Mildred composedly, 'but I have walked far enough. It would not be good for the baby.'

'But—' William stopped and stared at her.

'Yes, William, early next year.'

'By heaven,' he roared, enfolding her in his arms. 'Another Potts invention. We shall launch the new kite on his birth. We will make a start to— morrow,' he hastily amended, seeing the look on Mildred's face.

A pink frock. How she hated this frock, with its high neck and smocked front, with the dark woollen stockings, and the hat crammed on to her rebellious brown curls and kept there by a ribbon under the chin.

'Look at Polly,' Mildred said in despair. 'She knows how to be a little lady.'

Rosie enviously eyed Polly in her neat primrose-coloured dress. She wanted to be a little lady too but somehow there

14

was never time. There were more interesting things to do. Especially in Papa's workshop. But for all that the day was a glory. The day when Rosie became seven years old, and Mildred had for once relented in her efforts to keep Rosie's mind off aeroplanes. It was the day she saw man fly.

31st July 1894 started badly, with that frock, and Polly refusing to come at the last minute and Auntie Mildred sympathising with her. It got worse on the long ride in the railway train to Bexley, during which Rosie was sick over Mildred's new spotted lawn dress. Only the inducement that something very special in the way of kites lay at the end of the journey had made Rosie climb on board that puffing monster of death. She shut her eyes tight, hoping that once she opened them the railway train ride would be over, just like a magic carpet in *The Arabian Nights* that Mildred read to them on special occasions.

But once they were there: 'Where are the kites?' she cried, disappointed, looking round the huge Baldwyn's Park. None to be seen, only a funny set of railway lines going into the distance. They were raised a little off the ground and encompassed by a taller, higher set of rails.

'There's your kite, Rosie,' William pointed.

Disgusted, Rosie had been gazing at the rails. Now she looked up and along them. There was the biggest, strangest kite she'd ever seen, so big she'd missed it. It was towering in the air, a huge big kite on wheels behind something like a tractor engine.

'It's a flying machine, Rosie.'

She clutched William's hand in excitement. 'Like our kite?'

'Just like it, only bigger, much bigger, and it doesn't need a cable. One day soon it will fly just like a bird.'

'Like Icarus?'

'Just like Icarus. Only this machine will stay up as long as it likes. It will have its own little engine like a horseless carriage. Not today, but soon. Today it's just going to fly along the rails.'

Mr Hiram Maxim's flying machine. He was a manufacturer too, of guns, and this was his hobby. William had met him at a meeting of the Aeronautical

Society which he'd joined unknown to Mildred. He had a feeling Mildred would not approve. Kites were one thing, flying machines another. Yet all over Kent, pioneers were beginning to think of powered flight. They'd had near misses. Cayley had been the first, fifty years ago, then Henson, Stringfellow and a score more. Lighter-than-air flight had been mastered with airships and balloons. But heavier-than-air flight remained still unconquered. He'd gone as a boy in 1868 to the Crystal Palace to see the Exhibition of Machinery connected with Aeronautics, and there his interest in kites had been kindled, to remain dormant till Rosie came.

At the exhibition they had offered £100 for an aeroplane capable of lifting a man to 120 feet. No one had won it. Engines were the problem for powered heavier-than-air flight, for steam engines were too heavy. Since then William had kept a vague eye on what was happening in the aeronautics world. He'd heard with interest about Kaufmann's machine with its flapping propeller; heard about Thomas Penn who had set up a wind tunnel for measuring pressure at speed. Many attempts, but no breakthrough. Then the first flush of enthusiasm vanished, and membership of the society was down to forty now, but they were all keen; he remembered a project for using jet propulsion for aeronautical purposes in the 'eighties. Came to nothing, but interesting. Now Maxim was really on to something at last.

Those big wings made it look like a great big seagull, thought Rosie, ready to flap towards them. It looked like Auntie Mildred's new dress, with its huge, huge sleeves bulging out on either side. Perhaps Auntie Mildred too would fly. Fly away and not come back . . . An uneasy feeling grew inside her. The big bird thing even had a sort of beak, was it going to fly right over their heads? Then huge windmills began to turn, there was a hissing of steam and people beginning to shout. Suppose it wasn't a flying machine? Her terror grew. Suppose it was a railway train roaring towards them. It would crash, *crash*! Now men were shouting far behind the machine, marking something on a large board, then the noise increased, and the bird

16

was running towards them, the wind in its wings, like a huge bird of prey. It *was* a railway engine. She screamed, shutting her eyes as the monster roared past them, hiding her face against the nearest object, which was Mildred's skirt. Then she opened them cautiously to see everyone running after the monster. Suddenly brave, she joined them, following the thing with its huge wings roaring along the track. No – yes, it really *was* a seagull . . .

'Mildred, look, *air*!' William cried.

Something had happened to the big bird, the upper track it was running along had broken, and Rosie could see air under the machine. It wasn't on the track any more, it was a bird flying to its nest – flying. But the steam subsided, and the machine sank down, heavily, a wounded bird, on to the ground, with splintering and crashing of wood.

'Don't cry, Rosie,' said William, surprised she did not share his joy. 'It lifted. You saw it, didn't you? It lifted itself into the air. Now we *know* it's possible.'

Polly had refused point-blank to go to Baldwyn's Park, arguing that Rosie had not been forced to go to Polly's birthday treat two weeks earlier – a visit to the National Gallery. Polly was a dreamer. She'd welcomed Rosie's arrival into the household, for everyone was so occupied with her, they didn't have time to wonder what Polly was doing. As soon as lessons were finished she would collect her paintbox and pad and disappear into the gardens, wandering all over the estate and into the adjoining fields. She had her own hideaways, some quite near the house where no one would find her, especially Rosie. She liked Rosie but she did have a way of storming into her solitariness and disturbing her concentration that was very irritating. Mama understood, and never bothered her, but she was a little frightened of Papa – scared of the way he would scoop her up and say heartily, 'Now, little Polly, why don't we go and fly a kite?' She didn't want to fly kites – they were a waste of time. She wanted to paint. Nothing, but nothing, was going to stop her.

17

The winter of 1894/5 was long and hard, with piercing never-ending cold, and snow. They huddled round the fires at Brynbourne Place, and the fisher merchants brought tales of how the sea itself had frozen over. Mildred Potts bore her second pregnancy stoically. Patience was a virtue of hers much exercised after her marriage to William, but even her resolute spirit quailed with Rosie in the house. Polly quietly went her own way, and when with them was biddable and loving, but even her influence could not always calm Rosie who, despite her passionate devotion to William, remained intractable and opinionated, until Mildred reached the point of explosion. It was a battle of wills: Mildred intent on turning Rosie into a model little girl; Rosie resisting all such endeavours. Rosie was intelligent, but having learned precious little in her six years in Bethnal Green, she was at first more concerned to cover this fact up in front of Polly than to rectify it. In their free time they separated, Polly to paint or watch birds, Rosie to make a beeline for the workshed, constantly getting under Mr Fisherbutt's feet. Sometimes she could be found in the stables, not with the horses which at first scared her, but with the carriages themselves, particularly the old ones mouldering away in the barn. She was forbidden to go as far as the farm, but the sound of a tractor was a magnet. Anything with an engine attracted her, and it was this led to the worst conflict yet with Mildred.

Investigating too closely the workings of the fascinating steam engine and boiler with which William was experimenting in the workshop, inspired by Mr Maxim's experiments, Rosie's serge skirt became entangled in the casing and her tiny hands got badly burned in her efforts to remove it. Her screams brought William and Mr Fisherbutt running, and her arrival home in the former's arms in search of help made Mildred as white-faced as Rosie herself. When the wounds had been dealt with, the time of reckoning came.

'No more,' said Mildred. 'Either you give up these

ridiculous experiments, William, or you forbid the worksheds to Rosie.'

'My dear, they are not ridiculous experiments. Man is on the threshold. I cannot – Rosie my dear, I think for the moment, you had better do as your mother wants and—'

'She's not my mother,' bawled Rosie, shock setting in and settling on Mildred as the scapegoat. 'I'm going to Home! I want to—'

'You can't. There is no home,' snapped Mildred, more cruelly than she intended, hurt by the rejection.

'There is – There is—' And Rosie set out to prove it that night.

She trudged three miles to the railway station, convinced that if she could find the dark place then she would be taken to Home. Home was a place where the sun shone all the time and birds and kites flew, and Ma and Pa were there and – that other dark thing was not. She escaped the stationmaster's notice, and bravely climbed aboard the London train, before her absence was discovered by Mildred, and William set the telegraph wires clacking all the way to London in a shrewd guess as to her whereabouts. He collected her at Victoria railway station next morning, and bore her back to Brynbourne. A compromise was decided upon. Workshop visits were allowed provided lessons were attended and due study given to the niceties of femininity.

'I've got something for you, Rosie,' said Mildred one afternoon, as Rosie prepared for her usual afternoon dash from lessons to the workshop.

Facing the inevitable fact that Rosie was never going to be parted from her workshop completely, Mildred constructed Rosie a pair of coverall bloomers for safety, so that her petticoats should not get caught in machinery.

'Oh,' Rosie said when she saw the blue serge baggy pantaloons. Her eyes shone. 'Look at me, look at me, Mama.' She danced around when she had donned them. She ran to Mildred and threw her arms around her. A pair of bloomers had achieved what the last eighteen months had failed to do.

19

Rosie did not mention home again, but she did not forget it.

Fleeting, isolated moments, passing shafts of sunshine on a pathway to the sun . . .

'How shall we make our flying machine, Rosie? Shall it have rounded wings like a bird, or look like our old box kites?'

Seven and a half years old, several pairs of blue bloomers worn shiny now: 'Like the kite, the kite.'

'Then wood, wire and warp, if you please, Mr Fisherbutt. Let us commence. Mr Fisherbutt, if you please, we require a wind tunnel . . . Follow me.'

Eight years old: 'It had forty wings one above another. What do you think of that, Rosie? It had a steam engine, and was tethered of course, but it flew a load, so the Aeronautical Society tells me. Yet the French did that in '79 with the compressed air models of Victor Tatin. It's not the answer. Oh no. Not steam. Steam is too heavy for our Pegasus. We require an engine such as drives the new horseless carriages—'

Ten years old: 'The gliding aeroplane is complete, Rosie. I shall glide like Mr Wenham in '66, like Otto Lilienthal. I shall soar like a large bat. Like Percy Pilcher at Eynsford. All it needs is for Mr Fisherbutt and Mr Harris to run down the hill. And we must hurry. I hear Mr Ader in France has constructed two powered machines now, and one, I believe was successful in rising from the ground.' Then William's face fell. 'But I'm being selfish,' he cried. 'To you, Mr Fisherbutt, should go the honour of the first flight. Just lie down with the controls in your hands, then tilt yourself forwards, till the balance is shifted. I will cut the cords, and you glide down adjusting the—'

'Me, Mr Potts?' Fisherbutt interrupted, alarmed.

'Why yes, you deserve it.' A pause. 'Ah,' said William Potts. 'It should be me, for there is, some might say, an element of risk.'

'Oh no, Mr Potts, I like to help in any way I can.'

20

'If you're sure, Mr Fisherbutt—'

This duet continued to Rosie's intense fascination until the glider was in position at the top of Bourne Hill. It did indeed look like a large bat - or a bird. One day she'd fly . . .

'William, *what* are you doing with poor Mr Fisherbutt?' Mildred demanded, appearing in the donkey cart with two-year-old Michael beside her and observing Mr Fisherbutt lying precariously, white-faced, in the contraption.

Mr Fisherbutt was removed. 'I should never look Mrs Fisherbutt in the face again,' declared Mildred and William eagerly took his place.

But the glider failed to rise, despite Mr Fisherbutt's and Harris's best efforts. William climbed disconsolately out. He and Mr Fisherbutt conferred, while Harris, the coachman, stood by nervously, awaiting his fate. A brief discussion, then the problem was solved.

'Mr Harris - a moment of your time.'

Four months later: 'The wing fabric, Mr Fisherbutt,' moaned William. 'It is not taut enough. The varnish is not sufficient.'

Mr Fisherbutt inspected the problem carefully.

'Tapioca,' he remarked presently. A man of few words. Rosie clapped her hands in glee; she hated tapioca.

William Potts eyed him doubtfully.

'Very drying, tapioca,' added Mr Fisherbutt, seeing his word was doubted.

'Rosie, pray run to the house and request Mrs Fisherbutt's entire stock of tapioca—'

'I only record the sunny hours,' proclaimed the old sundial in the walled vegetable garden. What did that mean? Rosie often wondered. She did not discover for some years, but when she and Polly were twelve, a cloud crossed the sunny skies that had set fair on their childhood. A cloud that started small, and gathered momentum . . .

'Where are you going, Polly?' Rosie asked plaintively. She was bored. William was at the factory, Mr Fisherbutt

21

was otherwise occupied and, forbidden the workshop without them, there was nothing, but nothing, to do.

'Just out,' said Polly, flushing slightly.

'Can I come?'

'If you like.' Polly eyed her crossly, then, since she was kind-hearted, she grew more friendly, gathered together her paints and sketchbook and they went out in the grounds. Intrigued by the prospect of this rare excursion into Polly's life, Rosie followed her across the gardens and fields, then into the woods, until they came to a part where Rosie had seldom been. She and Polly had been companions, never close. They were too different. Polly came from another world. Polly, who always knew how to use her knife and fork properly, who knew how to speak properly, had been born into this life, not had to learn it bit by painful bit as had she. Looking back now, she saw how difficult it had been for Polly, yet she had been always kind, always helpful, never showing any resentment of this intruder thrust into her life without her say-so. As Rosie grew older, she wondered at it, and realised gradually that it came naturally to Polly, that she saw no need to fight with life, as Rosie did – not outwardly at any rate. Of her inner struggles, however, Rosie came to glimpse a little that afternoon.

'Where now?'

'We follow the stream now,' answered Polly matter-of-factly. Rosie was still a little in awe of Polly with her lovely, long, fair hair, and blue eyes and composed serene features, so different from herself. Their cambric dresses were identical save in colour, but Polly's always managed to look neat and tidy, whereas Rosie's frills managed to get caught up in every bush they passed. The stream was hung over with willows and bushes and, following the direction of Polly's pointing finger, she saw a screen of misty greens and yellows that hid the stream from further view.

'Where does it go when it disappears?' asked Rosie curiously.

'Come on,' said Polly, 'I'll show you.'

Galvanised and almost excited now, as if on a voyage

to a far unknown country, Rosie plunged after Polly as she scrambled along the bank of the stream, pushing through clumps of meadowsweet and willowherb, through straggling willows, through a fringe of trees bordering fields which deepened into woods. There was no sound save the trickling water, the occasional cry of a distant bird and the sound of crackling undergrowth as they pushed forward.

'Here,' said Polly finally, pushing through some bushes and halting. They were in a small grassy glade, by the side of the stream, surrounded by trees and clumps of rosebay willowherb. 'Do you like it?'

Rosie nodded, entranced, suddenly envious of Polly whose place this was. They threw themselves down on the ground, and Polly produced two apples.

'It's so hot,' complained Rosie, wriggling inside her warm dress. 'Let's take our stockings off. Or better still,' greatly daring, 'we could take *everything* off. Wouldn't it be nice to feel the sun all over?'

'We couldn't,' said Polly scandalised.

'There's no one to see,' said Rosie. 'Don't look, if you're embarrassed,' and she tore off her clothes, flinging the hated frilly dress carelessly aside. Why didn't Mama understand she hated frills? *And* these horrid black stockings and boots! Polly followed suit hesitantly.

'There, isn't that better?' proclaimed Rosie, wriggling luxuriously. 'It's all part of today. It's a sort of Garden of Eden here, isn't it?'

Polly hugged her knees to her chest, and then gaining confidence, the sun warm on her back, she lay down.

'What do you do here?' asked Rosie.

'I paint, of course.'

'But it's always the same scene. Don't you mind?'

'Oh no, it's never the same. It's always changing. Lie down and close your eyes and I'll show you.'

Rosie obediently did so.

'Now open them quickly, look towards the stream and tell me what you see.'

Rosie opened them, the sun put a haze before her eyes, a filter between her and the stream. She saw a blur of greens and yellows and greys, and patches of pink from the rosebay. A flash of blue of a dragonfly. It was a sea of misty colours.

'That's what I try to paint,' said Polly. 'It's very difficult,' she added wistfully. 'I'd like to learn properly how to do it. I've been reading a book about the painters in Paris who just paint impressions, not shapes. One day I'll be able to paint too.'

'But you paint now,' said Rosie.

'Not really,' Polly said impatiently, languidly stretching out in the sun. 'Not properly.' She changed the subject. 'What do you want to do?'

'I want to fly.'

Polly laughed.

'I really do,' said Rosie, hurt.

'You're as bad as Father.'

'But there's a big future for it, it's so exciting, don't you see?'

'Let's promise each other,' said Polly suddenly, 'that we'll help each other get what we want if we can.'

'All right.' A pause. 'Do you want to get married and have babies, Polly?'

'Some day I suppose we'll both have to, that's what Mother says,' said Polly practically. 'I'd like to have a little baby like Michael was.'

'I wouldn't,' said Rosie decidedly. Four-year-old Michael had a passion for Rosie, following her around, and she quite enjoyed playing with him now. But babies, ugh. Aeroplanes were much more interesting. 'And what about a husband?'

'He'd have to like painting,' Polly said firmly, wriggling luxuriously as the sun beat down.

Rosie frowned. 'If I had a husband he wouldn't stop me doing anything I wanted. So perhaps he'll have to want to fly too. Or else – Polly,' she screamed, simultaneously rolling over on to her stomach. 'Someone's watching us.'

There was a scampering, rustling in the bushes, trampling as somebody tried to get away. Rosie seized her dress, pulling it quickly over her head and rushed into the wood. There were sounds of altercation, and

Rosie came back dragging a short tubby boy of about their own age, pink-cheeked and definitely smirking. By that time Polly had hurriedly dressed and was pulling on her boots, regardless of stockings.

'You were peeping, yer scuffy squirt,' words dimly remembered from Rosie's early years came back in her rage.

'What if I was? It's my land.'

'Your land,' Rosie retorted. 'Who'd yer think you are then? The King of Kent?'

'I'm Robert Bellowes and my father owns all this land. So let me *go*!' With a jerk he freed himself from Rosie's grasp. 'You're the tenement child old Potts took in, aren't you?' he jeered. 'That's why you don't speak properly.' Rosie went white. 'Hopper, hopper, hopper,' he chanted.

A gasp, and Rosie flew at him; they tumbled together on the ground, rolling over and over, as she endeavoured to pull out fistfuls of his hair, pummelling and averting his retaliatory weak fists with ease.

Polly rushed up. 'Don't, Rosie,' she cried, pulling her off. 'And you,' she turned to Robert as he scrambled to his feet, 'you ought to be ashamed of yourself. You're supposed to be a gentleman. Peeping like that and being rude about my father. Fine gentleman you are.'

Robert opened his mouth to retort, then something about Polly's face made him shut it again. 'You're trespassing,' he pointed out sullenly, then turned and ran off.

'Ugh,' said Rosie graphically. 'He's a horrible, horrible slug. If that's a gentleman, I'm glad they never call on us. Let the toffs keep themselves to themselves.' She was trembling. What did he mean, 'tenement child'? Was that – could it be something to do with that tiny pit of fear that still recurred like a dark shadow every so often? Father had explained to her about the accident long ago, and that her father and mother had died in the crash, that her real home now was at Brynbourne, and in the daylight she no longer wondered about another home, lost long ago. But at night sometimes, when she awoke and saw the branches of the trees waving black against a midnight sky, the moonlight turned certainty to doubt and safety to shifting sand. Then, oh then, she recalled the dark place, and buried her head in the pillows as if by so doing she would be safe from it for ever.

'He's away at school, so Father said,' Polly was saying, as she did her best to tidy the ruins of Rosie's dress. She looked round the glade sadly. 'I don't think I shall want to come here again,' she said.

Rosie hugged her. 'Don't worry, Polly. We'll find another secret place. Even nicer than this. It will be *ours*. Magic places are wherever you want to find them, you know.'

'This, Rosie, is an elevating rudder on the same principle as Major Renard used in *La France*, his airship of some years ago. This little beauty will go up and down as it moves on its axis.' Potts's hand moved over it lovingly. 'And here is the steering rudder. Now the problem is, should we place the elevator at the stern or the bow?' He bent over the drawing board worriedly.

'And the wings. We still have to discover how to prevent lateral incline on turning. To offset the effect of turning, we must provide counter-resistance. If we had something like a set of birds' feathers in a fan shape that could be controlled by the pilot – unless, of course, one could provide that the corners of the wings be pushed up to offset the difference in thrust . . . I wonder . . . A wooden batten perhaps—

'I think perhaps the fan first, to enlarge the surface of the inner wing as it dips, and reduce the outer. You follow my reasoning, Mr Fisherbutt? Rosie?' He broke off as someone came in, someone he vaguely recognised. 'Good afternoon,' he greeted him courteously. William did not like uninvited guests in his workshop, but was prepared to be polite. Besides, hadn't he seen the fellow before? Then his face brightened. 'Ah, you're the cooper, aren't you?'

Sir Lawrence Bellowes almost danced with rage. He was no taller than Rosie, certainly no more than five foot. But what he lacked in inches he made up for in pugnacity. Ginger-haired and bearded, he was like an overgrown leprechaun, Rosie thought, amused. But a fearsome one.

'I have the misfortune to live at Court Manor, Potts,' he barked, 'as you well know. Misfortune in that we border your estate and I demand to know why my son has been attacked in his own home by this - er - person,' he pointed disdainfully at Rosie.

Potts absent-mindedly wiped his hands on one of his pocket handkerchiefs, vast quantities of which were newly imported every year by Mildred.

'My daughter, Sir Lawrence,' he pointed out mildly.

'A hopper's child,' Bellowes snorted.

'No, Sir Lawrence. My daughter. Suppose you tell me what happened, Rosie?'

Somewhat shamefacedly, Rosie explained. William listened in silence, then remarked, 'It seems to me, Sir Lawrence, your son got somewhat less than he deserved.'

Sir Lawrence grew purple. 'She's an evil influence,' he almost screamed. 'Keep her away from our land and—' he cast a scathing eye round the workshop '—kindly recall we're used to decent living round here. These dangerous things you're tampering with could contaminate our land, if they ever worked. I've seen warnings in the newspapers. I'll put a stop to it one way or other. Oh yes.'

They didn't take him seriously. That was a mistake, for Sir Lawrence took himself very seriously indeed. After a while, however, Rosie came to suspect that Papa almost enjoyed his feud with the Bellowes, glorying in his regular visits to the Canterbury offices of Messrs Foggett, Whistle and Featherstone, solicitors, to discuss the latest summons by Sir Lawrence.

Her first flight, drifting above the green fields of Kent in a tethered balloon basket, was a treat for her fourteenth birthday. Despite the brown woollen coat and scarf Mildred had insisted on her wearing for all it was high summer ('It'll be cold up there, my love') it was just as she had imagined it would be. A deep sigh of satisfaction, and knowing beyond all doubt that this was where she

27

needed to be. High, high above the world. Unafraid, Rosie peered over the edge of the basket, hanging on to her cream straw hat as she felt the breeze catch at the ribbon strings. Down below her stretched the patchwork fields, the streams snaking across their green magnificence, a picture that never ended. She exulted in her Olympian position, as the balloon swayed with the breeze.

If it was so wonderful in a balloon, how much more glorious would it be to be in a real flying machine? William had talked to her for hours about flight and its possibilities. Ever since the glider had at last achieved some measure of success in controlled flight six weeks ago, William had beavered away every spare moment, with Rosie and Mr Fisherbutt as eager apprentices.

'The clay is there, Rosie,' he'd roared. 'We have but to breathe life into it, like Pygmalion into Galatea. And in this case life is *power*. Balloons can achieve much, Rosie; look at Colonel Brine, who crossed the Channel in one, nearly twenty years ago now. Look at the use to which they can be put. But we need speed and power to progress. And that means heavier-than-air flight. We're in a whole new century now, and a whole new world beckons to be conquered. As the great poet Browning said, "Ah, but a man's reach should exceed his grasp or what's a heaven for?" Reach, Rosie, always reach upwards.' He sighed a little wistfully. 'It will be for you to do it. Not me. There's not enough time.'

'You won't die?' cried Rosie.

He laughed and patted her hand. 'You'll have to find your own wings eventually. Always remember a great privilege has been granted to us: a lease on the skies. You must never abuse it, Rosie.'

'Abuse? I don't understand.'

'This country rules half the world, yet it seems to me we can't rule ourselves properly. War will come sooner or later. They'll need these balloons then, and aeroplanes too. They'll use the skies as a new element in war.'

'Use aeroplanes for warfare!' Rosie cried horrified. She looked down once more at the peaceful landscape slipping away beneath them. A shiver ran through her, as though the dark place had suddenly reached out a tentacle to remind her that the night was not its only kingdom. 'No,' she cried fiercely. 'We'll never do that, will we, Father?'

'No, Rosie, no, but it's already beginning. They used balloons and kites in South Africa. And now everyone it seems is busy building airships and man-carrying kites.'

'We'll only use them for happy, lovely things, won't we, Father?' she cried.

'Yes,' William said decidedly. 'But be careful, Rosie. For the world has a way of forcing its will on those who stand against it.'

'Not on me,' she said confidently.

The Pegasus was Rosie's name for it, the winged horse of mythology. William said horsepower would be needed, and so Pegasus was born. A new century, a new horizon of man's achievement. Pegasus grew to dominate their lives, a new and intrusive member of their family to be discussed endlessly until Mildred rebelled. She had never been fully reconciled to Rosie's absorption in the ridiculous goings-on in William's workshed, and now that Rosie was growing up, redoubled her efforts to mould her in ladylike activities. But painting, music and embroidery were dismal failures which Mildred ascribed to lack of attention, not ability, and the atmosphere grew strained. Rosie did not notice. Pegasus, however unpromising to look at, took all her attention.

How proud she was when after months of work they gave Pegasus, then only a boxwood frame, its wings, which she was allowed to help construct. Squat, with its two wings on each side braced together with ugly wire, Pegasus looked less like a flying machine than a monstrous set of square bookshelves. But to Rosie it was a thing of beauty, and when the fabric was added to the wings and tautened with the ever-faithful tapioca, it flew already in her vivid imagination, no longer a passive object on the workshop floor, but a winged living creature soaring through the heavens.

William worked from instinct, not from books or mathematical calculations. Rosie, on the other hand,

29

could be found poring over issues of the Aeronautical Society journals, reading learned papers sent from France and America, her French, hitherto deemed by her to be pointless, suddenly improving.

'Listen, Papa, it says here that Colonel Renard claims that if one could find an engine weighing less than five kilogrammes for every horse power then the problems of heavier-than-air flight would be conquered.'

'Patience, patience,' William murmured. 'Let us make our Pegasus ready first. Now I need a foot-rest to place my feet on—'

'Won't you lie on your face like in the glider?'

'Far too undignified. I'm too old. No, I shall—'

'I'm not,' she cried eagerly.

William regarded her indulgently. 'Leave something for us men, eh Rosie? It's far too dangerous for ladies to fly.'

'Why?' The word shot out, challenging William. 'You can't know – you haven't flown yourself yet. Why should it be more dangerous for ladies than gentlemen?'

'Because I say so,' said William, boxed into a corner in bewilderment. Perhaps Mildred was right – perhaps he was encouraging Rosie too much.

'But Father, what about all we talked of? You said the future would be mine,' she cried, unable to leave well alone.

'Yes. Knowledge – that's what's important. Knowing how to build—'

'But what's the use of building without flying?' she retorted impatiently. 'I want to fly, you know that,' unable to believe that indulgent, kindly Father was so short-sighted.

William busied himself with his tool chest, turning away from conflict. There was no question of Rosie flying; his womenfolk had to be protected. That was his role, and he wasn't going to be able to protect them by letting them fly around in aeroplanes.

'Answer me, Father! You can't, can you?' came her triumphant voice behind him.

Flustered, William flew into a rare rage. 'Your mother's right. This is no place for a girl. You can spend some time

30

at home learning to run a household, that's where a young lady's future lies—'

'What about Charlotte Dod, Isabella Bird, Florence Nightingale?' she challenged.

'Don't you Dod me,' William roared, shaken. 'Go back to the house at once!'

She was in disgrace for a month, only Polly sympathising with her. At the end of the month she was allowed back into the workshed on sufferance, and on condition that she spent as much time studying to be a young lady as to be an engineer. Ever-optimistic, Rosie put Father's strange attitude down to a touch of dyspepsia, and if any slight apprehension remained, it was buried deep – as deep as that dream of home.

As the months went by, William felt his way towards a solution of one problem after another on Pegasus. Weeks of tension, during which everyone, especially Rosie, learned to creep about quietly, would be followed by a triumphant, 'By George I have it. To the workshop, Mr Fisherbutt, *if* you please.'

In after years she would think of him standing in front of Pegasus for hours, pondering. 'One propeller, or two, Rosie, do you think?'

'How many engines?' she asked practically. 'One or two?'

He turned a look of surprise on her. 'Why, I—' he paused. 'You're right, Rosie. One engine. One propeller, I think. Suppose after all one propeller were to break. Would not the one still working cause serious inbalance? Yes, my love, one propeller. I shall ask Mrs Fisherbutt for muffins for tea. We shall celebrate our decision.'

But it was not all muffins. Much of it was feud. In 1902 Sir Lawrence brought a case for actionable nuisance, and lost on the grounds that he had not objected earlier and that any aeronautical device must necessarily carry the implication of an engine being added at some stage. But it had been touch and go.

Mr Featherstone mopped his brow as they emerged from court. 'Mr Potts, pray take care, I beg. I do not share your taste for such exciting life. A third case might easily go the other way.' The first case, also brought on grounds of actionable nuisance, had centred on Sir Lawrence's hastily repaired eighteenth-century belvedere on the edge of his property, the view from which, he claimed, was now impaired by the new workshed William had erected some way from the house on the large flat Bred Field on the top of the downs.

'Calm yourself, Mr Featherstone, if you please. I am caution itself.'

He would not think Papa was caution itself if he saw what went on at home when he and Sir Lawrence met, thought Rosie, giggling to herself.

By 1903, however, Pegasus still lacked a workable engine. Steam was completely ruled out; early experiments in motor engines had been disappointing. In the summer, however, this last and vital problem was overcome.

In June the Aeronautical Society held a meeting on the downs in Sussex at which a prize was offered for man-lifting kites. William had now lost his competitive instinct so far as kites were concerned, but at Rosie's pleading, they went. For her, kites symbolised the beginning. However, William's interest was rekindled when he met Colonel Samuel Franklin Cody. 'He should have won,' said William sadly, shaking his head. 'The wind just wasn't strong enough, but he's the only one knows what he's doing.'

Long hair, big hat, long moustache, Cody looked like the buccaneer showman he had been rather than a famous aeronautic who was greatly respected for his work on kites and balloons.

'Now if *he* were to build an aeroplane, we might get somewhere,' said William. 'I'll have a word with him—'

'Don't you want *us* to be the first?' said Rosie curiously.

He paused. 'Do you know, I don't think I mind. Provided someone does it, and does it soon. And provided I get up in the air sometime. Now Colonel Cody,' he said, reverting to practical matters, 'would have the problem of engine weight solved in no time. Five kilogrammes horsepower, that's what Renard says, that's about eleven pounds. But it doesn't work,' William said crossly.

'It needs less, much less. Three, two perhaps,' broke in a voice at their side. A tall, thin, serious-looking young man, impeccably attired in boater and blazer, was listening to their conversation with intense interest.

'Two's impossible,' said Rosie immediately, annoyed at the intrusion, especially by someone of his patrician air.

The young man regarded her worriedly, pushing his gold spectacles up his nose. 'It's not, you know. Perhaps not yet. But we could work towards it.'

Half impressed that this elegant young man was taking her seriously, half annoyed by 'we', Rosie was about to answer when William forestalled her.

'Tell me more, young man. *If* you please.'

Harry Clairville Jones became a frequent visitor, and then part-time paid employee. Jealous of her own preserves, Rosie objected until William had pointed out his role was solely engines. She was the general assistant on whom he really depended. After that, she got on well with him, and was impressed by his possession of one of the famous Clairville motor cars, the product of the Clairville factory in Chatham owned by Harry's uncle and his partner. They had taken Harry on as a poorly-paid apprentice to learn the trade and reaped their reward when he developed a keen and rapidly expert interest in petroleum engines. Now at the age of twenty-two he was solely responsible for engine design. Restless, he strove for more, but his father, although the son of an earl, had made the mistake of being a penniless younger son, and a younger son who saw no reason why his more industrious brothers should not support him in the way to which life should have entitled him. Harry, repelled by a childhood of patronising hand-outs and dismissive shrugs, resolved that the world would remember only one Clairville Jones: himself. No matter how.

William's eyes gleamed when Harry told them he was working on a new six-cylinder engine for the new model Clairville Lion for 1904. Yet Harry's passion was the air, not the ground. He longed to build aeroplanes, and preferably to build and fly the *first* aeroplane. But his finances did not allow this, and to build engines for an aeroplane – even someone else's – would be the next best thing. His own ambitions must be laid aside while he did the next best thing. Learn.

'Harry?'

Rosie looked up, calling out, as she saw the familiar two-seater red Clairville arriving with a squeal of brakes. Harry's lean lanky figure leapt out in great excitement as he whipped off his goggles and deerstalker, brandishing a newspaper at her, his studious face unusually animated. It was cold for mid-December, but she stood transfixed, regardless of anything but these stark all-important words tucked away in a corner of the newspaper: *Balloonless Airship. From our own correspondent, New York, December 18th. Messrs Wilbur and Orville Wright of Ohio yesterday successfully experimented with a flying machine at Kittyhawk, North Carolina . . .*

And so it had happened. It was no longer a dream. It was within man's power, he had reached towards the stars. Now Pegasus too might fly. The skies were opening before her and the players in the drama that lay ahead had taken their places on the stage.

Only one was yet to come – and he the explosive force that lit the powder keg.

# Chapter Two

Excitement battled with reluctance as Rosie forced herself just for once to acknowledge a social world where aeroplanes were not all-important. On that warm July night on which Brynbourne Place was to celebrate the eighteenth birthdays of the daughters of the house, the future seemed an enchanted, exciting adventure. How strange, Rosie thought, that although Polly was oblivious to everything save a paintbox and she herself immersed in aeronautics, here they were preparing for a ball. To Rosie, it was strange in itself that William and Mildred had insisted on this grand gesture, since social functions were not high on their list of favourite occupations, but they had thrown themselves with their usual energy into its organisation. When in fact Mildred decreed the ball should be given, William had acquiesced without protest for to him it went without saying that the ladies of his household should be introduced formally into society. It was his duty to ensure the rules were followed.

'I think I've got more underpinning than Pegasus,' Rosie complained, twisting this way and that to see herself in the mirror to the despair of Trott. Trott was nearly of the same vintage as Mrs Fisherbutt and as much of a fixture. Where Mrs Fisherbutt was plump and apparently approving, Trott was thin and apparently disapproving. Both assumptions were liable to be proved wrong without warning. The corsets required for the correct fall of Rosie's hand-embroidered satin skirt came hard after the freedom of her breeches, which, to Mildred's impotent despair, had long since replaced the coverall bloomers.

'I'm going to give up trying to look like a Gibson girl. You look like the swan, and me the gosling,' Rosie sighed, admiring Polly's statuesque golden slenderness, and the fair hair piled high on the head as she disappeared into one petticoat after another dropped over her head by Trott.

There was a muffled reply.

'What?'

'I said,' Polly emerged flushed, as the last blue folds of her skirt, bedecked in frills and flounces, swirled round her slim figure, 'that that pink dress suits you. Harry won't be able to take his eyes off you.'

'Huh.' Rosie grimaced at her lively reflection in the mirror, the heart-shaped face surrounded by its curly mop of brown curls, more battered than swept into shape by Trott. 'He'd only notice me if I had wings, and then they'd have to be biplane design. I don't think he knows I've got shoulders.' She gazed at the unfamiliar sight of her thin shoulders emerging from the rose-pink satin bodice, and began to feel excited. Perhaps there was something to be said for all this fussy feminine attire after all. She tugged at a recalcitrant shoulder strap. Would it really stay up? Then Polly took quick advantage of Trott's bustling out of the room for flowers.

'Do you mind – about his being so serious, I mean?'

'Mind?' Rosie threw back her head and laughed. 'Poor Polly, you see romance everywhere. Harry and I work together on Pegasus, that's all. We both love aeroplanes. If I marry, I won't marry till I've got what I want,' she explained matter-of-factly.

'But what if Father and Mother insist?' asked Polly wryly. 'Mother is always on about it.'

'They can't force us to,' Rosie pointed out. 'Anyway you wouldn't mind marrying, if you met someone nice, would you?'

As so often she spoke unthinkingly, and was totally surprised by Polly's strong reaction. Red spots of anger flushed into her pale cheeks. 'Mind?' Polly cried angrily. 'Of course I'd mind. Just as you want to fly aeroplanes, I want to *paint*. Don't you remember what I told you?'

'But you do paint—' Rosie said in bewilderment.

She was so used to Polly's apparent placid acceptance

of the daily vicissitudes that this exposure of a different Polly – a Polly who might care as deeply and passionately as she did herself about life – was disturbing.

It was the wrong thing for Rosie to have said.

'You're just like Father,' Polly choked. 'I don't paint, I – I dab, doodle, that's all. I want really to paint, really to draw, really create. That's what *he* always says: I can paint here. He doesn't understand. And nor do you,' she added simply.

'I'm sorry,' said Rosie, dismayed and helpless. To her, painting was simply creating a drawing. She tried hard to put herself in Polly's place. 'Can't you do something about it? I would. There are schools, aren't there? Or what about Paris?'

'Not for gentlewomen, Father says. I asked him. He refused. And as I cannot pay for myself, that is that.'

'But he's always so reasonable with me,' Rosie blurted out, then wished she hadn't. Rosie could never understand why she (usually) got on with Father so well and Polly so badly. Polly was his real daughter, and she was adopted. And yet there was always tension between Polly and Father. Polly went her own way. Mother seemed to understand that, whereas Father did not. With her it was the other way about; Mother had never been fully reconciled to Rosie's ambitions and persisted in believing it was an aberration of youth which would vanish once young men replaced aeroplanes in Rosie's consciousness, and she would turn again to the traditional pursuits of a young lady. Polly's painting was after all acceptable within that classification and Mildred blinded herself to – or perhaps did not appreciate – her ambitions.

'With you, yes,' snapped Polly. 'You can talk about aeroplanes. All the same,' she said, calming down, 'I should take care, if I were you. He won't let you too far off the reins, you'll see. He'll tether you like one of your blessed kites. You'll see.'

'Nonsense,' Rosie retaliated. 'You just have to discuss things with him, that's all. And you never do. You just accept anything he orders.' Her words were sharper than she intended, perhaps to still the unease that Polly's accusations had left.

'Don't you think we have to, while we're still living at home?' Polly said quietly.

That was Polly's way, not her way.

They finished dressing in silence, donning thin long silk gloves and doing up the twenty buttons, picking up their lace fans, adjusting the bows in their hair. Then Rosie broke the silence by giving Poly a quick hug and the misunderstanding was over. But that last word lingered: home.

Neither Mildred nor William had made Rosie feel she was less dear to them than Polly. Yet somehow, long after she had forgotten the language of the costermongers, there was still within her a sense of difference, a tough inner core. It consisted of a concept of home that had nothing to do with that crowded damp house in Bethnal Green that had at first filled her dreams with a mixture of attraction and repulsion. A concept that never entirely vanished with the years.

Brynbourne Place was flaunting itself, bedecked in unaccustomed finery. The drawing room doors were open on to the terrace, to enlarge the dancing space. Later it would be candlelit. A huge marquee in the gardens had been erected to house a lavish buffet supper. Roses blossomed everywhere, between balustrades, draped round aspidistras, in huge tubfuls in every corner. Rosie had wickedly suggested they might be placed in Potts Pedestal Wash-down WCs and William had been on the point of taking her seriously when Mildred firmly vetoed it. In compensation, William, diverted for once from Pegasus, had invented a platform for the orchestra, whereby each of the eight players was arranged at varying heights and in such positions that they resembled the figure eighteen. The conductor's remonstrances when he saw it were swept aside with a 'You'll manage, my dear fellow'.

Brynbourne Place in its Georgian heyday had often entertained the gentry of the neighbourhood, but it had never hosted an event such as this. Tonight the local gentry had come, startled by the unexpected invitation and unable to resist attending this den of iniquity. Even the Bellowes had received an invitation. Sir Lawrence had seen in it a deep dark plot by William, but his wife had insisted on acceptance. As her friends were going, she must perforce follow suit if she were to participate fully in the inquest afterwards. The gentry, however, were first surprised, then shocked, then titillated, to discover that the majority of their fellow guests were local traders and factory workers. Mr Featherstone was similarly horrified at the unprofessional sight of suer and sued under the same roof (the latest writ had been delivered but yesterday).

The Sittingbourne factory staff, uncomfortable in their dress suits and white collars, were standing rigidly at the side of their stiffly corseted wives, the younger men painfully aware that etiquette demanded they ask Miss Polly and Miss Rosie for a dance. Miss Rosie was all right, but Miss Polly – what could they say to her? They would have been surprised to know that Mildred had no less rigidly drummed their social obligations as hostesses into Polly and Rosie. And on no account, no account whatsoever, were they to commit the solecism of refusing a dance to *anybody*.

Michael, banished, partly to his disgust, partly to his relief, to bed, was compromising on direct disobedience by leaning over the landing balustrade into the well of the hall to gaze down on the colourful dresses of the arriving guests. It was here that Rosie spied him, and he shrank back sheepishly at having been discovered. She sped up the stairs, aware of just how strict Mildred's ruling had been.

'You'll be part of Pegasus's bracing if you don't watch out,' she warned him. 'Off to bed with you.' Then she laughed as she found herself leaning over the balustrade at his side, watching a particular fat vision in yellow enter the front door.

'I'll go, if you dance with me first,' he declared. His slavish devotion to her had not slackened over the years.

'Very well, my lad,' she surrendered, and with the music now clearly audible from below, performed a spirited cakewalk with him. She planted a kiss on his cheek and ran back downstairs, disregarding his 'I don't want anyone else to dance with you – *ever*'. What a child he still was, she thought idly. Of average height for his age, thin and with nondescript brown hair, it was hard to remember that Michael was ten years old, and that childhood was passing. Only those intense eyes made him look any different from hundreds of other boys, and they, had she thought about it more often, were always fixed on her.

Where was Harry? thought Rosie impatiently. Her card was already nearly full. Surely tonight he'd dance, though she knew he didn't like it as a rule. She wanted him to see how different she looked in her ball dress. She pirouetted on the last step, ridiculously pleased with herself in this pretty rose-pink dress with the lace bows dotted everywhere.

As she entered the drawing room she saw Polly. How beautiful she was looking, almost ethereal, as she waltzed in the arms of a young man as fair as herself, and with brown eyes, an unusual combination. He was a stranger – he must be the friend staying with that boring young man from Meadow House in Borden. He was as startlingly good-looking as Polly, and Rosie wondered what he could be saying to her that she looked so alive and absorbed.

Ah, there was Harry; he was standing in a corner with a group of men, earnestly talking. She frowned. She could distinctly hear the words 'dihedral', 'bracing' and 'wing-warping'. Normally she would have joined in with alacrity, but tonight was a little different. Harry looked up, his long serious face dissolving into a smile. He left the group and came towards her, taking both her hands.

He grinned, his eye running over her. 'I didn't recognise you without the grease and tapioca. Are you going to give me a dance?'

'Considering,' she answered with dignity, obscurely offended because he had said nothing complimentary on her appearance, 'that Mother says I can't refuse *anybody*, I can hardly say no.'

'That's all right then,' he said blandly. 'I see you've left the supper dance free.'

'Only because I want to talk about something sensible during supper, that's all. There's a problem on the propeller and—'

'I can't talk about propellers while you're wearing pink satin – it's ridiculous.'

'Maybe I'll be wearing it to fly in one day,' she laughed unthinkingly. 'You'll see.'

He stared in amazement. 'Fly in?' he repeated slowly. 'What on earth do you mean?' His voice was oddly flat.

'Just what I say. Pegasus in pink satin. I shall look rather splendid.'

'You're ribbing me, aren't you.' It was a statement, rather than a question. 'You don't seriously think you're ever going to fly Pegasus yourself?'

'Of course,' she said, surprised. 'Why else do you think I've spent all these years helping to build Pegasus, if not to fly it myself one day? Father doesn't know, of course,' she added blithely.

'I should think not. It's a man's sport,' he muttered, his face suddenly flushed.

'It's not anyone's sport yet,' she said, puzzled at his reaction. 'Apart from the Wrights, no one has left the ground in a machine fully under control. Papa and I might be the first. Harry, what on earth's the matter?'

She stared at the muscles beating in his cheek, a sure sign that something was displeasing him.

He made an effort and grinned at her. 'Nothing. I keep forgetting you're a New Woman. We'll see you marching with these suffragists soon. I can see it now—' he slipped back into the Harry she knew '—Vote for Rosie. Your member for Much Dreaming in the Air.'

'Well, why not?' Rosie came back vigorously, nettled at his jesting.

Not for a moment would she let him see that his approval meant anything to her. Ever since the day when he'd first come up to them at the air show, she'd been slightly in awe of him, though she would have died rather than let him see it. Flattered that he treated her as an equal, although she had then been only sixteen to his twenty-two, she had come to depend on him now as

41

one of the team, far more than just the supplier of an engine. She enjoyed riding in the smart red Clairville Lion, motoring round the Kentish lanes, its horn honking at every rabbit. He'd even shown her how to drive the motor car and on the straight roads would sometimes let her take the wheel. Why therefore should he be surprised that she wanted to fly Pegasus? Odd that you could work with someone for two years and not know something as basic as that.

A small unease grew within her. She glanced at him. Was it a trick of the light? Or were his eyes watchful, rather than warm, behind the spectacles. No, it must be imagination because the next moment he was saying to her easily, 'Remind me to talk to you about castor oil, Rosie. Not here. I'll come over next week.'

'*What*?'

'Castor oil,' he repeated laughing. 'Castor oil and engines. I've had an idea.'

The fair-haired young man had managed the impossible – a second dance with Miss Potts. They were dancing very slowly and talking very hard.

'You should see the light in Cornwall, Miss Potts; it's different every day, in the rain, in the sun, in the mist – Oh, it's like no other place in the world. It's hewn of granite, its people carry the past with them, reflect the sea in their blue eyes – Miss Potts, I wish I could describe it to you properly.'

'And you attend the famous painting school?'

'Yes, Newlyn School. Oh, Miss Potts, if I am still for a moment, I can hear the seagulls calling, I hear the sound of the sea crashing on the rocks; it's a place of dreams set in a blue bay with a castle rising out of the sea. Miss Potts, if you wish to paint, you should come to Cornwall. Come to attend the school. There are several single young ladies there.'

Her face lit up with a sudden wild hope.

Gabriel hesitated. 'Perhaps if you would allow me to call, Miss Potts,' he continued, 'I could tell you more.'

She flushed. 'That would be very nice, Mr Marriner,'

she said coolly, trying to keep the tremble of excitement from her voice.

'To the workshed, gentlemen. Home to the future.'

William, swept away with champagne and the exhilaration of the evening, waved a lordly hand to the gentlemen guests, many of whom were eager to view Pegasus. The flying machine and the dreadful doings at Bred Field were a byword of the district, and they could not miss a rare opportunity to gain first-hand knowledge.

Rosie frowned. 'I don't like it,' she said to Harry uneasily. 'They're just going to mock. If they don't do it to his face, then they will afterwards. Just like all the newspapers. Poor Papa, he doesn't realise. I think we should go to stand by him.'

'If you like.' Harry shrugged. 'It hardly matters. They'll change their minds soon enough when Pegasus flies.'

'Yes, but look, Sir Lawrence is going with them. We *must* go.' She tugged Harry's arm and they followed the band setting off for the workshed.

'I sometimes think,' she commented, watching the small red-headed man in front, 'that the entire British Government is composed of Sir Lawrence Belloweses. They're so blind, Harry. I just don't see how they can be so foolish as not to see that heavier-than-air flight is the way to the future.'

'They're only interested in war, that's why,' said Harry. 'They don't think that flying machines will ever have sufficient strength or stability to drop bombs, so they're not interested.'

'Well, that I'm glad of,' declared Rosie forthrightly. 'They show some sense there. That's not what we're doing all this for, is it?'

He glanced at her, knowing her views. 'Of course not,' he agreed. 'All the same, until they come to their senses, I'm afraid the Press will go on laughing us out of court. Laughing at people like Mr Potts.'

Rosie glanced ahead to where William was animatedly chatting to Sir Lawrence. He was so *innocent*, she thought fiercely, protectively. Didn't he realise that everything he said would be pounced upon secretly by Bellowes and used against him afterwards?

'The Wright brothers apparently offered the Government the chance to develop their Flyer – the new one they're just testing now. They've turned the offer down because they see no future for aviation,' Harry was saying. 'They're going to regret their lack of interest, I fear. Just as they let France and Germany get ahead in developing the motorcar by their ridiculous legislation about the need for a man to walk in front of the vehicle with a red flag, they'll let them shoot ahead in aviation development,' he said gloomily. 'In other countries, the Government's given the pioneers their official blessing. Yet here, where we've had an Aeronautical Society for forty years, where we invented the wind tunnel, where Stringfellow, Cayley, Henson all worked, we get people like him—' He jerked his head towards Sir Lawrence, now sniggering openly with his son. 'Well, they'll know soon enough,' he said with satisfaction as William opened the doors of the shed.

'Yes, but—' Rosie broke off, unable to put into words that Pegasus was their own private creation, not for mocking public consumption, not till they were ready to spread its wings. Besides, there was Sir Lawrence. William might joke about him, but he was sly and devious. The whole feud was one big joke to William, but a deadly serious matter to Sir Lawrence. When Sir Lawrence diverted his stream so that it flowed over and through the workshed, William retaliated by inventing clockwork foxes, smeared with fox scent, that popped their heads up from behind bushes to confuse the hounds. When Sir Lawrence removed a wall to which William's greenhouse had been attached for fifty years, William hit back with cleverly motored flying papier-mâché pheasants which he put up for the benefit and subsequent fury of Sir Lawrence's guests.

'If only,' he had remarked wistfully to Rosie, as they watched the winged creatures take off, 'Pegasus's mechanics were so easy to solve.'

In the workshed now about thirty men managed to

squeeze round Pegasus, Rosie hopping up and down in anxiety lest the fragile structure be damaged.

'And you think this will actually fly, Mr Potts?' breathed the Bredhill butcher Ted Sanderson.

A snort from Bellowes was ignored by William.

'Power is still the problem, my dear sir. How to have a light enough engine for the structure, but which will nevertheless have enough power to sustain flight.'

'Let's see you in it, Potts,' suggested Sir Lawrence smoothly. At his side was the plump figure of his son Robert with whom through gritted teeth Rosie had agreed to dance later. He was finished with school at last, and had come back into their lives. Her heart sank again, studying him. He was still like a slug. He was taller now, at least taller than his father, about her own height of five foot five inches, but he was still podgy with full face and thick lips, staring at Pegasus. What he was thinking was impossible to tell. She gulped, mindful of Mildred's strictures about the duties of the daughters of the house.

William clambered proudly into Pegasus's seat. As a large man, he had insisted on its being a proper wicker seat rather than a perch like that of the Wright brothers. With his feet stuck out at the front, and his hands clasping lateral controls and rudder controls, Rosie realised that to most of these people he must look a figure of fun. Only she and Harry knew that like a swan in motion, one day he and Pegasus would soar in flight. But of course these idiots had not the vision to see that.

'We cannot,' said William, clambering down again, 'be sure that it will fly first time. After all, it took the country a long time to get a workable railway engine. It just needed one simple invention and then – boom – the Rocket. And look what the railways have done for us.'

And look how everyone round here opposed them, thought Rosie. Just like aeroplanes now.

'And that's what flight will achieve, too,' William finished proudly.

'Shoot birds from this contraption, can you?' Sir Lawrence rapped at William. 'Take up passengers? Shoot?'

William looked mystified.

'Game,' explained Sir Lawrence impatiently. 'My pheasants. New idea, eh? Take this thing up and catch them on the wing. What do you think of that?'

'Just the sort of damnfool idea you would come up with, Bellowes,' declared William roundly, to the great delight of the local population. 'Firstly, you could not manoeuvre Pegasus quickly enough for bird shooting. Secondly, you'd be too high for most birds. And third, it's a damnfool notion. We aren't using these machines for death. Thou was not born for death, immortal horse,' he declared dramatically, misquoting, and patting Pegasus lovingly. There was a round of applause in which Bellowes did not join.

'You may laugh, Potts,' he said slowly, 'but you'll be laughing on the other side of your face before long.'

'Come, Bellowes,' William retorted. 'Forgive my outspokenness. What do you say we forget all this nonsense?' He held out his hand. Bellowes glanced around, caught the temper of the assembly, and took the hand unwillingly, clearly calculating. His eyes remained angry.

'Very well, but take care, Potts. It's a dangerous thing to meddle with the Lord's elements. No good will come of it. You'll see.'

Dancing with Robert Bellowes was as bad as Rosie had feared. His plump moist hands revolted her. After all, it was only a dance, she reminded herself.

'How long are you home for?' she inquired stiltedly.

'I go up to Oxford in October,' he said casually, patronisingly. 'You'll take up governessing, I suppose.'

'*What?*' Had she heard correctly? 'I shall go on working on Pegasus,' she said coolly.

He grinned, his hands hot on her back, his breath hot on her face. 'Hardly a job for a lady. But then you're not, are you? Just a hopper's daughter.'

Horrified, she jerked back instinctively, but he pulled her to him again, his pale eyes alive with enmity. So he had not forgotten their earlier encounter either, she realised ruefully, biting back words that came to her lips.

'Just because you're decked out in that,' his eyes swept down her making her shiver in disgust, 'that doesn't make you a lady. Underneath,' he grinned, 'and I remember what's underneath - and her—' his eyes went to where Polly was dancing with Mr Featherstone.

Polly? He dared to think of *Polly* that way?

Blind with fury, she forgot all about etiquette and Mildred's lectures. She delivered a stinging slap on his face and walked away, leaving him standing there in a sudden hush. His face was pale with fury, save for a flush where her hand had struck. He stood still, as people stared, mesmerised by the breach of convention.

Appalled, not knowing the reason, Polly rushed to rescue the evening, putting her hand on his arm. 'A sudden sickness,' she said lightly. 'Pray dance with me, Mr Bellowes.'

He looked at her, the flush still on his face. 'I'd be delighted to, Miss Potts,' he replied evenly.

Just a hopper's child. Why the 'just'? What did it matter who her parents were? Surely it was she who mattered? Rosie smarted. Ever since that dreadful evening she had been in disgrace, lectured by Mildred on her appalling behaviour, sympathised with by William and Polly. No matter how great the justification, a lady should behave like a lady, and a hostess never, but never, offended a guest. All the halting explanations she made to Mildred were inadequate by the side of these social dictates. Public disapproval still hung in the air. The local gentry seized happily on this incontrovertible evidence of the Potts's social shortcomings.

Even now Rosie shuddered at the very thought of Robert Bellowes, who crept like the snake he was into their Arcadia. Thank heavens he was going away to university. They had another three or four years virtually free of him and by then who knew what might have happened? Pegasus might be flying, and she in it. Her natural buoyancy began to restore itself, and would have done so completely had it not been for the wound that Robert Bellowes's remarks had reopened; they had brought her inexorably up against the dark pit within her that she had never dared explore. For twelve years ever since she had been brought back from Manning's hop farm she had kept away from all hop gardens and hop-pickers, staying on the estate during that six-week season, shutting her mind to all save aeroplanes. Now his words had forced her to think back to that dark place which had so rarely haunted her in the last few years. But it was still there. Always there. Only when she had pulled it out by its roots, would she be free of it – free to fly, she smiled, remembering it, like that bird on the privy roof. Only then would she know she was Rosie, an aeronautical engineer, and free to choose her own path. Those early years were a blur now, a mingling of warmth, fear, smells and noise – and something else, that darkness she could still not define.

She walked down the lane, half drawn, half repulsed by the thought of Manning's farm. The hoppers' annual season was midway through now, and the village of Bredhill had put up its barricades, mental and physical, against this invasion of gypsies, Cockneys and other strangers. The shops had barricades between their goods and hoppers' nimble fingers; the pub had its sign 'No Hoppers Inside'. When she was a child she had found herself at Manning's farm one day on a walk not long after she arrived at Brynbourne Place and cried, she knew not why. It was then that William had gently told her the reason. Then she had run away there, hoping to find her parents, to find 'home', but once there had been terrified. It had been big, and empty of life, and she had been overjoyed when William came to fetch her.

Now she knew it would be full of hoppers settling into the small huts built by the farmer – old Manning was progressive in his treatment of hoppers. As far back as 1890 he had built some special huts for them. As a result his band of pickers from the East End of London was remarkably faithful. All the other girls in the village helped at hop-picking, but Rosie never did. They thought it was because she was from the big house now, but that wasn't the reason.

She walked past the two oast houses, smelling of the sulphur they fed to the furnace underneath the drying hops. Although picking had finished for the day, the oasts were still throbbing with activity as pockets of hops were loaded on to waggons on their way to the brewery, and the dryers were still keeping their twenty-four-hour vigil on the fires. She entered the hop garden, which was almost deserted now, only a cheap toy, a broken umbrella, a scarf caught on a hop pole to indicate that merely an hour ago these rows had been full of life. She began to feel happier. There was nothing here to daunt her and perhaps much to discover. Yet the inexplicable fear still haunted her, both attracting and repelling. In the huts themselves old demons might yet lie. Oddly, since she recalled so little of those early days, she could remember the inside of the small hut the family had occupied clearly; its picture of the Queen on the wall, the chipped dancing shepherdess Ma insisted on bringing with her for luck each year. Poor Ma, it hadn't worked in the end. The few pots and pans and hazy impression of bodies milling everywhere, falling over each other, getting dirtier and dirtier, the smells of the cooking pot, of the beer the men drank, the constant noise . . .

Almost by instinct she found her way to the huts. She must eradicate for ever this nagging idea that home lay elsewhere, other than at Brynbourne. She must forget everything that Robert Bellowes had said. Better a credit to a hopper's family than a disgrace to the gentry like Bellowes, Mother had said comfortingly afterwards when she considered Rosie's penance had gone on long enough.

The rows of huts stood at the edge of the garden in the next field. There were not many, only enough for the privileged few families who supported Manning loyally year after year. Was it really here, with the sounds and smells of cooking, the noise now that work was over for the day, that she had spent those days of childhood? Rosie had taken care to wear an old frock today, so that she should not stand out among the pickers, but even so curious glances came her way. Was she once part of this, she wondered? Was it still part of her, deep down, part of her home, her heritage?

She stopped still. *That* was the hut, that one there. There was a sick feeling in her stomach suddenly as she remembered the view of the tall oak tree, the old brick wall beyond it. The nausea swelled up, and she shut her eyes to blot out the sight.

'What's up, luv?' a woman called out, concerned. At the sound of her voice a group of men looked round, staring. Then one of them, whistling thoughtfully, roughly dressed in corduroy trousers and threadbare jacket, costermonger's scarf at neck, came over to her.

Rosie stared at him, mesmerised by his straggly side whiskers, rough face and mocking eyes, the feeling of menace towards her so strong that she took a step back. He shot his hand out: 'Nah you see him, nah you don't. Take one,' he thrust the three cards forward.

'What do you want?' she cried.

'Take a card, luv, that's all.' He grinned at her with blackened teeth, regarding her mockingly, as she swayed as if in a dream misty and faint, and reached out automatically to choose a card. Then she pulled her hand back, as though this committed her in some way, and giving up, he put the cards back in the pocket of his shabby, food-stained waistcoat.

'Read the leaves, Doris.'

It was mad, quite mad. The woman who had spoken to her first held out an old cracked cup. In a mist Rosie swirled the leaves round, unable to refuse, yet frightened inexplicably by the sense of menace. This woman was a Cockney, not a gypsy. Why the tea leaves?

'I must go.'

Thrown back twelve years into the childhood she didn't want to remember, a childhood before the security of aeroplanes, she turned in panic.

'You go, luv,' the mocking voice called after her. 'But you'll be back soon enough, Rosie.'

Rosie, he'd called her *Rosie*.

She spun round, inexplicable fear engulfing her. The

man executed a neat, mocking double shuffle and swept off his ancient bowler hat, bowing low.

'How do you know my name?' she cried fearfully.

'How do we know the lady's name, Doris?' the man reiterated to the woman.

'*Please*!' Rosie almost screamed.

A sardonic smile came to his lips. 'Well now. As if I wouldn't know it. I'm your Uncle Alf, luv, that's 'ow I know yer name. Know yer anywhere we would.'

Waves of sickness swept over her again and she leaned against the hut for support.

The woman eyed her, glancing into the teacup. 'You shouldn't have told her, Alf,' she said sharply. 'Look at her. All to pieces. She's not our Rosie now. You go, luv. *Go*!' she shouted at Rosie. Petrified, Rosie turned and ran.

'You'll come to me, Rosie,' Alf called after her matter-of-factly. 'Oh yes, sometime you'll come back 'ome.'

It all flooded back, the misery, the pain. She ran, as though by so doing she could blot it out once more. When she was far enough away from the hop garden, she threw herself down on a haystack, and cried. She was eighteen and she cried the tears that she should have done twelve years before. She remembered the two dark, damp rooms, Ma and Pa in bed behind the curtain, she and others – sisters? brothers? – all in one bed, rolling, smelling, shouting, until she longed to escape through that grimy window and fly off after that bird to where the sky was blue. She remembered the beatings, the hugs, the smoke, the smell of drink and perpetual hunger. She remembered all this dispassionately, and it was past. But that other terror – why then this dark place still remaining? The dark place and Uncle Alf? And why did his words still echo round her mind: 'You'll come to me, Rosie . . . you'll come to me.'

'Let me see, Polly.'

Gabriel sat up suddenly, taking the painting from her as she spoke. Polly snatched it back. She had thought him

51

asleep on the grass, but his eyes had been on her all the time.

'Why do you do that?' he asked surprised.

'Because – because you're a *real* artist,' she said. 'I'm not.'

'Don't you think what you do is good? Is that why you won't let me see it?'

'I don't know,' she said. 'Oh, I don't *know*. It pleases me. I think it's good but—'

> 'He either fears his fate too much
> Or his deserts are small
> Who dare not put it to the touch
> To win or lose it all.'

He quoted lightly, gently. 'Anyway, I'm not God to say this is good or bad.' He looked at her watercolour. It was a scene of where they were sitting, showing the undulations of the downs, and the hop garden where the pickers were working. To him it gave an impression of timeless life amid nature. He looked at it for a long time, then gave it back to her.

'It's bad,' she said desperately.

'It's good, Polly, you know that, don't you? But—'

'It *is* bad.'

'No,' he said violently. 'No. But you need technique. You need to be taught, and not by a young lady's drawing master. You need a school and proper teachers. I see what you're striving for, but I think you're going about it the wrong way. You've seen too many Monets, too many Sisleys and you're using their techniques. You need your own. You need the technique for you have the art, so the question is, what are you going to do?' He lay back on the grass. He chewed a piece of grass contemplatively.

'Do?' said Polly, fencing.

Gabriel sat up again with an exclamation of annoyance. 'Yes, *do*, Polly. You need to join us. Come to the school with us in Cornwall. Or if you don't want to be with me, go to Paris, go anywhere where there's a school. You have real gifts, you must use them, and you can't do that alone.

You need other painters around you, to discuss the newest techniques, or you'll never develop.'

'My father won't let me,' she said dispiritedly.

'Have you asked him?'

'Not recently, but—'

'Then do it. There are plenty of lodgings in Newlyn.'

'He wouldn't,' she said carefully, looking away from him, 'allow me to go to Cornwall unchaperoned. And there's no one to chaperone me.'

Gabriel gave an exasperated '–tch!'. 'You've no idea how respectable we all are. It's painting we love and the girls *are* chaperoned. They live together and the married couples chaperone them.'

Three months she'd known him, three months of delight, of talking with him about painting – no, she was deluding herself; it was Gabriel she wanted to see, to be with; but painting was part of it, bound up with her love for him.

'I'll ask him,' she cried, fired with enthusiasm.

'And I'll come with you so that he can see how frightfully respectable I am, and that I have no dastardly plans to sell you to the white slave traffic. I do have some dastardly plans, though,' he added after a moment.

He caught her in his arms and gently took her into his embrace, as if he held a fragile butterfly that would flutter between his lips. At first she was rigid in his arms, then her arms crept round him, as her lips softened under his.

'One day,' he whispered slowly, 'I'll write a poem about you. In fact I think I'll begin it tonight.'

'Pushing party away,' called William, waving a hand at the controls.

Rosie, Harry and Michael, designated 'pushing party of the day', trundled Pegasus on its large bicycle-type wheels out on to Bred Field. At last the trials day had arrived for the new engine, the fourth Harry had produced. Rosie should have been bursting with anticipation, but something was niggling in her mind, stemming from what William had told her yesterday. 'Harry's been pressing me to patent Pegasus,' he had said quite casually. 'Do you think it a good idea, Rosie?'

Why should that have worried her? It was eminently sensible. Yet she had always thought of themselves as part of a group, working towards a common purpose: flight. What did it matter if someone took your idea, if thereby the objective came nearer?

'He believes that when the age of flight really dawns we could lose a lot of money with our invention if it is not patented,' William continued. He looked half irritated and annoyed. The businessman in him had to look after Potts Pedestal WCs, not aeroplanes. He had not considered the commercial aspect before and disliked the idea of doing so.

'There's his engine, I suppose,' said Rosie. 'He should patent that, perhaps.'

'He wants a joint patent, Pegasus and its engine.' Was it from this the niggle stemmed?

'He's right, I suppose,' she had said reluctantly.

'I'll think about it,' William said absently. 'Do you like Harry, Rosie?' he went on unexpectedly.

'Of course,' she said, startled he should even ask it. 'Don't you? Or do you mean do I want to marry him?'

He looked surprised as though such an idea in connection with Rosie had never occurred to him. Then he ruffled her hair and said no more.

They'd had four engines since they met Harry, and still had not achieved sufficient horsepower to sustain Pegasus's weight in flight.

'The Wright brothers had only a twelve horsepower engine, but we've a heavier structure altogether,' she'd said to Harry once.

'So you know about engines too?' replied Harry cheekily.

'Don't be patronising,' she said amicably. 'Flying is an art, not a science, so you have to know *everything* about it.'

'Science. It's a matter of mechanics, and nothing else. Solve the mechanical problems and we'll be able to fly. Simple.'

'I don't agree,' argued Rosie. 'It's like the driving you showed me. It's the last little bit of it which makes it art.

54

Feeling part of the machine. And being *up* there is what flight is going to be about, not *how* you get there. You'll see, it will make all the difference in the end.'

'You're a romantic, Rosie,' he said lightly.

'Don't you feel romantic when you think of flying?'

'No,' he said shortly. All he knew was he was going to conquer the air, and he was going to be the first to do it, if he could. And that was all there was to it. Motor cars were all very well, but air was a new element. A challenge that could not be resisted. Nothing would stand in his way, not old Potts and certainly not Rosie. She'd understand. It was just romantic nonsense, her wanting to fly. She'd been reading too many girls' magazines. His time with Potts had taught him the principles of aviation and, one day, he was going to put them into practice. And Rosie was not going to get there first – or at all, if he had anything to do with it.

Just before Harry met the Potts, he'd visited Paris and there at the Aero Club he'd heard an elderly American engineer, Octave Chanute, lecturing about the principles of gliding and how from these you could proceed to powered flight. It was then he'd known what his future was. Not just engines, but the aeroplane itself. Chanute was an enthusiast of the Wright brothers and their ideas, but he believed now they were busy barking up the wrong tree. In Europe they'd got the right idea, and their way was going to be his way: inherent stability. In the Wright brothers' machine, the aviator had to do all the controlling; but in Europe they were after letting the machine do it for you. Much safer. The purpose of flight control was adjustment, only your controls provided all stability. He knew he was right. Interesting the way old Potts groped and stumbled his way to something by instinct, whereas he reasoned it out from facts. Potts had a touch of the true pioneer in him, but it was to people like him, Harry Clairville Jones, that the laurels would go in the end. Relentless, determined men, who would brook no obstacles in their path. And that path meant building and flying one's own aircraft. Between them with Rosie's help, they could make Pegasus fly, he was sure of that.

And by the time they did so, he would have persuaded Potts he was the man to fly it. It would make sense for Potts as he was far too heavy. As for Rosie – he laughed.

'Isn't she beautiful?' Rosie exclaimed, looking at Pegasus on Bred Field. It was a weird kind of beauty. It was built as a biplane, rather like their old box kites, but with extended wings, as they learned from the glider; the driver was well forward of the wings with his controls. The tailplane looked impossibly top-heavy, but William swore he was right in designing it this way.

'Ready,' William signalled.

Pegasus looked like an albatross, thought Rosie as she panted, pushing hard. It might have huge ungainly wings on land, but in flight, why, it would prance the skies. She had thrown herself into working every minute she could on Pegasus, to rid her mind of that dark shadow that hung over her. She worked vigorously, convinced that it lay behind her, that Uncle Alf was wrong. She'd never go back, never. She was Rosie Potts, aeronautical engineer.

Unwillingly, slowly, memories of Uncle Alf had returned to her, however much she fought against them. *He* was the shadow that had crossed her life when she was a child, her father's brother, who, whenever he visited them, seemed to leave Ma crying and Pa violent. She'd hated him, hated him. The evil web he spun around her cocooned her in fear; he would trap her alone, and whisper, looking at her and always those words, 'You'll come to me Rosie, you'll come to me. You and me, Rosie.' She'd cried out in the night when she remembered this and Polly, hearing from her room next door, had come in to her, soothing her as though she were still a child. Rosie had tried to explain, but could not. Did Uncle Alf ever touch her? She could not remember. She only remembered the threat of some dread secret shared between them, some horrible thing that awaited her, a fear that made Pa's beatings almost welcome as a tangible evil to be faced. Not like this dark something waiting to spring at her unawares.

*'You'll come to me, Rosie. You'll come to me.'*

No, no, *no* . . . It was over, a new life had started, her path lay elsewhere. Away from the darkness for ever.

The engine coughed into life, and Pegasus began to travel along the ground under its own power. Michael ran behind it, cheering, while obediently Rosie and Harry flung themselves flat on their faces in order that they might determine the slightest lift of Pegasus from the ground.

'On, on,' Rosie willed it, her chin on the grass and almost feeling part of the machine as it struggled to lift.

'Tally ho, Jorrocks,' carolled William Potts, bent forward grimly, the controls clutched in his hand. But with all Rosie's prayers, Pegasus failed to lift. A hop, another hop, but nothing more. It raced on towards the edge of the field, where to their horror they saw Sir Lawrence waiting by his boundary fence. As William slewed Pegasus round at the last moment the wing tip brushed over Bellowes's fence, so that he was forced to duck.

'It was worth it just for that,' chortled William, as he clambered out chuckling. Then he noticed their downcast faces.

'Why, what's the matter? You're surely not worried about Pegasus not flying, are you? I'm sure I felt a little hop,' he said encouragingly. 'Yes, a very positive hop, and next time,' he said firmly, 'it will hop higher.'

'We'll have to wait till I get the new engine sorted out,' said Harry gloomily. 'If I ever do, that is.'

'The castor oil one?' asked Rosie. 'I'd forgotten about that. You hadn't mentioned it recently.'

'I wanted to wait till I got it right,' said Harry. 'We'll give this one another go. Lighten the load some other way. I could try going up in her.'

'Or me,' put in Rosie. She was ignored.

'No,' said William, unexpectedly firmly. 'Good of you, Harry, but if there's to be any risk to life, in my aeroplane, I'll do it.'

'Trespass?' shouted William unbelievingly at Featherstone. 'What the devil do you mean?'

'Trespass on his property, Mr Potts,' said Featherstone unhappily. 'I must admit to some concern. Sir Lawrence claims the space above his land is just as much his as

57

underground mineral rights would be. I must say,' he said, his legal mind suddenly warming to the idea, 'it opens up many interesting possibilities. If he succeeds, then could landowners charge balloons for floating above their land? No common law exists of course, and so the arguments would be most absorbing. I could quote—'

'I don't want you to quote,' said William testily. 'I want you to rid me of this ridiculous nonsense, so that I can spend my time doing what I should be doing.' Whether by this he meant the factory or the workshed was not clear.

'It may not be easy. He claims your aeroplane trespassed on his land when your – er – wings crossed the hedges and nearly knocked him off his feet. He generously forwent the assault charge,' Featherstone added without a trace of irony.

'Most generous,' muttered William, goaded. 'I'll go to see him.'

This he did but failed to move Sir Lawrence.

'The fellow's quite mad,' he complained grumpily to Rosie on his return. 'He's going to sue for trespass unless that son of his has an equal share in Pegasus.'

'What? The slug? Oh, Father, you didn't agree?' cried Rosie alarmed.

'Of course not,' said William indignantly. 'I said no. I said I had Harry and you and that was enough.' It was a paraphrase of his actual words which were: 'The mechanics of aviation do not yet cater for dead weight, Sir Lawrence.'

William regarded Gabriel Marriner cautiously, as if sensing an invasion on his property.

'Good morning, Mr Potts.' Gabriel was dressed in his best suit, not his usual blazer and flannels, in order to impress with his sobriety. The library at Brynbourne Place was a sober enough place in itself, increasing his nervousness.

'Father, I want to go to school,' Polly stated without preamble.

'To school, my dear?' William fenced for time, fiddling

with his Albert watch chain. He was quite aware of what was coming.

'In Cornwall, Father, with Gabriel,' she rushed on, already realising she'd made an error. 'To join the Newlyn School of Painting. It's all perfectly respectable. I mean, there are lodgings for single girls and there are chaperones.' Her words fell over each other.

'Painting?' William looked craftily nonplussed. 'But why?'

'You know I wish to be a real artist, Father, I always have. Like you and aeroplanes.'

'Pollykins,' he looked unhappy, 'you really cannot, you know.'

'I'd look after your daughter, sir,' put in Gabriel.

'No doubt,' said William drily. 'How old are you, young man?'

'Twenty-one, sir.'

'Polly is eighteen. You propose that she should come to live with you in Cornwall, and you want my blessing?'

'If you do not approve of that, sir, then not Cornwall. But let Polly go to art school somewhere,' said Gabriel impetuously. 'There are excellent ones in Paris and London. She should not be stifled.'

William turned on him. 'You seem to be unduly interested in my daughter's future, Mr Marriner,' he said mildly. 'I could not possibly permit her to go to art school alone. *Or* with you, unless she were married, of course. It would be most improper, however respectable you say these lodgings are. I take it that you would see a lot of each other. And I assume that you are unmarried, Mr Marriner. Do you wish to marry my daugher?'

Repressing the desire to point out it would be more improper if he were already married, and ignoring Polly's outraged 'Father', Gabriel replied stiffly, 'Miss Potts comes from a comfortable station in life. I am not yet able to offer her the same advantages, not till I make a name for myself. And I have not yet done so. But I will.'

'Very proper sentiments, young man,' observed William approvingly. 'So I suggest you go away and make a name for yourself and then come back and discuss taking my daughter to Cornwall.'

Gabriel turned white and as he was clearly dismissed, gave a despairing look at Polly and took his leave.

'Father, you don't understand,' Polly burst out once he had gone. 'It's not just Gabriel. It's painting. I must paint. Don't you understand?'

'I don't understand all this talk about painting,' said William, annoyed. 'You can paint here.'

'It's not the same. I must learn to develop technique.'

'That sounds like something that goodlooking young man has been planting in your head.'

'He didn't need to plant it, I've always known it. I've asked you before. I gave way then because—'

'Because then there wasn't Mr Gabriel Marriner to influence you. If you want to paint,' said William, upset at Polly's despair and struck by a happy thought, 'you could paint Potts Pedestal WCs. We could call them the flower range, how about that? They're all the fashion. You could paint flowers inside the bowl and paint over embossed ones outside too. Or – *here's* an idea – how about armorial bearings, individual WCs for each landed gentry family. Now there's an idea. How about that?'

Polly burst into tears and ran from the room, leaving William staring after her. There was no way she could go, of course. Children, the pair of them. The very idea. Who would chaperone her all day long? Painters had a bad reputation. Polly said the fellow came of a painting family. Unreliable, all of them. In love with their models. He'd be asking Polly to model before long. No, he'd had no choice, William thankfully decided. Having settled this in his own mind, he cheered up. That a desire to keep his womenfolk firmly under his own domain had anything to do with his decision, genuinely did not occur to him – for he took it as a tenet of his role in life that this should be the case.

'Rosie, it was terrible,' Polly wept. Rosie held her close. That calm, gentle Polly should show such grief. 'I hate Father. I *hate* him. He just didn't understand. He just made it seem as though Gabriel and I were—'

'Were what?'

'Wanted to go to Cornwall to be with each other.'

Rosie was already fond of Gabriel and thought romantically he and Polly were ideally matched.

'Father says I've got to paint at the factory,' Polly cried.

'I suppose it's better than nothing,' said Rosie practically, if unhelpfully.

'It's not *real* painting,' Polly wailed.

'Are you in love with him, Polly?' asked Rosie, going to the heart of the problem.

A short pause. 'Yes,' she whispered. 'And Father made it seem something shameful. Gabriel has never mentioned marriage, and Father cross-questioned him as though he'd asked for my hand. Now he's driven him away and I'll never see him again. I'll never love *anyone* else, ever.'

'If he loves you he won't be put off by Father.'

'But I don't know if he loves me.'

'Has he kissed you?'

'Yes.'

'Well, then—'

'He might be a philanderer,' said Polly, clearly not believing this for one moment.

Rosie thought about this. 'What do you feel inside when he kisses you?'

Polly thought carefully. 'As if I'd put the last touch to a perfect picture; as if all the bluebells in the world were calling out to me to paint them—'

'That's how I felt when I went up in the balloon and when I think of flying in aeroplanes—'

'Don't you feel that way with Harry?'

'Harry's never kissed me, so how would I know?' answered Rosie, cornered. One day she'd marry Harry, but not yet. Pegasus was the important thing at the moment.

'I should make sure he does, then,' said Polly now the practical one. '*Then* you will.'

The new rebuilt engine with the extra horsepower was

installed by the spring of 1906 and Pegasus was ready for its trials yet again. Rosie stood rapt in admiration, for the sturdy biplane wings with their struts and bracing arranged in giant squares, like a box-kite, were nearly all her own handiwork. The huge elevator attached by long booms in front of the flying machine was Mr Fisherbutt's contribution to the manufacture, the other controls all William's own work. William, as befitted his position, signalled Pegasus was ready and stood aside as Rosie and Harry trundled it out, Michael as ever her silent, faithful shadow.

When it was on the field, Harry stood back panting from the exertion and gave Rosie a quick grin. By now she had thought over what Polly had asked her about Harry. She liked him, she decided, loved working with him, sparring with him, and admired him. He took her into a world she would not otherwise have known. Having badgered him, she had toured the Clairville factory, and had even worn a dress for the occasion; she had surprised the engineers by talking knowledgeably about crankshafts and pistons.

Yes, Harry was part of their world now, part of Pegasus, part of her own ambitions for flight. Their destinies were bound up together in a glorious bid to explore the skies. What mankind could achieve with flight, to harness the air lovingly, not take it by storm, that was the important thing. She would ride it as she would a horse, on Pegasus.

She wished Polly would take some interest in Pegasus, but she refused pointblank. Painting the Potts Pedestal WCs had proved an unexpected success; Polly had enjoyed both the painting, and the companionship of the workshop; and the armorial bearings range provided a boost to the business. But it was her delicate flowers that Rosie loved, the graceful harebells that clambered up the sides of the bowl, the climbing roses that flocked over one another, the yellow sunflowers that turned their faces to the centre.

Pegasus was gathering speed now; heart in mouth Rosie raced after it with Michael, as if by so doing she could will Pegasus off the ground. So many aircraft were now performing short hops, flight was getting nearer, *surely* Pegasus must work? It was powered by a new forty horsepower engine. It must fly, it *must*. Pegasus gathered speed and William yanked on the controls as behind him the engine responded. Pegasus's bicycle-type wheels were lifting from the ground. Yes, no, yes they *were* lifting, surely they were lifting? She felt as excited as in Baldwyn's Park so many years ago.

Pegasus lifted perhaps a foot into the air, before disaster struck. What happened they could not see, but the aircraft catapulted, dug a wingtip into the ground and somersaulted, throwing William out.

It was Rosie reached him first, knotted in fear at the sight of that still figure on the ground. There was no sign of movement as she got there, and bent over him. Fear leapt at her, then relief came as an 'ouch' was followed by his rolling over and painfully struggling to his feet. He had a deep cut on his forehead where he had been thrown through the bracing wires.

'It was the tail,' he muttered worriedly as he dusted himself down, and hobbled over to the pile of splintered wood and fabric that was all that remained of Pegasus. 'The tail,' he repeated thoughtfully. 'But it nearly worked, didn't it?' He managed a brief smile as, clinging to Harry and Rosie, he stumbled back to the house, holding a handkerchief to his forehead.

From the ashes of the old, grew the new. More determined than ever, William designed new wings with less camber, but was still muttering about the tail. 'Initial lift, that's what we need,' he said. 'Lift to clear the tail from the ground.'

Rosie started work in the shed on her own. It was just an ordinary day, a day like any other. Harry was busy with the new motor car, and they hadn't seen him for weeks; William was at the factory. She was working on the piano-wire bracing struts, kneeling on all fours on the high platform, whistling, an unladylike accomplishment that Mildred had tried in vain to rid her of, and her hair pushed into a cap to keep it from falling over her eyes.

Gradually she had a sense of being watched, a sense that there was someone in the workshed with her. From her all-fours position, she glanced over her shoulder.

There standing down below her, inspecting Pegasus closely, was a man. A man she did not know and who was quite unlike anyone she had ever seen before.

# Chapter Three

'Pa, what's the matter with you?'

Alarmed, Jake Smith shook his father's shoulder roughly. His father was staring as if hypnotised into the pan he held at the edge of the creek.

'It's gold, boy, gold,' he said slowly, not taking his eyes from the pan. 'That's what the matter is with me. Yippee!' He sprang up, laughing and carolling his joy aloud, seizing hold of Jake in his exuberant way, just the way he did after a win at cards back home in Spitalfields – before things went wrong. 'Yippee.' He took off his wide-brimmed hat and waved it aloft, in thanks to the skies that had rained this fortune on him.

'Just the sun again, Pa,' Jake said quietly. He might be only fifteen, but he had learned quickly out there in the Klondyke. This had happened so often before in the six months since they'd arrived in the New Year of '98. His father, like everyone else it seemed, had impetuously rushed to the Yukon after the SS *Portland* had docked at Seattle in July '97 with its cargo of gold, and the story of how George Carmack, Skoojum Jim and Tagish Charlie had struck gold at Bonanza Creek in the Yukon almost a year earlier had flashed round the world, sparking off another Gold Rush. It was California '49 all over again.

Pa had been unstoppable. Just a few months, he'd said, after he'd lost his job in the docks, and they'd have made their fortune in gold and be back with Ma and Katie. He always had some wonderful scheme to make money. Wonderful schemes that could never fail – not until they did. Then would come the depression, the black moods, the drinking away what money they had, then the resolutions that he would create a better life for them all.

65

So he and Pa had joined the Klondyke Gold Rush and all the rest of the thousand upon thousand crazy bums in the world.

When they'd left Liverpool Jake was a Cockney fourteen-year-old who reckoned he knew it all, but by the time they reached Dawson three months later he knew he was only a raw recruit in life. They'd picked up a Yukon Express coach at Montreal, then run out of money, and had to work their passage on ship from Vancouver, then work on the dog-sled run to Dawson. By then he'd learned to keep his head down and his wits sharp. Part of the way they'd travelled with a herd of reindeer bound for Dawson. He never knew such animals really existed. He'd seen a model of one in a shop up West once, pulling a sled with Father Christmas in it. There weren't any Father Christmases out in Spitalfields – or in this wilderness. Nothing came for free down chimneys. It was hard work just to live, let alone finding gold. It hadn't taken Pa and him long to realise that the 'hunks', the foreigners, got the raw end of the deal every time. They were fair game at first for the North American hobos and miners from the south, making their way to the riches of the Klondyke. So they promptly lost their accents, young Jack Smith became Jake and they swopped their English clothes for rougher American duds. But that didn't mean they'd forgotten home. They learned to drawl, to chew tobacco, to drink, and to use a gun. Flooded by the hopeful, Dawson's population grew from 10,000 to 35,000 in a year, every man jack hoping to make the lucky strike. More dead than alive when they arrived, Pa and he had made their claim, registered it, staked it out and waited for spring.

'I tell you that's gold, son. And no fool's gold, neither.'

Jake stared into the pan where flecks of gold shone amidst the gravel. Slowly he moved so that he stood between the pan and the sun. The flecks still shone.

'Pa, it's gold.' His voice trembled, then ended in a shriek of joy. 'You've done it, Pa. We're rich.'

News travelled fast in the Yukon, especially in the summer of '98, with gold fever at its craziest, outstripping even Dawson's attempts to keep law-abiding, spurred on by its increasing importance as the capital of the new territory of the Yukon. Properly built houses replaced wooden cabins and shacks, and gold became a big, organised business, run on well-regulated lines. But no system gets going perfectly all at once. In its quest for the survival of the whole, there was precious little time for the victims of the system.

Jake stopped on the threshold of the ramshackle hut he and Pa had built when they arrived. It wasn't bad for a first attempt at building, although thrown together in desperation, but it was already beginning to fall apart. Now today he knew something was wrong. He could smell danger as surely as he could outside the pubs of Spitalfields. You learned that instinct early, if you were going to survive. He'd learned back home you had to fight to protect your own; then you could relax a little, sort out some better sort of world, where you didn't need to fight, not if you didn't want to, and whether folks had money didn't bear relation to whether they got well again. Like Ma, back home. Never been really well for years, but they didn't have the money to put things right. Now they would.

It was all quiet in the hut and yet . . . He opened the door cautiously. The first thing he saw was Pa slumped on the floor and still, very still. The next was the two hobos, one either side of the one-room shack. He'd seen them before, for they'd staked out a nearby claim to theirs, looking for placer gold just like them. Miners? Ex-convicts? Hunks from overseas? It didn't matter. Everyone was on his own up here. In the search for gold, some had no scruples how they got it.

The next moment Jake was yelling, shouting, 'Pa!', flinging himself down beside that still figure, rolling it over. He didn't need that drunken bum of a doctor to tell him Pa was dead. The unseeing eyes would have told him even if the blood spurting from the wound hadn't gushed all over him. The hobos closed in on him menacingly, standing one either side. A huge hand yanked him up.

'If you know what's good for you, boy,' he hissed, '*git*. Git right out of here now.'

Blindly Jake turned on him. He was already six feet tall and the punch he swung would have done damage if it had been controlled. As it was, it caught the hobo glancingly on the cheek. He staggered back, and his companion caught a blow under Jake's chin, forcing him back, and in his dizziness he fell over the box that served them as a chair. Then they were on him, pulling him up, one holding him, the other knocking him half senseless. He could taste the blood in his mouth, one eye was closed and in the murky distance, he could hear:

'If you wanna end up like him—' a foot kicked Pa '—that's okay with us. Or else you git now. Your pa was good enough to sign over his claim to us afore he left, so don't go getting no ideas. It's all legal.'

He heard their laughter fading away as he painfully picked himself up from where they'd dropped him, and left him with Pa. The men from neighbouring huts started to come around then, creeping from their shacks, helping him to bury Pa. He tried to report it, but no one wanted to know. It was happening all the time. The authorities were sympathetic, but, 'Your pa signed the claim, kid. Ain't nuttin I can do. It's all legal.' There was relief in the man's voice. One problem the less to deal with.

Jake left the office and went back to the hut, sick with misery. At least he still had the gold left. They didn't know that was there. He could sell up, get back to England, go back to Ma and Katie to look after them. Pa wouldn't have gone for nothing. But first he was going to find those hobos and make 'em pay for what they did to Pa.

He walked over to the place where they'd had their log fire. Then he saw the logs thrown around all higgledy-piggledy and he knew they'd made Pa tell them where the gold was. It had vanished along with the hobos.

It had been May who saved him then. Perhaps she had another name beside May, but Dawson never knew it. She was just May behind the Hoffman bar. If she could carry on another business privately, it was a discreet one. May was ageless with her painted face, inscrutable eyes and fussy bright-coloured frocks. But she had two major assets. She was a shrewd businesswoman, and kindhearted. She had been the best friend Pa had had.

So he went to May, vowing vengeance and sobbing his grief out on her lap. She listened in silence to his wild outpourings in the little room behind the bar, then she said dispassionately, her eye running over the lanky boy with his long honey-gold hair and straggly young beard and dark blue eyes, 'Jake, if they told you to git, then you gits.'

'That's running, May. I don't do that, not from Pa's murderers.'

'The fool's way is to stay, Jake. You want to do the right thing by your pa, don't you? I remember he told me he was mighty fond of your ma back home. And ain't you got a kid sister?'

Jake nodded. How would he get enough money now to get himself back home, let alone take money back with him? He gulped.

'That's the man's way, Jake. Not getting yourself dead too. Think your ma would want that?'

A mulish silence.

'Jake?'

'Reckon I'll stay,' he muttered.

May sighed. 'I'm moving on, Jake. I'm heading south to Colorado, where my sister is. This town ain't no fun now. You know mining, now that's good mining country. You come on down with me and earn enough money to take you home again to your ma. There's money to be made down there. I'd be mighty glad of the company on the journey, Jake. I'll pay your travel costs, if you come with me.'

A longer silence this time.

'I'm gonna stay, May.'

Three days later he came back to the hut to find it cleaned out, his belongings gone. When he'd taken this in, he ran for the Colt his father had kept. It too was gone. He'd hardly taken this in, before he was jumped by three men, bound and tossed over a horse, jolted to the outskirts of town, and thrown unceremoniously into the Yukon Express coach that the pack of swell women came in. A group of charitably minded American and English ladies had banded together to make life more comfortable for the miners in the Yukon. It wasn't May's sort of comfort, and they had little time for someone they clearly set down as a woman of pleasure. Not that May had appeared to care. She hitched her dress a little lower and laughed.

He glared at May sitting there beside him. 'Mighty sorry it had to be this way, Jake,' she said, grinning. 'But you didn't leave us no option.'

They didn't untie him till they were fifty miles from Dawson. By the time the coach had jolted its way through the White Pass, hundreds of miles towards Juneau and the Pacific Coast steamship, she'd talked some sense into him, and not only about not making his way straight back to Dawson.

'Jake,' said May, looking at his straggly beard, unkempt clothes and none-too-clean face. 'You look plug-ugly. We're heading for some swell place at Leadville and I sure would like to think of you arriving the way your pa would be proud of you.'

He took the heavy hint. The Jake Smith who arrived at Seattle harbour might not be smart, but he was tidy and the buckskin and shirt as clean as he could get them.

'I sure am grateful to you for paying for this,' he managed to mumble, as they jolted through the wild open countryside. It wasn't all by coach this time, but by railroad, not railways like back home, but full of strange-looking men with even stranger accents than he heard in the Yukon. The railroad sped through hundreds after hundreds of miles of nothing but empty plainlands, or mountains and rock, and never a sign of habitation, only the occasional halt. On these occasions he slept rough to save May's money while she took a room at the cheap hotels set up for travellers. Save one night. They were sharing a supper of beans and beef when May remarked casually; 'It looks mighty cold out there tonight, Jake.'

He shrugged. 'Don't notice it no more.'

'I reckon you'd find it warmer upstairs, Jake.'

'You can't afford no room for me, May.'

'Wasn't reckoning on taking no room for you, Jake.' A pause. 'Not when there's mine.'

'But where—' he stopped, hurriedly stuffing a mouthful of beans into his mouth, so he wouldn't have to speak.

'I like company at nights from time to time, Jake,' she said matter-of-factly. 'You ever been with a woman, honey? You're fifteen now and mighty big for your age.'

Crimson, he shook his head. Been with? Like Ma and Pa? He thought of the furtive fumbling, the muffled groans and sighs, listening to Pa and Ma the other side of the dividing sheet in the bedroom. He used to lie awake at such times and stare out of the small window at the small patch of sky he could see above the chimney pots, wondering what it was like up there, where you could look down on this ant-heap of a world as if you were part of the stars. Then he got older, and more knowing. No, he'd never been with a woman. Not really. In Spitalfields you had to get to know all about sex early. You saw enough of it; the huddled couples and the girls with their skirts up, the fourpenny ones they called them. There'd been that flower seller he'd been with, mistaking the beauty of her flowers for something more than a fourpenny one. But she'd laughed at him for being too hesitant, too clumsy, and she'd pushed his hand away impatiently, and the flowers had looked somehow tawdry.

He followed May into the small unswept room with its narrow bed, watching mesmerised as clothes began to fly everywhere, and white shoulders, huge white breasts emerged from her chemise. Half fascinated, half repelled, he took a deep breath, stripped off his clothes and jumped into the bed beside her, pulling up the one thin sheet to cover his nakedness. Then her large arms enfolded him and he was lost in flesh.

'Jake,' she said to him afterwards, when he lay exhausted and panting in her arms: 'Jake, you know something? There's a whole jungle of loving waiting for you, honey, and love up every damn tree of it.'

Leadville was at first a disappointment, after all the tales May had been telling him how the town had sprung up after the silver mining had begun, and the characters that had passed through, like Wyatt Earp and Doc Holliday, and she told him of Governor Tabor who made a fortune and lost it in the silver mines. But while he had money, he spent it. Spent it on building the Tabor Grand Hotel, and building an opera house to bring some culture to the place. And it had. Oscar Wilde had come, opera singers from all over. She had fired Jake's imagination. He'd pictured Wyatt Earp walking the streets, beautiful society women, and streets paved with silver, not this rather dull town with its rows and rows of houses. Then they drove down Chestnut Street, after getting off the Denver–Leadville–Gunnison railroad, and he changed his mind. This was Dawson grown up. Fashionable hotels, saloons, real respectable women. This looked like a town where he could earn money. May's sister, an older, primmer version of May, ran the Bellevue Hotel; it wasn't up among the top-notch hotels, but May's sister was aiming to be grander than the Tabor Grand itself. She and her husband owned the saloon next door too, but pretended they didn't. She eyed Jake with disfavour.

'Don't want no work-shy critters here, boy.'

'I don't want no poke-outs, ma'am. I want to work.'

'Times are hard since the silver crash. Even the saloon ain't doing so good, what with the strike.' There had been a miners' strike in progress since '96. 'You get your keep, that's all.'

'That'll do, I reckon,' said Jake steadily. 'For the moment,' he was thinking to himself, exchanging looks with May. Inside he was boiling with rage. He'd come all this way – and no money. He couldn't mine, because of the strike. But he'd find something else, that was for sure.

But it wasn't going to be soon, that was for sure as well. He'd no sooner found his feet in the saloon, learning to give as good as he got, deal gently with the drunks, and straight with the tricky customers, compassionately with the bums, than the snows came. That winter of '98/9 was the worst for snow Leadville could remember. It began in November, and piled up five feet high. Then it stopped awhile. In January it started again and hardly stopped for four months. They were digging railcars out, the miners' camps got cut off, and the snow just went on coming. Food ran short, and money shorter. But he was imprisoned there. He took up faro, in desperation, but May talked him out of it.

'There's better brains than yours at it, Jake. Bat Masterson played here, just like he still plays back in Denver, and the folks round here learned a lot from him.'

Even Jake had heard of Bat Masterson of the Wyatt Earp era, so he stopped. Maybe that wasn't such a bright way to get money to send back home. So he passed the time another way. He took on a job as cleaner at the opera house just so that he could get to every production, both plays and operas. He goggled at the actors and singers and colourful scenery, and it took him into a world completely new to him of which he'd heard back home in England, but never seen. Into a life that so far had known only struggle, it fed both romance and a longing for something he could not yet define. When he wasn't at the opera house, he was reading, to catch up on his inadequate schooling. They wouldn't take him at the school, but the schoolmaster took a liking to him and gave him lessons in the evenings. And it was there he met Florence.

He'd never seen anything as beautiful as Florence, the schoolmaster's daughter. Long ringlets, pink and white skin, pretty silk and lace frocks that showed her flouncy petticoats when she walked, and two dimples that showed when she smiled. She was a whole year older than him, nearly seventeen, and somehow she always seemed to be around when he came in the door, hat in hand, tongue tied, just staring at her. Then she disappeared with a smile and a whisk of her skirts, as he began his lessons.

One day she took him into the garden, sitting herself on the hammock, swinging to and fro while he gazed. She laughed. 'You're always staring so, Jake. Why? Do you think I'm pretty?'

He gulped. 'I guess you're the prettiest thing I ever did see, Miss Florence.'

'You could kiss me, Jake, then tell me all about England.'

It was a royal command. Kiss this fragile lovely thing? He put his arms round her, like she would break in two if he did it harder, and hesitantly placed his lips over hers. She giggled. 'Your moustache is tickling me, Jake.'

'I'll shave it off, Florence, if you don't like it.'

'Silly. Of course I like it.' She nestled against him and the birds sang their songs just a little sweeter that day.

Sometimes they'd go for walks after that. He never went any further than just kissing her. It wasn't like with May, and indeed he never connected the two. He kissed her fingers hidden in the little muff, in the cold snow, sat by her feet before the warm fire, and worshipped her.

Every day was full of Florence. May noticed and sighed, for she knew Florence Brown. Then came the spring, and time for him to go. Now there was Florence he didn't want to but, head over heels in love, he told himself it was part of the quest.

'I'll make a fortune, Florence, send some money back to the folks at home and then I'll come back and – marry you.' Greatly daring.

Florence giggled, and nestled closer. Two little hands stole round his neck, and enmeshed his heart. 'Do you love me, Jake?'

'You know I do, Florence,' he answered fervently, all the love of the world in his eyes. 'You'll wait for me, Florence, won't you?'

'Of course, Jake. For ever.'

* * *

In the two years that followed Jake grew up. He'd gone
west like so many before him. He learned how to survive
physically and mentally on his own in a tough world
where survival was a struggle. He roamed north to
Wyoming where he became a ranch hand, learning to
ride adequately enough; his only previous experience had
been the milkman's nag. From here he found his way to
Texas where he learned to use the bullwhip proficiently,
enjoying his mastery of it. Even the cowboys would gather
round to watch him flick a matchstick from a hand sixteen
feet away with the popper on the end of the lash, and never
touch the holder. Tiring of Texas, he travelled up to Kansas
on a cattle drive, working his passage, earning enough to
send a little back home. He kept to himself as much as he
could in this masculine society, the thought of Florence at
the end of his quest keeping him going. In Kansas, his use
of the bullwhip came to the attention of Buffalo Bill, who
took him on for his Wild West Show where, dressed in
outlandish cowboy clothes, he travelled from city to city.
He made a friend in the show. Old Will was so much a
part of it, so much a grizzled old hand, he was taken aback
when he said to him one day, 'Ever go to the Canterbury,
Jake?'

'Why, that was pulled down years ago.' Jake stopped.
'Hey, how come you know? You visited London?'

'I'm as English as you boy, that's why. Just bin out
here longer. Came out to California in '49, never did find
no gold, and somehow I never got to go back. Mind that
don't happen to you, boy. Ain't no good forgetting your
country.'

Nor Ma, nor Katie. A pang was replaced by thoughts of
Florence.

'I'm sending money,' he told himself fiercely. 'That's
what they need, ain't it?'

'That little Albert king now?'

Jake stared amazed. 'King? We got a queen. Queen
Victoria. Ain't you heard, Will?'

'Well now. She still going? She was just a pretty little

75

thing when I left. Never reckoned she'd still be alive. Ain't that something. Like me, eh? A stayer.'

'What made you stay, Will?'

'Oh, I dunno. Kinda appealed to me. Back home it's all closed in. You don't see the sky like you do here. Just you look up there now.'

Jake looked up, and shrugged. 'It's just the sky, Will.'

'Look again, boy. Don't you see nuttin else? Haven't you ever got to wondering what it's like up there, looking down?'

'Reckon I have,' said Jake slowly, all the old memories flooding back again of that little patch of sky that meant so much in his youth.

'I just sits here and looks at it. I ain't beholden to no man when I looks up there. One day I reckon we'll find out what it's like. Maybe even fly just like a kite. What do you reckon, Jake? Possible?'

'Yes, Will. Must be. One day I'll find out.'

What the hell made him say that? Him, Jake Smith? He must be plumb crazy. Yet he knew he wasn't. He was quite certain he'd be up there. Heading for the sun.

Just after Christmas that year, the old queen died. Jake read the news in the Chicago newspapers where they were holding the show that week, and went to tell Will.

He took the news calmly, then said at last; 'Reckon it's time for me to be moving on too, Jake. Now the old queen's dead.'

Will died quietly and without fuss a month later. 'Time for you to git, boy,' were his last words to Jake.

Time to git. Yes, now he could go back to Florence. He'd saved enough now.

May hadn't changed. A little more paint and a few more wrinkles, but the same warm smile. She looked up, showing no surprise as Jake came through the door.

'Ain't you surprised to see me, May?'

She looked at him; he'd fleshed out a bit, still lanky though, but the eyes held knowledge now.

'I knew you'd be back, Jake. You reckoning to stay?'

'Sure am, May.'

She came out from behind the desk and hugged him. Then the tears came. 'Darn it, that's my paint running. How are you, Jake?'

'Doing well, May.' A pause. 'How's Florence?' he burst out.

'Florence? Why, Jake, well. Baby coming soon now.'

'Baby?' He looked puzzled.

She saw the look. 'You mean to say she didn't tell you, Jake? She didn't write you that she married 'bout a year after you left? Lives in a big house up on Harrison.'

The world spun round. He thought he kept his face straight, but she knew him well. 'Things don't stay the same, Jake.'

That was for sure. Nothing was secure, not even May. They treated their women well in America, that had always impressed him seeing how it was back home, remembering the beating up they got at home on Friday and Saturday in Spitalfields. Here the women were treated like goddesses. Like he had Florence. But they didn't treat May like a goddess the night she got shot.

'Never get between a man and his cards,' she told him once. She broke her own rule. She aimed to break up a game in the saloon, but got in the way of a bullet. Just like Pa. May was still alive when he reached her.

'Jake,' she whispered, her eyes already clouding. 'You git back home now and find yourself a girl. A whole lot of loving, that's what you need, boy.' Then she'd died. Went and died on him, just like that. Slowly Jake straightened up on his heels and looked around. 'Sheriff's coming, son,' said one of the onlookers awkwardly.

'I ain't waiting,' said Jake slowly. He'd seen the killer slinking out of the door. He walked behind the bar and brought out his bullwhip from where he kept it, and walked out of the saloon. He caught up with the killer round the back of the saloon and left him half dead. Then he told the sheriff where he was. Three days later he put up a stone over May's grave. He'd given a lot of thought to it. It read: 'A lovely lady lies here'. Then he went to old Pap Wyman's saloon and got drunk.

He was still there six hours later when a hobo came in, singing, waving a bottle of rye in one hand.

'Uncle Sam done it again, bud.'

Jake recognised him out of one bleary eye. 'You're drunk, Joe. Drunk. This is a respectable house.'

'I'm not drunk,' said Joe carefully. 'I'm just congratulating Uncle Sam. You know, Jake,' he continued as if he'd seen him only yesterday, 'I seed a man fly.'

Jake snorted. 'Too much whiskey, Joe.'

'Listen, Jake. Don't you want to hear?' He lurched slightly. 'I just got back from Carolinee, Jake. Six months I bin there, and I tell you out there in Carolinee, it's mighty different. Why, I seed a man fly with great big wings.' He took both arms off the table to demonstrate and fell off the chair. 'I sure did, Jake,' he burbled anxiously, head reappearing over the table level. 'And that's God's own truth.'

'Tell me, Joe,' said Jake, resigned.

'You'll listen to me?' said Joe, charmed. 'Why, I tell you, Jake, you're the first as has.' Jake listened with half an ear to his ramblings. 'Out on the sands on them Kill Devil Hills, they got this contraption. And one of them lay on it, and other fellows pushed and off it flew. You do believe me, don't you?'

'Sure do,' said Jake absently.

'Like a kite it was.'

Jake's attention riveted on him. A kite? Soaring in the sky. Suppose this lush was right. Suppose he really had seen something. Before he left England there'd always been talk about man flying, trying to build machines, even gliding like birds. Suppose someone here had actually done it . . .

'Tell me again, Joe,' he said excitedly. Perhaps it was going to be possible to get right up there in the sky and look down on this old world after all. 'Tell me again, *slowly*.'

That was July. In August 1901 Jake was discreetly standing on the huge expanse of sand known as Big Kill Devil Hill, one of four such dunes, constantly shifting shape with the wind. He was trying to keep in the background for he'd already learned in the nearby village of Kittyhawk that these men didn't like strangers around. He'd travelled hard and rough to get here, and he had a sense of anticlimax. He could see something like a huge box kite being carried up the dune by four men. Old Joe must have been imagining things. This contraption wasn't going to fly!

But it did – after a fashion. One of the men clambered prone on to the bottom wing, grasping some sort of controls. Then the rest rushed down the hill, releasing their hold. Yawing wildly in the wind, the contraption was on its own, coming right past him now. With no engine, it was just like a huge box-kite in many ways. And it was flying. It must have flown three or four hundred feet before it came to rest burying its nose in the sand. It wasn't a long flight, but it was enough. If man could achieve that in non-powered flight, what could he not do with power?

Kittyhawk, North Carolina, the day he knew he wanted to fly above all other things. In the two years that followed he went back to the Wild West Show, determined now upon a course of action. He'd sent money back home, and in the meantime found out all he could about these men and their machine. It had not been easy for they were reticent, scientists rather than showmen. But he'd found out all he needed to know. They were two brothers who ran a bicycle factory up north, a place called Dayton, in Ohio. He'd read all he could about aircraft, engineering and the principles of flight in those two years, he visited Chicago and talked to an engineer called Chanute, whose enthusiasm for flight had helped and encouraged the Wright brothers. It was he who had got the Wrights interested in building their own glider, and he who fired Jake's determination to join the world of aviation. He put in two years of hard work and late in 1903, when he was twenty, he went back to Kittyhawk.

He found his heart beating with excitement almost as if

he, Jake, were to take off in the flying machine. For this was no glider. This was powered, albeit by a hand-built engine of only twelve horsepower. If it worked – perhaps this would be the first fully man-controlled flight ever.

The machine was sitting on skids as before but they were on a support on two small wheels which would run about eight inches from the ground along a wooden rail, facing into the wind. By this time he knew why, thanks to his reading. He'd been here now for a month, paying his way by helping out at the general store and diffidently offering a hand at the Wrights' workshed whenever he could. The weather had been bad, and it was again today. But it might be the last chance until spring. The brothers, immaculately and correctly dressed as they always were in suits, ties and stiff white collars, appeared as cool and calm as ever. The first flight this morning with Orville at the controls hadn't worked well. Instead of soaring into the air, the machine plunged right into the sand; but somehow Jake didn't lose hope. It was only a matter of time. Now, at twelve o'clock, Wilbur was ready for the fourth flight of the day. The official witnesses, five in all, were silent, almost as tense as the brothers themselves must be. Now the engine was being run up with the machine still tethered; now it was being set free; it was running along the rail, faster and faster. When it gained sufficient power . . .

*It flew.* Up and along . . . The cheers had scarcely left the onlookers' throats before it was down again. But there was no doubt about it. For fifty-nine seconds it had flown, covering eight hundred feet. It was a modest start, but quietly, confidently, the two brothers turned to face the future.

The press reported the event, without great excitement, and the world, save for a few far-seeing men, scoffed.

Orville and Wilbur Wright were different from Jake in almost every respect, but one: they went their own way. Serious, determined, Orville the more dynamic, Wilbur the quieter, the two brothers with the encouragement of their father, Bishop Milton Wright, head of the United

Brethren Church, had gone into the bicycle-selling business in the early '90s. They started by selling bicycles; in a year or two they were marketing their own invention, the Wright Special, which sold for just eighteen dollars. Ohio was forging ahead in industry and manufacturing was encouraged in Dayton. The Wright Special was a commercial success, but bicycles weren't enough to satisfy the brothers. They became fascinated by the concept of flight, and the principles of gliding inspired by the German pioneer, Otto Lilienthal, and the more they studied the more interested they became until in 1899 they got in touch with Octave Chanute, a Chicago engineer famous for his interest in aviation. With his guidance and encouragement, they progressed to building their gliders of 1899 and 1901. From there, it had been a short step to powered flight – a short step but a difficult one, which had culminated in the brothers designing their own engine for their assistant Charlie Taylor to build.

They had achieved flight, but the world took little notice. Not that that bothered Orville and Wilbur Wright. They went back to Dayton from North Carolina, to build another aeroplane.

This time Jake Smith followed them. The brothers had no need of and no desire for a partner, but the way Jake reckoned it, if he could get taken on in the bicycle business, he'd be one stage nearer. He found himself cheap lodgings in the town, wheedled a job from Charlie Taylor who ran the bicycle business for the brothers and built their engines. He spent every spare minute helping the Wrights as a general hand. Never obtrusive, never putting his own burgeoning views forward. But learning. When the Wright Flyer II was tested in the second half of 1904 at the Huffman Prairie, east of Dayton, Jake was there to help. He noted the problems, wondered about solutions, and was ridiculously pleased when they thanked him for his work. The tests went on for six months quietly making progress in beating the problem of turning the machine, although it was still liable to stall.

He had a lot of ideas about aeroplanes now, he knew how he would agree with the Wrights and where he differed. He itched to tell them, to argue it out, but he didn't. His whole life was bound up now with the quest for flight. If girls, like his landlord's daughter, eyed him wistfully, he either did not notice or ignored them. Somewhere buried inside him was the memory of Florence. And of May. It no longer hurt, but he remembered the lessons. The problem was put aside as part of some future when the real aim of life had been achieved. No woman would ever have the power to hurt him again, either by betrayal or by her loss. Not quite realising the reason for it, he gradually began to adopt his old style of dress, not to conform to the business wear of Dayton, but to work in his old Texas duds; that way he was left alone, an amiable companion but no close buddy.

By 1905, Jake was twenty-two and an accepted part of the small Wright circle. The famous Flyer III was tested that summer and autumn, with progress being made all the time; flights lasted longer now, but deep problems remained.

'You know, I still reckon you're wrong about linking that warp and rudder,' he burst out, unable to hold back any longer while they were discussing it on the field one day in his presence. The two brothers stopped and looked at him as if he had been so long part of the scenery that they had forgotten he could speak. They exchanged a look.

'Take her up,' said Orville laconically. 'Then, you tell us.'

Jake stared at them open-mouthed.

'Don't you want to?' asked Wilbur impatiently.

'Sure,' Jake managed to stutter, before doing what so often he had done in his dreams, slithering prone on to the pilot's seat, engulfed by his new world.

The machine had a better system of take-off now, relying on a derrick and rope system, willing hands hauling a weight into position.

He felt as if he was on a sled back in Leadville. But this was no sled. As the weight was released, and the engine roared to life, he felt the power under him as the machine began to move along the rails, he felt the Flyer gather speed, quicker and quicker, he could feel his heart beat. Raise the nose carefully now . . . He saw the rope slipping off the spin and the complicated rope arrangement released its hold on the aircraft, and then he felt the power surge beneath him as the machine rose and the ground slipped crazily beneath him, yawing violently. Power line ahead. Correct quickly. He warped the wings, bringing it back under control as it rose responding to his touch. Ah, this was love – perhaps that was what May had meant? His heart exulted, while his mind remained deadly clear, feverishly trying to remember all he'd learned, all they'd talked about the controls. Hell, it was going to stall, yes, no; by instinct he put the nose down to gain speed. That did it. He breathed again, and the fear left him. Sheer joy. King of all he surveyed. Yes, this was love. Women's love could never be like this. He stayed up ten minutes, then seeing the upturned faces beneath, tactfully decided to come down. This was surprisingly easy compared with the turning problems. He made it down, bumping over the uneven ground, but safe, though a little too near the barbed wire fencing for the brothers' liking. He saw the agonised tense faces relax in relief.

'What do you think?' they asked intently.

'I'd say,' said Jake, not quite suppressing the excitement in his voice as successfully as the tremble in his knees, 'pretty good. But I still think those darn warp and rudder controls need dividing.'

Now he spent less and less time at the factory and more and more at Huffman Prairie. In September they divided the warp and rudder controls, which left Jake bursting with suppressed pride. Occasionally they'd let him take the Flyer III up, and that was enough for him. And all the while he was sending money back to Ma and Katie. They had become part of a dream now, to be attained some day, like having his own aeroplane.

One night at the Wrights' home they talked more than usual about the future of flight. And more practically, the future of Flyer III. What was the next step? To the Wright brothers it was quite clear. Someone had to buy it, and who but the Government? But the US Government had turned it down earlier that year. The device must have been brought 'to the stage of practical operation without expense to the United States', the letter had run to their disgust. How to make them understand it *was* operating? So they turned to England.

Lieutenant-Colonel Capper, head of the British Army Balloon School, had come to Dayton earlier that year. Very excited, he had taken back photographs and details to the British Government. Who had not been interested. So the Wrights approached the Government themselves. Again nothing. Neither the War Office nor the Admiralty was seriously interested. 'The Flyer,' Wilbur quoted bitterly, 'would not be of any practical use to the Naval Service.'

'They're crazy,' said Jake forthrightly.

'You tell them that, Jake. You're English.' The Wright brothers were going to build no more aeroplanes until someone bought one. Design them, maybe. Build and fly – no.

The biggest decisions come in the simplest way. Jake was to go to England to try to persuade the Government once more. If he failed, he'd stay there, for there would be no more flying at Dayton. If he succeeded, he could choose what to do.

The old familiar sights and smells, the wet claustrophobic warmth of London closed in around Jake as soon as the railway train drew in. The fields on the way up from Southampton looked like patchwork after the vast prairies of the States – unreal; cottages and small villages like a picture postcard – and left him unmoved. But London did not. The foggy wet clammy smells, the muddy pavements, the crowded streets, haphazardly laid out, tugged at his heart. It was like taking a step back in time. He'd bought special clothes so he didn't stand out too much and wouldn't attract notice, yet somehow he did. Maybe the way he walked, with that long loose stride. Maybe his tall figure with his long deep-golden hair and deep blue eyes. Or maybe the drooping long moustache.

Montague Street looked much the same. There were

no motor cars here yet. Just house upon house crowded together. He knocked on the door, feeling strangely calm, children in ragged clothes staring at him. Then the door opened and Katie stood there. She'd been only twelve when he went away and now she was twenty, but there was no mistaking that brown curly hair; though she was thinner now and handsome. My, she was handsome.

'Jack,' she said faintly. 'You're Jack.'

He opened his mouth, but no words came. Instead he scooped her up off the ground and hugged her. It had been a long time since he hugged anybody, and he knew as his arms went round her that regardless of the success of his mission he was back to stay.

'That you, Jack?' A roar from upstairs. A well-remembered roar. So dear to him.

'Yes, Ma.' He almost choked.

A gaunt figure appeared at the head of the narrow staircase. Mrs Smith regarded her son grimly.

'Took your time, didn't you?'

'Yes, Ma. But I guess I'm home now.' He began to walk, then run up the stairs towards her.

Jake did his best but the English Government remained English. Armed with his letters of introduction, backed up by support from Capper, he still failed to convince them of the potential future for flight. He spent two months trying to persuade them and he'd given up. He felt an alien here. These English didn't know whether to laugh loudest at his clothes or what he had to say about man flying. He kept his buckskin and check shirts for private, but still he stuck out like a sore thumb in London. And he got nowhere. The offer of trials failed to impress the Government. It was good of the Messrs Wright, ran the policy, to offer to come to show them the aeroplane, but that suggestion had already been put forward once and rejected. The purposes of flight for war were adequately fulfilled by the man-carrying kites of Mr Samuel Cody at the Army Balloon School.

At the Aeronautical Club Jake received a warmer welcome, but hidebound by insularity they were only really interested in English flight and their own experiments. The wider concept – what was happening in France and in America – failed to grip their imaginations. Only one man gave Jake a hearing, apart from Capper, and that was Samuel Cody. He was no relation of Buffalo Bill, but a naturalised American. He lived in England now, and he too had ideas about flight. They talked long and hard about the Wright brothers, but when Cody mentioned a friend who might be interested in Jake, Jake was so conditioned to pessimism that he forgot all about it.

He heard the noise in the street outside, as the large chauffeur-driven motor car drew up. It was just as well it had a chauffeur in that neighbourhood, for Clairvilles were rarely seen in Montague Street.

'Jack!' Ma came rushing in, bright as a bee. Thanks to the money, her health had much improved. 'Someone for you, Jack.' She couldn't get used to calling him Jake. He stood up as a portly middle-aged man, smartly dressed and with a slightly absent air about him, bustled in.

'Mr Smith? Delighted to meet you. I'm Potts, William Potts. You may have heard of Potts Pedestal WCs, if not, never mind, it's aeroplanes we're here about, aren't we? My good friend Mr Cody says you—'

His eyes were still flicking round taking everything in, including the buckskin.

Aeroplanes? Potts? Wasn't that a name he'd heard of at the Aeronautical Club?

'Sit yourself down, Mr Potts.'

'Thank you, my dear man, thank you.' But William preferred to stand, shrewdly summing up the young man with the long golden hair and straggly moustache, as if coming to a silent decision.

'I understand you've worked with the Wright brothers?'

'Why, yes.'

'And you want to work with aircraft?'

'Why, yes, I—'

'Good, good, I have one. You're hired.'

'Now that's mighty good of you, Mr Potts, but I—'

'You want to know what sort of aeroplane. I suggest you come and look at her.'

'You want a mechanic?'

William looked surprised. 'I've got a mechanic.'

'An engineer.'

'I have an engineer.'

'What then? General hand?'

'No, Mr Smith, I'm getting old and I'm getting fat. I want someone to help me fly it and to be in charge of the whole project. I'd give you an assistant, naturally.'

Jake stared. The man was crazy; ten to one his aeroplane was nothing but a collection of strings and wires and a paper design.

William Potts flashed him a charming smile. 'I daresay you think I'm quite mad. I see it this way, Mr Smith. Now the Wright brothers have flown, very soon so will many other people. And then the Government will wake up. There will be a great many people, all wanting a share of the Christmas cake. Indeed there are already,' he added as an aside. 'It needs a strong hand, and a true hand, Mr Smith. I want to keep my ideals and I can afford to do it. I don't want my aeroplane a stepping stone to individual power. It's to help mankind, that may sound a trifle grandiose, but I understand,' he paused and looked at Jake shrewdly, 'from what Mr Cody tells me, you might share my views?'

Jake was bereft of words and could only nod.

'I should like it if you would join us, Mr Smith. I warn you, it will not be easy. But it will be rewarding. Oh yes, it will be rewarding. So you'll do it.' It was not a question. 'Splendid. Come down to Kent and have a look at Pegasus.'

# Chapter Four

The boy just stood up there, grinning from ear to ear like the Cheshire Cat in that story Ma had told him once. He was clearly trying hard not to break into laughter. A lively enough youngster, and ordinarily Jake wouldn't have reacted. But today was different. Dressed in his buckskin as befitted a working day for him, he'd come down by the railroad to check out this flying machine, this Pegasus, full of suppressed excitement. Even now he could scarcely realise it had happened. No ifs, no buts, but 'you're hired'. He would have taken to William Potts straightaway even without the confidence William had placed in him.

The journey had been far from enjoyable. He'd been unable to concentrate on his thoughts about how he'd go about things to make sure this Pegasus was in the forefront of development here. The railway carriage had been full of prim and proper types who had inched away from the tall foreigner as though he might contaminate them. At Newington Station he'd found a strange reluctance in the cab drivers to bring him to Brynbourne, and in the end he had been forced to beg a ride from a farm waggon. It wasn't the way he'd have chosen to arrive.

And now this slip of a lad, thirteen, fourteen, maybe, was laughing at him. Jake took a deep breath. If he was going to run things here, he'd start right now.

'Something amusing you, boy?' he asked mildly.

At the sound of the soft American drawl, the grins gave way to a peal of laughter, which set the kid down to even younger than Jake had thought, twelve maybe. The boy opened his mouth to speak, perhaps an apology, but Jake forestalled him, flushing red.

'If you're aiming to stay around while I'm here, boy, I reckon you need to be taught manners,' he said softly.

In two strides he had reached the scaffolding, swung himself up, and caught the boy up under one arm. With a squeak, the boy, as quick as he was, wriggled out of his grasp, gave him one horrified look, and seeing the grim intent on Jake's face, swung down the scaffolding and doubled out of the shed, with Jake in hot pursuit.

Jake caught up with the boy on the far side of the field, swept him up, screaming in anger, and held him over the enormous cattle trough; he suspended him aloft for one moment, the boy's legs kicking wildly but ineffectually, then deliberately lowered him into it, dropping him the last few inches. It was a deep trough with plenty of water, and the boy yelped and spluttered. Then one strong hand hauled him out like a wet bedraggled puppy, gasping, and wiping the water from his eyes.

'I guess you're going to enjoy working for me, boy, ain't that so?' Jake enquired mildly.

Not taking in the words, reacting only to the hated voice, the boy aimed a weak fist up at Jake's face.

'Whoa there,' Jake caught the hand, knocking off the boy's cap in the process. A mop of sodden dark curls clung round the boy's face. A puzzled look crossed Jake's face, a moment's uncertainty before a look of horror followed it. His eyes travelled down his victim's soaked figure, but before he could speak, the full extent of his unspeakableness swept over Rosie.

'Why, you – you – monster.' Blind with fury, she put her head down and charged this mountain of evil before her, ramming him amidriffs, knocking him backwards, and transferring some of the wet to his buckskin jacket as he caught her and held her to prevent another charge.

'How was I to know you was a lady, ma'am?' he said contritely, as she struggled impotently in his arms.

'I'm surprised *you* think it would have made any difference,' she stormed.

Jake considered, still grappling with her. 'It might not at that,' he said, a slight smile on his lips.

'Only an American would behave like that to a lady,'

she cried uncharacteristically, and almost weeping with rage.

'You ain't no lady,' he replied, matter-of-factly, taking off his buckskin and putting it round her shoulders, trying to keep his eyes away from the thin overalls clinging to her breasts. 'Ladies don't laugh at other folks that cruel way.'

He had no way of knowing just how this struck home as shades of Robert Bellowes swam before her eyes. Rosie was inarticulate with rage, all the more so because she knew he had right on his side. But he had caught her on the raw.

She flung off the coat, then appreciating why he had put it round her, flushed and put it on again. 'I'm Rosie Potts, William Potts's daughter, I live here, I work here and I'm not going to be taught manners by a – a – Hiawatha,' twitching disdainfully at the buckskin coat.

Mr Potts's daughter! Jake groaned aloud. What a helluva way to start the new life. It seemed the fates were dogging him. Be darned if he was going to grovel though. The girl deserved it, so he told himself, though he would never have laid a finger on her if he'd realised her sex. Deciding that his conscience was clear, he said calmly, 'You ought to get some dry clothes on, miss. We can talk later.'

'I sincerely hope you'll be gone, when I come back, and that whatever you're doing here, you'll do it and disappear back to the *Mayflower*,' she shouted.

A silence. 'I – reckon I'll be around for a while,' Jake said hesitantly, ''less Mr Potts says otherwise naturally.' Ten to one, this girl would dish any hopes he had of staying around. An awful thought struck him. 'Would *you* be the assistant Mr Potts said I'd have—' he asked slowly.

The girl stared at him, dark eyes filled with horror. 'If you mean do I work on Pegasus, I do,' said Rosie stiffly. 'What do you mean – *the assistant you'd have*?'

An appalled silence, then: 'Why, ma'am,' said Jake slowly, 'didn't Mr Potts tell you he'd put me in charge of the Pegasus project?'

91

* * *

Rosie stormed back to Brynbourne Place shivering with cold and shock. Smarting from the sense that she had not behaved well and that he could not be blamed for taking her for a boy, she was still indignant at her treatment. It was an insult to be treated so by someone who looked as if he were out of a Wild West show. Worst of all, either he was some kind of lunatic, or William had really appointed him to work on Pegasus. Not as leader, she couldn't believe that, there must have been a misunderstanding. He may have assumed too much, he must be boasting. He *must* be. After all, Father wanted to keep everything under his own control. Even so, why should she have to work with such an oaf at all? And why was it necessary when they had Harry and Mr Fisherbutt? And *why* hadn't Father told her? She stormed into the library without even changing, spoiling for a fight, but William was at the factory. Instead she found Mildred who ignored the tirade that Rosie directed at her, and ordered that she should get out of those wet clothes.

On her way to the bedroom, Rosie met Polly – who stared, and then the corners of her mouth twitched.

'Don't laugh at me,' said Rosie anguished. 'Come and find some dry clothes if you want to help.'

'But what happened?' gasped Polly, unable to hold back the peals of laughter. 'And *where* did you get that jacket?' She executed a neat little dance, humming 'Where did you get that hat?'

Rosie had forgotten she was still wearing his coat, and flung it off as if it were contagious.

'Take it back to him,' she ordered, flinging it at Polly. 'Tell him I thought he should have it *before* he left. And leave he *will*. I'm not working with *him*!'

'Who, what, where?' asked Polly, bewildered.

Rosie explained jerkily, ending: 'I don't care *what* Father says, I'm not working with *him*. And what will Harry say?' Her voice rose in anguish.

'I wonder why Father did it?' said Polly. 'He must have had some reason.'

'Perhaps he didn't,' said Rosie hopefully. 'Oh I hope, I hope he didn't. That *man*!'

Just as shaken as Rosie, Jake watched the small belligerent figure stalk back towards the house. What an end to all his hopes. William Potts would hardly forgive him treating his daughter that way. He'd be out on his ear before he'd even so much as seen the aeroplane properly. Hardly knowing what he was doing, he began to walk towards the road to walk back to Newington station where he'd left his luggage. Well, he wouldn't need that luggage now. He'd just take it back to Spitalfields.

Then, his despair increasing, Jake remembered his ticket and all his money were in the jacket that he lent to the girl. He'd have to go to the house after all to face the music. Or rather laughter, with him in his check shirt sleeves, breeches and boots. Damn it, he might as well have a look at this aeroplane while he was here. He'd been so caught up with Miss Potts he'd hardly glanced at it. Irresolutely, slowly, he turned back towards the shed. It couldn't hurt too much just to look. Or could it? Suppose it were just as good as William Potts described? It would be mighty hard to walk away from it again, to see all his dreams in front of him, only for them to be snatched from him. All because of a slip of a girl. Women were nothing but trouble in his life. For a moment he stood irresolute, then arguing once more that it wouldn't do any harm to have a look, he walked quickly back to the shed.

Jake drew in his breath sharply. It *was* every bit as good as William had said. He could see that at a glance. A biplane of the same basic box kite design as the Wright Flyers, its span was roughly the same size, about forty feet. Marked emphasis on elevator – good longitudinal stability – interesting. Though he was beginning to have doubts about forward elevators. But Pegasus had no wing-warping, or ailerons, only inadequate balancers. He frowned. So that meant little lateral control. The engine was a beauty though. He was looking forward to meeting this Henry Clairville Jones – though William hadn't told him much about him. He got the impression William Potts wanted him to find his own feet. That suited him.

Then he remembered. He wouldn't be here to find his own or anyone else's feet. By one unlucky chance he'd thrown away his future.

He ran a hand down one of Pegasus's ash struts, overwhelmed with despair. He wasn't used to girls like Rosie; the ones he'd met were ladies like Florence, or good-time girls like the landlady's daughter. He'd never met any that were interested in aeroplanes. Working with a woman, he thought uneasily. How the hell could you do that? Especially his employer's daughter. Kate worked as a school-teacher; that was all right, but this was different. Here he'd be dependent on Miss Potts's help – and in charge or no, he couldn't sack her. Anyway, he wasn't going to get the chance to find out once she saw her father. He sat down abruptly on a pile of wood, tearing his gaze from Pegasus by burying his head in his hands, fighting the hot tears of misery welling up in his eyes.

A soft cough made him look up, quickly brushing his sleeve across his face. The most beautiful girl he'd ever seen stood before him, golden-haired, blue-eyed and gentle of face. Like Florence – no, not like Florence. This girl was looking at him with compassion, and gentleness had been a stranger to Florence's face.

'I've brought your coat back, Mr – er—'

He leapt to his feet. 'Why, thank you, ma'am,' he stammered. 'I'm Smith, Jake – that is, Jack Smith. That's sure good of you, ma'am.'

'And I'm Polly Potts, Rosie's sister.' Polly hesitated. 'Forgive me, Mr Smith, but you look upset.'

'I guess I am, ma'am. I kind of annoyed your sister.'

'She'll recover from the wetting, Mr Smith. But she says you'll be working with her on Pegasus?' asked Polly doubtfully.

'That's so. Your father put me in charge of the project – but I guess he won't want me now.'

'He's an unusual person, Mr Smith. I should wait to see. Please do come to the house to wait for him. I'll keep Rosie out of the way.' She smiled. 'I think – forgive me, Mr Smith, but Rosie won't like having you – anyone,' she amended hastily, 'in charge of the project. Not at all.'

'But, Father, he threw me into the cattle trough!' cried Rosie, outraged.

'Why, my dear?' inquired William with interest. 'Did he have some reason?'

'No,' she flashed.

'Now that is strange. I shall certainly inquire why he took this precipitate action.'

Rosie glared, then said reluctantly. 'He took exception to my – oh, Father, I couldn't *help* it. He looked so strange. But—' returning to the main charge, 'Father, he says he's to work for us. With *me*.'

'More than that, my dear. I'm handing over my work on Pegasus to him. He is to be in charge of the project while I devote more time to the factory. I shall still be involved on design of course, and naturally still fly Pegasus. But—'

'Father—' Rosie was thunderstruck. 'Why didn't you *tell* me? Do you really mean I have to work *for* him? You can't! Pegasus is *ours*. And you didn't even *tell me*,' she wailed, hurt beyond measure at this betrayal.

'I hoped to introduce you first,' William said vaguely. In fact he believed that a *fait accompli* was by far the easiest way of solving the problem that had been causing him concern for some time. The problem was to clip Harry Clairville Jones's wings before they got too ambitious; before they could lay claim to take to the air. 'I did not realise you would be introducing yourselves. Unfortunate. However, at dinner tonight you may find he is not the monster you imagine.'

'Dinner,' she snorted. 'I have to meet *him* at dinner?'

'Certainly,' said William, unexpectedly firm. 'And you will be polite to him as our guest, Rosie. Harry will be there too, and we shall discuss our plans then.'

'Does Harry know?' muttered Rosie, still mutinous.

'Not yet,' said William loftily. 'I shall tell him before dinner.'

He was rather looking forward to it. He couldn't explain to Rosie that she was too young, too impetuous to see

95

danger ahead. It needed an outsider, and Rosie's interests needed to be protected. Harry was a good servant but a bad master. Harry with his own ideas, his own ambitions. Ever since Harry had mooted the suggestion of a joint patent – which so far he'd kept at bay – he'd realised there might be danger ahead. At that moment it was in Harry's interests to stay with Pegasus. He hadn't the technique to build his own aircraft – *yet*. But soon he would have, and then it might be too late to avert trouble. Rosie wasn't a good enough judge of character yet. She needed to be protected. Above all, when he was too old, Pegasus would need a flyer. And it needed a man, not a woman. A man with the strength to control a machine, a man who could outwit Harry – not a girl.

William did not question his reasoning more deeply. His parents had taught him that ladies had to be protected and cherished and he had never doubted this was a rule of civilised society. Men were to achieve, women to support them. Polly and Rosie should be protected as far as he could; they should remain under his control until they were married and could be handed over to the responsibility of a husband. It was a simple philosophy, but a well-tried one; it had been so over the centuries, and neither he nor the majority of his countrymen saw any reason that the twentieth century should change it.

Rosie deliberately chose her most feminine-looking dinner dress for the evening ahead. She charmed Trott into putting away the severe blue satin, casually taking out instead the diaphanous-sleeved, low-necked pale pink moiré. A pendant to match the ornamented clasp on the belt lay demurely on her breast. Jake Smith would regret his accusation that she was no lady. *Jake!* What a ridiculous name! Well, this *Jake* would not recognise in the stately young lady that greeted him the girl he had treated so badly that afternoon. She would make polite conversation and ask him all about America. But not about the Wright brothers, with whom William had told her *Jake* had flown. She would not give *Mr*

*Smith* the satisfaction of showing her interest in their achievements. And, for all Harry said about the Wright brothers being outside the general tenets of aviation theory and development, she was very interested indeed in the Wright brothers. Particularly in their theories of pilot control. But never, never would she display her eagerness to Mr Smith. She would treat him as Father had suggested.

The sight that greeted her in the mirror suggested her efforts in the matter of appearance had been well rewarded; she was almost looking forward to meeting Mr Smith again and seeing his expression change – if one *could* see for that ridiculous long golden moustache. She smiled again at the thought of it. She looked at herself again in the mirror, this time more critically. She could not rival Polly for beauty of course, but at least tonight she looked reasonably attractive. For once, her curls were obeying her wishes, more or less. She twisted sideways, glad that the tight-waisted corset had at least given her a prominent bosom, whatever its other discomforts, and becoming annoyed once more that Jake had failed to recognise her sex that afternoon.

She would go down early, *now*, to see if Mr Smith were here already. Perhaps she could impress him before dinner with her forgiving charm. Inspired by this idea she ran downstairs quickly. It wasn't Jake Smith, however, but Harry whom Rosie found in the library. Of course, she thought, William had been going to break the news to him before dinner. One glance at his face told her that he had done just that. Harry was standing quite still, glass in hand, one arm propped on the overshelf, apparently lounging, yet she could see he was very angry. For all his anger, however, he looked defenceless, and at once all her loyalties and sympathies boiled up anew. How could Father do this without so much as consulting Harry, who'd devoted so much of his time to Pegasus? Harry looked up, saw her and came towards her, kissing her quickly on the cheek, a rare gesture on his part. She'd often joked that she thought he saw her as an animated spanner. 'Adam's spare rib,' she'd laughed once, as she battled on the scaffolding with a piano wire ferrule for Pegasus's bracing.

'So,' he said, making an effort at his usual grin, 'we are to be taught how to build our own aeroplane by some latter-day Buffalo Bill.'

'Oh, Harry, it's not fair on you,' she cried impulsively. 'You know I had nothing to do with his coming, don't you?'

'Of course,' he answered instantly. 'I knew you'd feel just the same as I do.'

'It *needn't* make any difference,' she said stoutly now, defensive of William. 'Not if we can get on with him.'

'Certainly not to me,' Harry said carelessly. 'I hold the patent on my engine.' He glanced at her.

'Harry, you wouldn't do anything to spoil Pegasus's chances, would you?' she cried, appalled.

No, he wouldn't do that. No one in Britain, apart from perhaps Samuel Cody, was so near to completing a flyable powered aeroplane as William Potts.

'And you wouldn't desert Pegasus *now*, would you?' Rosie continued, horrified.

'Of course not.' Harry gave her a warm smile. 'Besides, what would I do without my very own spanner adjuster. And you wouldn't work for anyone else, would you?' If there was a faint interrogation in his voice, she did not hear it.

'Do you really enjoy working with me?' she asked ingenuously, rather wistfully. After William, Harry was the person she most respected in the world. He was a real gentleman, not like Robert Bellowes; he was well off, talented, even famous through his uncle, and his approbation mattered a lot to her. She had never forgotten Robert Bellowes's stinging remark. The immediate hurt healed long ago, but deep inside was a small pit of uncertainty.

'Rosie, you *are* Pegasus to me.' He was laughing, but her heart warmed all the same. 'You have wings all your own. Now, tell me the worst before we have dinner. I gather you met the gent.'

'In a way,' she said unwillingly. She wasn't going to

confess to Harry what had happened. 'He's tall, golden-haired, and he does dress like a cowboy,' she began reluctantly.

'Trust a woman to describe his hair. What I mean is: does he know about aeroplanes? According to your father, he worked with the Wright brothers.'

'I don't know. We – er – didn't discuss Pegasus.'

Harry raised his eyebrows, but luckily at that moment William bustled into the room escorting Mildred, followed by a nervous Mr Fisherbutt doing his best to pretend he wasn't there and looking uncomfortable in an ancient tail coat and false dress shirt front that he glanced down at from time to time to ensure the tell-tale edges were not on display.

'Mr Smith needs to meet the whole team, does he not?' William explained grandly. Then Polly arrived, breathless and flushed, and looking as if in spirit she were miles away. Last of all came Jake Smith.

Rosie blinked. Far from his not recognising her, she hardly recognised *him*. He was wearing one of the new short dinner jackets – Harry wouldn't approve of that, she thought instantly, with his insistence on tradition. His unruly hair was combed into order and the long moustache had vanished. She could even see the faint red of the skin where it had been – until, aware that she was staring, she greeted him with elaborate politeness, conscious of his eyes flicking over the dress and pleased that he had indeed noticed. She watched Harry as he shook Jake's hand. Did she imagine already a tense undercurrent? From whom did it stem? From herself, from Harry, from Mr Smith or from all of them? Except Polly, of course, at whom Jake was gazing in open admiration. Who wouldn't indeed? In lavender chiffon with early pinks bound into her hair, Polly had the kind of beauty of which it was impossible to be jealous.

At first the dinner went reasonably well. Everyone behaved impeccably, Mrs Fisherbutt had produced her best baron of lamb, as if determined to support her husband by this method if not by her presence, Mr Smith appeared to be getting along very well with Mr

Fisherbutt, and had all but ignored Rosie, seated next to him. It was through embarrassment, if she could but have known, but she took it for arrogance. Jake had persuaded himself he could just treat her straightforwardly, like any of the mechanicians in the Ohio factory, but this girl in the flimsy pink dress with the formal glassy manners bore no relation to his resolutions. Those frills and flounces reminded him of Florence.

'Tell me, Mr Smith,' said Harry, apparently eagerly, leaning forward, 'do tell us about the Wright brothers. Is it true they've now acknowledged their failure in flight?'

'Failure?' echoed Jake, stupefied.

'They have given up building flying machines now, have they not, now that no one can be found to purchase their invention?' Harry pressed.

'Their only failure is in not convincing a lot of hidebound politicians that the future of their countries could well rest in the Wright Flyers.'

'But if no one wishes to buy it, Mr Smith, then surely it is failure?' Harry said smoothly.

Jake frowned. 'They are years ahead of anyone else anywhere, Mr Jones.' The dropping of the Clairville was unintentional, but Harry did not see it as such.

'Or behind it. Their so-called aeroplane is inherently unstable, is it not?'

'Sure, but—'

'They place the responsibility on the flyer to control the machine in the air?'

'Yeah, but—'

'Here in Europe we have travelled beyond that concept, Mr Smith. We believe that the aircraft should be made inherently stable in itself; the flyer is needed for adjusting control using elevator and rear rudder. The machine does the work, not the flyer. In Pegasus, we believe in engine power for lift and thrust and are well on the way to having solved the problems of control. That's the way to go.'

'And suppose it's the wrong way?'

'I hardly think you can yet judge that.'

'I ain't heard that the machine has flown yet. I'll judge it when I see it,' said Jake evenly, but trembling.

'But Pegasus is almost ready for trials,' said Rosie sharply. 'You can't change it *now*.'

William sat silently, pensively playing with his glass of wine. Jake glanced at him. No response. All right, if that's how Mr Potts wanted to play it, he would go along with it. He took a deep breath.

'Only if it's necessary, Miss Potts.'

'Then you'll have to change the engine, too,' said Harry coolly.

A split-second pause. William looked up sharply, ready to intervene. There was no need.

'I've been checking the papers, Mr Jones,' said Jake, coolly forestalling him. 'Seems Mr Potts bought that engine fair and square.'

Harry flushed. He hadn't counted on that. 'Not the patent,' he said. 'That's in my name. And when you need an update on the engine, we'll need to discuss it. Not to mention the new concept I'm working on—'

'The one that uses all the castor oil?' broke in Rosie eagerly.

Harry cast her a look and she subsided, realising too late he hadn't wanted this mentioned.

'*Castor oil?*' said Jake. 'Are you serious?'

'That's the disadvantage,' said Harry, patently displeased.

'And its advantages?'

'Will be seen in my good time, Mr Smith.'

Torn between fierce indignation on Harry's behalf, and a sneaking feeling he was going too far, Rosie sat silent, appalled. Flight was meant to be pure, to bring benefits, to sublimate the souls of mankind, not bring wrangling and bitterness. It was all this Jake Smith's fault. Couldn't he see he was barging his way into a happy team and was breaking it up? Was he going to ruin everything?

Jake met Harry's eye and said more coolly than he felt: 'Listen here, I like the look of your engine, Mr Jones, but there are other engines. I can build my own, come to that. Done it before, I can do it again. And, Miss Potts—' the deep blue eyes turned in her direction and she stiffened. 'I ain't never worked with a woman before, not on an aircraft at any rate. But I don't see any reason I shouldn't try.' As he looked at her in that pink silk the idea was ridiculous, but he had to show he was willing at any rate. But how could he concentrate on machines with those brown eyes staring at him in indignation all the time? Perhaps she'd get married, he thought hopefully. Marry this swell and disappear.

'That's a nice speech, Mr Smith,' flashed Rosie, 'but how do *we* know you know anything about aeroplanes? It might be all talk on your part.'

Jake nodded slowly. 'That's right. You take me on trust till you know. Anyone disagree?'

Mr Fisherbutt broke the silence. 'Mr Smith,' he said timidly, 'if Mr Potts says it's all right with him, why then it's all right with me.'

Rosie took a deep breath, thinking of Pegasus. 'I'll work with you, Mr Smith,' she rushed out, carefully not saying 'for'. Take orders from him? The idea was abhorrent. From Father yes, but not him.

The dark-blue eyes met hers head-on. '*For* me, Miss Potts,' he said, his eyes holding hers firmly. Then he grinned and his face lit up, as if aware he'd already won. Approval showed on William's face. Rosie bit her lip, glanced at Harry for support, and a small nod reassured her.

'Very well, Mr Smith – just so long as it's in Pegasus's interests,' she said stiffly.

Was that relief in those blue eyes? 'I guess that will do for now.'

'I want to see Pegasus fly as much as anyone,' said Harry quickly. He paused, then, 'We'll leave the question of a new engine in abeyance.'

Rosie held her breath. There was the sound of a Chippendale chair scraped back fiercely as Jake got to his feet. She held her breath, waiting for an explosion. All eyes were on him. 'Excuse me, Mr Potts, ladies. I'll bid you good night.'

'You're leaving us, Mr Smith? Do you feel you are not suited to Pegasus?' Harry asked straight-faced, a mocking tone in his voice.

Jake looked at them all slowly, then addressed William. 'It's the finest thing I seen since I got to England, Mr Potts.' His gaze swept over them once more as they waited for his words – it was a trick he'd learned at the show, none the less useful because used unconsciously now that he was in deadly earnest. 'I'll get that Pegasus flying real soon for you. I want to do it with all your help – but if you don't choose to give it to me, I'll do it alone. I'll put you in the air, Mr Potts, don't you worry. And mighty soon.'

'This is it,' said Rosie shortly, pushing open the rickety wooden gate.

Jake followed her into the overgrown cottage garden and stopped still, gazing in admiration at the house.

'It sure is beautiful,' he murmured.

'Beautiful?' she echoed, surprised. The tumble-down Old Lodge was hardly her idea of beauty. Plaster falling off, windows broken, tiles badly needing repair. She and Polly used to play hide-and-seek here years ago, enjoying its poky corners and mysterious cupboards. It hadn't been occupied for many years, not since they altered the main entrance to Brynbourne House in the 'seventies to the Bredhill Road. Now this corner was almost forgotten. She had been amazed when Father offered it to Jake – and even more surprised when he eagerly agreed, until she thought about it more deeply. He'd stayed with them at Brynbourne for one night, then moved out to the village to find lodgings. It only took three days before he mentioned to William he was looking for a place of his own, nice and quiet. Rosie had sniffed contemptuously. No wonder he wanted peace and quiet after Peggy Wilkins, the daughter of the house at his lodgings. She was not known for backwardness in her dealings with men. And precious little discrimination at that.

Jake ran his hand over the wood of the old lintel and door. She noticed to her surprise the long sensitive fingers and thought of them on Pegagus's struts. He might have an understanding of aeroplanes. He'd certainly impressed her so far; strive though she might, she could find little to object to as he quietly went about making himself acquainted with all Pegasus's controls and fabric.

'Wouldn't you be better finding a cottage to rent in the village?' she asked doubtfully. 'You could find one there that didn't need work on it.'

Jake grinned. 'Kind of work I enjoy.' He pushed his way inside. The door wasn't quite hanging off its hinges, but if the Big Bad Wolf came along and started huffing she wouldn't give much for its chances – or the house's – Rosie thought, as she followed him in. He inspected the two plastered rooms downstairs with the neat fireplaces from mid-last century. 'Give me time,' he said at last. 'You see that fireplace? Now that was never there when they built the house. And I wonder what's behind it?'

'Probably a dead body,' she muttered. 'We're like that in Kent. We tend to treat invaders rough here.'

'I've noticed that, Miss Potts, he answered absently, disappearing into the kitchen built on the end of the cottage later and covered with a catslide roof. Then he made his way up the small boxed-in staircase with a false ceiling. But when she followed Jake up all she could see was his long, lanky legs; his head appeared to be in the attic as he stood on an old trunk. She heard a muffled whistle and he jumped down.

'Reckon they knew about building in those days,' dusting himself down.

'You've got a spider in your hair,' she commented, reaching up to pick it off. He bent his head submissively, and she was disconcerted by his nearness as she extracted the insect from the honey-coloured hair. 'There,' she said unnecessarily, carrying it to the far side of the room, before setting it free on the window ledge.

'Oh,' she cried, and Jake's 'What?' brought him to her side, where she was staring out of the dormer window. 'I thought I saw someone,' and his hand was on his hip instinctively as two figures emerged from the long grass of the overgrown garden and looked up at them.

'Polly,' Rosie cried in amazement. 'And – oh, Polly,' she tried to repress a smile, 'Mr Marriner.'

'I – we were sketching,' called out Polly weakly, blushing bright red, until Gabriel saved the day by roaring with laughter.

'Good afternoon, Miss Potts,' he said, and looked inquiringly at Jake.

'Jake Smith.' Jake squeezed in beside her at the window. 'I guess that's what we were doing too, isn't that right?' He grinned at Rosie, who opened her mouth to retort fiercely, then realised she was leaning out of what might be termed a bedroom window. Furious with Jake, whom she unfairly blamed, she muttered, 'Yes. Um – Polly, does Father know you're sketching with Mr Marriner?'

'Not exactly,' said Polly blithely.

'Polly won't let me talk to him,' explained Gabriel ruefully. 'She is ashamed of my sketching, you see. It's too bad to present to your father.'

'Oh, Gabriel,' Polly turned indignantly to him, then joined his laughter. 'We usually meet in London,' she said, 'but with the summer coming . . . this seemed nicer. You won't tell him Rosie, will you?' she ended anxiously.

'Of course not.'

'Your sister sure is beautiful,' said Jake absently, as he watched them departing into the fields.

'Yes,' snapped Rosie, looking at Polly's graceful figure in its simple white sprigged muslin dress. 'So everyone tells me,' elbowing her way from the tight window space. And then, ashamed for having displayed a jealousy of Polly that she did not feel, asked hurriedly, 'Do you have a wife, Mr Smith. Or a sweetheart?'

His eyes went blank. 'I have a mother, and a sister. That's enough women for me,' he said quietly. 'Shall we get going?'

'Do not trespass' was the clear warning sign, thought Rosie. As if she were *interested*! He made her feel like Peggy Wilkins.

She followed him crossly downstairs, since he had clearly signalled that her part in the afternoon was at an end. He didn't even bother to usher her through the front door first, but once across the threshold stopped abruptly so that she cannoned into him.

'What's that?' His eye had been caught by a carving above the doorway almost hidden by wisteria. He swept the leaves aside to look more closely.

'Some kind of rose,' said Rosie stiffly, determined to show no interest and walking off.

'No, it's not, Miss Potts. Well now, just you look at this.' Unwillingly she turned back. His fingers were lovingly tracing out the carving. 'It's a sunburst.'

'A what?' she asked ungraciously.

'The heraldic badge of a couple of mediaeval kings. The sun bursting out from the clouds. There's another badge depicting the sun full out with rays all round – in glory. I wonder now—'

'You can get Polly to paint them on a Potts Pedestal WC for you,' she quipped sourly, still smarting from his rebuff and from being caught by Polly and Gabriel in such a compromising situation, however innocent.

Fortunately he did not take in what she had said, for he was murmuring, almost to himself, 'How about that! A sunburst.'

'Miss Rosie's our wing lady, our little angel, Mr Smith.' Mr Fisherbutt made the joke proudly, as he had every time a stranger came to the workshed for the last five years. 'And the wind tunnel's all her work too.'

Jake had at last declared himself ready to inspect Pegasus officially. 'Is that so?' At last a look of respect. 'You built that, Miss Potts?' Jake inspected the canvas and wood contraption, while Rosie hovered near, anxious lest he condemn it with faint praise or condescension. At last he straightened up. A nod.

'You're very generous, Mr Smith,' she replied demurely.

A straight look and, 'And the wings are your speciality too?'

She nodded.

'The struts, bracing? You can use the jig? The fabric, too?'

She nodded again.

'Adhesive?'

106

'Jel - isinglass.' She pulled herself back in time. She had nearly used the private joke between herself and William that had developed as Mrs Fisherbutt's stores had been raided, first for tapioca and sago for dope and then for isinglass for adhesive. But not to Mr Smith. He wouldn't understand.

Satisfied, Jake turned back to Mr Fisherbutt for the rest of his tour. It slightly annoyed Rosie how quickly Mr Fisherbutt had given allegiance to the tall American, following him around as if he were Father. She, Rosie, had managed to maintain what she considered a polite aloofness.

Jake straightened up, and there was a tenseness about him. 'I see you've opted for small balancers rather than warping or full ailerons.' It was a statement of fact, so why did she sense danger and wish Harry were here?

'Harry believes that, after the engine, longitudinal and directional stability come next in importance.'

'He doesn't reckon lateral control important?'

'Naturally,' she said, annoyed. 'That's taken care of in pitch by the elevator and by the rudder for directional control.'

'So you reckon to use it only for correction in roll, and not for control of flight?'

'Father used to believe ailerons were the way,' she said reluctantly, for she still had a sneaking feeling he was right, 'but Harry convinced him they weren't important provided you had correct dihedral by the wing angle.'

Jake thought of how he'd felt up in the Wright Flyer – the roll as he turned it, the pull on the wings, the struggle to keep the aircraft up as it obeyed its natural tendency to drop as the outer wings moved at a slower rate than the inner. And that was *with* the Wrights' wing warping. He'd have gone for ailerons – not wing warping, but the Wrights were adamant. Just as Clairville Jones had been about using balancers and William had given way over using ailerons. After all, it was Harry who went to all the European shows; no one mentioned lateral control as a problem there, he had told Jake off-handedly. Provided you had inherent stability you had a safe aircraft. Fine, thought Jake, listening to his arguments – provided you had fine weather too . . .

'Once we've achieved flight,' Rosie shouted to Jake's unresponsive back as he climbed the scaffolding to inspect the balancers, then wriggled down under the fuselage, 'then control can be adjusted by experience in flight, but the machine must do most of the work for the flyer, or it isn't safe. That's sense, isn't it?'

'Is that so?' came Jake's muffled voice, as he crawled out from under the wicker seat and stood up – to find himself face to face with Harry.

'That is indeed so,' said Harry. 'I don't think that's a disputed line of argument.'

'I reckon I could dispute it all right,' said Jake.

'There's only one way to prove it,' said Harry nonchalantly. 'We test it out. Now.'

'I'm not ready for that yet.'

'Whether you are or not, Mr Smith, Pegasus *is*.'

'I'm not sending an aeroplane up in the air unless I'm satisfied it can be controlled in wind.'

'I think you'll find Mr Potts *is* satisfied.'

But this time Jake had his way.

Mostly Rosie found Jake possible to work with, provided they both ignored the undercurrent that lay beneath the surface. In everyday work he was demanding in some ways, easy-going in others. It both relieved and annoyed her, however, that he took little notice of her sex. It seemed to her that the moment she appeared in trousers, he simply forgot her except as an adjunct to Pegasus. Just what she wanted, she told herself firmly. Only on one subject did they clash openly, though: 'Harry says,' she would begin, only to be smoothly interrupted.

'And *I* say this is how I want it.'

'Why won't you even *listen* to Harry's ideas?' she flashed once.

'Miss Potts, when you're up there flying, you feel *with* the machine. It's a partnership between you or it don't work. Now the way *he* talks, he just wants something to get him up there and keep him up there. A cow would do if it had wings. But it ain't just enough to drive Pegasus into the air like it was a London omnibus.'

Rosie laughed.

'What's so funny?'

'I was just imagining how many struts I'd need to plane to sustain a London omnibus up in the sky.'

'Oh, one day it will happen.'

'I'd be happy flying anything,' she said wistfully.

'You?' he said, surprised.

'Yes.' She turned to him, belligerently, spoiling for a fight. 'What's wrong with that? You're just like Father, I suppose. You think women have to be protected: they can sew, they can teach, they can look pretty, even hold spanners, but in the end their domain is the kitchen and—' she stopped.

'Bedroom,' he finished for her matter-of-factly. 'That what you were going to say?'

'Parlour,' she snapped. 'So that's what *you* think too, is it?'

Memories of May and Florence flooded his mind. Perhaps that was what he might have thought once. Now he didn't, having met Rosie. Thank the Lord she was different. Thank the Lord, when she wore those trousers he could forget she was a woman, his resolve to avoid ever again becoming entangled emotionally with a woman unshaken. Flight was the consummation of desire for him; the aeroplane the only partner he could ever envisage now.

'I guess you don't know too much about how I think,' he said uncommunicatively, and she stalked back to her work.

'This darn engine is too hot,' muttered Jake some time later, switching off the dynamometer.

'Have you looked at the condenser?' she yelled from the table on which she was planing a rib.

'Nope.' When she glanced round a few minutes later he was staring into the innards of the Clairville, hands in pockets.

'Well,' she asked impatiently. 'Have you— You don't know where it is, do you?' she accused him, flabbergasted.

Jake looked disconcerted.

'I thought you said you knew all about engines,' she accused him. 'You don't know *anything*, do you?' she suddenly realised. 'That was just bluff to get Harry to give way over the Clairville engine and the patents. You *tricked* him—'

He flushed angrily. 'It wasn't that way, Miss Potts, and I reckon I know as much as the next man about engines. Charlie Taylor was teaching me—'

'You cheated him,' she repeated sternly.

He shrugged. 'Miss Potts, I promised your Pa I'd do everything I could in Pegasus's interests, and the way I see it what I did *was* in Pegasus's interests.'

'I can see it was in Jake Smith's interests to keep Harry out of the way,' she said tartly. 'You're jealous of him, aren't you? Afraid that he might fly before you,' she added to her own surprise. What had made her say that?

'Fly?' Jake took up the word sharply. 'He wants to fly?'

'No, he doesn't,' she said uneasily, 'but even if he did, what's wrong with that?' she came back at him, eyes flashing.

'Why nothing, nothing at all. If you do it for the right reasons.'

As soon as she heard the familiar toot of the Clairville's horn she rushed down the steps of Brynbourne Place before Harry had a chance even to step down from the motor car, regardless of the rain.

'Don't you mind?' she asked indignantly, when at last she finished, disappointed at the results of her news.

'Of course I mind,' he replied absently, tossing his sports cap and gauntlets back into the Clairville and following her back into the house. 'He bluffed me. I'm thinking about what to do, that's all.' But inside he was raging with fury. He'd been tricked by a mere Yankee and, what's more, if he wasn't careful, he'd find his status over Pegasus usurped. Pegasus would fly – and without him. Nor had he time to build his own aeroplane now. There were signs at last that the British were waking up to the possibilities of aviation. And he was going to be the first man into the air here. He and no one else. The name of Clairville Jones was going to mean more than a motor car in the history books.

'Rosie darling,' he said as he struggled out of his umbrella coat, 'the clever thing to do at the moment is to allow our Mr Smith to do all the work, then arrange at the last moment to outwit him. Suppose you wanted to fly Pegasus? Mr Potts couldn't refuse you.' Let her think he was going to encourage her ridiculous notions. The important thing was to ensure that Jake Smith proved no threat.

'Yes, he could,' said Rosie forthrightly. 'And has. Anyway, Father will be flying Pegasus himself. But I don't like it, Harry. Shouldn't we have it out with Mr Smith? Isn't it underhand not to?'

'Isn't that just what our Mr Smith is?'

She could think of no response to this and seeing he'd won his argument, Harry put his arm round her shoulders. 'You won't desert me, will you, Rosie?' he said quite seriously.

'Why should I?' she asked, surprised that he could even ask it. 'You're as much part of Pegasus as I am. I can't think what Father was thinking of to ask that awful man here.' Harry laughed lightly, then leaned forward, drew her to him, and kissed her lightly on the cheek and then the lips. She could smell the stuff he put on his hair, a slight rubber smell lingering from the umbrella coat, a faint aroma of tobacco emanating from his tweed jacket, the comfortable, familiar smells she'd associated with him for three years now. When she did not object, he kissed her again, harder and harder still until finally she drew away.

'You don't mind, do you?' he asked, but, occupied in bringing his spotted silk cravat back to its former neatness, did not seem to need an answer. 'It seemed so natural somehow. And you look very pretty today.'

Pretty? In this old blue skirt and blouse with the scarf tied round her hair? Rosie felt bewildered as if there were something she did not quite understand. Then she forgot that in her pleasure at Harry having kissed her. A real kiss too. Not the passing pecks she'd exchanged at dances over the years with one partner or another, kisses so butterfly light that lived as long.

'Father, I could fly her,' pleaded Rosie. 'I'm so much lighter than you.' And I know Pegasus better, she could have added, but wisely didn't.

Jake interrupted firmly. 'Neither of you is going to fly. I just don't reckon it safe, Mr Potts, whatever Mr Clairville Jones maintains. So if anyone's going to risk their life, it's going to be me.'

Just as they thought, Rosie winked at Father, but Jake wasn't going to be first in the air if they could help it. They had made a plan. But Rosie's usual lift of the heart at seeing the familiar white wings emerge, was absent, so caught up was she in this battle.

The men were trundling Pegasus out, Harry was standing with folded arms a little way away. 'I'd offer my services,' he said blandly, 'but Mr Smith seems not to approve of me as an airman.

Jake glanced at him. There seemed an air of suppressed excitement about him that he could not pin down, over and above the natural expectation of seeing Pegasus in the air. Jake climbed into the wicker seat and prayed to whatever gods might be looking out for him today that they take special care. He could look after the controls, but Pegasus's inbuilt inefficiencies would leave him at the mercy of fate.

Jake felt excitement well within him as the men swung the propellers and the Clairville started up, throbbing in anticipation like Jake himself. But then Rosie was shouting. Damn it, what did she want?

'Jake, the rudder. There's something wrong—' Half a mind to ignore her. No, he couldn't. Impatiently he jumped down and strode round to look behind Pegasus. A sixth sense, perhaps something in Rosie's tone, stopped him. But it was too late. The engine accelerated, and he had to fling himself to one side as Pegasus roared away with William Potts at the controls. Horrified, Jake rushed after him, joined by Harry. Odd, his brain recorded. Why?

There was nothing he could do, but watch helplessly, as William Potts, proud as punch and eager as a child, drove the Pegasus relentlessly towards the Bellowes's estate.

'Lift, damn you, lift,' Jake exhorted the machine through gritted teeth. It should be *lifting* now. Was it? He couldn't bear to look. He must. Surely it was hopping, no, back on the ground, the engine straining to lift. What the hell was wrong? Even with William's weight, it had plenty of motive power. William had counted on Pegasus lifting too. But hopping only a few feet from the ground, he saw the Bellowes's boundary wall coming up fast. He was only eight feet up. He wrenched on the control lever to turn her, but without sufficient height and without warping or full size ailerons, Pegasus was a clipped dove, not a flying horse. As it turned, a wing-tip touched the earth, Pegasus pivoted for a moment, then collapsed in a heap above its pilot.

Ashen-faced, Rosie found her legs would not move. As in a dream, she saw Jake and Harry running towards the wreckage, but she still could not move. It was her father. She'd connived at William's taking over his aeroplane. And now he was dead, instead of Jake. Dead because of *her*. Her legs began to obey some unconscious command and she ran. *Ran*.

Then they were tugging at the wreckage to reach the still figure underneath.

'What the hell happened?' cried Jake in anguish. Harry said nothing, but glancing at him Jake knew that whatever had gone wrong had stemmed from Harry.

# Chapter Five

'Nine lives, that's what they say,' said William proudly, sitting up in bed, his broken leg strung up in front of him. 'That's roughly four left.'

'And four you won't be risking in an aeroplane,' said Mildred sharply.

' "Ah, but a man's reach should exceed his grasp or what's a heaven for?" as your favourite poet says,' he declaimed. 'Good heavens, my dear. Could that be an early peach from our greenhouse? You spoil me, Mildred. Ah, Rosie, come in—'

'I said you should have let me fly, Father,' she said lovingly, rushing across to kiss him.

'It seems to me,' William commented severely, 'everyone wants to fly and no one wants me to. You all forget it was my idea to build a flying machine. Why shouldn't I have the privilege of flying it first?'

'Because you're too fat and too heavy,' said Mildred forthrightly.

William was silent as he thought this over. Then he came to a decision. He laid the peach aside. 'I shall become thinner,' he declared happily.

Polly lay in Gabriel's arms on the hillside. Hitherto, Gabriel's visits had been arranged on the days on which William was at the factory and Polly was not. William's broken leg had put an end to that, and William and Gabriel Marriner had come face to face once more. At Mildred's urging, reluctant permission had been given for Mr Marriner to continue to call. To forbid him the house was unwise, she had pointed out. Polly could be obstinate. This way she might tire of him. Personally

Mildred doubted it, but there was no reason for William to know that.

'I keep hoping I'll love you less each time I come,' complained Gabriel, pulling the last petal off a daisy. 'But no, there you go. Making me love you more each time. I resent going back to Cornwall. And if that's not bad enough, you don't even have the decency to supply the right number of petals to your daisies.'

Polly laughed, the sunlight lighting up her face, as Gabriel pulled her into his arms again, and said joyously, 'I sold six whole paintings last month. At this rate we could be married by the time you're forty-five.'

'Six. Why that's wonderful! In Cornwall?' she exclaimed.

'Better than that. To a London gallery. So you see, my fortune's made, I can go to your father and say I have a secure future of six pounds a month on which I can offer his daughter a share in my fame and fortune.'

She giggled. 'Don't forget I work too. If I paint three Potts Pedestal WCs a week, I can contribute almost as much.'

'Two Marriners for the price of a Potts Pedestal. Alas! Would you have me supported by my wife,' he moaned, clasping a hand to his forehead. Then he swiftly turned to her, holding her gently, passionately. 'Every time I come,' he whispered, 'I keep fearing your father will have found someone else for you to marry.'

'He may try, but he won't succeed,' said Polly simply. 'I want to marry you, Gabriel.'

His fair head bent over hers, and he laid her back on the grass, two figures entwined, passionately embracing.

'It's only your corsetière coming between you and a fate worse than death,' he said after a while. The sky was very blue above them and the afternoon sweet.

'She can be overruled,' said Polly shyly. He laid his head down on her breast and clenched his fists.

'No,' he said. 'Not for you, Polly. When I love you, there'll be no doubts before, no regrets after. We have a dream, and wait for it we shall.'

116

Jake had gone down to the workshed very early on the morning after the accident. He'd lain awake all night puzzling over what could have gone wrong with Pegasus when the engine seemed to be running so well. Exhausted, he'd fallen asleep and when he awoke the answer was crystal clear. It was the propeller. It had to be. Easy to think of the engine, so easy to forget its counterpart in thrust. In order to perform to the required standard, it had to meet the air at the optimum angle, and be inclined at about forty-five per cent – *at one particular point*. And that was the blade-tips. Now, they were just fine when he last checked Pegasus – but what if something – or, with growing certainty, someone – had changed that? Changed the angle of bend so that the aircraft wouldn't lift; so that he, Jake Smith, would look a fool. No one could have laid the blame on the engine – the blame would be on his shoulders. No wonder then that Harry had looked so pale when William Potts took over.

Jake rushed to the workshed to verify his theory. He had all the proof he needed. The propeller had vanished, so there wasn't a damn thing he could do about it.

The meeting was held in William's bedroom where he presided like an emperor. It was short, for Jake was in no mood for compromise:

'We're starting again with a new configuration. Much of Pegasus will be included, but this will be *my* way. With full lateral control. Keeping inherent stability though. I agree you're right there.'

'What do you propose to use for an engine?' Harry asked coolly.

'Your new one if it's ready.'

'It isn't,' said Harry flatly.

'Then we'll use the old one.'

Rosie gasped. 'But she failed to lift.'

'I reckon we can fix that,' Jake said coolly, lifting his gaze to hold Harry's eyes.

'And if I disagree?' Harry grated, his eyes glinting.

'Like I said, we've got the old engine. We'll make out.'

And he would too. This time Harry knew it. He wavered and acquiesced, but marked up another score to even with Jake Smith.

William turned purple when he saw who the new visitor was.

'No more writs, Featherstone, I beg of you. Can't you see I'm ill?' he said plaintively.

'The law, I regret, takes no account of that. I'm afraid this time we have little defence.'

'Yes, yes, I knocked down part of his wall – I'll pay, I'll pay, only leave me in peace.' William sank back on his pillow, head sagging, eyes closing.

Mr Featherstone was not taken in. 'More than that, Mr Potts,' he said loudly. 'He's taken out an injunction to stop any more aeroplane building or trials on your land, and I greatly fear, Mr Potts, he will obtain it.'

Jake wandered over to Manning's hop garden, to watch the last day of picking, curious to see hop-picking again. He used to go hop-picking in the Weald as a boy, revelling in the freedom, the strangeness of the country, the horses and the people. Now, tired, after puzzling over plans for the new Pegasus, he found the hop garden a good antidote, throbbing with life and excitement. No one here cared about aeroplanes, they cared about family, enjoying themselves, honest brokers and villains alike.

He noticed Peggy Wilkins, clad in an overtight cotton skirt and blouse. She saw him too. With mixed feelings, as she winked at him, he strolled towards her. As Rosie had surmised, he had moved from her mother's comfortable lodgings to avoid her overzealous attentions.

'Coming to hopkin tonight, Mus Smith?'

That had not been his intention, but Peggy was an attractive girl, and it was a long time since he'd held a woman in his arms, even if only to dance. Maybe that was what was missing from his life. And to be casual suited him just fine.

Gabriel and his friend David Barratt arrived promptly to escort Polly and Rosie to the hopkin. For once this was an official visit by Gabriel blessed by William, and Gabriel had persuaded the girls to attend. 'You'll see,' he said excitedly, spinning Rosie round, 'it'll be a lark. Oh, it will, I want Polly to enjoy it. I go to the fisher folk dances in Newlyn and oh my word, it's such fun. I'll show you my canvases. I sketch while I'm there – to get the movement, the excitement, and then work it up afterwards. And the hopkin will be just the same, you'll see. I keep telling Polly to try to put people and life in her pictures. But she never listens to me.' He pulled a face.

'Landscapes are easier,' laughed Polly. 'I could never—'

'Yes, you could,' said Gabriel firmly. 'Look at those lambs you drew. Why, I've never seen such a gambol in paint. You should try now. Now shouldn't she, Rosie?'

The hopkin was held in a huge mediaeval tithe barn, lent by the farmer with many admonitions as to the use of candles. Villagers and hoppers were for once united, old animosities forgotten in the happy knowledge that the hoppers would return to London on the morrow. So the villagers cooperated willingly in the baking of huffkins and brewing of ginger beer and cider. Music was provided in the form of accordion and violin, though it could scarce be heard for the chatter of voices.

Gabriel promptly whirled Polly into the middle of the dance and Rosie, having conquered her sudden fear at the remote possibility her uncle might be there, soon followed suit with his shy friend from Borden who had brought Gabriel to their eighteenth birthday party. A studious young man, David Barratt had no interest in aeroplanes. He did not scoff; he simply was not interested. How could *anyone* not be interested, she wondered, desperately racking her brains for something to say.

Then suddenly, swirling in the middle of the crowd, she noticed Jake energetically swinging one of the village girls round in the dance, catching her again by the waist in exuberance. It was Peggy Wilkins of all people, dressed

119

outrageously in a very low-cut dress of cheap red moirette. Rosie noticed with a sniff that the narrow skirt was slit to knee height. It would be. She was amazed to see Jake looking so animated, and so much for her theory that he disliked women. He must have been friendly with Peggy all along; what a secretive, sneaky man he was. And what taste!

'Mind if I have this dance, Miss Potts?' Jake asked solemnly, appearing before her as the next dance started. He hardly knew why he asked. He supposed it was polite. Before she could answer no, her partner, taking one look at Jake's confident six foot, relinquished her and she was sucked into the dance, surrounded by whirling bodies and hot steamy breath from every direction. Jake's hand was warm against her back, until he gave her a hefty push with it to indicate she'd forgotten to turn. She cannoned back into him, and he held her there.

'What did you say?' he yelled in her ear.

'I said we're not in Texas *now*,' she answered, aware of how close she was to him.

'No, the steaks are smaller,' he agreed, loosening his hold, to her slight annoyance. 'And the women.' He meant her slimness, but glancing at Peggy's prominent chest Rosie took it amiss and was about to retaliate when something happened that took her mind off Jake Smith. A man loomed at her, jerking his face sideways between them.

'Wotcher, Rosie! Now yer sees me, now yer don't—' and he whirled away with his partner. Before she could recover he was circling them again, leaning towards her, whispering to her, 'You'll come to me, Rosie. You'll come to me,' the last words swallowed in a hoarse chuckle.

Jake pushed him away, just as Rosie gave a choking cry. 'Easy now. You all right, Rosie?' he asked in concern. She was aware of his leading her outside the barn into the cool evening air. 'Sit down,' he said, 'put your head between your knees.'

'It's all right, I'm not going to faint,' she said swiftly, struggling up, but he forced her down again.

'Who was that coster?'

'My uncle Alf,' she said, bitterly choking, speaking without thinking of the effect her words would have.

'*Who*?'

'Not Father's brother,' she said, stiltedly, forcing herself back to normality and realising she owed him some kind of explanation. 'I'm adopted. That man's my real uncle, he says. He's down here hop-picking. That's how I got here in the first place, after a railway accident. My parents were killed.'

He squatted down beside her, and put his arm round her. 'Where were you born, Rosie?'

'Bethnal Green, I think, I don't remember much – only the rooms – I try to forget it.' Her voice rose. She didn't want to talk about it.

'Why?'

She stared at him blankly, wondering how, and whether, to put it into words. And how to explain without talking of Alf. 'Because it's home,' she said at last, 'and I don't want it to be home. I want this – Brynbourne – to be home. And, Uncle—' she choked, and started again, moving away from his encircling arm, as though it threatened not protected her. 'Because *he* says I'll go back one day,' she whispered. 'Back there.'

'I guess home is where you want it to be,' he said absently. 'Not where other folks tell you. Nothing wrong with Bethnal Green anyway. That's where I come from too, you know. Near there – Spitalfields.'

'*You?*' she asked in amazement. 'But you're American.'

'No – English. I was in America for eight years though. I was christened Jack Smith. Changed it to survive.'

She would have found it funny any other time. Now she found it oddly moving.

'I thought you were the great American cowboy, and you come from within the sound of Bow Bells.'

'Yup. And I thought you a Fair Maid of Kent,' he replied simply. 'So I reckon we're quits.'

'Is that where your parents are? In Spitalfields?'

'Mother and sister, yes. Pa got killed up there in the Yukon.' His eyes darkened.

'I'm sorry, Jake.'

121

He grunted. Then he said curiously, 'Why does he scare you? And what did he mean by "you'll come to me, Rosie"?'

'He doesn't scare me,' she retorted immediately. 'He did when I was small, but not now. It was just a shock seeing him again. And I don't *know* what he meant.' Her eyes defied him to disbelieve her.

'Maybe. I'd say that he still has some kind of hold over you. Did he—' He broke off, wondering how to put it.

Her defences broke. 'No,' she shouted. 'No, he didn't.'

Did he? She couldn't remember and it didn't matter very much now. What mattered was the dark caul he had woven around her. His words 'you'll come to me' made no real sense. He had no power over her now. But the past still had, and the past was epitomised by Uncle Alf. A past where violence and fear were heightened, rather than tempered, by the animal needs of man for woman; where Ma and Pa's sporadic outbursts of affection were no match for the menace of Uncle Alf - a menace that grew all the stronger in the suspense of waiting for the next visit.

'I always used to reckon that I'd as soon a bear tackled me from the front as from the back,' Jake remarked, putting his arm round her once more.

She turned her head toward him, and found it buried in the rough check of his red shirt, smelling as sweet as if just washed in a running brook which, she thought hazily, remembering the Old Lodge, it probably was.

Robert Bellowes was paying the customary squire's visit - brief - to the hopkin on his father's behalf. The first thing he noticed was Polly dancing with Gabriel. The fellow he'd seen her dancing with at her eighteenth birthday ball. He didn't know who Gabriel was, but it was clear from Polly's animated face that now at least she knew him well, and liked him more than a little. A blind unreasoning jealousy took hold of him, as if his honour were somehow impugned by seeing Polly with another man. He had waited too long; it should be put right. Soon.

Robert drew up the gig, doffed his hat, and leapt down beside Polly as she walked back towards Brynbourne Place from the village one day.

'Good morning, Mr Bellowes,' she replied composedly, preparing to walk on.

'Allow me to drive you home, Miss Potts.'

'Thank you, I do enjoy the exercise.' Her soft voice robbed the words of sting.

'I insist, Miss Potts. My father would never allow—' Then, belatedly realising this was hardly a cogent argument in view of the feud: 'I cannot be permitted to ride while you walk.'

Seeing he persisted, Polly gave in, and he handed her up into the gig.

'I should enjoy escorting you to the concert in Maidstone next week, Miss Potts.'

'Thank you, Mr Bellowes,' she said evenly. 'I regret I am engaged that evening.'

'Then the following week.'

'Thank you, but no.'

A silence.

'It's that artist fellow, isn't it?' he burst out vengefully.

A silence. Her cheeks flushed. 'I believe it is no business of yours, Mr Bellowes.'

'Ah, but it is.' He seized her hand. 'I dislike seeing you throwing yourself away on a fellow like that.'

'You feel yourself more worthy perhaps,' snatching her hand away.

He stared. 'Of course.'

'Fortunately,' she said tartly, 'that is for me to decide, Mr Bellowes. Please stop.'

He refused to do so and she was forced to continue in silence till he halted at the doors of Brynbourne Place. She jumped down, and went inside trembling without a backward glance.

Rosie kept away from Jake as much as she could, regretting the weakness that had made her break down. This was not hard since the new Pegasus, as Jake was calling it, as yet existed only on paper, a few struts and wing ribs lying on the flat table. They had still found no alternative site for testing now Sir Lawrence had obtained his injunction.

Polly had flown to her in tears to tell her that Robert Bellowes had come to Father with a distressing offer. The injunction would be lifted, if she, Polly, were to consider Robert Bellowes's advances favourably.

'The indignity,' she moaned to Rosie. 'As if I could even touch him. Ugh. Slug he was and slug he'll remain. Well, I've told *it* I love Gabriel and I'm going to marry him.'

'What did he say?' asked Rosie uneasily.

'Nothing,' said Polly triumphantly. 'What could he say?'

Distrust the snake in the grass, thought Rosie. The silent enemy. The sleeping slug.

'A thaw, my dears. A positive thaw.' William beamed, waving an invitation. 'Sir Lawrence has invited us for New Year's Eve. Mr Marriner is included too, Polly.'

'I don't like it,' said Rosie decidely. 'Beware the Greeks bearing gifts.'

'They aren't Greeks,' said Polly doubtfully. 'And they *have* invited Gabriel, so perhaps their intention is to show goodwill.'

'You'd see goodwill in Bluebeard,' commented Rosie forthrightly, and Polly laughed.

In honour of the occasion which William chose to see as a triumph, he bought both the girls and Mildred new dresses, and even Rosie became interested as Trott pinned and poked at her, fitting the heavy cream lace over the satin underlay. Polly stood obediently still, Rosie fidgeted, twisting and turning while Trott snapped at her impatiently. She tugged at the boat-shaped Berthe neckline, dragging it lower in the fitting, determined that Harry should see her at her most beautiful on this rare excursion into femininity. At any rate, Jake wouldn't be there to upset the evening, even had the Bellowes invited him. He had chosen to spend the New Year in London, but in an odd way she found herself almost missing his presence. There was something about his personality, as if, almost without meaning to, he became the centrepoint of a carousel, as horses and their riders whirled up and down around it in a carnival sparked off by him. She laughed to herself. What a ridiculous notion. Trott looked up and frowned as she wriggled inside the cream dress, obscurely disappointed that he would not see her in it.

When they arrived at Court Manor, Rosie on Harry's arm, William still limping slightly from his injury and Polly openly hand in hand with Gabriel, Rosie's suspicions were confirmed.

'Look at Robert's face,' she whispered to Harry. It was completely blank, as he watched Polly and Gabriel together. It was he who had persuaded his father into this seasonal gesture of apparent goodwill. He wished to observe his rival once again at close quarters.

'Robert's all right,' said Harry reasonably. 'He seems to be going out of his way to be nice to Gabriel. You're so prejudiced, Rosie.'

'No wonder. He hates me,' said Rosie robustly.

'Nonsense,' said Harry, squeezing her arm. 'No one could hate you, Rosie.'

Later in the evening, after dinner, dancing to a small orchestra began and she was separated from Harry. It was some time before they danced together, and then it was not a conspicuous success.

'Ouch!' she said, as he trod on her foot, shod only by cinnamon satin shoes. He exclaimed in apology, and led her hopping into the conservatory.

'Here,' he said, 'let's have a look at the invalid.'

He put her on a chair and lifted up the foot with the dark mark on the light satin. He caressed it to her embarrassment. 'There,' he said lightly. 'Better now?' He sat down beside her and put his arm round her. Had it been anyone but Harry, she would have suspected him of engineering the situation.

'Happy New Year, Rosie. Our year, shall it be? Shall we get married this year?' he asked, smiling at her.

She gaped, not sure she'd heard aright. *'Married?* But

125

Harry,' she stopped, and started again. 'Harry, you don't want to marry me?'

He laughed and tweaked a curl.

'I love you, you must know that.'

'Love me?' she repeated doubtfully.

'Oh Rosie, you don't doubt that, do you?' He was hurt. 'Ever since I first saw you – how old were you – just sixteen I suppose. Such a quaint face and those eyes, always glaring defiance or laughing. Up to now I couldn't afford to settle down, but now I can. My uncle's taking me into the business as a partner. After all, you'll be twenty this year.'

'I'm not quite an old maid,' she said, nettled.

'It's a good age to get married,' he said firmly. 'Especially for us with so much to look forward to.'

'One day perhaps,' said Rosie. 'I'd really like to one day, but not yet.' She meant it. She couldn't imagine anyone she'd feel more comfortable with than Harry. But somehow, *not yet*. There was so much she wanted to do.

'Give me one good reason,' he challenged, holding her uncomfortably close, his fingers accidentally digging the bones of her corset into her skin.

One good reason? An irrational panic took hold of her. Wasn't this what she'd wanted? Did still want? Why then this sudden dart of doubt when faced with the prospect of it becoming reality? She needed time to – time to what? She did not know. She cast around wildly for a reason. She could not find one for herself, let alone for him. Then she did: 'Not until Pegasus has flown. We must get into the air first, don't you see, Harry?'

With the coming of spring came good news – the hint of a possible testing field, with William looking mysteriously content. Robert Bellowes was back at university, and had not troubled them further. Now, Harry had invited her to join him on a visit to Colonel Capper in London to discuss common progress on aeroplane development. The Clairville arrived promptly at ten o'clock, Rosie dashed out, forgetting her motoring hat as usual, and had to dash promptly back again.

126

'I almost forgot breakfast, I was so excited,' she said as she tied the veil under her chin. 'You are an angel to take me with you, Harry – you know how much I want to meet him.' She was slightly surprised to see that he was dressed in a smart reefer jacket with his flannels, rather than a formal suit. She was even more surprised when the Clairville turned its graceful way on to the Dover Road. She frowned. 'Why have you turned right, Harry? London's the other way.'

'Even Clairvilles need fuelling. I need some petroleum. I can buy some along here.'

But they didn't stop for it in Sittingbourne.

'Harry,' Rosie cried, twisting round to look at the town disappearing behind them, the wind blowing through her curls as the hat blew backwards on her head despite its anchorings. 'Where are you going?'

'My dread secret must out,' he sighed. 'We're not going to London.'

'We're not? Where are we going then?'

'France.'

'*France*? Harry, are you crazy?'

'I thought it would be a nice surprise. Monsieur Voisin is testing a new biplane hang-glider at Le Touquet today. It's only just across the Channel. We'll take the steamer to Boulogne, then have a pleasant luncheon in Le Touquet, watch the gliding tests and return to Brynbourne. *Voilà*.'

She frowned. 'Father won't like it,' she said dubiously.

'Your father won't know,' he said cheerfully.

'But there might be people we know there,' she said. 'What will they think? And don't I need a passport?'

'Oh come, Rosie. Everyone knows you want an aeroplane. They'll know you're there professionally. And no, you're English. You don't need a passport, not unless you're planning to elope with me and take up residence in Paris?' He cocked an eye at her. 'How about that? Would you like to see Paris? We could always go on there.' He was laughing at her and her anxiety was laid to rest. How ridiculous of her to have made a fuss.

Conscience wrestled with excitement at the thought of the trials. After all, Jake always said that gliding principles were behind the success of the Wright brothers' aeroplanes. She might learn something to help Pegasus II. Aviation was leaping ahead in France. The flights – or hops as Jake called them scathingly – of Mr Santos Dumont in that funny-looking aeroplane built like flying cardboard boxes strung together, had spurred the Europeans on. Now the French were the nearest to achieving full free-powered flight in Europe. Today she might see their competitors perhaps, talk to them, gauge how far they were ahead compared with Pegasus. Was Harry right when he said Pegasus should be rebuilt as it was, but with a stronger engine – even wait for him to develop the new rotary engine, or was Jake right when he said a different configuration was needed altogether, based on full lateral control? Jake should know – and Father trusted him. But Harry seemed so sure. Santos Dumont had no lateral control, and *he* flew.

By the time the motor car had reached the Channel steamer at Folkestone she was looking forward to the day ahead with excitement. She had travelled to France only once before so the sea journey was still a novelty, and she had conquered her fear of railways by now, so the journey to Le Touquet held no fears. The wind was brisk, however, and the sea choppy for all it was May, and by the time the steamer rolled into Boulogne she was very white, and feeling decidedly unlike luncheon at all. By the time the short railway journey to Le Touquet was over, however, her interest revived, sharpened by the exotic and wonderful smells emerging from the hotels and restaurants, quite unlike England. And so were the people, though many seemed to be English.

'Have you thought again about what we talked about at Christmas?' asked Harry casually, as Rosie worked her way through an enormous plateful of oysters and other seafood. 'Mind you, I don't know if I can afford to keep you, if you eat that amount all the time,' he added.

She grinned at him, then said hastily, 'Of course I have, Harry. But I'm sorry, I really don't want to get married *yet*. Not to anyone. I expect I will though,' she added brightly. She really did not want to take this talk of marriage seriously when there was so much else to talk about. Mr Voisin's gliding biplane, for example. How exactly did the airmen hang from it? And what kind of tailplane did it have? And exactly how did the man control the glider by his movements?

The trials were being held on the soft sand-dunes of Le Touquet, and as the sand clung to the flared skirt of her green gabardine walking dress she wished not for the first time she were free to wear her trousers on such expeditions, and not be encumbered with these stupid heavy skirts.

'Why,' exclaimed Rosie in astonishment, 'it's *Jake*!' He was striding towards them with a face like thunder. 'Jake – have you seen the hang-glider yet?' she called to him, this being uppermost in her mind.

'To hell with the hang-glider,' he said grimly. 'I'm here to get you back home just as quick as P & O can arrange it.'

The muscles in Harry's cheek were twitching violently. 'Aren't you overlooking the fact that I'm escorting Miss Potts, not you?'

'And I'm here from Mr Potts,' said Jake quietly. 'Unfortunately for you, Clairville Jones, Colonel Capper telephoned Mr Potts this morning – and seeing you was not part of his day's plans. He told him that he'd discussed Le Touquet with you, so we guessed where you were heading. By that time I'd missed the Boulogne boat which set me back a while, otherwise your joy ride would have been a whole lot shorter. Come along, Miss Potts.'

'Just how do I know Mr Potts has asked you to escort Miss Potts back? And just why do you think I'd entrust my fiancée to a cowboy?' Harry said coolly.

'Harry!' said Rosie, really furious that he should have referred to her as his fiancée but determined not to let him down in front of Jake. 'Harry's quite right,' she amended. 'How do we know Father's asked me to come back immediately? It's so stupid not to watch the gliding trial now we're here.'

'And cut it awful fine for the last Boulogne boat,'

said Jake sarcastically, looking at her coolly, almost contemptuously.

'Nonsense,' said Harry sharply.

'Which of you is going to explain that to Mr Potts?'

A silence. 'Harry, perhaps we'd better go,' said Rosie uncertainly.

'If I discover when I see Mr Potts that this charade is unnecessary,' said Harry slowly, 'then you will answer for it, Mr Smith.'

'That so?' said Jake evenly, leading the way to where a cab awaited them in the roadway.

In the short train journey to Boulogne, they sat all three silent, glowering at each other.

Once at Boulogne, Harry descended from the train. Before Rosie could follow, however, Jake forestalled her, standing on the platform as if to help her down and blocking the way for Harry to fulfil this duty himself. Thus it was that Harry, stalking grimly to the exit, turned to see the railway train steaming out with Jake and Rosie once more aboard, after some swift movement on Jake's part.

'Reckon we'll be a lot happier now Mr Harry'll have to wait for the Boulogne boat.'

'How . . . can you?' she cried.

'Easy now. You don't think I'm taking you for the white slave traffic, do you? I tell you, lady, they'd sling you right back,' he said feelingly.

Rosie glared at him, as he sat with folded arms, long legs stretched out in front of him.

'And you're safer with me than with Mr Clairville Jones. We're getting the Calais boat right back to Dover; you'll be home for dinner.'

'But this is ridiculous. You behave as though Harry's a vile seducer. Oh Jake, how *silly*.'

'You're his fiancée. Reckon you know.'

She stopped laughing. 'I'm – I don't know. We're not formally engaged. But Harry wants to marry me.'

'Does he though? And you the daughter of the owner of the Pegasus patent.'

She stared at him, unable to believe her ears, then burst

130

out: 'He *loves* me. *Me*, not Pegasus. Don't you believe that?'

'Nope.'

She bristled, taking this as a personal slight. 'You're wrong. And you and Father are wrong to drag me back from France, as though Harry would do anything to hurt me.' Even as she said it, Harry's words echoed in her mind: 'Would you like to see Paris? We could always go on there.' But he'd been laughing – that was just a joke.

'There are plenty of folks you know at Le Touquet today. It sure is one way to put pressure on you to marry him—' When she did not reply he said, exasperated, 'I tell you, you act so darn stupid, I think you're well matched.'

'At least he doesn't pretend to be someone he isn't,' she snapped.

Anger filled his eyes and he said no more.

The sea was even choppier on the return trip, and by the time the steamer reached Dover Rosie was ill as well as bad-tempered, only just avoiding the indignity of losing her luncheon to the sea in front of Jake. It was early evening by the time the train drew in to Newington Station and there were no cabs to be seen.

'Tenderfoot!' Jake said tersely. 'Can't you walk three miles? Only a mile and a half over the fields. Let's see your boots,' and he had calmly got down on bended knee, lifted her skirts and examined her boots before she realised his intention.

'Do they pass inspection?' she asked sarcastically.

'Sure. Nice boots too.'

They branched off the lane into the fields, still in silence. The ground was damp from the evening dew, the bushes green with promise, and the air full of the smells of May enchantment. A light drizzle was beginning to fall.

'Are you still mad at me for saving your honour?' Jake broke the silence at last.

'You can't really think Harry would have tried to seduce me?' she cried indignantly, her loyalty welling up again.

'I guess not. He's got engine oil in his veins, not blood.'

He'd given up a full day's work on Pegasus to go and collect this fool of a girl. If it wasn't for the aeroplane, he'd go back to the States – or better, to Europe where they weren't playing at aviation; at least they were *trying* to get in the air. Then: 'He's a gentleman,' he heard the girl say.

That did it. The humour of the situation overcame him and he roared with laughter.

'Gentleman? Rosie, you couldn't tell a gentleman from a horse thief.'

She stopped still. 'Who said you could call me Rosie?' she shouted at him, overcome with misery and her skirts wet with drizzle and beginning to cling to her.

'I don't know,' he answered, surprised. 'I guess that's how I think of you.'

She glared at him. 'It's *raining*!' she shouted. 'I'm *wet*!' He looked at her. She was right. Dress limp, hair tousled under the sodden gabardine hat, set above a mulish face.

'So it is. It's got worse. We'd best shelter under a tree awhile.' The scent of the apple blossom in the orchard brought out by the rain filled the air with perfume, the leaves were sleek with water and lush in colour.

'The rain's dribbling down my back,' Rosie complained crossly.

'And mine.'

'I'm not interested in *your* back.'

'What makes yours so special?' he inquired politely. Then the corners of his mouth twitched.

'What are you grinning about?'

'There's raindrops running down your nose, only they can't fall off the end because it's stuck right up in the air. As always.'

'It's not.'

'You're making a habit of being soaked through when we're together.'

'Oh.' She turned on him in fury for reminding her of their first meeting. Jake automatically seized her arm, which was flailing towards him in anger, and whether it was the smell of the fresh rain in the apple blossom or the green of a May evening, he gave a surprised gulp, turned her face up to his, bent over and kissed her; drew back with a frown just as her mouth opened wide either in surprise or to shout, then kissed her again so that she could not speak, so that apple blossom was spinning round her, and there was nothing but the sound of Jake's heartbeat close to hers and a tingling all over her body that had nothing to do with the pattering rain. His hands held her closer and lower so that her whole body arched into his and there was nothing but he and she in the whole wide world save for an uninterested yellowhammer chattering its unending song in the hedgerow.

# Chapter Six

Jake looked at her, half amused, half worried.

'Well,' he said slowly, 'I guess that answers why I called you Rosie.'

He released her, and so dazed was she by what had happened that she almost staggered. He caught her by the arm. 'Steady,' he said with a catch in his voice. 'You're as rickety as Pegasus.'

'It's only my longitudinal stability,' she said inanely, looking up at him, waiting. If he kisses me again, she thought wildly, please, *please* . . .

But he didn't. Perhaps hesitating for an explosion of wrath, every inch of him wanted to seize her again, kiss her again, and, darn it, more than that. Rain or no rain, he wanted to lay her down in the green, wet grass and love her till the apple blossom fell. All this pulsed through his mind and body, side by side with a memory of Florence. Hell, she'd do the same as Florence, wouldn't she? *Wouldn't she*? Despite Clairville Jones, Rosie was no Florence. Looking at her, how could he doubt it? But he could not move; the willing warmth in his eyes died. Instinctively she turned slightly, proud and unwilling to make the first move. And the moment died.

Turning points, he wondered savagely – like with Pegasus. Too late to cry now: *mine, all mine*. There came moments when you could break through the clouds into the blue sky and sun above, but they crept up on you and like ghosts tiptoed away.

'Rosie,' he said abruptly.

If he apologises, she thought wildly, I'll – hit him.

He didn't apologise. 'We'd best be getting back,' was all he said, uncommunicatively.

'Yes,' she said coldly.

Michael Potts, now twelve years old, followed them at a distance. He had not seen what had happened, but seeing them climb over the stile together, was well enough versed from his observance of Polly and Gabriel to know that this was no casual meeting. Jake took a terrific tumble in Michael's estimation. When Jake had arrived a year ago, looking like Buffalo Bill, with his long hair and moustache, his expertise with the bullwhip had been all that was needed to gain Michael's adoration. Jake had spent long hours teaching him just how to crack it to get the popper right on target, and to both their pleasures, Michael had shown some proficiency in the art. He was touchingly grateful to Jake, for this acquired skill gave him a status at his Rochester school that he would not otherwise have merited. Being a friend of a Clairville Jones gained him some respect at first, which he promptly lost since he knew little about motor cars; and being the son of William Potts was a distinct disadvantage. Already named (out of official hearing) Pisspotts, Michael suffered even worse indignities when his father's penchant for flying machines became general knowledge. Sketches of flying WCs thrust under his nose were the mildest of them.

Michael sometimes thought there must be something wrong with him. He wasn't interested in that flying machine Father and Rosie were so keen on, nor did he like looking into motor car innards. Taking a spin with Harry was all right, but Harry never seemed to have time for him these days. What Michael liked doing best, though he never let on about this at school, was poking round the Potts factory, seeing how things worked, admiring the Potts Pedestal WCs lined up, embossed and painted, ready for despatch to their customers by railway. Polly made them look all right. Lately she seemed more interested in that Gabriel, who wasn't a patch on Jake or Harry. He only seemed interested in Polly and art. Art wasn't a real man's thing. Up to now, he could have sworn Jake was only interested in aeroplanes. Michael could put up with

that, because Jake had seen the world. Sometimes he'd tell
him about gold hunting in the Yukon, sometimes about the
Wild West and the stories about Doc Holliday. When Jake
got on to the Wright brothers Michael quickly lost interest
and, sensing this, Jake let it drop. Michael knew Jake was
a wonderful storyteller, funny, clever and always keeping
him on tenterhooks.

'What happened then, Jake?' he'd cry.

'Why, then this li'l ole bear,' accentuating the accent,
'just held out its paw like it was a kitten. And I just didn't
have the heart to kill it, though I could have done with
some good bear meat in the pot that night—'

Now his idol was interested in Rosie. *His* Rosie, who
always had time for him, even if she was interested in
aeroplanes first and foremost. Rosie was lovely; and she
wasn't his real sister, so he might even marry her when he
grew up. That way he'd always have her to talk to. Thus
he watched jealously for any sign that Rosie might marry
before he grew up, though she had frequently assured him
that she would not. He'd always kept a careful eye on
Harry, but it had never occurred to him that Jake might
be a threat. He felt deeply ashamed. That the two people
he liked most in the world were perhaps kissing behind his
back. Jake never so much as mentioned women when they
were together. He'd been brought up in a man's world
and that, assumed Michael, was how it would remain. His
possible desertion seemed a kind of betrayal. He kicked
moodily at a stone. The way he looked at it it wasn't fair
on Harry. Harry had first claim. A brainwave occurred to
him.

William was unexpectedly firm with Rosie, despite her
indignantly pointing out that there was absolutely no proof
of Michael's accusation or of Father's wicked thoughts.

'A lady does not place herself in a position where
unfortunate events *might* occur,' William pointed out
pompously, without a trace of his usual gentleness. He
was indeed shocked to the core. He couldn't believe
Harry would go so far as to kidnap his daughter, but
nevertheless, the shock of realising that Rosie might have

been manoeuvred into a situation where he could not protect her made him severe. She had too much freedom, he argued unfairly. She was abusing his trust.

Smarting under injustice, Rosie rushed for solace to Polly. Now she was beginning to appreciate what Polly had so often suffered, remembering her warning. Not for many years had she transgressed his code, and only now realised just how strict this was.

'It's quite understandable, I suppose,' said Polly, commiserating in her bedroom. 'He just wants to keep us here under his eye all the time – till we get suitable husbands.' She pulled a face.

'Surely Harry *is* a suitable husband?' raged Rosie.

'More than Gabriel,' said Polly mournfully.

'I thought he approved now.'

'I think he at least tolerates him now. He's stopped talking about greenery-yallery Grosvenor gallery young men.'

Rosie collapsed with laughter. The thought of Gabriel with his sparkling interest in people and life itself as an effete hangover from the decadent 'nineties, as they were called, was very funny.


'Where are the sackcloth and ashes?' asked Rosie of Harry, somewhat warily, as he appeared in the drawing room after his interview with William. She had felt embarrassed at the thought of facing Harry, as if she had been somehow to blame for what had happened.

'The way I see it, young Rosie, you're the one who should be wearing the sackcloth – though I don't think it would suit you as much as that green thing you're wearing. Giving me the slip at Boulogne.'

'This green thing is new,' said Rosie sharply, glancing down at the figured muslin, 'and it wasn't my fault. What did Father *say*?'

'Nothing much,' replied Harry cheerfully. 'I explained it was a pre-birthday surprise for you, that our bull-in-a-china-shop Smith had obviously helped him to the wrong interpretation and that we would have easily made the connection back to England. Don't worry,' he touched her hair lightly, 'all's well. Except that I don't feel amiable towards your gallant friend Smith.'

'He's no friend of—' she began, then stopped, remembering an apple tree and how she felt then. The memory dazed her for a moment, a sense so strong that only her feeling of ecstasy when in the balloon all those years ago could compare.

But he wasn't a friend. '—mine,' she ended. Whatever Jake was, friendship played no part. Where was the confidence, the trust you needed between friends? What did she know of him, or of his past life? The only one of them he talked to was Michael, and even Polly probably knew more about his past than she did. Not that Rosie wanted to.

'I have an idea, you see,' said Harry slowly, 'that your friend Jake might have engineered our fiasco. He might have put the idea in your father's mind, offered his services to hare after us, kidnapped you to make himself appear a hero by saving you from a fate worse than death — ' he glanced at her '—with the intention of seeking your favours himself.'

Rosie gasped. 'But— ' She stopped. Could say nothing. The *apple tree*. Surely not a traitor's kiss?

'It would suit Mr Smith nicely, wouldn't it, to marry you.'

'But,' she said ingenuously, without thinking, 'that's what he said about you.'

'Did he indeed?' said Harry smugly. 'Doesn't that just prove my point? He'll stop at nothing to blacken me. Now, Rosie darling, don't let's waste all this time talking about that bounder. Where would you like to go today? To Canterbury?'

'Not today, Harry. I want to get to work on Pegasus now J— Mr Smith has finished the plans. I can't wait to start.'

He sighed. 'Always Pegasus first. I think it's almost preferable to be forsaken for another man than a warped wing.'

'But Harry,' she began indignantly, 'we're not warp—' then she saw he was laughing at her. 'You are an idiot,

Harry,' she said laughing. 'Anyway, you want Pegasus to fly as soon as possible too, don't you?'

'Oh yes,' he said, 'I want Pegasus to fly.'

'Care to give me a spin, Harry?' asked Michael importantly.

'Where to?' Harry, already clad in his summer dust-coat and goggles, having left Rosie in the drawing room, was not pleased to be thus buttonholed by Michael in the midst of cranking the Clairville's engine.

'Anywhere,' said Michael mysteriously. 'I've got something to tell you of great importance.'

Harry sighed. He'd tell him to scram if it wasn't for the fact that he was William Potts's son – and Rosie's brother. He was well aware that Michael had his favourites – and he, Harry, was not among them. But when the Clairville was away from Brynbourne and Michael began to talk, he quickly changed his mind. It amused him to think he might have been more accurate than he thought when he accused Jake of philandering, for Michael had embellished the truth of what he had seen more than somewhat. He had to be careful. He would just store up the information till the right time came. If he mishandled it, however, it might send Rosie straight into Jake's arms, though he couldn't imagine she'd be attracted to Jake rather than himself. But she was a hot-headed little thing, and might throw herself where her sympathies lay. Rosie could be unpredictable, always the question mark in his plans.

They seemed to be making painfully little progress with Pegasus in the summer of 1907, but Jake refused to be hurried. This time it was going to be right. Finally they got to the point of constructing the scaffolding so that Rosie could work on assembling the wings with Mr Fisherbutt, who now worked somewhat slower owing to his arthritic fingers. She was in a fever of impatience, and when she peered over Jake's shoulder to see him regarding such fascinating symbols as

$$b = \frac{f}{P}$$

she found it hard to be convinced that Pegasus's future depended on the solution of such equations. What did impress her – and alarm her – were reports in aviation magazines of events in France, more flights by Santos Dumont, the increasing mention of the name of an Englishman working there, Henry Farman, and another building aeroplane after aeroplane, Louis Blériot. None really successful – *yet*. But they were hopping, they were flying, after a fashion, like young birds leaving the nest. This was their spring – soon would come summer and young birds would soar into full flight.

Here, too, such birds tried their wings. Jake hooted with laughter at one young cuckoo. 'Look at this, sir,' he chortled, thrusting a picture under William's nose, Rosie craning to see. 'Remember his multi-plane Venetian Blind of 1904? Horatio Phillips has produced another one. Look!'

It looked like four enormous barnyard fences braced together one behind the other with a propeller in front and an engine in the middle.

'It has flown after a fashion, Jake,' William pointed out. 'Who are we to scoff at it?'

Jake was silent, put away the magazine without a word and returned to his equations.

He disappeared for a week in the summer, and when he returned was both elated and depressed. Another Englishman had tested an aeroplane, Mr J.W. Dunne. Built on gliding principles with only a twelve horsepower engine, it had stayed aloft for only a few seconds and, as had Pegasus, had been damaged. The race was hotting up. And still Pegasus consisted of wings, engine, tail-plane, and a burning ideal still to be forged to its conclusion.

Harry, as if anxious to avoid confrontation, came rarely to the workshop now, but accompanied them to the new site they had leased for testing.

'There,' said William proudly, sweeping his hand in lordly fashion in a semicircle. On the Isle of Sheppey, there was much flat land and he had come to an agreement with the farmer to lease an area twice the size of Bred Field.

'And there are no neighbours to say we're overflying their land,' William pointed out helpfully.

'Only the sea,' said Jake drily. 'I guess we'd better include floats on Pegasus.'

One day in late August, Rosie hunted in vain for Jake. Why wasn't he around? He knew the wings were approaching a critical stage and that she was worried about stress now they were being assembled.

She walked over to the hop garden to see if he was there. It had not been easy. Lurking at the bottom of her mind was the stupid fear that Uncle Alf might be there. If he were – so what? She told herself firmly that she could just walk away. His physical presence would bring back the past and contaminate the present only if she let it. The dark place was in her mind, and nowhere else. Pegasus was much more important than childhood horrors.

She found Jake, once again, with Peggy Wilkins, just like the last time. He was still in his thick cotton working overalls, so it was clearly a spur of the moment decision to come here, which somewhat mollified her – until she realised the decision might well have been made for him by Peggy. They were working closely side by side, just as before, stripping the same plant, working into the same basket, she with her blouse hanging half open. Jake's eyes were alight and laughing, as he tickled her bosom with a scratchy hop branch, while peals of laughter issued from her.

Then he glanced up and saw her, and a kind of shutter came over his face. He lay down the hops, with a joking aside to Peggy – about her? Rosie raged instantly – and came over to her.

'You looking for me, Rosie?'

'I was, but you seem to be busy here,' she said disdainfully.

He looked embarrassed, which made her irrationally crosser. What did it matter to her if he kissed every girl in Kent? Nothing, except that she had clearly been but one among that number.

'I get ideas up here – away from the workshed.'

142

'Peggy Wilkins can give you ideas about aeroplanes?' she asked ironically.

'That isn't what I meant and you know it,' he said mildly. She noticed he was losing his American accent now, and only the occasional word betrayed his unusual upbringing. 'Clears your mind being out here in the air.'

'I saw that,' she muttered, then, as if there had been no barb in her words, continued hurriedly; 'I wanted to tell you the wings are nearly ready, but I've run into a problem with fairing in the spars.'

'I've got the plans back at the Lodge. We'd better go back and look at them. It may be tied in with the general stress problem we've got.'

She sensed he was unwilling to leave and jumped to the wrong conclusion. He didn't want to leave Peggy – or perhaps he didn't want to be alone with her, Rosie.

It was a half-mile walk to the Old Lodge, but enjoyable in her comfortable trousers, and she walked by his side, hands in her pockets.

She had not been to the Lodge since he had moved in, and was amazed at the transformation. The old thatch had been replaced by peg tiles, the garden tidied up and even planted with sunflowers. Inside, the old fireplace had been stripped away to expose a huge old inglenook like those she had seen in some older houses that had not been renovated. How strange that he had chosen to expose it. It looked nice, and she told him so.

He was clearly pleased at her approval. 'I reckon this old cottage may have been part of a much bigger house once – that sunburst, you only get that where a king has stayed. And stayed pretty often. I like getting to the bottom of things – like this old fireplace. I like things simple, like they were built to be,' he said. 'Straightforward, not covered up.' He glanced at her. If he thought of Harry, he did not mention him. 'I have the plans upstairs. I'll go get them.'

He bounded upstairs while she looked around the room. It was ruthlessly tidy like Jake himself. Nothing to betray personality, except a photograph in an old wooden frame of a simpering girl with long ringlets and bows in her hair. His sister perhaps, she thought – hoped.

143

A shout interrupted her thoughts. 'Hey, Rosie, come up here.'

Without thinking she ran upstairs, and stopped in surprise. The whole of the upper floor he'd made into one large bedroom – but without a ceiling. Now the room was open to the roof, the huge tie-beams and timber framing exposed. He was standing, legs apart, hands on hips, on the bed, staring up at the beams. 'Up here Rosie.' He leaned down and with one strong hand pulled her up beside him on the bed. 'Look at those beams.'

He was gazing up at them entranced. 'That's it, Rosie, that's *it*. The king-posts. I reckon old England has shown us the way. That's how men solved the stress problem in the old days. And that's how we'll solve it in Pegasus. The ash wood by itself will take too much stress for the resistance when it's in the air, but if we strengthen it with a king-post arrangement on each side, why, that's the answer.'

'You know,' she said excitedly, nearly falling off the bed as she craned to see, and steadying herself by holding his arm, 'you might be right.'

'Now don't you be so cautious, Rosie. It's the answer, you know that.' He leapt off the bed, put up his arms and jumped her down. She thought he was going to kiss her, and was irrationally disappointed when he didn't; he simply grabbed her hand and pulled her down beside him sitting on the bed, as he seized the plans to demonstrate his point.

He talked non-stop for five minutes as if he'd forgotten she were there and when she eventually said something, looked at her in surprise and said awkwardly: 'I guess I should take you downstairs. It isn't really fitting—' he gestured to the bed. 'With those trousers and all, it's hard to remember sometimes you're a lady.'

'You don't have the same trouble with Peggy Wilkins,' she said tartly, embarrassed. 'Can't you recognise a woman unless she's got ringlets and a – a – big chest?'

'Ringlets?' he repeated blankly. Then: 'Ah.' His face

went pale, and she knew she'd blundered into uncharted territory.

'Jake,' she said quickly, warmly, rightly, 'that's one mistake each we've made. Neither meant, neither remembered.' She put out her hand and took his; after a moment it closed around hers.

Then he stood up, scooped up the plans and said abruptly, 'Let's work on this in the garden.'

It was a truce; she thought he did not wish to be too close to her; she was right, but she did not realise this was because he did not trust himself; that with a few simple words she had temporarily driven the memory of Florence back into the mists of time.

Once in the garden he breathed again, once more under control, spreading the plans out unnecessarily carefully on the grass.

'This Pegasus has got to work this time, Rosie. We've got to fly.'

'But,' she said wistfully, 'you've flown already.'

'Yes, but with the Wright Flyer. What I want – what I feel is—' he broke off, unable to express it, and she did not speak for fear of interrupting him. She wanted to know. 'I want,' he said as much to himself as her, 'a partner in the air, not a slave. A lover, not a servant. It's a dual triumph; man and aeroplane together, setting out on a quest with an endless horizon. It is not really a question of who flies first, or when or on what. It's how it's done, and why. And the why has got to be for good, not evil; to create, not to destroy.'

'But that's the way I feel,' she interrupted, surprised.

'Do you, Rosie?' he paused and smiled at her.

'Why, yes,' she said eagerly. 'I've always wanted to fly. To find out what's above the clouds. Ever since I saw a kite as a child. It's not a question of overcoming engineering problems, of scientific achievement, that's only the means; it's spirit that is the end. It's the exaltation of life, it's like – it will be like – it's like—' she cast around in her mind '—it will be like that kiss – it carries you on, soars you above the experience itself, and into new horizons; we won't be limited by what we think of as the boundary

145

of achievement any more, but soar beyond it. To – to the heavens, to God if you like—' She stopped, wondering why he stared at her so strangely.

'What kiss, Rosie?' he asked quietly. Inside, his heart was pounding. His kiss, their kiss under the apple tree. Had she, could she have felt the same as him? Had she tried to ignore it too, as had he? But if they both—

'What kiss—' she repeated, stunned. He had to ask what kiss. With all the Peggys, all the women who must lay their charms so willingly at his feet, how could he possibly remember just one kiss – theirs?

'Harry's,' she blurted out defensively. 'Last Christmas.'

'Harry, do stop. There's some wonderful blackberries there. *And* a cobnut tree.' Rosie was almost jumping down from the Clairville before it had stopped.

Harry tried not to show his exasperation. 'I'll sit here and wait for you,' he said as patiently as he could.

Rosie was constantly surprised that he did not share her passion for the countryside – perhaps because he was born into it, she thought perceptively. Those first six years of her life had made a difference. She should try to appreciate his viewpoint. For herself, she loved the mellow ripeness of the September sun, of the fruits offered by God's bounty free to all who could linger awhile. The sweet cobs, blackberries, even the sloes, with which Mrs Fisherbutt would make wine, all part of the excitement of autumn. If only Harry would share it.

'I thought you liked blackberries,' she said wistfully, hoping he'd come to help her.

'In a pie,' he said firmly, getting out his pipe and a magazine. 'Not getting scratched to pieces picking them.'

'All right, lazybones, I'll pick them for you.'

She picked handfuls of blackberries and brought them back to him, wrapped up in an old scarf.

Harry eyed her critically. 'You've got red stains on your blouse.'

She laughed. 'I think you believe I should sit in the parlour and sew a fine seam all day long. Aeroplane grease is worse than blackberry juice, anyway.'

'How long do you intend to go on working on aeroplanes?' he inquired politely.

'I told you. Always. And,' she added for good measure, licking her fingers, 'I'm still not thinking of marriage. Not until Pegasus flies.'

'You could be pretty old the way Mr Smith is carrying on.'

'He's doing his best,' she said shortly.

Harry saw he'd made a mistake, and immediately rectified it. Time enough to think out its causes later. 'Come here.' He took her in his arms and kissed her. It was very pleasant, she thought. Undemanding – quite unlike Jake's. She pushed this uneasy thought from her. It would be very tempting to say she would marry Harry now. After all, he represented all she could ever want. No surprises, no puzzling undercurrents. And Harry worshipped her. *Her*, not a hundred others. She sighed and settled back in his arms, despatching an indefinable anxiety from her mind. 'Pegasus will fly very soon now.'

'We could be engaged.'

'When Pegasus flies, Harry. When Pegasus greets the sun.'

Michael frowned as he saw them kiss as they said goodbye. Now Harry was as bad as Jake. And it meant Rosie was fickle. At least she'd told him she wasn't engaged to Harry. And a good thing too. She was promised to him, Michael. It was hard on Jake though. Michael pondered on what was best to do.

Rosie was still trying to dismiss that uneasiness from her mind. It had now taken shape. Surely Harry would not expect her to sit in drawing-rooms all day if they married? He must realise that she would always want to go on working on aeroplanes? What a stupid question to ask her. Suppose she'd asked him if he intended to go on working on cars all his life?

Then she cheered up, remembering the jokes, and how well they got on together, they could always talk things over. He was not uncommunicative like Jake. She managed

147

to forget that Harry's kiss, though enjoyable, had been a poor substitute for Jake's, persuading herself that it was natural that Jake could kiss well. He'd had plenty of experience. That simpering girl in the photograph. And Peggy and doubtless hundreds of others. Harry was a hard-working, sincere young man. He'd spent his time with engines, not women. So his kisses were to be valued far more highly. And that was what she wanted, not some American Romeo.

In the spring of 1908 there was an air of suppressed excitement in the small enclosed world of British aviation. Cody's airship *Nulli Secundus* had flown successfully last year, and the scoffers were less vocal thereafter. Even the Government were reconsidering their attitude to powered flight now. If engines could assist in making lighter-than-air flight not only possible but safe, perhaps it was but a short step to powered heavier-than-air flight.

In France, Mr Henry Farman had succeeded in flying a kilometre, turning his aeroplane, flying back to the starting point, landing safely and bearing off a prize of £2,000 in triumph.

At Brooklands motorcar race track other pioneers besides Potts were hotting up their race. A young man called Alliott Verdon Roe was indefatigably edging towards flight, and in a neighbouring shed a glider designed by Mr Moore-Brabazon was being modified and having an engine installed. But more than these, if anything was needed to spur Mr Potts's venture on, it was the letter from the United States that Jake came to the workshed clutching excitedly one day.

'They've started,' he called out to Rosie.

'Who's started?' she yelled back, cross at being interrupted in the middle of adjusting the propeller.

'Orville and Wilbur Wright. They're flying again at Kittyhawk. And what's more, the US Government is buying the Flyer at last – and the best news is that Wilbur is coming to France to fly there.'

Harry stood unseen in the shadows, thinking rapidly. He held no brief for the Wrights, but he knew as did Jake that for good or ill Wilbur's coming would give aviation in Europe a push forward.

And still Pegasus was only at the ground trial stage.

'Why, Gabriel, you look so – *sober*,' Polly said, stopping short as she flew into the morning room to greet him.

His fair hair was neatly plastered down; his whole mien was subdued as he stood there in his sober suit and high starched collar, bowler hat in hand.

'Do you think I look a reliable sort of fellow?' he asked anxiously, craning to view his appearance in the mirror.

'Reliable – you certainly do,' she said. 'You look very boring indeed.'

'Oh.' He looked downcast. 'I don't like the idea of that. I don't think you'd like a boring husband, would you?'

'Boring – Gabriel, what do you mean?' she cried.

'It means,' he said, sending the bowler hat spinning into a corner, and catching her round the waist, whirling her round, 'that I am a rich man at last. Well, reasonably rich. I have a commission to paint a whole series of paintings, and if they are acceptable, many more will follow. It means, dearest, *dearest* Polly, that I can ask your father for your hand, and it means, dearest, sweetest, loveliest Polly,' whispering in her ear, 'that I can love you in the long, long grass, and kiss you under the blue, blue sky for ever. And what's more,' he added, 'it means we can be married. And that shall be,' he threw open his arms joyously, 'just as soon as Trott can make your bridal dress.'

William tried very hard to avoid giving a definite answer; postponement was talked of, and making secure plans for the future, but even he could not hold out against a united front of Gabriel, Polly, Rosie and, above all, Mildred. Gabriel had long been a favourite of hers.

Even Michael was in favour of the match, though personally he couldn't see why Polly was so keen on the fellow. He was only a painter. But provided it didn't put ideas into Rosie's head, it was all right with him.

He watched suspiciously for signs of her favouring either Harry or Jake, but she showed no signs of the moonsick love that he could see displayed in Polly's eyes, and she continued to laugh robustly at the idea of marriage. There was far too much happening for her to get married yet awhile. She and Jake continued to work together as if nothing had happened and a polite formality reigned on the rare occasions Harry put in an appearance at the workshed.

Late in the summer of 1908 came the day that Pegasus was partially dismantled and transported to its new testing ground near the village of Eastchurch on the Isle of Sheppey. Flat, with few obstacles, it was ideal for their purpose, though the rough shed that they had had quickly created there lacked the facilities of Brynbourne Place. It had the advantage of there being no one to object to or spy on their manoeuvres save seagulls and a few sheep. The villagers, dependent on land and sea for their living, were uninterested in a new element when the old ones served them well enough.

Rosie and Mr Fisherbutt pushed Pegasus out. The ground was muddy, and Pegasus did not move easily. Jake watched frowning as they pushed, steadying the wings supported on the tiny bicycle wheels.

There were times, thought Rosie wrily to herself, when she wished Jake *did* take more notice of her sex. Only when she slipped and fell into the mud did he come; not to assist her, but to take her place with the pushing. Scrambling up, knees and hands covered in mud, she was tempted to transfer a sizeable portion to the immaculately jacketed back – the buckskins had at last been replaced by more conventional attire.

When Pegasus was waiting, Jake climbed in and the Clairville started its familiar hum. Smooth as ever, Pegasus began to move but, strain as it might, it did not lift. A short hop of a few yards was all it managed. It was a disappointing end to their hopes of a bright summer of promise.

Face like granite, Jake drove William's Sunbeam back to the house, having graciously allowed her to accompany him. It was another source of irritation to Rosie that she was never allowed by William to drive the motorcar. To her fell the indignity of bicycling to Sheppey, or worse, the governess cart, since Jake preferred usually to take his own motorcar, and it never seemed to occur to him to offer to take her as a passenger. *Why* shouldn't she drive, and *why* shouldn't she fly?

The next day Jake came to the workshed looking tired. 'I've worked out what's wrong,' he told Rosie and Mr Fisherbutt, 'and it's bad. With the new configuration, we've increased the aeroplane's fineness. We increased the plane area, so you had to stay it more strongly, Rosie; that improved the fineness but so far as I can make out, that's now diminishing our power and thrust.' He paused. 'In other words, we need a stronger engine after all. We're going to have to talk to Harry.'

Gabriel and Polly's engagement party at Brynbourne Place confirmed the local gentry's worst suspicions; artists from dens of iniquity in London had invaded by means of the renamed Southern Eastern and Chatham Railway, filling the house with chatter and outlandish clothes, bringing a life and spirit to Brynbourne it had not seen for decades. Artists were all very well in the middle of fields with an easel quietly painting horses, ran the local thinking, but on a social occasion in civilised society, their exuberance was another matter. This evening would provide grounds for talk for the next year. Polly did not notice. Shy, having met so few of Gabriel's friends, she quickly warmed to their enthusiastic charm, and was overwhelmed when they talked to her seriously about art, taking her for one of them, instead of admiring her beauty and asking her to sit for them, flattering though that was. Quickly finding their way uninvited into her small studio at the top of the house, they examined her paintings with frank curiosity and constructive criticism.

William, in his usual spirit of forgiving generosity, had invited the Bellowes, and to Rosie's great surprise, Robert was announced. How did he have the nerve, thought

Rosie indignantly, after what his family had done? But William bustled forward to greet him courteously.

'I've come on my father's behalf. He's not well,' announced Robert blandly. Rosie thought Robert looked like a black toad ready to spring, with his flickering dark eyes and dark straight hair liberally plastered down with Macassar oil.

'Slug,' hissed Polly in Rosie's ear, taking her attention from Jake, and she giggled. She heard Robert say, 'He wanted me to come to say he's willing to let bygones by bygones. You've found somewhere to test your aeroplane, I gather,' he said patronisingly. 'Well, we shall not object to a certain amount of noise emanating from Bred Field while you are engine testing. So far as we're concerned, we feel it right that neighbours should be tolerant of one another.'

'What's he up to?' whispered Rosie to Harry. 'He must have something nasty in mind.'

'Not like you, Rosie, to be so ungenerous,' said Harry, frowning. 'I think he means it.'

William certainly seemed to be taking it in the spirit in which it was intended.

'Welcome, my boy, welcome,' he said expansively.' 'Come in and enjoy yourself. You've met Mr Marriner, our Gabriel, of course.'

'Indeed I have, many congratulations, Mr Marriner.' The smile did not reach his eyes, Rosie noticed, and she felt uneasy as she saw Robert take Polly's hand, then lean forward and kiss her on the cheek.

'The privilege of an old friend,' he murmured to Polly smoothly, setting Rosie's teeth on edge. 'He's a very lucky man.'

Rosie could almost feel the chill emanating from him. Or was it her imagination as Harry implied? Perhaps Harry was too preoccupied to think of Robert, for he asked while they danced: 'Doesn't all this melt your stony heart, Rosie? Would you not like to be married yourself?'

She looked at him in surprise. 'You know what we agreed.' But was it Pegasus or the knowledge that Jake Smith's eyes were on them that was uppermost in her mind? 'When Pegasus flies—' she said unconvincingly yet again.

'And suppose it never flies?' he asked.

'You know what Jake says, it needs a new engine. When we get that—'

'Rosie, forget about the damned plane. Think about us,' he said angrily. 'It's important.'

'Why?' she asked, surprised.

But he did not reply.

Rosie walked into the workshed the next morning, unprepared for the surprising scene that greeted her. Jake was working on Pegasus as usual, stretching up to adjust an upper boom. What was not usual was that he was stripped to the waist, the muscles standing out on his shoulders, and apparently stationary.

'Hey, what are you doing?' she shouted, concerned for her precious bracing.

At the sound of her voice he straightened up, clearly swearing under his breath. 'That's enough, darn it,' he said, irritated, to some third person – and when Rosie turned there was Gabriel busily sketching.

'This is not my idea,' Jake threw at her, embarrassed and hunting for his shirt.

'Mine, Rosie,' shouted Gabriel cheerfully. 'I've finished the first sketch now anyway, thanks. I persuaded him to abandon Pegasus for half an hour while I promised him immortality. I shall call it "Man and Machine",' he announced gravely. 'The dignity of man's naked struggle against the elements. I wanted Jake to strip but he refused. So I'm stuck with those ghastly grey corduroy trousers. His shoulders are enough, though. Aren't they splendid, Rosie? Don't you admire them?'

Rosie reached the shirt before Jake did, waving it at him and whisking it away as he grabbed at it, blushing red. 'No wait,' she cried dramatically, 'one more glimpse of those splendid, splendid shoulders, I beseech you.'

'How would you like another dip in the cattle trough?' Jake inquired dangerously.

Gabriel looked up, bright-eyed. Fearing for one awful

153

moment Jake meant it, Rosie turned and fled, forgetting she still held the shirt. He caught her before she had gone ten yards from the shed, pinioned her from behind against his chest with one arm and removed the shirt with the other.

She could feel his heart thudding and for a moment the smell of apple blossom seemed to fill the air, lingering on the breeze, seducing her into turning irresistibly towards his lips. But only she was aware of it, it seemed, or perhaps it was Gabriel's presence as he strolled out towards them. All Jake said was: 'You should have more respect for the dignity of labour, young woman,' apparently engrossed in putting his shirt on.

Rosie walked quickly back to the workshed, with Gabriel following her thoughtfully.

'I could paint you two. Standing together like that. I could call it "The Threshold". '

'No,' she said fiercely, polishing Pegasus's wheels with great attention to detail.

'Beatrice and Benedict.'

'*No*.'

'Love's Denial?'

'Definitely not,' she snapped, her face red.

She stood up, to escape this inquisition, to find Gabriel laughing at her, and Jake returning. Had he heard? But if he had, he showed no sign. All he said was: 'Where did you leave those pliers yesterday, Rosie?'

William presided miserably at the table in the library, having been hauled in at Harry's insistence to the conference on Pegasus's future. He liked discussing with Jake how Pegasus was going to fly, talking about flight itself; he didn't want to get embroiled in the business side of it. And it looked as if there might be ructions ahead. He was almost pouting.

Jake strolled in, slipping into the seat beside Rosie, nodding to her casually. She sensed he'd been deliberately avoiding her, just when – she did not finish the thought. Now there were four people here. Each with different hopes for one aeroplane: Pegasus.

'We asked you for this meeting, Mr Potts,' Harry said quickly, 'because we're all three of us agreed, are we not' – quick glance at Jake – 'that Pegasus needs a new engine. An increase of power to fifty horsepower, and there's precious little time to get it installed now that Cody and Roe and now Moore-Brabazon are almost ready. I have the engine prepared, of course—'

'What's the problem then?' asked William testily.

'The problem is, Mr Potts, that I'm not prepared to sell it to you.' Harry dropped his bombshell quietly and with precision.

Jake looked up sharply. A moment's sheer bewilderment seized Rosie, as she took this in.

'Won't sell it?' William asked. 'Why not? Isn't Jake offering you enough?'

'Monetarily, yes.'

'He won't sell it, Mr Potts,' said Jake, holding himself in control, but his eyes glittering dark, 'because we don't agree over Pegasus.'

'Correct. Not to beat about the bush, Mr Potts, I won't sell you the new engine – which I have patented – while Mr Smith is in charge.'

Rosie was aghast. Why oh why had she always assumed that though they did not like each other, both put Pegasus first?

'Harry, you can't do this, not at this late stage,' she cried.

'I can and I will, Rosie. I'm sorry – but I have no confidence in Mr Smith – nor in his version of Pegasus.'

'It's blackmail, doing this now,' said Jake angrily, pounding his fist on the table in frustration. He knew he was going about this the wrong way, but whatever he'd expected, it hadn't been this bad. And he had no answer for it.

William interrupted. 'I agree with Jake over the configuration, Harry, and the principles on which Pegasus was to be built. In any case I can't dismiss Mr Smith because you won't supply an engine. It would hardly be fair.'

Harry shrugged, but Jake intervened before he could

reply. 'I put it the other way round, I'm not prepared to accept any more of Clairville Jones's interference. We buy the engine – and that is that. He has no other say in Pegasus.' It was a gamble, banking on Harry needing the glory of being associated with an aeroplane in which his engine was installed.

'No.' The word came out flatly, definitely, almost smugly.

He's got something up his sleeve, thought Rosie instantly, realising to her surprise she was regarding Harry almost as the opposition.

'Then we'll have to manage without your engine.'

'Before you try to bluff me that you'll build your own,' said Harry calmly, 'Rosie's explained just how deep your knowledge of engines is. Don't try that one.'

The deep blue eyes turned to her coldly, as if she were a stranger, then away again.

Rosie, furious with Harry and furious with herself, burst out; 'Why shouldn't I have told him? You were deceiving him – taking an unfair advantage.'

Jake didn't even bother to reply, not even to acknowledge she had spoken.

It was Harry who did. 'You're right, Rosie, I'm afraid. Deceit seems second nature to Mr Smith.'

The deep blue eyes blazed, and William barked, 'Harry, you go too far.'

'Do I?' he replied. 'I doubt I could. If Mr Smith had been less lucky, you would not be alive today, sir.'

A hush. So now it comes, thought Rosie. This was what it had all been leading to. The two men faced each other across the table, engaged in a deadly poker game.

'Justify that remark,' said Jake abruptly. 'Do you hear me? Justify it,' he shouted.

'Certainly. Though you know very well. Doubtless you had not counted on my producing evidence.'

'Of what?' Jake's voice was a whiplash.

'Of your altering the bend of the propeller tips so that the engine lacked the power to lift sufficiently,' said Harry coolly, holding Jake's eyes. 'It was unfortunate for you that William, heavier than you, was flying when Pegasus

156

crashed. Undoubtedly you had planned a somewhat more spectacular failure at the trials. With you at the controls, calculating what would happen after you had interfered with the propeller, Pegasus would still have crashed, but you could have ensured that you escaped unhurt. The result, however, would have been the same – that Pegasus would have to be rebuilt according to your design.'

'You'll prove every word of that, Harry,' William said. His instinct never let him down. He'd always suspected Harry might bring trouble in his wake, and now he was showing himself in his true colours. Let him prove this ridiculous story.

'Certainly. Here are the photographs I took of the blade tips before the crash. The blade tips themselves are now in my Rochester workshed if you wish to see them.' He threw the photographs on the table.

Jake did not even bother to glance at them. Rosie looked quickly, before William picked them up and studied them. The blade tips were undoubtedly bent in those photographs more than they should have been. But that was no proof that Jake had done it. He would deny it. He *must* deny it.

But he didn't. Jake scraped back his chair and stood up, smarting with hurt as he looked scornfully at the faces of those he'd worked with, trusted. They were waiting for him to deny it. Clairville Jones was daring him to come out with the truth, that it was he, Harry, who had tampered with the blades, hoping to force them into having to acquire the new engine – on his terms. Couldn't they see that? It was obvious. These photographs were no evidence of anything – except to those who wanted to believe him guilty. How could Mr Potts believe it? And how could Rosie? Rosie, the betrayer. Rosie, like Florence. Swayed by the snake in Eden. A Cressida ready to sell herself to the highest bidder. Just like Florence.

None of these bitter thoughts showed on his face, as he said coolly; 'What difference would it make if I denied it? Your verdict's already made.'

'Jake—' said William sharply. 'All you have to do is tell me you didn't do it. There's no proof—'

But Jake was already at the door. 'Pegasus is all yours,

Jones. I'll be gone by morning,' he said offhandedly, and the door closed behind him.

Harry drew a deep breath. 'I'm afraid there's no doubt, no doubt at all. I saw him doing it. That's why I took the photographs just in case. I never dreamed Mr Potts would fly Pegasus himself.'

'Why have you said nothing till now, Harry?' cried Rosie in anguish.

Harry shrugged. 'I wanted to give him the benefit of the doubt. But things have got out of hand.'

William pored over the photographs as if even yet some defence might reveal itself. But Jake hadn't bothered to defend himself, so that was that. He sighed. He was getting old. He could have sworn Jake wasn't that sort. But he was a young man, ambitious – as ambitious as Harry. The temptations were great. It didn't seem like Jake's way of doing things, but why not deny it if he had nothing to hide – he knew William to be a fair man. No, there was no getting round it. He'd better get back to keeping an eye on things himself, or young Harry would be heading for the stars, not him.

Rosie was choked with tears, on whose behalf she did not know. She stayed in the library sobbing after the men had gone. Jake, all the time a schemer, a self-seeker, and all the time she thought this she could still feel his arms about her, the touch of his lips on hers. What a fool she'd been. She should stay with the tried and true, like Pegasus itself.

She heard Harry come back into the library and looked up with a face blotched with tears. 'Harry, when Pegasus flies, I *will* marry you. And let's make Pegasus fly soon, Harry. *Please*.'

# Chapter Seven

Rosie threw herself into the endless modifications of Pegasus that Jake had deemed necessary after the trials, leaving Harry free to concentrate on the installation of the new engine. The harder she worked, the less time she had for thinking, for endlessly mulling over the events that had led to Jake's departure, endlessly wondering . . . convincing herself that she had done the right thing in becoming engaged to Harry. Was it possible to love one person, and still be attracted to another? For she did love Harry – she must. And how could she have been attracted to someone like Jake – and, she thought dismally, not only 'have been'. Was still, and he'd gone, like the roving buccaneer he was.

How could he have done such an underhand thing? And she had been blaming herself for Pegasus's accident. But it was Jake himself. He hadn't denied Harry's accusation, hadn't even glanced at her for support. She was nothing to him. Harry was right. She was merely a pawn in his chess game of power. She should stick to the people and places she knew. What else could one expect from a man reared in the backwoods of Canada and America, Harry had asked. He had tactfully refrained from saying Spitalfields, she noticed. Everything fitted to point to Jake's guilt and now she was happily engaged to Harry. He'd wanted a double wedding with Polly's in September, but for some obscure reason it now seemed all the more important to Rosie that first Pegasus should fly. She became even more obsessed with the idea. Now the scoffers were falling silent, it being quietly assumed that one day soon man would fly in England. Every day counted now. She didn't expect Pegasus to be the first, but it had to be among the first;

they had to be among the pioneers to share in the first thrill and joy of flight.

Harry could never understand her point of view. He was set on being first in the air in Britain. And that, she realised, was the only reason that he did not insist on redesigning Pegasus so that lateral control should be subordinated once again to absolute inherent stability. Harry never mentioned Jake now, except in passing, all that was finished, and he obviously assumed that everyone else felt as did he. He had presented proof; they had accepted it, and the affair was closed.

So why did she feel this emptiness inside, why when she had occasion to walk by the Lodge did her stomach lurch slightly, why did she still feel that justice had not been done? Father pointed out to her when she tried to talk it over with him, that all the evidence was against Jake, whatever their previous opinions about him. He had been determined to fly, a self-made man who had had a hard life. Who could blame him if he tried every means in his power to achieve his ambition, William said kindly. That settled it; if even Father believed in his guilt, and it would be against his principles to speak before he was sure, then her own doubts must be laid to rest. She must face the fact that Harry was right, Jake had deliberately courted her, that kiss had been the kiss of a traitor, given in the hope of winning her away from Harry; perhaps even, she swallowed, in the hope of marrying her and making his future in aviation secure for ever. And yet, and yet that look on his face as Jake realised she had revealed to Harry his lack of knowledge of engines – as if she, not he, had been the Judas.

'Oh damn,' exploded Rosie, bringing the hammer crashing down on the table.

'If you're going to be in that mood,' remonstrated Harry mildly, 'I'd as soon you left now – you said Polly wanted to talk about weddings. It'll do you good to get away from Pegasus.' Harry had stepped into Jake's shoes easily, and spent nearly all his time now at Eastchurch, working on testing Pegasus's new engine.

She flinched slightly as she saw his hands wrenching

160

at the control lever to test it. There was a world of difference between his impatient hands on Pegasus, however knowledgeable, and Jake's long sensitive fingers. And Pegasus was only at ground testing stage. What would happen if for some reason William could not fly, and Harry had to take Pegasus up? He'd never manage her, for all his confidence. It needed an artist, not an engineer, to ride a winged horse.

She had pleaded with William to be allowed to be second pilot, instead of Harry, but he would not hear of it. And nor would Harry. Even Jake had encouraged her to ground test from time to time. Harry simply forbade it, and when she got upset, he teased and laughed her into submission, so that his point of view seemed quite reasonable, until she went away and thought about it. She pushed the disloyal thoughts away that Harry would be one of those flyers categorised by Jake who just needed a machine to get them into the air, not a partner of Pegasus but master. Pegasus should be free, as free as was the mythical winged horse after which he was named, and responding willingly as Bellerophon urged him on.

'Perhaps I will,' she replied to Harry dispiritedly. 'I don't seem to be aviation-minded today.'

'Do you like it?' said Polly, swirling round to Trott's annoyance as, on painful knees, she endeavoured to pin the hem of Polly's wedding dress. Its silk underskirt was covered at the back and sides by an overskirt of white Charmeuse which formed a short train at the back. Its low square neck was bordered with silver beading, as was the high waist and the edge of the train. The sleeves were long and wide at the wrist where yet more silver beading edged the cuffs.

'Oh Polly, it's beautiful,' breathed Rosie, fingering the soft white pleated silk. 'You're very clever, Trott.'

A grunt from a mouth full of pins.

'And there's yours—' Polly nodded to the bed where the rose-pink silk bridesmaid's dress in a somewhat similar style lay ready to be fitted.

When the fittings were over and they were alone, Polly

showed Rosie the trousseau she had ordered. Rosie was envious. Delicate white lawn chemises, flounced silk princess petticoats, slim to fit the new skirts, French knickers with lacy frills and cambric *directoire* knickers for her straighter skirts, white silk nightdresses with Brussels lace . . . She picked them up, exclaiming at each.

'You should start ordering your own,' said Polly, blushing slightly.

'Yes,' said Rosie absently, putting them down hastily. It was hard to imagine herself in white silk and Brussels lace – and Harry. What would she feel like when he touched her? An unwelcome memory of his hands on Pegasus . . . Resolutely she turned her thoughts away. All prospective brides must have such qualms, she thought stoutly. Even Polly perhaps. But somehow she could not believe Polly was having any qualms at all about Gabriel. She gave her a hug. 'Oh Polly, are you looking forward to it?'

'So much, I daren't think about it. It seems,' Polly paused, then said shyly, 'as though I'm walking along a green, green path, bordered with flowers on either side, but the path is so long I can scarcely see the other end. I know that at the other end is Gabriel – but however hard I run, I can never reach him. Yet I also know that on the day we marry, Rosie, I *will* be there.' Her eyes filled with tears.

'Why, Polly, you're crying,' said Rosie in wonder.

'Only in happiness,' Polly laughed. 'Wondering how the angels sent one of their own down here by mistake to marry me.'

'You're the angel, Polly,' said Rosie warmly. 'You deserve every bit of the happiness, you always have.'

Gabriel had finished his studies at Newlyn now and was spending more and more time at Brynbourne Place – unfortunately when Polly was busy at the factory, he passed some of his time with Robert Bellowes, much to Polly's dismay. Robert, it appeared, had sought him out, and Gabriel, friendly to everyone, saw no harm in him.

'Robert's all right,' Gabriel told Polly disarmingly.

'You see good in everyone,' said Polly. 'But he *isn't* good.'

'Now that's not my Polly.'

She stilled her misgivings, and concentrated on the plans for the wedding. She told Rosie casually, 'Father says we may live in the Old Lodge if we wish, to begin with – before we move to London—'

'The Old Lodge, but that's Jake's,' said Rosie without thinking.

'He won't need it again,' said Polly in surprise. 'He's hardly likely to show his face here, not after what he did. I was so sorry, I did like him so.'

She was right of course, and yet Rosie could not bear to think of anyone living there now, not even Polly. She wandered over there to see once more. Empty of Jake and his few possessions, the Lodge was soulless; only the work he had done remained, and she had to suppress an instinctive 'You can't do that' when later Polly talked of altering something. Perhaps Father would offer it to her and Harry when Polly no longer needed it. *No!* She could never live there with Harry. He wouldn't like it anyway. He would not understand its honesty. Why then was she marrying him, she suddenly asked herself? Because they knew each other, for one thing, and had a common goal in life. And she loved him. Didn't she?

William was as eager as a schoolboy when in mid-October Pegasus was trundled out on to the Eastchurch testing grounds. There was a big crowd assembled to watch the official trial. The flights of the Wright brothers in France had been taking place since August – was Jake present at Hunaudières on 8th August when Wilbur Wright had first flown in Europe and started off the new enthusiasm for flight? wondered Rosie with a pang. Not a word had they heard of him – scarcely surprisingly she supposed, but she could not stop herself thinking about him, however unwillingly.

In England, Samuel Cody had hopped his aeroplane off the ground only a day or so ago. He had risen ten feet, so the newspapers said, before crashing. Harry had been determined to beat him to it, but William had sharply refused. Samuel Cody deserved the honour of trying first;

and he, William Potts, would not rob him of his glory. Harry had been forced to acquiesce, but he did not like it.

'By George, look at it, Rosie,' William said proudly, as Pegasus was trundled out of its shed by Mr Fisherbutt and his assistants (he had progressed to two now). The reporters began to inch forward, impressed by what they could so far see.

William had already done several test runs in Pegasus, and was eagerly looking forward to the moment when he could achieve flight. He had no doubts now, no lack of confidence.

'Are you sure you wouldn't prefer me to take her up?' asked Harry worriedly.

'You?' William queried, somewhat rudely. 'My dear boy, I haven't waited eight years and more to see someone else fly my aeroplane.'

Harry bit his lip and said no more. Rosie squeezed William's arm to show she understood, then returned to stand by Harry.

'It is safe, isn't it, for Father?' It was a rhetorical question for she knew as well as anyone that Pegasus was safe.

But Harry said slowly, 'We don't yet know the effect of those ailerons in flight.'

'I know how to control them,' called William testily, from the airman's seat. 'They were my own idea, I should know how to use them.'

'With Mr Smith's help,' murmured Harry. 'If I had my way, they'd be off.'

Ignoring him, William strode forward and clambered into Pegasus's seat; Rosie took up her appointed position lying on the grass to signal if – when – she saw air under the wheels; Harry swung the propeller as the Clairville roared into life and William's eyes gleamed.

'Tally-ho,' he breathed. 'Oh my paws and whiskers.' Pegasus began to bump forward, faster, then faster, and faster still.

'He's left it too late,' shouted Harry.

'No, he hasn't . . . it's lifting, it's lifting,' Rosie cried, waving madly to William and scrambling to her feet; she didn't know whether to laugh or cry and settled for a jig of triumph.

Mr Fisherbutt was leaping up and down in excitement, waving his hat, as though William were off to distant lands instead of a brief hop over the Isle of Sheppey.

She could see *real* air under the wheels, at least three, now six – why, he must be ten feet up now. Up in the air, William was glued to the controls, filled with a satisfaction he had never felt before, as the landscape wavered and slipped beneath it. It was worth every penny, everything he'd waited for.

He'd turn now; right he thought happily, gently easing the control stick to the left, pulling the wires which operated the ailerons. Careful now, he could feel Pegasus turning without inclining inwards. He risked a glance to see the ailerons raised on the outer port wings; the starboard ones he could see had lowered at the same time. Pleased with himself, delighted with Pegasus, he over-reacted in centering the stick after the turn. The countryside around him started turning topsy turvy, as Pegasus inclined to the right. In a panic he centred the stick again, he pushed the lever too hard, catching the turn, but Pegasus lurched, juddered and dipped. A gust of wind caught it and tipped it to one side. He righted it, saw a tree approaching, banked again. Pegasus, responding dutifully to the controls, turned too tightly for its forward motion, tipped, lost forward speed and crashed, its pilot flung forward to hit the ground heavily.

With leaden feet as in a nightmare, Rosie tried to run, seeing almost in slow motion the crowd moving towards the still figure. It would be like last time. He would get up, brush himself down and laugh. Wouldn't he? *Wouldn't he*? But he didn't. This time, Father just lay there.

It was two weeks before they knew whether William would live or die. Two weeks in which it seemed Mildred never left his side, and Polly and Rosie tiptoed in and out of the bedroom, and the still silent bandaged figure in the bed did not speak, hardly opened his eyes or moved except to take broth. It was three weeks before the doctor was able to give a definite verdict.

'Everything else will mend, Mrs Potts, but his legs will always remain useless. I am afraid he will be paralysed from the waist down.'

'Father, I'm here. You wanted to see me, Mother said.'

The wan face on the pillow, almost unrecognisable in its thinness, turned towards her, and said with an effort, 'I wanted to talk to you about Pegasus, Rosie.'

'Yes, Father. But you mustn't—'

He made an impatient movement. 'I've been told all that. Listen, my dear, it's important. It wasn't Pegasus's fault, you know. It was *my* fault this time. Don't let Harry change those ailerons. They worked, Rosie. Just the way Jake said. I made a mistake, that's all. We just don't know enough yet about what it's actually like in the air. We don't have the experience. But it will come. And you'll go on, won't you? I won't be able to fly again – but you'll support Harry. He'll have to fly Pegasus now.'

'But Father, I can fly—' Rosie stopped as she saw the immediate anger spring into his eyes.

'No, Rosie, *no*. Not you. I forbid it. You hear? It's too dangerous for a woman. Harry will do it. Harry's a good boy—'

With one blow he was taking away for good all she'd wanted most. 'Promise me, you'll do everything you can to help Pegasus, Rosie. Help Harry fly her and forget this nonsense of flying yourself.'

She gulped, trying to smile bravely, 'Yes, Father, I promise.'

Harry and Rosie regarded the wreckage of Pegasus despondently. It was all very well to say carry on and get Pegasus flying again, but what remained was simply a tangled mass of wood and fabric.

'Well, that's that,' said Harry gloomily. 'Half of England is about to soar up into the sky and all we have is a pile of firewood.'

Rosie held back her misgivings, trying to conquer her own despair. 'For Father's sake, Harry, we've got to try. Unless we get her in the air at roughly the same time as the others we'll lose precious time. We won't be able to keep up, in order to move on to the next stage.'

'If we can't be the first to achieve a reasonable distance at a reasonable height in this country,' said Harry, muttering, 'what's the use of a lot of work for nothing?'

'What's the use?' she cried, suddenly believing her own words. 'I'll tell you what use it is. It matters that what we've worked for is successful, that Pegasus actually goes into the air and stays there under control, that we're up there with the other pioneers. That we'll know what it's like. We'll be part of the whole new world opening up. Part of it. It doesn't matter who's actually first.'

Harry was thinking fast. Maybe Rosie was right. Even if he wasn't first in the air, there were other ways to fame. There was a future in aviation, and a rich one, once this stage was over and they travelled on to the next; there were going to be lucrative contracts, a future for men who could fly *and* build. He would break away from Potts. Or at least threaten to. Now he was in a position to call the tune, it would be Clairville Potts Aviation at least and preferably just Clairville Jones instead. Once Rosie was his wife he'd make a good case for it, now the old man was out of it.

He kissed her. 'What would I do without my muse? Always so right.'

'So we race to the finish?' cried Rosie. 'We won't be first, but we'll be there. Let's start now on the new Pegasus.'

'We can't today – I'll have to show you the designs and they are at home.'

'Designs,' said Rosie, a pit growing in her stomach. 'No,' she said firmly, bracing herself for a fight, 'none of your ideas about switching configurations. We rebuild Pegasus just as it was – Father says it was his mistake, not the aeroplane's.'

'I'm not so sure he would know,' objected Harry. 'If I'm going to fly—'

'We have to assume he does. I won't help you otherwise.'
She could not add '—or pay'; it was too demeaning.

'I—' he opened his mouth to argue.

'It's decided, Harry,' said Rosie quickly, anguished because she was forced to oppose him, and because speaking for William she must prevail in the end.

Expediency made Harry submit, but he would not forget. After they were married, Rosie wasn't going to so much as set foot near an aeroplane again. He'd see she started a family right away which would settle all argument.

They had an unexpected helper in their plans to rebuild Pegasus. Michael offered his services during weekends and evenings. Harry viewed the offer suspiciously. The last thing he wanted was another member of the Potts family, particularly Michael, taking an interest in Pegasus, but Michael was adamant and Rosie delighted. The way Michael saw it was that he had a duty to help his father, and furthermore Rosie needed him. He couldn't have cared less about aeroplanes, but he wanted to keep an eye on how things were progressing between Harry and Rosie. No one had noticed how hurt he'd been when Harry and Rosie announced their engagement, and his loyalty had swiftly moved to the now vanished Jake. No one would tell him exactly what had happened, but now that Harry had double-crossed him and taken Rosie from him, Jake had received instant reinstatement in his affections.

It started so calmly, that late day of Indian summer, as though the winds of tragedy facing the Potts family had spent their force and given way to conciliation. But it was a false impression, for they were but pausing in their efforts, gathering strength for the day that was to catapult them all into the whirlwind.

With William's incapacity, the wedding had been postponed until Christmas and Polly found herself more and more embroiled in the factory, acting as messenger between William and his manager, and carrying out more and more of the business herself.

'Rosie,' she called one day, before leaving for the

factory. 'Would you take this list over to Gabriel? It's the new guest list. He's gone over to Court Manor,' she explained. 'The Slug asked him to go fishing on the lake. I don't like it, Rosie. Why does Robert want to be with Gabriel so much? What's his reason?'

'Perhaps he wants to be near at hand in case you break your engagement,' said Rosie idly. 'He's a very strange man.'

'I'd sooner break his neck,' said Polly forthrightly.

It was a sunny day, so Rosie decided to walk over to the lake by the footpath linking their estates. The large artificial lake in the grounds of Court Manor was stocked with trout for the Bellowes's table. All was still as she walked through the fields towards the woods bordering the lake. As she neared the woods, she could hear the sounds of Gabriel's laughter echoing off the water from the lake beyond, and the occasional deeper sound as Robert said something.

She entered the woods and the trees branching above her shut out the sun. She shivered without reason for it was not cold. As she came towards the edge of the wood, the sun was there full-strength before her, shining straight into her eyes, shimmering and dancing on the water ahead. What happened then she could never be certain of, though the horror haunted her day and night thereafter, trying to remember exactly what she saw in the sunny mists of the lake as it telescoped back into unreality. Was it her imagination that she saw Gabriel leaning far over the side? Her imagination that Robert leapt up, overbalancing the boat? Her imagination that he stood quite still watching . . . as Gabriel flung a hand out for help? That then the hand stretched out once more in supplication, and disappeared? Fleeting impressions crowded across her sun-dazzled eyes, but when she blinked and rubbed them, she saw Robert alone in the boat. Then her feet, her voice took action. Pounding to the lakeside, wading into the water impotently for the surface of the lake was unrippled now where just before she had seen a hand. Crying, screaming, but the sounds did not leave her

169

throat, and she was held back by weed from wading further.

'Gabriel,' she screamed in one great cry that broke free from her at last.

Robert looked round, saw her, and his face changed. 'You,' he cried malevolently – did she also see fear? – '*You*, always *you*.' Then he crouched over the oars and rowed swiftly towards her, leapt out and dragged her back to land.

'Gabriel,' she croaked again.

'He's gone,' Robert replied flatly, staring at her. 'We'll get help but he's gone. Drowned.'

'No—' A wail of horror, as she tried to push past him into the boat, to seek out Gabriel. That bright spirit drowned? It was not possible. But Robert held her back, as if hypnotised by her.

'You,' he hissed again. 'Always *you*.' And his great weight was bearing down on her, arms round her, forcing her back on the bank.

'What are you doing?' she cried, unable to free herself. 'He might still be alive.'

'You,' he muttered again, his breath steaming over her, almost bearing her off her feet, and seeming quite crazed, and strong with it, the strength of the mad. He was pushing her back into the trees, then forcing her down on the earth, and he on top of her, shutting out the light. The dark place had come, was engulfing her, trying to possess her for ever.

She wrenched her head aside, and screamed, which maddened him more. She tried to force his head aside, but he bit her hand, and as she cried in pain, forced up her skirts, ripping at her thin dress and underclothes, pinning her underneath him so that she was crushed in a seething mound of flesh. She moaned as the Slug's hands found her bare flesh, and he was forcing her legs apart under him.

Suddenly a trampling in the path, and she gasped as the whole weight of his body rolled on her and then off her, writhing in pain, and the blessed sky was above her again. She lay there gasping, conscious of someone standing over her, of Robert howling like a wounded dog, and a snake-like object whirling through the air that she could not at first identify.

Then she did. Jake had taught Michael Potts the use of the bullwhip to good effect. And still that howling, still the lash.

She dragged herself to her feet, gathering her torn clothes around her, and saw a hysterical Michael standing over a prostrate Robert, lashing viciously, uncontrollably. She seized him but he tore free, lashing out again.

'Michael, come home!' In the end she had to tear the whip from his grasp, take his hand and force him away; then run, run away from the nightmare to seek help, then face the horror that must follow.

A kaleidoscope of unreality as police marched in and out of her consciousness as, shuddering, she tried to inch herself out of the dark place. They found Gabriel's body five hours later and by that time Polly was a still, carved statue of granite, staring glassy-eyed into an endless void.

Beside the loss of Gabriel, how could Rosie raise her own ordeal? And just what had she seen of what happened on the lake? She had not seen Robert Bellowes push Gabriel, could not swear he had deliberately left him to drown, that he had deliberately upset the balance of the boat. That for her his guilt was confirmed by the look on his face was her torment and one she could not share, not with Father, for he was too ill, not with Harry, lest he speak to her in patient reason, and she had to explain further, not to Polly, *never* to Polly.

Only to Mother. Rosie poured out the whole story, incoherent, choking, finally leaving nothing out. Her suspicions, her fears, her horrors.

'You believe me, don't you, Mother?'

Mildred was silent, the true implication of what Rosie was telling her freezing her mind for a moment, then simply weighing up her knowledge of Rosie's dramatic outbursts that she had had to cope with for fifteen years, her known hatred of Robert Bellowes, her own inability to understand Rosie, against her honesty, her painful need

171

for truth. And against what she herself had always feared about Robert Bellowes.

'Yes,' she said slowly. 'Oh, I believe you.'

Rosie gave a choking sob and flew into her arms. 'What shall I do?' she whispered. 'Oh, tell me what to do.'

'There's nothing to be done over Gabriel,' said Mildred, 'only remember. You can't swear to what happened, so you can't accuse him to the police. But if in your heart you're sure, then it's your duty to tell *him*, Rosie. No matter what the cost. Or he'll think he's triumphed. And above all, *remember*. Tell him—'

Rosie looked up fearfully. 'And me, Mother?'

Mildred took Rosie's face between her hands and kissed her cheek. 'You could go to the police, Rosie, but think before you do.'

'Why?' Rosie burst out. Mildred did not answer, but looked at her beseechingly. Then Rosie understood. If she were to go to the police – what about Michael?

And Robert came, still apparently bland and smug, that same day, perhaps a little paler than usual under the one vivid red scar that showed on his face. But he walked stiffly, and malevolence walked with him.

Rosie saw him alone in the morning room.

'I've come to convey my condolences to Miss Potts,' he informed Rosie unsmilingly, as she tried not to flinch from his very presence.

'The doctor has forbidden visitors,' said Rosie shortly.

'Indeed?' Staring at her. 'The police will be visiting you, Rosie—' He used the name studiedly to underline the Miss Potts for Polly. 'In my concern for Mr Marriner, I did not mention the vicious assault on me—'

'The what?' she cried, then took control of herself. This was a game, a deadly game that she must play carefully. '—And will not, if I do not lay charges against you for trying to rape me.'

He stared at her. 'A crazed boy,' he said off-handedly, 'who should be in an asylum. That leaves your word against mine, and you so distressed at Mr Marriner's death.'

172

'Which you caused,' she said quietly.

The look on his face told her all she needed to know; guilt, surprise – and then calculation.

'As crazed as your brother, I fear. How sad for Mr and Mrs Potts. But then your father is well known—'

'No!' she interrupted in a voice that cut through the air. 'I'll lay no charges, to spare Polly distress and to spare Michael from appearing in court to tell what he saw. But I tell you this. I shall not forget. And as long as I live, every time you see me, or hear my name, you'll remember I know the truth. I'll not tell Polly – unless you make one move towards her. If you do, she shall hear how Gabriel died.'

'You saw nothing, for there was nothing to see,' he said flatly.

'In your eyes, there is. And Polly will believe me, if I speak.'

She expected a rejoinder, a recovery, but none came. He simply took his hat and departed, leaving her trembling with shock and relief. It was not until later that it occurred to her that it was unlike Robert Bellowes to cede victory.

'Did I do wrong, Rosie?' asked Michael anxiously.

'No,' she hugged him.

'He was hurting you, wasn't he?' he said diffidently. He looked away. He didn't want to think about what Robert had been doing. They'd been fighting, that was all, *fighting*, because they didn't like each other, he refused to think beyond that – and beyond the fact that some day he'd meet Robert Bellowes again. And then there'd be no one to stop him punishing him as he deserved.

'Yes, and I thank you, Michael, for saving me,' said Rosie gravely, anxious not to be too serious about it. He must forget what had happened as soon as possible. But she would not forget how much she owed to Michael.

'Mother's taken my whip away.'

'Perhaps that's best.'

She slept in Polly's room that night and every night following. Polly did not speak, beyond the necessary niceties, did not apparently cry. She existed that way until the funeral held at Gabriel's home in Hertfordshire. Rosie, Michael and Mildred accompanied Polly to the funeral; it was like travelling with a composed, detached stranger who sat there in the railway train so neatly clad, so remote. Only a grip of Rosie's hand that tightened till Rosie had to grit her teeth against crying out with pain, as his body was laid to rest in the churchyard, betrayed the fact that this was more than the sad passing of a casual friend.

Only on the return journey did she speak, quite naturally, as if she had been conversing continually. 'Mr Bellowes called to pay his condolences.'

'What did he say?' said Rosie, heart beating, exchanging looks with Mildred.

' "I would have given my life for his, if it could have avoided your unhappiness," ' she said flatly.

The cold hand of horror fastened over Rosie's heart.

'I said to him,' continued Polly, ' "I'm sure you did all you could." '

A chasm opened before Rosie, as her stomach churned. Was that a query in Polly's voice, an appeal? She should speak. No, she could not. Not now. It would only make things worse for Polly. Tears gathered in Rosie's eyes and she bit her lip to prevent them falling, but Polly remained dry-eyed.

That night she slept in Polly's room again, and awoke, to find Polly sitting by her bed staring at her, chatting as if it were the middle of the day. 'You remember the long green path, Rosie?' she said excitedly. 'I've been wondering, how to learn to reach the other end. It seemed I never could. That Gabriel had gone for ever, for though I know he still awaits me at the end of that pathway, I didn't know how to get there. But now I *do*.' She said no more, but got back into bed, and for the first time Rosie heard the sound of tears, heavy, harsh sobs. She got out of bed, and this time it was her turn to sit by Polly's side, holding her hand as she sobbed for the loss of Gabriel's golden light.

Polly made her announcement casually the following lunchtime with just Mildred, Michael and Rosie present, and William in his wheelchair, slowly recovering his health if not his spirits.

'I intend to leave to study in Paris, Father, Mother—'

William dropped the carving knife which he had insisted on wielding as usual. 'My dear—' he began to say in his usual reasonable tones whenever anyone wished to do anything that was obviously out of the question. 'Your place is here where we can look after you.' His eyes were pleading as though this time he knew it was a lost cause.

'No, Father, my place is where it is right for me to be. And that is Paris. I intend to take up studying art.'

'Now we've been all through this before, my dear. You're very upset, naturally—'

'Father, I'm quite decided,' she interrupted. 'I like living here, I like working at the factory, but I have a duty to Gabriel. He told me I should paint – you remember, Rosie.' She smiled fondly at her sister. 'How he said that day that I should paint from life. Now I shall. Not retreat from life, but share it with Gabriel. And where else than Paris? I shall carry on his work . . . And first I have to learn.'

'The long green pathway,' said Rosie slowly.

'What are you two talking about?' shouted William, scarlet.

'Oh, Polly, now you've upset Father,' said Mildred.

'I'm sorry, Mother,' said Polly unemotionally, 'but I have no choice, and I must do it now.'

'I'm not supporting you,' said William furiously.

'Of course not. I am twenty-one now,' said Polly. She had obviously expected this, thought Rosie, and had planned for it. 'I have what I've saved from the factory. And my income from grandmother's estate. And I have more.'

'Indeed?'

'I have Gabriel's paintings. His parents have given them all to me. I shall sell them, establish his reputation and with the proceeds, pay my fees. Living is cheap in Paris.'

'Romantic rubbish,' William glared.

'No,' said Rosie intervening. 'She's right, Father. Oh, she's right.'

'Then you're both out of your minds. Look, my dear, this sadness will pass,' he said pleadingly. 'You'll settle down eventually, find a nice husband—'

Polly looked at him as though he were quite mad, smiled politely and said, 'I really don't think so, Father,' and the tone of her voice silenced them all.

Polly left in December, on what should have been her wedding day. Her going left a vast emptiness in Rosie's life, which even Pegasus could not fill. She tried to talk to Harry, to share her feelings, but preoccupied as he was with Pegasus, he had little time for discussion. 'We'll be married soon,' was his stock answer, 'then you'll be happier.' She was forced back on Michael's companionship, now a shared secret existed between them; she could not talk to him for at thirteen he was too young, but his fierce loyalty was comforting in this new world in which laughter and joy seemed to have vanished. Michael worked diligently and hard on Pegasus whenever he had time, though without real interest or understanding. He was doing it for her, she realised, and was too discontented to wonder if this were wise.

She received brief letters from Polly, stating nothing but facts: she had found suitable lodgings, and a school willing to take her; she had companions, there was no need to worry about her. But Rosie did worry.

'That's it,' cried Harry, early in January, throwing down his working gloves and straightening up. 'Pegasus is ready. We'll organise the trial for next week.'

'Oh Harry, I'm so pleased. We've done it,' she said, weak with relief that the grim ordeal of work, work, work was over and there was something to look forward to.

'I'll ground-test it now, just to be sure!'

She stood on the field, watching as he taxied, trying to fight down envy and to remind herself they were working for a common cause. She ran up to him as he came to a stop.

'That was splendid, Harry, but you have to try the ailerons in the air soon. You don't understand that—'

'Of course I understand,' he cut in sharply. 'For

heaven's sake, Rosie, this isn't your aeroplane, you know.'

'Nor yours,' she said swiftly, before thinking.

He drew in his breath sharply, fighting for control. 'Our first quarrel,' he said lightly, 'and we're not even married yet.'

It was he who attempted to breach the gap between them that evening when after dinner Mildred discreetly retired for the evening, leaving them in the drawing room. He crossed over and sat next to her on the sofa, putting his arms around her. 'I hate quarrelling with you,' he muttered thickly. 'Make up?'

She turned to him, as eager as he that the cloud should be dispelled, and he seized her in his arms, kissing her harder than he ever had before, his hands moving to her breasts, then lower down. Demanding lips, and hands that had no gentleness behind them, carrying no request for shared love.

'What are you doing, Harry?' she asked bewildered, pushing his hands away. She was trying to fight revulsion, and an inexplicable comparison with the Slug.

'I can't help it,' he said thickly. 'You're very lovely at times, and it's been a long wait . . . You don't mind, do you? After all, we're getting married in a couple of months.'

Ridiculous to say wait till Pegasus flies, so she let him kiss her again, letting his hands rove until involuntarily she found herself pushing them away again. To her relief he did not object, merely swallowing hard and taking out a cigarette. After a minute or two he began to talk. She was depressed, he said, naturally enough after the events of the autumn. But it would be all right. When they were married. And that would not happen until Pegasus flew!

'He'll fly it all right, don't you worry, Miss Rosie,' said Mr Fisherbutt, noting her frowns as Harry tested Pegasus again. 'He'll be safe enough.' He mistook her worries, but she knew he shared her concern.

Together they watched as the ground trials commenced, William sitting in his wheelchair, watch in hand. Mr

Fisherbutt glanced at her as Harry did a short test and came to a halt. 'Hasn't got your touch, Miss Rosie. I wish you could have a go.' She winced. If only—

William forbade the trials to be held before Mr Cody had tested his Army Aeroplane, much to Harry's annoyance. On 20th January, Cody's aeroplane flew for four hundred yards at over twenty feet – and then—

'You see,' said William sadly when he read the reports, 'it's the turning again. "The aeroplane crashed after trying to turn. Mr Cody was unhurt." Jake was right to insist on those ailerons.'

Harry compressed his lips. 'Are you prepared to test Pegasus now?' he asked.

William smiled. 'I think we've all waited long enough and we haven't taken Mr Cody's glory from him. We don't want everybody in the sky before us, do we? Let's unrein Pegasus.'

Late in January, officials from the Aeronautical Club, press representatives and enthusiasts made their way to Eastchurch early one morning for Pegasus's trials.

Rosie's heart was pounding as she tried hard to concentrate on convincing all these people how wonderful Pegasus was. 'You can do it, my warhorse,' she had patted it affectionately in the workshed. 'You can do it.'

Hearing Pegasus's engine roar, she put on her goggles and hat against the breeze and dust, so that she could help in this all-important day, and glad of the comforting warmth of her self-designed serge working suit and long leather boots. She ran up to join Mr Fisherbutt, determined not to be left out on this day of days. But unease was growing. Harry was in a very restless mood; eyes glittering, issuing orders, strutting about far from his usual self. He climbed up into Pegasus and down again several times, checking various things. Then yet again as the engine warmed up: 'Rosie, get a spanner.' One hand was yanking on the ailerons control lever.

'Harry, take care. That doesn't need adjustment.'

'Rosie, don't argue; just do it.'

'No, Harry,' she said steadily.

His lips pursed. 'Very well, I'll get it myself.'

178

The ailerons would work correctly. She could not, would not see Harry alter them, ruin Pegasus's chances. It wouldn't be fair to Jake. To *Jake*? And the light came. She knew just what she had to do, regardless of anything and anyone, remembering only that hillside long ago when she'd given her heart to flight.

She saw Harry's back disappearing into the shed. Not stopping to think, she cried to Mr Fisherbutt: 'Now. Swing when I give the sign.' His eyes lit up.

She leapt into Pegasus's seat, glanced quickly at the controls. She knew them all so well. Be quick. Harry would be returning. *Now*. She gave the sign, and then she was off in Pegasus bumping over the grass, seized with the excitement she always had when she tested it. Faster now and faster, she was aware of the watching crowds, of cries in the distance, of William in his wheelchair – what had he said? He'd made her promise she'd never fly Pegasus. But he'd said more. 'That you'll do everything you can to help Pegasus.' And she would, she *would*.

The engine was accelerating; she knew it was almost ready now. She glanced back to see Harry in the distance still racing after her. She almost laughed; his face was crazy with rage, just like Robert Bellowes's had been. But she had no time to think further, only to concentrate on Pegasus. Now my proud beauty, lift the nose, now, now, *now*! The ground slipped sideways, no bumps, no noise save the engine and the wind singing through the wires. Pegasus was in flight, rising high, sure and steady, a winged horse to greet the rising sun.

Oh, the glory of the world. Down below her, the fields, the upturned faces, the river snaking beneath them, and the sea stretching to meet the blue of the sky on the horizon. And around her the silence. The air beneath Pegasus as steady as the Dover Road. She must be twenty – twenty-five feet up, turn, turn now. Lovingly she pulled the control lever, glanced to see the ailerons on the wings responding, and Pegasus wavering but faithfully turning. Oh yes, Jake had designed him true. He was sure and strong. Him? How strange. All these years Pegasus had been 'It', a thing created of wood and fabric. But here

179

in the air, Pegasus had come into his own, had come alive.

Jake, oh where are you . . . Jake should be here to share this. This should have been his flight, he should be here to glory in Pegasus's freedom. Time seemed of no importance. How long had she been up? Ten minutes? Fifteen? She should go down. Slowly she began to descend, hearing the cheers that were for Pegasus.

And she began to laugh, to sing out in joy to the wind for the culmination of their dream. Flight had begun. Pegasus had burst through the clouds and greeted the sun in glory.

# Chapter Eight

Clown-like, crazily tilted faces upturned towards her as Rosie came in to land Pegasus gently on its wheels and skids.

'Whoa, my beauty,' she cried, exhilarated. One face in particular she half glimpsed, half sensed, distorted in rage, and then forgot it as the adrenalin flowed from her and tired happiness replaced it.

'Five minutes, twenty-five seconds,' William shouted, waving vigorously from his wheelchair, urging the man pushing it, 'faster, faster, man. Do I have to fit wings to it?' and almost toppling out, to Mildred's alarm, as they hurried towards Rosie as she jumped down from Pegasus. She covered the distance before they did, hugged Mildred and then bending down, threw her arms round William.

'Father, we did it,' she cried. 'Pegasus did it. *Your* Pegasus. At last.'

'Now didn't I always say we'd fly?' William crowed, as the Aero Club officials began to gather round them, with newspapermen hard at their heels, staring at the unusual, and shocking sight of a woman in trousers. 'Why ever did you doubt us?' he said happily to Mildred.

'I didn't,' she replied, for once her composure gone and tears of joy running down her cheeks. 'I just didn't want you to break your necks in the process. Not you, William, nor,' she said firmly and somewhat grimly to Rosie, 'you, my girl.'

Rosie looked abashed, but nothing could dampen her spirits for long today. 'Oh – and Pegasus is not an it, Father, today he was a *he*. Pegasus was a real horse of the air; he was alive.'

'Pygmalion and Galatea,' laughed William.

'Or Frankenstein,' she quipped. Frankenstein's monster – why think of that at this moment of triumph? A monster meant for good that turned to evil. An explicable shiver ran through her as she watched Pegasus being examined by the Aero Club officials, his mainplanes bright in the sunlight. She shook herself out of this strange mood.

'*Flight* magazine, Miss Potts. How do you assess the performance of the balancing flaps?'

'Miss Potts, you seemed to be having trouble on that figure of eight?'

'Miss Potts, I see you're using continental rubber-proofed fabric on the wings—'

She answered questions as politely and speedily as possible, then seized an opportunity, while they were engaged in taking details of measurements from a Mr Fisherbutt bursting with pride, to speak to William on the one matter that worried her.

'You don't mind, do you, Father, about my having flown Pegasus and not Harry?' She crouched by his wheelchair.

'Why should I?' asked William blankly, then said wonderingly, 'my word, I'd quite forgotten that I ordered you not to fly.' His face looked so comically dismayed that they both burst out laughing. 'After all,' William said stoutly, 'the important thing is Pegasus, not who flies him.'

'Oh, Father,' Rosie said simply, hugging him again.

'Mind you,' he said thoughtfully, 'I think you're going to have some explaining to do to Harry.' He glanced at her as she stood up guiltily. He was going to have to do some thinking on the subject himself – but he wouldn't spoil today for her – or for himself.

'I don't think Harry will be very pleased, but *you* know why I did it, don't you?' she said anxiously. 'You saw some of the short hops he made in Pegasus. He just doesn't have the right handling ability and he doesn't appreciate the importance of being able to control turns – he expects Pegasus to do all the flying for him.'

Full of contrition now that she had compounded her

misdeeds by not finding Harry to explain right away, Rosie ran to see whether his motor car was still on the aerodrome. She must apologise, try to explain why it was so necessary that she flew Pegasus today. There he was, just cranking the engine of the Clairville. She ran towards him as he cast one look at her, then continued his task. She was checked for a moment by his face, full not just of anger but of some other emotion. She ran forward, laying a hand on his arm.

'Oh Harry, I'm so sorry – won't you forgive me – but isn't it marvellous that Pegasus flew?'

He threw her arm off, his face suddenly convulsive. This was a stranger, the stranger she had sensed as he had kissed her that time. She stepped back as almost physical waves of anger emanated from him.

'*You*,' he almost spat out, 'all the time you were planning to steal a march on me. I certainly underestimated you—'

'No, Harry,' she cried, alarmed, her mind flashing back involuntarily to the horror of Robert Bellowes and his 'You, always *you*'. 'I'm sorry, but you must see it was for the best. You were too heavy-handed on those tests last week and in today's conditions it needed a gentler touch. We had to make sure that Pegasus flew well today. Don't you see? What with the Europeans so far ahead and now at least three or four British aviators catching us up, we had to be up there with them. I didn't *plan* it. You're wrong, and I won't do it—' she stopped her headlong rush of words in time. Won't do it again, was what she'd been going to say. But how could she with honesty say that? Today had confirmed the dreams she'd had as a child. She'd worked unconsciously for this for years, not just to build an aeroplane, but to share with it the joy of the skies. And now she was only just beginning.

Harry looked at her with cold, angry eyes. 'Again,' he finished her sentence. 'It's no concern of mine if you do or don't. But today! A *woman* to fly before me.' There was more in his eyes than anger – a dislike that must always have been there.

Then her own anger boiled up. 'Because I'm a woman?'

Then she was wrenching off the engagement ring and handing it to him, half hoping, half dreading the apology that must surely follow . . .

But it didn't. He hardly looked at it, merely took it and put it in a pocket. 'Aren't you going to say anything?' she blurted out aghast.

He smiled, with the same easy-going smile she'd thought she'd loved.

'Dear Rosie, there's nothing to say. You can hardly imagine there would be any point in our marriage now. No point in a wife that prefers to be in the air to where she should be, or one that imagines she can do better than me.' Despite his words, he was speaking coolly, absently; instinctively she knew this not to be the true source of his anger. And she was right. Suddenly his face flushed angrily. 'I could have kept Pegasus up for half an hour or more, if you hadn't bungled it. You congratulate yourself that you're so clever, making me look a fool, but it's you that has wrecked Pegasus's chances.'

She was unable to speak for a moment, at this double-edged attack.

Satisfied, he cranked the engine again, hardly glancing at her as he said matter-of-factly, 'If you want to fly Pegasus again you'll have every opportunity. But you'll fly it without my help *or* my engine.'

With blinding, sickening clarity she saw the truth. 'You only wanted the glory of flying Pegasus, didn't you? Of being in the air first?' she said quietly. 'And I was part of that because I'm Rosie Potts. Married to me, you would have complete charge of the project now that Jake's gone.'

An odd look on his face. A shrug. 'You have to get used to the realities of the world, Rosie. It was a suitable marriage.'

'But we were friends,' she cried, bewildered, 'we loved each other—' Had that been true? Of course not. She could see that now. She'd convinced herself it was, for she thought they shared a vision of the future that surmounted everything else. That married to Harry, she would be free for ever of the shadow of Uncle Alf, for she would be

184

established in the life she wanted. Well, now she knew differently.

He leapt into the Clairville saying casually, 'I feel sorry for any man who marries you. Like kissing a spanner.'

'Go away,' she shouted childishly, a red mist in front of her eyes. 'I never want to see you again. *Ever*.'

'I'll send for my engine,' he said with a smile of triumph as the Clairville eased away and then roared on to the roadway.

Dizzy with shock, Rosie did not take in the full meaning of his words as she walked back to the shed where Pegasus was being wheeled back. She touched him lightly.

'At least *you're* real,' she whispered to him fiercely. '*We* understand each other, *need* each other.'

But the scene with Harry left a sick feeling in her stomach that remained there even while she joined in the technical discussions between William and the Aero Club officials. They knew most of them well now since they had their headquarters nearby at Leysdown, and talking of elevators, drift and thrust distracted her from the scene that had just passed, and filled her with pride for their achievement in Pegasus. To her delight, no one thought it strange she should have been flying the aeroplane. She had long been accepted by the Aero Club as part of the Pegasus team – they probably no longer even noticed her sex, she told herself incorrectly. The newspapermen, on the other hand, *were* curious and she concentrated therefore on talking to the technical press and not the daily newspapers, even the *Daily Mail* with its keen enthusiasm for aviation.

Why should she be surprised at their attitude, she asked herself somewhat bitterly? Was it just that she was William Potts's daughter that her opinions were being sought so avidly? Was that why Jake too had listened to her and appeared to respect her judgement? She had thought Harry did too – until this afternoon. But he didn't want her at all. He wanted only the daughter of William Potts, and a wife who knew her place, who would not rival him. Perhaps she had been expecting too much. Perhaps that's what all men wanted from marriage.

She had thought Harry and she had so much in common, but the person she had thought of as Harry did not exist. Instead of the easy-going companion of the years, there was a calculating determined stranger and the discovery was shaking at the roots of her life. Now that it had happened, relief was setting in. She stared at the place on her finger where Harry's ring had been, then ran to a tap to wash it as though it were still contaminated with fool's gold. An overpowering relief swept over her that she would not have to face Harry again, not in her arms, nor in the worksheds. He wanted no more to do with them . . . She shivered as his words came back to her and she realised what he'd said. '*I'll send for my engine.*' But he couldn't do that. It was theirs, not his. They'd bought it, hadn't they?

'So there it is,' Rosie finished matter-of-factly, looking despondently round the table at William, Mildred and Michael. 'Pegasus is ready now to take on anybody – with the small exception of having no engine. I'm afraid Harry only loaned us the engine, not sold it to us, as he told us.' She gulped. How could she have been so gullible? Why had she not kept an eye on the paperwork?

'I blame myself,' said William heavily. 'I distrusted him, but did nothing – and after all, he'd done nothing but help us. There was no real reason for distrust – so far as his work on Pegasus went, that is.' His eyes were on her, as he burned with indignation at this betrayal. It was not something that often happened to him.

'I never did like that man,' commented Mildred forthrightly.

William turned to her in surprise. 'That's unlike you, Mildred.'

'It's exactly like me, William,' Mildred said crisply. 'You never listen, that's all. Too busy in that faraway world of yours.'

William's eyes clouded. Once it had been a world of never-ending wonder and possibility, where with his inventive mind he opened up new horizons, where he could use his gifts for a better world, whether it be sanitary ware or aeroplanes, spittoons or kites. It was a world he had trodden with confidence as a Colossus but now, racked with pain, he found the horizons narrowed. The brain was tiring and the will was fading.

'Harry did give us a lot of help over the years,' said Rosie defensively, with some remnant of vanished loyalty.

'Certainly. It was in his interests,' Mildred pointed out.

'I'm glad he's gone,' put in Michael stoutly, keeping quiet at his first important family business meeting, but unable to conceal his delight at the broken engagement. Not quite fourteen, he was gaining rapidly in height but his lean looks were fixed on Rosie as intensely as when he was ten. They were closer now, for they shared the experience they never spoke of. Indeed, Michael had almost put it out of his mind. Almost but not completely, for every so often the memory of Robert Bellowes bending menacingly over Rosie would haunt him. Older now, he knew now what Robert had been about, and in his mind wielded that whip still more fiercely as though with it he could erase memory itself.

'You've achieved what you set out to, my dear. I'm proud of you,' said Mildred slowly. 'But you realise, all of you, don't you, that there's going to be a lot of money involved now? The odd flight is no use if you're to take part in the aviation world of the future. You have to decide whether you are going to be part of it or not. And if so, how.'

'We must be there,' said Rosie pleadingly. 'To have come this far and not go on would just be breathing life into Galatea and then shutting her up in a box.'

'You and your romantic notions, Rosie,' said Mildred robustly. 'How are you going to do it, with just you, Mr Fisherbutt and no engine?'

Rosie stared helplessly at the three pairs of eyes fixed on her, waiting for her answer. She realised she was the leader now. William was handing the torch to her by his very silence. For a moment she panicked, wanted to run to him, for him to tell her all would be well, that he would take care of everything, just as when the kite had trailed so forlornly on the grass all those years ago. She pulled herself together; if that was how William wanted it to be, needed it to be, then so be it. She owed it to him not to turn back now.

And then the idea came. 'Listen,' she said eagerly. 'At the end of August there's going to be a big air meeting at Reims in France, the first ever where all countries will come to fly their aeroplanes, all together. I want to take Pegasus there. Fly him. Show the world what we can do.'

William's eyes lit up, then dulled again. 'Rosie, my darling, even if we had an engine, we're so far behind Europe in aviation we'd be laughed to pieces.'

'No matter, we'd *be* there, and people would see Pegasus fly,' she came back eagerly. 'It would establish us as serious competitors.'

'Why not, Father?' said Michael enthusiastically. 'Yes, oh *yes*.' His eyes were bright. He would not be due back to school until September, and Rosie would need someone with her as a chaperone.

'I don't know,' said William wearily. 'That's only a few months away. Not long to find a new engine, adapt it, and get Pegasus up to competition standard.'

'It's not like you, Father, to give up,' Rosie pleaded.

'You're right, Rosie,' he smiled with difficulty. Then, 'Right,' he pounded his fist on the table in some semblance of his old self. 'We'll crate Pegasus up, ship him across and, by thunder, we'll show them.' He beamed round the table.

'And what about the engine?' enquired Mildred drily.

William hesitated, brain working furiously. 'I'll ask at the Aero Club. There's a company I've heard of who deals in engines from failed aircraft, either those that have crashed, or sold by people who've got bored with the project. We might get one to give Pegasus his oats until we get something permanent sorted out. Perhaps Mr Smith might assist us,' he added casually.

It was as though a pit had opened in front of her into which she had stumbled on a clear blue day. Jake? Rosie had consciously repressed all thoughts of Jake since his departure, telling herself that his guilt over the accident to Father exonerated her from the instinctive feeling she had that she'd let him down. And guilty he must surely have been for he had not even bothered to deny it. He was as bad as Harry. *As bad as Harry.* An icy hand clutched her inside, as she pushed away an unwelcome – welcome? – thought. She looked up to see it mirrored in William's face.

'If Clairville Jones was determined to take over Pegasus in order to fly it himself, Mr Smith was in the way, was he not, my dear?' he said slowly. 'Do you not think that it is quite possible that he engineered Mr Smith's departure by accusing him of doing what he had done himself – interfered with the propeller?'

Rosie licked dry lips. 'Mr Smith did not deny his guilt, Father,' she pointed out. The thought tore at her through and through that they had driven him away unfairly, that she had even been the instrument of his going, that she had betrayed him in some way. She remembered the apple tree, the sunburst and, sharply etched on memory, a hundred moments that would not come again.

William sighed. 'Mr Smith is a proud man, Rosie.'

'But he too wanted to fly, Father, just like Harry,' she said hesitantly. 'He too is ambitious.' Deny it, Father, she was willing him. Tell me I am wrong.

'Not quite like Harry, my dear.'

'There's no proof either way,' she said, anguished. Yet in her mind's eye she saw again that odd smirk on Harry's face when he drove off from Eastchurch in the Clairville. Yes, it was all too likely. 'What shall we do?' She looked round the table helplessly.

'We can write to apologise,' said William. 'And hope.'

He wrote a carefully worded letter, signed by them all, to Mr Jake Smith at his London home address. He had put much thought into it. If Jake Smith was the man he thought he was, he'd come marching in one day.

But there was no reply.


Polly trod a calm path amid the hustle and bustle of the Paris boulevards surrounded by laughing, extravagantly dressed students and the *beau monde* of Paris. Her path was calm only because she was all but oblivious to it, seeing it, appreciating it, but not part of it. She shared an atelier with another girl student, Lise, in the Boulevard des Italiens. It was very small, and it was on the seventh floor, but it had two advantages. Although it had many artists' studios in it, the boulevard was a highly respectable street even during the evenings, and above all, the atelier, facing north, had the light so highly prized by painters.

At first Polly had preferred to live on her own, but now she was glad of the company as well as realising its practicalities. She had begun her lessons at a private atelier teaching establishment run by a fashionable painter where she was the only female pupil amidst twenty men and, more to the point, the painter displayed more interest in her potential as a model than a pupil. Her fellow students, sensing her remoteness, left her alone, but the maître did not. Repelling both advances and requests for modelling from life, as he put it, she applied to the vast Ecole des Beaux Arts, more impersonal but safer. Here in the workshop atelier to which she was first assigned, she had met Lise, daughter of a French count, who like Polly had come against the wishes of her family, and at her suggestion left the hotel in which she was living and joined her in the Boulevard des Italiens.

From here it was quite a walk to the Ecole but it was one Polly loved even in the rain or under the frequent grey skies: along narrow streets, past sprawling markets full of shouting and jostling crowds, the diverse wares making a profusion of colour everywhere she looked, past the majestic Louvre with its awe-inspiring legacy of the past, and across the River Seine to the Left Bank, often to linger on the Pont des Arts and marvel at Notre Dame, the endless succession of graceful bridges, and the cold precise beauty of the Paris skyline. This latter was what she loved most, whereas Gabriel would have revelled in the street markets and the cafés, with their thrusting, urgent life. Was there a reconciliation of the two, she wondered? Could she fulfil his wish and paint from life, convey that optimism, belief in mankind's potential which he had so firmly held, and of which he had through cruel chance been deprived?

Lise was the only person who knew her story; sensible and understanding, she left it at that. With a good command of English she bullied Polly into sharing part of the student life, coupled with the need for caution. Not that Polly had any desire to spend much time in the thousands of cafés and theatres that Paris boasted, especially those frequented by the students, but she yielded to Lise in visiting the occasional café with her fellow students. Only at night would the agonising grief tear at her, when she stifled her racking sobs silently into the pillow to avoid disturbing Lise, and when she was glad of the dawn that she might be free for a while from memory. In the day she presented a calm confidence.

The life class drew from the Ecole's splendid collection of classical casts to begin with and then graduated to live models. The professeur was adamant that she should remain with the casts. Polly was equally adamant that she should not.

'I must learn to draw from life,' she told the professeur.

He was shocked. 'But young ladies *always* learn from casts.'

'This young lady does not,' said Polly firmly, quite unintimidated, since she was driven on by what Gabriel would have expected of her.

'For the female body perhaps, but it is quite unfitting that young ladies should draw from the male unclothed body.'

'Why?' asked Polly, 'when the male students draw from the unclothed female body?'

'That is different,' he replied stiffly. 'That is accepted.'

'And so will I be, you'll see,' said Polly serenely, for nothing could touch her.

'Very well,' said the professeur grimly. 'You will try and when you see what these rough students are like, you will enjoy the return to the plaster casts.'

For all her brave words, Polly was trembling when she arrived at the Ecole promptly at 8 a.m. for the first class in her new atelier, nodding to the uniformed gardien watchdog, who eyed her suspiciously, having been warned by the professeur.

Polly had dressed as inconspicuously as possible, her golden hair almost entirely hidden beneath a dark blue hat, clad in a two-piece woollen costume of the same colour, with a decorous bolero style jacket. As she hesitated on the threshold, intimidated by the noise, there was a sudden silence as they saw her.

Then: '*Vous vous êtes trompées, mademoiselle,*' they cried out cheerfully, laughing and pointing towards the dais where the nude middle-aged male model was already being posed.

'*Non, c'est la classe de Monsieur Duran, n'est ce pas?*' Polly replied as composedly as she could.

Another silence. The beginning of sniggers. Then a roar as the laughter and comments burst out. She could not understand what was being said but its ribald nature was clear. She advanced, crimson in the face, looking for a spare easel. No one helped her and the laughter began to change to a resentful muttering. She was almost ready to turn tail and flee when a tall well-built man with prematurely grey hair and steady grey-blue eyes spoke from behind her, having just entered and taken in the situation. He spoke in English with a heavy German accent: 'Permit me, Fräulein. If you will take my arm, there is a spare easel for you.'

She glanced round at his serious kind face in gratitude and took his arm, as he led her ostentatiously to an easel which to her horror was well to the front of the room. He murmured a few words of welcome, including a soft suggestion that as a newcomer she would be expected to pay for drinks for all the students today, and that until a newer student arrived she might care to consider arriving first and preparing the studio for the day, including cleaning it.

'It is the custom,' he said apologetically. 'It would help.'

'I will do it,' said Polly determinedly.

He smiled at her. 'I am Thomas Dietrich,' he announced, and sat down at a nearby easel carefully leaving her to herself except to explain, 'I am the *massier*. I will see you have no further trouble.' He had not passed on to her the general tenor of the earlier remarks which was that the old initiation ceremony of requiring each newcomer to fight a duel naked with paintbrushes should be revived.

As *massier* elected by the students, Thomas Dietrich was responsible for booking the models, for seeing that the students agreed the pose, and was the acknowledged leader of this high-spirited quarrelsome varied group of young men, and he would see this lady had a fair chance to study if she were serious about her work. Thomas Dietrich, whatever his private problems, believed everyone, male or female, should have an opportunity to prove themselves. Besides, there was a look in her eye, however composed she looked, that made him think of the wounded animals he had so often restored to health on his father's estate in Bavaria after the ravages of so-called sport. Were students so very different?

'Oh Michael, look, the black flags are flying,' Rosie cried, her spirits sinking faster than ever Pegasus could, as she looked out from her hotel window on the Place Royale in Reims. The concierge said that meant there would be no flying today. Indeed the wet ground and general greyness of the sky would have been sufficient evidence in themselves. But optimistic as ever she had donned her new glaće silk dress. It looked smart, but the narrow skirt, even with its short fashionable length, was constricting.

'You wouldn't want to take Pegasus up in this, would you, Rosie?' Michael gave a disgusted look at the grey clouds and steady drizzle falling on the first day of the Reims meeting. 'Perhaps it will be better tomorrow. We could look round Reims today and—'

'Oh, Michael, you're joking. You must be,' she cut in, eyes bright with alarm in case he was not. 'We must go to Bétheny to see what is happening. We can at least meet people and look at their aeroplanes – oh, I can't *wait*.'

When the cab arrived at the Bétheny plains five miles outside Reims it was worse than they had expected. Rosie's feet, even in the stout boots she was wearing, sank down in the mud on the road leading to the stands that had been erected for the public, and she was only grateful that fashion now decreed skirts could clear the ground. Oh, for her flying clothes which she would wear the rest of the week. Michael pulled her out of the mud with a squelch, laughing at her exclamations of disgust mingled with cries of excitement. But she forgot her caked boots, as she saw the aeroplanes, sitting in their wood and canvas, protecting them from the weather, waiting for the skies to clear. Pegasus was not booked to fly at the qualifying trials today for the big Gordon Bennett race, as William had advised caution – not flying too high, as he put it. But this did not dampen Rosie's enthusiasm.

'Can't you smell that special smell?' she cried to Michael, closing her eyes.

'I can smell wet mud, oil, petrol and garlic,' said Michael provokingly, wrinkling up his nose. 'I'd rather smell Potts Pedestal WCs.'

'You've no imagination,' she said scornfully, hopping up and down in excitement as a hint of a break in the clouds coincided with the first machine, a red one, being wheeled out. But it could not lift off the ground, so it was followed by: 'A Wright,' she cried knowledgeably to Michael, who remained unimpressed, but tried to show willing.

'Is that Wilbur flying it?' he asked grandly.

'No,' said Rose, glancing at the programme, watching as fascinated as if she were in it herself, as the little machine rose into the air. A catch in her throat. So like Pegasus and so unlike. So this was what Jake had loved so much, been so committed to. She could almost believe that was him at the controls now – no, how stupid, it was nothing like him.

'I say, isn't that Blériot?' Even Michael was excited, seeing the familiar monoplane being wheeled out. Everyone in England knew the Blériot and its now famous flier after his historic flight over the Channel in July.

England will never be the same again, pronounced the cynics. Her island supremacy is gone.

'It is the beginning of a united world,' cried William, the optimist.

And now Louis Blériot himself was here, and shortly to fly.

But Rosie's attention was not on Monsieur Blériot. It was on a tall, golden-haired figure walking towards the Wright Flyer. A walk she knew, a back she knew. At once her stomach was hit by the same feeling she had in the air with Pegasus, a crazy lopsided half-sick, half-excited, half-scared feeling, that sent the world spinning into a kaleidoscope of dreams.

Jake Smith had only half his mind on the Wright Flyer and why Tissandier had flown it for only a minute. The other half was on Pegasus, which he had just seen with mixed feelings in the shed. Why the hell hadn't he thought before that Pegasus might be here? The Potts kept up with the aviation world. He knew that Pegasus had flown – with Rosie as the pilot. That had rocked him on his heels at first. Rosie fly? A woman? Then he had wondered at his own surprise. She'd always talked of when '*we* first fly', she knew as much about it as any of them. But how on earth had she got William Potts to sanction it? And even more to the point, how had she persuaded Harry Clairville Jones? So it had come as no surprise to hear the rumours that Clairville Jones and Potts had parted company. He'd heard no more and darn well wasn't going to ask any questions. That was all over now. But here at Reims to be faced with both of them . . . he cursed softly to himself. He'd make sure he stayed well out of the way.

The past loomed up sickeningly before him, as try as he might he recalled the agony in tearing himself away from Pegasus, which had become his project as much as Potts's. Then had come a later realisation, that it was more than the loss of Pegasus tearing at him. It was the Potts themselves – no, he was deceiving himself. It was Rosie. The way she stuck with Clairville Jones, not him, had struck him hard, but he didn't know why. He'd heard they'd got engaged. Perhaps they still were. He didn't care. He didn't want to think about any of that. Any more than he wanted to think about Florence. The present was the only thing that counted. The past was always pain, so why dredge it up again? Thank the Lord he wasn't the same unconfident man that he'd been in Kent. After nearly a year of aviation in Europe, flying round Europe with Wilbur Wright and, after he'd gone, teaching at the new Wright flying school in Pau, he was a respected figure in aviation circles. Now that Orville Wright had come over to Europe he might join him. He'd had a brief spell with Blériot too – and how interesting *that* had been. Yet Pegasus was still the best. For it had been his. Sometimes he wept for it.

And for Ma. He couldn't bear to think of her. She'd died. Quite unexpectedly, without him even being able to see her again. Kate's letters caught up with him too late, as he travelled round Europe with Wilbur. He'd rushed back to England and all that was an unreal blur, the funeral, seeing Kate was all right, selling the house, moving Kate in with Pa's sister, and then back to Europe and blessed oblivion in flight. Up there you could be above pain and grief – and that suited him.

'But monsieur, I don't understand.' Rosie was aghast. Pegasus had qualified on the Monday for entry into the Grand Prix race in a flight of 15 kilometres in 14 minutes 13 seconds, and moreover she was particularly proud of her achievement in performing a tight figure of eight. How right Jake had been to insist on the ailerons. Only that control had managed to get her through it. She'd tell him – flushed with excitement she had rushed to find him, but whether by accident or design there was no sign of him. Someone else unknown to her had observed her achievement however, and the results were now confronting her.

She had changed into her dark blue serge trousers and jacket that she wore for flying and come early to make sure Pegasus was ready for the big event on Wednesday. She was busy checking Pegasus when the race organiser came up to her. She could not believe what he appeared to be saying, and he repeated it slowly, impatiently, in broken English.

'I regret, mademoiselle, that the rules of the competition do not permit a lady flyer.'

'But that's nonsense,' she cried, outraged. 'Why?' she exploded.

'It is not decent,' he replied stiffly. 'There have been complaints. About you—' he hesitated '—your attire, mademoiselle.' He kept his eyes averted from the serge trousers.

'Do you expect me to wear a ballgown?' she enquired scathingly. 'Would that be *decent*?'

'You will treat this race with the respect it deserves, mademoiselle. The Fédération Aéronautique has ruled that you are not permitted to compete.' He had no idea why, not knowing of Harry Clairville Jones's rapid behind-the-scenes contact with the Paris official he knew. Conscious that this was inadequate, the official began to walk away, mopping his brow. Rosie was so overcome with shock that she had not noticed someone join the group of mechanics who were listening sympathetically.

'I'll take Pegasus up, monsieur,' said a slow cool familiar voice. 'If Miss Potts would permit me, of course.'

'You, Monsieur Smith?' Amazement in the organiser's voice. Jake was clearly well respected and known here. Every nerve on edge, fighting between tears and anger, this was all Rosie needed. She turned sharply, eyes flashing, to face Jake Smith, ashamed he should witness this scene, conscious of all that remained unspoken between them – such as the letter of apology he had not even bothered to acknowledge. She longed to refuse, but she had to think of Pegasus, not herself. She swallowed, hating to admit defeat.

'Any reason I cannot fly Pegasus?' Jake challenged.

'Non, monsieur,' the *chef* said doubtfully. 'There is no rule that says only the owner must fly.'

'Miss Potts?'

The familiar blue eyes on her, impersonal, cold. 'That would be good of you,' she said stiffly.

She hovered anxiously as Jake swung up into Pegasus on the field and was surprised to find that she didn't feel the qualms she had when Harry sat at the controls. It seemed entirely natural to see Jake putting on his goggles and cap, checking Pegasus's controls, as the men started to swing the pusher propeller. She noticed his hands resting on the controls, long and slender hands that knew and loved Pegasus as did she, gentle and understanding hands that would coax, not insist, respond not override.

'Remember,' she said anxiously as the engine roared into life, 'we reduced the rudder area since – since – you went. You'll have to compensate. And the engine hasn't quite the power. It's an old Curtiss and it's feeling its age.'

'I heard. I guess I'll manage,' he said shortly, embarrassed, knowing how Rosie must feel and anxious to be away. Why the hell had he not been able to resist? He'd just given in to the temptation of a quick look at Pegasus – and run straight into this muddle. He didn't want to have to see Rosie's anxious, familiar face.

Rosie flushed. Didn't Jake realise she was only doing her job? Even if he disliked her so much, he need not make it so obvious. She backed away as Pegasus trundled then roared away, watching with tears of pride not mortification as Jake lifted him into the air, experiencing almost as if she were there too, the thrill of soaring upwards, willing the little aeroplane onwards as it surged forward.

Yet however many flights Jake made and however successful they were, she knew Pegasus had no hope of winning the prize. She had seen enough already during the four days' flying to realise how far behind British aviation was, although she was not despondent. They would get there in the end. It was exhilarating to see the Wrights, the Voisins, the Blériots, because where they were now, Pegasus would surely soon be. Meanwhile Pegasus would be seen, admired, discussed and that was all she wanted.

Jake stayed up for an hour – too long – too long, she thought in anguish. He must have crashed. But no. The dear beloved shape of Pegasus soared into view and he landed him gently on the grass.

She forgot Jake's dislike for her as excitedly she ran up to the aircraft to congratulate him. 'That was wonderful, Jake,' she said, balancing herself by the wicker seat and throwing her arms round him to hug him before she could stop herself. 'Oh, Jake, didn't you feel like a god soaring through the air? A curlew. That's what I feel like. And scared. Just a little scared. And did you feel the left aileron just needed a little adjustment – too much wing flexibility?'

He sat very still until she self-consciously drew her arms away after a few seconds, leaving the smell of her perfume lingering in his nostrils. Darn it! He should be used to flying now; he did enough. Yet he felt as excited in Pegasus as if this had been his first flight. And he should be used to women throwing their arms round him by now. But inside every nerve was telling him that this was Rosie, Rosie whom he'd kissed under the apple tree, that he saw in dreams linked in his mind with the clouds and the sun and flight itself, and who had betrayed him to Clairville Jones and never so much as apologised.

He glanced at her. 'Yes, I agree with you. A little shaky on the right turn,' he said offhandedly. 'Otherwise, not bad. Let me know if you want me to fly again for you this week.' He hopped out of Pegasus and stripping off his gloves, walked away.

'I know the important thing is that Pegasus actually flew and oh, Father, people were so nice about it – impressed. But it was so terrible—' Rosie paced round the library at Brynbourne Place, running her fingers through her curls in agitation; left free of restraints they tumbled round her head chaotically. '—to be refused permission to fly, just because I'm a woman!' Even now she was incredulous. 'Women do *everything* now. Lottie Dod won the Wimbledon championship when she was *fifteen*. And she was a golfer, and she climbed mountains, and a hockey player and a dozen other things.'

'But she did not compete against men, my dear,' William pointed out.

'But what does that *matter*?'

'I'm getting to be an old man, and I see things as an old man sees them. It's the way things have always been. I only changed my mind about you flying when I actually saw you in the air; then it didn't seem to matter. The important thing is that somebody did it, man or woman. But other people still see things differently.'

'But why did it have to be Jake Smith who helped us?' she wailed, remembering the look in his eyes as he walked away. 'He hasn't forgiven us for what happened – he didn't even mention our apology.'

'Then there's no more we can do,' said William flatly. 'He clearly has no interest in the future of Pegasus now he's established in France.'

Why that bleakness that swept over her at his words? Why that sudden emptiness at the thought of the future? She swallowed. Jake was gone, and would not return.

'Rosie, I've had some worrying news, my dear. Of Harry.' William cast a look at her almost as if to see whether even the name still had the power to hurt.

'Harry?' she said blankly. 'Hasn't he gone back to his uncle's factory?'

'No. In fact, the contrary. He's left Clairville Cars altogether and leased land near Ramsgate. He's setting up in business on his own account. He's formed a company already, and work is in progress. He's going to design, build and fly aircraft, Rosie.'

'And he's in partnership with Robert Bellowes,' William finished flatly.

Shock deprived the words of their sting for the moment.

'Robert Bellowes?' she repeated blankly. 'But he's not interested in aeroplanes.'

'Apparently he is. Remember his father's original proposition to us? He's interested enough to put up the money anyway. He is to run the company while Harry designs and flies.'

'We'll never be free of them, never,' said Rosie dispassionately, despairingly. Was Robert Bellowes to taint all that was good and pure in their lives? He'd blighted Polly's life. And now he seemed to be reaching out and casting his shadow over the thing Rosie held most dear.

'We will ignore them, my dear,' William was saying.

'It's dangerous to ignore people like Robert Bellowes,

Father,' she said slowly. 'Or they grow insidiously and strangle from the inside.' She braced herself. This was something that had to be faced, then: 'What sort of aeroplanes are they planning to build, Father?' she asked briskly.

'I don't know if he's begun yet. But I fear, my dear,' his face grew unhappy, 'that Harry will be a fearsome competitor. It cannot be chance that he has chosen Robert Bellowes as a partner.'

'Father, there's you, me and Mr Fisherbutt against Harry and Robert Bellowes. And Michael. He was wonderful at Reims. We can get Pegasus ready for the Blackpool Meeting in October between us—'

'And where then, Rosie, where then?' If he was right, from what Rosie had told him about Reims, Pegasus could not much longer be modified to keep up with modern aviation. 'We need new designs. And where do we get them?' He thumped the edge of the wheelchair in frustration, cursing again his ill health. All the magazines in the world, all the books, could not make up for actually circulating in the aviation world, discussing ideas, getting the whole smell of the thing. 'I can't do it, Rosie. Not any longer,' he said defeated.

'I'll be your eyes and legs, Father, and between us we'll do it.' He said nothing, only stroked her hair as Rosie bent down to kiss him.

Jake sat at a café table in the Rue de Bonaparte on the Left Bank. Was it chance or purpose that had brought him here? In Paris for the Aero Show early in October, he had happened to meet there the Comte de Mirapré whose daughter was studying at the Ecole des Arts. Listening politely, he was alerted by the name of Mademoiselle Potts, with whom she shared an atelier. It could be no other than Polly, surely. Perhaps Gabriel was here too? He suppressed the instant desire to find her, but finding himself near the Ecole he found himself hesitating . . . She might after all have news of Pegasus, he argued. He had been surprised not to find Pegasus at the Aero Show - indeed there was no one from England. And not entirely surprised to hear the news of Clairville Jones and Robert Bellowes.

In the aviation world there was still amazement that Great Britain with all her resources was still so behind in its flying machines, that just as with automobiles she lagged far behind France. He was sure now his future lay here, especially now that Ma was gone. All the far-seeing Englishmen interested in aviation were here, Claude Grahame-White had started a flying school, Henry Farman was building spectacularly successful flying machines. He himself was working at the Wright School. But England was slowly becoming more aware of the potential of flight. Pegasus alone showed him that. And ever since the Channel Crossing he'd heard that new companies and pioneers were two a penny, all with their crazy ideas, usually based on nothing but sticks, wire, excitement and hope. And now there was Bellowes Clairville. Surely Rosie couldn't still be going to marry Harry now?

He saw Polly coming out of the Ecole with a group of students. She was even lovelier now, her face maturer than a year ago. The neat brown dress she was wearing with the Peter Pan collar set off her fine features. No wonder Gabriel was so in love. Where was he though? There was no sign of him. She was with a tall serious-looking man of about thirty. Slowly he stood up, left money for his drink and went towards her.

Polly saw him and started with surprise. She left the group with a few murmured words and walked towards him accompanied by the tall man, who bowed somewhat stiffly when introduced.

'Thinks I'm a rival,' thought Jake, amused, as he hailed a cab to take Polly to Rumpelmayers for tea. 'If only he knew.' All the same, where was Gabriel?

Polly plunged directly into the conversation. 'Mr Smith, I'm so *very* glad to see you here now,' she said earnestly. 'I've been so worried since I saw Rosie on her way back from Reims. You know, don't you, that she and Harry Clairville Jones are no longer engaged?'

Jake felt a red flush rising in his cheeks and carefully

stirred sugar into his thé de citron, so that he did not have to face the directness of Polly's enquiring gaze.

'I'm sorry,' he managed to say coolly.

'I hardly think any of us were *sorry*,' she said, 'least of all Rosie. He led us all up the garden path over his motives – all except you, Mr Smith.'

He looked at her closely then.

'Rosie told me they'd apologised to you, Mr Smith.'

'I don't remember any apology,' he muttered.

'They wrote—' she said.

His head jerked up. 'I received no letter—'

'To your London home.'

'I moved—'

They stared at each other.

'They need you back, Mr Smith,' she said slowly.

'My place is here, Miss Potts. I can't. There's no going back. *Ever.*' She saw the anguish in his eyes.

'I understand,' she said. A pause. 'You heard Gabriel died, Mr Smith?'

Dead? Gabriel? He groaned. Death took the best – it took them all – Pa, May, even Ma. Now Gabriel . . .

She watched him, then reached out and took his hand. 'Let life win, Jake,' she said gently. 'Give it a chance. I have.'


The Blackpool Golf Course aviation show in mid-October competed with a rival display at Doncaster. Suddenly the British people were waking up to aviation. Flying machines were hopping, running, collapsing, and the few were gloriously flying. The weather was warm and sunny, and the crowds flocked to both places. The A.V. Roe yellow triplane attracted most attention, but Latham and his Antoinette and the outstanding Farmans were close rivals. Rosie and Michael, who had insisted on taking time off school to come, proudly displayed Pegasus.

Now she would make up for Reims. Now she would show them. On the second day, Pegasus responded magnificently and she flew a five-minute stretch before uneasily deciding the winds were too strong and she must land. Pegasus was beginning to buck and rear like a bronco. Fear seized her, but she overcame it, bringing Pegasus down, down. She touched earth and relaxed. Too soon. For a sudden gust caught him before Pegasus halted, twisted it like a wooden toy; then there was a crazy splintering of wood, a wrench and pain, a fear that this had all happened once before, on a railway train, and then nothingness.

She opened her eyes, dimly aware of faces bending over her. With their help she staggered painfully to her feet. Two yards away lay Pegasus in a tangled mass of wood, fabric and metal. Vomit welled up in her at the sight. She was covered in blood from a cut on her head, her ankle ached, there was a sharp pain in her ribs, but she thought of none of these things. Only the total wreckage of Pegasus.

Receiving the crate with Pegasus's remains at the Eastchurch shed was almost worse than the crash itself. She and Mr Fisherbutt had spent the whole morning trying to see whether anything was salvageable, but even the engine was a write-off. 'Even if it hadn't been, we'd need a more powerful engine for our next one, Miss Rosie,' Mr Fisherbutt remarked in an effort to be cheering.

'Fine couple of aircraft mechanics we are, aren't we, Mr Fisherbutt?' She tried to smile. 'No aeroplane, no engine. Just a lot of hope and fine ideas.'

'I'd best be getting back to help Mrs Fisherbutt. Will you be all right, Miss Rosie? Briggs will be here to fetch you home at four.'

She was left alone with the empty jigs, the drawings that once seemed full of promise, and a pile of wreckage. She wandered disconsolately round the shed; all that work and it had come to nothing. What point building another Pegasus when they needed a new aeroplane for the future? What hope now? True, she had flown, but where had it got her?

Limping over to the pile of wreckage, she patted it affectionately.

'You did your best,' she murmured stupidly. 'It wasn't your fault. It wasn't mine. It just happened.'

But the sight of the splintered wood that she had helped so lovingly to carve, this heap that once had pranced the skies, that had caused so much joy, so many hours of patient love and care overwhelmed her. The tears filled her eyes. Perhaps she was still shaken from the crash, she told herself. But the tears would not be stayed and, as she clung on to Pegasus's shattered frame, sobs racked her body, shaking, heavy sobs which she made no attempt to control. Tears of sadness for the waste, for the empty future and most of all for Pegasus filled her eyes, ran down her face and fell unheeded on the tattered fabric of Pegasus's mainplanes.

And it was thus that Jake saw her, as he hesitantly entered the workshed. His heart thrust into life after the numbness of the last few years, as he saw the ruins of Pegasus, the slim slight figure holding on to them, crying in such abandonment.

'Do you always have to be drenched in water, when I drop by?' he managed to say.

Startled at the familiar voice, Rosie turned her head, scarcely able to see, for the drops still glittering bright on her lashes, Jake lounging with a nonchalance he did not feel against the doorpost.

# Chapter Nine

What had she expected? That everything would be just as it was before the snake had crept into their Eden? She and Jake working on Pegasus, with Mr Fisherbutt's eager, fussing help and Father always there quietly in the background, the omniscient mentor? A tenderness, a new understanding between herself and Jake? Rosie laughed at herself ruefully. How foolish that seemed now in the spring of 1910. Whatever she had expected, it wasn't what had happened – particularly as regards the last. Herself and Jake . . . What memory had obliterated was the quarrels, the constant edginess between them; once working together again, she remembered it all. Wherever the other tender Jake was, the Jake she thought she had once or twice glimpsed, imagining it 'the real Jake', had certainly vanished now. Not that she cared, she told herself, or only because it made working together the more difficult.

Those first few weeks after his return, despite the October sunny mists turning to the damp depression of November, the trees on the downs bending under the eastern winds of winter, had been a whirlwind of activity.

Jake's plans had been carefully formulated by the time he had arrived at Brynbourne. He had to know his path, or one sight of William's puzzled, loving face, one glimpse of Rosie's eager optimism and over-confident amateurism, and he would weaken, and the chances of forming an aviation company would vanish. He disciplined himself to concentrate only on the task before him. Personal considerations must be laid aside. Rosie must be regarded as his mechanic, his assistant and no more. There was no room for any emotion other than the pure thrill of the suddenly expanding horizons of flight and the need to be part of it all.

'It's sales we need, sir,' he announced to William at the first formal meeting to discuss their plans.

'And a new aeroplane,' William retorted somewhat drily.

'More than just one. I plan two at least, perhaps three. A single seat biplane on the lines of Pegasus but more modern of course. A passenger-carrying biplane – or perhaps triplane. And a monoplane. That's for this year.'

'A monoplane?' William's voice sharpened. 'No – I don't believe they're safe.'

'Reims has shown that that's the machine of the future,' Jake cut in apparently calmly, and held William's eyes. 'You should have seen the Blériots and the Antoinettes.' Too late he realised what he was saying.

William's face flushed red. 'Not in my factory.'

Jake stared down at his hands, forcing himself not to display weakness or compassion now. 'Sir, *if* I come back, I have to run things my way—'

'On my money, sir.' William knew this was the decisive moment as much as did Jake.

Rosie watched, helpless to contribute, agonising lest it all go wrong again. To lose Jake now . . .

'On both our monies, sir. It's not fair to ask you to underwrite all the risk, and we'll need a lot of money,' said Jake evenly, 'directly we get orders coming in for the machines.'

'Orders?' William repeated, perplexed. Orders were for Potts Pedestal WCs, not his beloved aeroplanes. He had never conceived that aeroplanes and commerce should be mixed.

'That's the only way we can push our way in to the future. Selling to order. How else do we get our money back? Hope for a fine day so that we win prizes in competitions, with only luck deciding whether we win or Horace Short, or A.V. Roe, or Cody, or Moore-Brabazon – no, it's on sales that we must depend. And of course once we get the new aeroplanes up and flying—' he hesitated, with a sidelong look at Rosie, then plunged, '—I plan to start a flying school.'

She caught her breath, immediately intrigued by the idea, her imagination leaping ahead. In France she'd heard them talking about Grahame-White's school at Pau and of others, and a sudden excitement at the thought of a school on Sheppey seized her. A group of people all wanting to fly, sharing the same goal, the same ideals, the same love of adventure.

William banged on the table, face red. 'Too fast, too fast, young man. I still make the decisions here.'

Jake swallowed. 'No, sir. As I said, I will only come back if I can do things my way. The way I know aviation is going, because I've seen it—'

'And I haven't, eh?' William glared. 'Because of this damned contraption.' He thumped the wheelchair in frustration.

'That's not what he meant, Father,' Rosie said gently.

'He may not have meant it, but that's the fact,' William snapped at her. 'So, young man, you propose we're partners, eh? Potts and Smith?'

'No sir, if anything Smith and Potts, but I—'

Rosie gasped. 'No,' she cried. 'No, no, no. This is Father's company – you can't just come in here—'

Those cool considered eyes on her. 'I don't mean the name literally, Miss Potts.' So impersonal now, revealed in his true colours. 'I mean that I must have control, though naturally I'll always consult you, sir. I thought we could call it the Kent Aviation Company.' Jake looked at the two unresponsive faces.

For William, a dream of old flared up briefly and died. He was a businessman, already beginning to concede Jake's arguments, already planning in his mind how best to safeguard his interests; how could a man in a wheelchair possibly hope to keep up with practical aviation? Besides, he was too old; it was a young man's adventure, a young man's hope. The horizons of the sky were the future; Jake was going to be part of it; so was Rosie. But his day was done. Rosie saw the lost look in his eyes, and misinterpreted it. In her a dream was still strong, and growing stronger. How could she know their dreams were different?

'How could you do it?' she stormed at Jake after an agreement had finally been hammered out whereby Jake would have forty-nine per cent of the shares and a contract for running the company, William forty per cent, Rosie nine. The other two were held by Polly by mutual agreement between Jake and William. For all practical purposes, therefore, Jake held control of the company. 'Have you no feelings for Father?'

He swallowed and said evenly, 'Your father understood, Rosie. There's no other way.' This was his reward for what even she must see as a compromise that left him vulnerable if the Potts family had not the integrity he credited them with. He cursed himself for having weakened at this first test. It would not happen again.

'There's always another way,' she cried scornfully. 'You just didn't want it, that's all. You want it all for yourself. Just like Harry—'

He turned white, his first impulse to walk away. Then he stifled it. 'Rosie,' he tried to reason with her. 'What do you want? Just to play with aeroplanes in a shed? Or to be a real aviator and march forward with the new world lying before us? I tell you, Rosie, you have to choose *now*.'

There could only be one answer to such a question, but she gave it grudgingly, feeling that she was playing into his hands. 'A part of it. But why your way? There are other ways.'

'My way is the way to get what we want,' he said quietly. 'Rosie, you still have it in your power to persuade William against my plans. I have to know.'

His deep blue eyes held her, disturbing her. How impossible to believe in him when he withdrew so completely from her. 'Just tell me one thing, Jake. Do you still feel about flying as you did on the Kill Devil Hills? Still hold the same dreams as when we talked about it first?'

'Yes,' was his emotionless reply.

'Then I'll agree,' she said slowly. 'I'll work hard, I'll fly hard, I'll do all I can to get the company going . . . but it's for the company and for Father, not for you.'

He flinched, the hurt showing in his eyes. She thought he was like Harry. Like Harry Clairville Jones . . . He nodded slowly. 'That'll do. That's all I want, isn't it?'

What had happened left a rage buried deep within her which she assuaged in work. And there was plenty of it. New staff joined them, a new factory was built adjoining the Sittingbourne sanitary ware factory, the drainage of the land on Sheppey was improved so that aeroplanes could have a long run without falling foul of ditches and holes. Sheppey suddenly burst into life as the Short Brothers also set up factory facilities there, building aircraft both for others and of their own design. Furthermore, there was talk that the Aero Club might also be interested in settling on Sheppey.

'If it does,' said Rosie, eyes shining, 'that would really make sense for us to have a flying school.'

For a moment she forgot that Jake was their enemy as his eyes lit up, pleased at her enthusiasm for the idea.

Taking advantage of the temporary truce between them, Jake said abruptly, 'I want you to design the new Pegasus, Rosie.'

'Me? But I can't—'

'I can't undertake all these new machines,' he explained quickly, in case she might interpret this as a sop to Cerberus.

'I could call it Astra,' she said excitedly, her attention captured, the machine already beginning to take shape in her mind's eye. But how to transfer it to paper, to reconcile it with figures and equations and calculations, and then to transfer those into material form . . .

'Call it what you like, but have it ready and built by the spring. I'll get you an assistant.'

'Mr Fisherbutt will help—'

'No,' he said impatiently. 'Mr Fisherbutt is not equal to it any more.'

'You can't get rid of Mr Fisherbutt,' she cried, appalled. 'He's always been part—'

'Did I say I'd get rid of him?' he said angrily. 'You do love sparking off like a catherine wheel in all directions.

Of course he'll be here as long as he wants to be, but you need more assistance.'

'Thank you,' she murmured meekly.

A glance, a quick smile as quickly suppressed. If only that damned row over the company hadn't happened. Only three feet between them and he was aware of every inch of them. A chasm as unbridgeable as the Amazon in flood. And did he want to cross it without being assured of welcome? No, he must stick to his resolve. Women could be insidious, draining you of emotion.

Rosie was glad Jake was no closer – she found it difficult to think clearly. She glanced down at the plans of Astra which they had been studying, then was aware of his breathing over her shoulder, looking down at them too. Unbidden the thought came to her that she had but to turn and her mouth would be on his.

His arm stretched round her, for a moment she thought it would embrace her, but it pointed at the front elevator.

'We'll have to talk about that,' he said abruptly. But not now apparently for he turned and walked away.

Every day now offered something new. New staff, each chosen for their interest in aeronautics, and a draughtsman to incorporate professionally their ideas for the new machines.

Every day an excitement, every day nearer to the day when she would fly again. And one day offered something very special indeed.

'Miss Potts, this is Monsieur Pinot. He's going to be supplying our engines,' Jake said.

*He's going to be supplying our engines.* Jake hadn't even had the courtesy to tell her something so important. Seething, she extended a hand to the tall young Frenchman with twinkling eyes and light brown curly hair who looked at her appreciatively.

'*Enchanté*,' he murmured, taking her hand and kissing it to her confusion, since it was covered with a generous portion of sticky dope.

'What kind of engine?' she asked sternly to cover her embarrassment.

'A rotary engine,' he answered. 'Run on castor oil—'
All the while his eyes ran up and down her body, amused, obviously, to be talking to a woman.

She groaned.

'You do not approve, Miss Potts?'

'Miss Potts is kind of old-fashioned,' Jake said steadily.

She flushed red in anger. How dared he? 'I'll consider it,' she said grandly. 'Do you have one you can install here for testing?'

His mouth fell open with astonishment. '*Mais*—' he looked at Jake. She caught the wink that passed between them.

So, it was too late. The sale had been made.

'Miss Potts,' that charming smile again. 'Perhaps you will allow me to take you to dinner tonight and I will tell you all about the engine. And tomorrow you shall see it.'

'Why I—' Jake began uncertainly.

Seeing him disconcerted decided her and a smile of pure happiness came to her face. 'That would be delightful,' she replied primly.

She wore her new Empire line dress that evening, conscious that the turquoise charmeuse suited her. This called forth great appreciation on Jean-Michel's part. She couldn't take his extravagant flattery seriously, which first disconcerted him and then made him laugh. His factory was situated on the outskirts of Paris, but he seemed to spend increasing amounts of time in Kent, and once or twice a month they had dinner together.

Jake never appeared to notice.

By the spring, the two biplanes were ready and the monoplane not far to go. Ground-testing had been in progress for some weeks and soon flight trials would begin. How far off those early days of Pegasus seemed now, compared with the businesslike organised work schedules of today.

'Do you regret what's happening, Father?' as she saw his wistful face when Jake took the two-seater Daisy Belle, as he'd named her, over the field. He'd called it

Daisy Bell after the song; it had been she who insisted on the 'e' at the end. 'Because she's beautiful, Jake,' she'd said honestly, admiringly.

He had looked at her then, a warmth in his eyes that she rarely saw now. 'Why thank 'ee ma'am,' he'd said, solemnly tipping his hat. But the warmth hadn't lasted.

'Yes and no, my dear,' William replied to her question. 'We couldn't keep going with fading dreams, but I worry about the future, I wonder whether even Mr Smith knows quite where he's going.'

She frowned. 'The flying school idea is wonderful and so is that of Daisy Belle taking up passengers.'

'I did not mean that,' he said slowly.

'And so is the King coming to the Aero Club and calling it Royal,' she continued from where he stopped. 'And now the Club is coming to Sheppey for its headquarters. Isn't it exciting? I want to take the Club's certificate tests just as soon as possible.'

'My dear, has it occurred to you just why His Majesty is so interested in aviation?'

'He loves motor cars, so naturally he's been interested in aeroplanes,' she answered, astonished.

'More than that, Rosie. He is a wise gentleman where international politics are concerned. Did you know that whereas last year we spent £2,500 on aviation for the defence of our island, the Kaiser Wilhelm II spent £400,000?'

'Defence?'

'War, Rosie. The Kaiser is building ships at twice the rate that we are, the Government is alarmed about it.'

'But ships are all that's necessary for our defence.' She was fighting, fighting off the words she knew must come.

'No longer, Rosie. Not since Monsieur Blériot crossed the Channel in an aeroplane. Now the War Office, for all their previous scornful words, are becoming interested in aviation.'

'They want to use aeroplanes for war?' Her voice sounded hollow. She supposed she had been naive to block the possibility so completely from her mind. But surely it would not affect them? 'You mean they might

214

use them like kites and balloons in the South African War for reconnaissance.'

He sighed. 'I suspect more than that, Rosie.'

'Bombs,' she said flatly. 'No, you must be wrong, and in any case there'll be no war. Everyone's agreed that this scare over Germany is a false alarm. The Kaiser loves England.'

'Does he? He flexed his muscles in Morocco five years ago. I suspect soon it will be time to flex them once more.'

'He's just like a schoolboy, Father, trying to show off,' she tried to convince herself. 'But Germany is run by its ministers and they have more sense. Now Father, do have a look at these designs.' She dragged her mind away from the thought of war. They had so much to do. So much to achieve that was good; why think of evil? Why think that the darkness of earth might stretch into the skies?

Jake taxied to a halt, jumped down from Daisy Belle and sauntered towards them, seldom at his ease now with them. 'I'll take Astra up tomorrow,' he said casually. 'I think she's ready for it.'

'You?' For a moment Rosie could not believe what she had heard. 'You?'

'Sure.'

'But she's *my* machine,' she cried, astounded.

He reddened and they faced each other like belligerents.

'And my company. If anyone takes risks, it's going to be me.'

'But it's my design,' she shouted before she could stop herself, unable to believe he could cheat her so. '*I* designed Astra. I take her up.' In her fury she had run to him, pummelling him.

'Don't be childish, Rosie,' Jake said quietly, fending her off. 'You nearly killed yourself in Pegasus. Do you think I could face Mr Potts—' He glanced at where he was sitting some way away talking to Jean-Michel.

'I didn't. And it's nothing to do with Father. It's you – you don't want me to fly because I'm a woman. Just like all the rest. And anyway, why should you care if I kill myself?' she shouted, switching tactics. 'You don't know whether I'm alive or dead half the time.'

215

A startled pause, then coldly: 'I care because I can't afford to lose a good mechanic. I take her up, and that's that.'

Raging impotently, she was forced to accept it. For a while she decided not to attend the trial next day, but made herself do it. How could she stay away when she had given six months of loving work to Astra? There were tears in her eyes as she helped run Astra out on to the grass. Jake saw her face, and hardened his heart. Why the hell had he stopped her flying? He couldn't face William, he didn't want to lose a mechanic. Rubbish. Hell, he couldn't bear to watch while she risked her life, that was why. In theory he saw no reason that women shouldn't fly as well as men; but in practice it wasn't so easy. For it would be Rosie in that flimsy bucket seat.

'And don't get any ideas on pulling that stunt you did on Clairville Jones,' he remarked coolly, glancing back to where she stood at Jean-Michel's side.

Astra performed perfectly. Torn between pride and regret, Rosie watched its box kite wings rising into the air, the misty air full of the smell of castor oil. Like Pegasus in its basic shape, but oh, how far in advance technically with all the knowledge they'd acquired, the mahogany propeller in which she'd put such hours of work, the elevator – how sharply she and Jake still differed over forward elevators, but she'd won her way this time, and the more substantial seat for the pilot since she'd saved so much weight elsewhere. Astra was a delicate lady, with a heart of steel. She glanced at Jean-Michel. He nodded. '*C'est bien, ca.*'

She lay on her back in a field near the factory next day, taking a short break. Astra had flown successfully, so why should she feel so dissatisfied this warm spring day? She should be looking forward to flying Astra, now His Majesty Jake had given her permission, she thought crossly, smarting anew at being under his control. Jake was always drawing William into the centre of discussion, but with her he was always the opposite. He seemed to go out of his way to make her feel awkward and unwanted. Yet that had always been the case, so why was she so restless now? Why this envy of Polly with her new life? Rosie had spent Easter in Paris, and found a new Polly, transformed with enthusiasm for her painting, and perhaps for that German man Thomas Dietrich. He clearly wanted to be more than a friend, but of that Polly seemed oblivious. He was obviously devoted to her. Rosie suddenly felt envious. The air was full of spring promise, the birds singing in their courtship, flowers dotting the fields, all nature was on the move for the new year save only she. Where were the queues of eager swains? Her girlfriends of youth were all married, Polly had had Gabriel's love, and now Thomas was there. Once aeroplanes had been enough for Rosie. But the restlessness in her body made her sigh for something more.

There was Jean-Michel of course, with his laughing eyes and his clowning mock admiration of her which he professed each time they met. She saw him every visit he made to England, partly because she had an obscure feeling that Jake did not like to see his engine supplier so friendly with his assistant, and partly because she was flattered, but mostly because she enjoyed his company so much. She always dressed with great care . . . and was always rewarded by his throwing his hands up in the air and exlaiming, 'Why, you are so lovely, my English Rose. Why do you hide yourself in trousers when a dress becomes you so much more?'

She'd laugh. And he would kiss her. Full on the lips now. She hadn't objected in the least. She tried to fancy herself in love with him, but knew it was untrue.

'Rosie,' he said, 'you make me think of my engines. Throb, throb, throb in passion—' His eyes twinkled.

'You mean kissing me is like kissing the Pinot II?'

'*Non*,' he said indignantly. 'Anyway, I do not kiss my engines.' And they always ended up laughing.

Yesterday had been different. They'd been to a concert in Canterbury, and he had driven her home, taking as usual both hands off the wheel to express some Gallic point, until she'd demanded to take over the wheel herself.

'*Non*, it is not fitting that I should be driven by a lady.'

'This lady is very fit.' She found herself hampered by her narrow skirt, however, and was forced to hitch it up over her knees, and found herself laughing so much when he spent the rest of the journey admiring her legs that he demanded that they changed places again.

Before she could climb out, however, he'd said, 'And now I thank my chauffeuse.' Swooping on her, he had kissed her quite differently, demandingly, softly his hands moving over her breasts until she pushed them away indignantly.

He merely laughed. 'You are so prim, you English ladies.'

'You mean French ladies allow you to do that?'

'Why not? With all this armour you wear, it is not wrong for them and little amusement for me. But if, my Rose, I were to lay you down in a large soft bed and take all this stupid armour off, ah then, *ma petite*, we will see what fun we should have. Does not Mr Smith do this?'

'What?' She grew bright red. 'No, he does not,' she answered flatly, for a moment imagining just that, back in the Lodge and lying down in Jake's arms on that bed. 'He is not at all interested in me – in women,' she said firmly.

'This I do not believe. Of course he is interested in women. Have I not seen him with many ladies in Paris? And he gazes at you like Signor Galileo at the sun. At first I think, Oh ho! I wait. Jake is my friend. I do not go where he wants me not to go, but he do nothing. I think why not? And so, my lovely Rosie,' he kissed her lightly and said thoughtfully, 'perhaps I will marry you. I will consider it.' He twinkled at her and she laughed outright.

'The day you marry, Signor Galileo will recant.'

Now she lay on her back in the field, her trousered legs splayed out in luxurious contentment, and thought about last night. Strange that though she was not in love with Jean-Michel, she enjoyed his lovemaking more than she had Harry's. And Jake – what would it be like . . .

A shadow fell across her and she looked up to see Jake himself looming over her. For a moment she just lay there incapable through surprise of moving, yet every inch of her was aware of his physical presence, and also aware, she suddenly realised, that she must look ridiculous, sprawled at his feet like a Sabine woman before her captor.

'Don't get up,' Jake said gruffly, and sat down by her side. She hastily scrambled into a sitting position, mentally preparing herself for another fight. 'I came to ask whether you wanted to come up with me as passenger in the Daisy Belle.'

She caught her breath, at first inclined to refuse out of pride. No, how stupid. She was longing to try it, even if only as the passenger. 'When?' she asked eagerly. 'Now?'

'If you like.' He smiled at her. 'We might as well take advantage of the weather. The wind's dropped.'

She jumped up eagerly, then turned to him, unable to bite the words back: 'Are you sure you want to risk my precious life?'

'It's by way of being a peace offering,' he replied steadily, to her shame.

'Minnehaha accept Big Chief's penance,' she said gravely, her eyes dancing.

'Then we'll both sing our song for the wind and be on our way.'

'Our *what*?'

'Old American Indian custom in some tribes. It appeases the all-important god of the winds. You can whistle him up or soothe him with song. But never ignore him.'

'He hasn't heard the way I sing,' she laughed ruefully, as she almost ran beside him back to the flying field.

She climbed into the passenger seat behind Jake, nodding slightly to herself as she appreciated the bracing and struts from this new angle. Jake jumped in, seating himself at the controls, and one of the mechanics swung the propeller. It was the first time that she had flown without being in control of the craft, and it felt odd not to have the joystick to cling to. She held on to the stout bamboo struts as the Pinot engine roared into life.

She was acutely aware of her closeness to Jake, of the smell of the stuff he used on his hair tucked in under his cap, peak towards her lest the wind catch it; she was aware of his lean body leaning in concentration over the controls, of the smell of the leather of his jacket, and excitement mingled with trepidation rose in her. Not that she didn't trust Jake of course. He was a wonderful pilot. But it seemed odd to be passenger, not pilot, and she was suddenly aware of vulnerability with nothing but the wood struts and a wicker seat to hold on to.

Daisy Belle began to bump along the grass.

Aeroplanes were a familiar sight on Sheppey now but even so a small crowd had gathered to watch the trial, a crowd that was suddenly slipping away beneath them as they rose into the air. The familiar tight panic in her stomach, and her hands shot out involuntarily to clasp Jake's waist.

'Cling on,' he shouted.

Then they were rising high into the sky, rocking gently and bumping occasionally with the sound of the engine roaring in their ears. Rosie looked down at the ground tilting beneath them, fear left her, replaced by exhilaration, as she saw the patchwork of green fields one way and the blue sea the other. Were they ships or clouds, those small white patches scudding along?

Jake began to bank. 'Hold on tight, I'm turning.'

'Jake, no. Try the left hand first.'

But he was already into the turn.

'Keep the nose down,' she shouted in alarm for the radial engines responded notoriously badly to right-hand turns, with a tendency to stall. For a moment it faltered, on the point of stalling, and she buried her face in his back, the world suddenly still, but Daisy Belle recovered and he turned to smile reassuringly at her.

'Jake,' she screamed into his ear against the noise of the engine, 'it's a winner.'

Joy swept over her again; Jake must be feeling as she did for he shouted back to her: 'Time for that song – Daisy, Daisy, Give me your answer do, I'm half crazy—'

'All for the love of you,' she yelled in his ear.

'You'll look sweet, upon the seat, of a bicycle made for

two,' he carolled back. 'Rosie, I'm taking her down now. Hold on to your hat.'

'I'd rather hold on to you,' she shouted.

'Well,' Jake said, as Daisy Belle came to a halt. 'What do you think?' he asked as he helped her climb down.

'I think we should get the flying school going right away,' she announced, 'just as soon as the Aero Club clears us.'

He expelled his breath in relief. 'That's what I think too.' He stood behind her, pointing. 'There – we can build *there*. Can't you see it already in action? How do you fancy yourself as a teacher?'

'You mean you'll let me fly and teach – oh Jake—' Rosie flung her arms round him; it felt so natural, so right.

'Listen,' he said. 'How do you feel about that competition – first to reach Exeter? Like they did in the Grahame-White versus Paulhan race to Manchester? We'll race each other – Astra against Daisy Belle – no, the new monoplane – and if we win the competition—'

'Yes—' she breathed eagerly.

'I'll get you that new jig you wanted for the workshop.'

The race would take place in July, by which time the monoplane would be ready too. In June another newcomer arrived at Brynbourne.

'My sister's coming to live at the Lodge,' Jake mentioned casually one day.

'Your *sister*?' She remembered now he'd spoken of one years ago, but had not mentioned her since.

'Yup. She's a schoolmistress. She's coming to teach at the local school. I persuaded her to leave London, now Ma's dead,' he added detachedly.

'Your mother – oh, Jake, I'd no idea – I'm so—'

'Anyway,' he cut her off, rejecting her sympathy. 'Kate is coming down to try the country air for a while. Would you—' he hesitated.

'Would I look after her?'

'Yes.' He looked at her. 'I'd be grateful. I'll be there as much as possible, of course. But sometimes a woman can help more than a man.'

If Kate Smith needed help, however, she gave little sign of it. The eyes that greeted Rosie when she called at the Lodge, eager to meet Jake's sister, were cool, as cool as Jake's could be, but less impersonal. Rosie had the immediate impression that Kate Smith did not like her. She was tall, five foot eight perhaps, and serious-looking in her sober high-waisted grey wool dress, with brown instead of Jake's blue eyes, with straight back and stiff of face. Handsome, but reserved for her twenty-four years.

'It's good of you to offer, Miss Potts,' Kate said in reply to Rosie's offer to take her to Canterbury to shop. 'I should enjoy that.' But she did not look as if she would enjoy it, and when the day came the conversation was stilted and awkward all the way to Canterbury in William's chauffeured motor car. Try as Rosie would, she could not seem to find a subject that would loosen the tongue of the ramrod figure by her side, and at the shops she noticed that Kate's purchases were meagre. Immediately jumping to the wrong conclusion, Rosie offered to loan her some money and was speedily rebuffed.

In fact, Kate Smith was desperately unhappy. She had had to leave London when her suffragette activities resulted in the loss of her teaching job, but here she felt like a fish out of water. Jake had told her so much about Rosie, she had been quite sure she would loathe her on sight and was too reserved to be prepared to find herself wrong. Rosie was so different, so used to money, she'd never known what it was like to go hungry; she behaved so childishly, prancing around in her ridiculous trousers and talking of nothing but aeroplanes, aeroplanes. Nothing to improve the lot of the working man. She knew Jake was eager to get her out of London, to get her away from the suffragettes. She had smiled to herself. As if distance could alter her views. Here she planned to start workers' educational classes. The poverty down here was different, however, and she wished now she hadn't come, no matter what. She'd have managed somehow, even without a job.

There was another reason she did not like Rosie. The reason was Robert Bellowes. She'd met Mr Bellowes on the train and been flattered by the courtesy he'd shown her, and the interest he'd taken in her affairs. It had taken little time before he discovered her relationship to Jake.

'A first-class chap,' he'd said, 'brilliant pilot. Pity he's got himself in with the Potts – especially the girl. A girl who goes round throwing herself at every man she meets,' he'd continued. 'You had better watch your brother, Miss Smith,' he had added with a light laugh.

'Fontainebleau.' Polly drew in a deep breath. 'I see what you mean, Thomas. No wonder so many artists chose to live here.'

'Yes,' agreed Thomas, as he stopped the Renault by the vast, impressive mounds of prehistoric stones in the forest. 'I thought you would like it. Once before she died, I met Rosa Bonheur who painted here all her life in the forest. She was a very old lady then, and no longer exhibited, but she talked to me of the forest, and its wonders; she described to me her pleasure in it.'

And now he passed that pleasure to Polly, content at the new look on her face, a happiness to replace the sadness that so often rested there. She jumped down from the Renault and ran over to the stones, exclaiming at their smoothness and weird shapes, feasting her eyes on them.

'Shall we go to Barbizon for luncheon?' Thomas enquired presently, not wanting to break the spell.

'What I'd really like,' said Polly, 'is just to stare and stare at those stones, wondering how they got here, what giant hand threw them, what potter moulded them.'

' "Who is the Potter pray, and who the Pot",' he murmured.

She smiled. 'You read FitzGerald in Germany?'

'Great poetry travels everywhere. Like art,' he replied. 'Why do you frown, Polly? Something displeases you?'

'The stones need life,' she said at last. 'They need people on them, these old primaeval shapes.'

'So, my Polly, now you are sure.'

'Yes,' she said simply. 'I know now that my landscapes mean nothing unless they are seen through people, with

223

people, speak to people. Even if I paint these stones alone without anyone on them, they must somehow be alive to have meaning.'

'You have heard of Van Gogh?' he asked.

'Isn't he the artist who painted yellows, who went mad? But he was never taken seriously?'

'Now people begin to look at his paintings, Polly. They see what you saw. The life in an old pair of boots, in sunflowers—'

'Or rocks,' she finished for him. She smiled at Thomas. 'Let's go on to the inn now.'

'Won't you tell me, Polly?'

'Tell you what?' she asked guardedly.

'Why you are so alone?'

She did not make some trite reply, for she knew very well what it was she must tell him. And now was the time. 'My fiancé, an artist, was drowned just before our wedding day, Thomas,' she began composedly. She would be objective, speak as though it were someone else that this thing had happened to.

Thomas did not murmur polite words of condolence. 'You loved him very much.' It was not a question.

A silence. 'Too much,' said Polly. 'So that when he died, I died too.' She turned to him and smiled. 'But now, thanks to you, I am coming alive again.'

'Thanks to me,' repeated Thomas wonderingly. 'If I have helped, if I have—' he choked before those blue eyes, then took her in his arms and kissed her, gently, holding back the dam of passionate love that threatened to overwhelm him.

At first she was stiff in his arms, then tentatively her lips opened to his, until she drew back, trembling.

'Forgive me please, Polly,' he said contritely.

'There's nothing to forgive you for. It's me,' she said awkwardly. 'It's too soon – I feel – Oh Thomas, I feel as if Gabriel were still here, telling me something. It's nothing to do with you. Can you understand that?'

'Of course,' he said quietly. He hugged to himself the remembrance that she had responded, if only for an instant. Some day, one day . . . She saw the hurt on his face, and put her arms round him. 'Kiss me again, Thomas,' she whispered. 'Please.'

And the strong warmth of his arms blotted out – for a moment – the memory of Gabriel.

Jake sauntered in to the Royal Aero Club headquarters and ordered a drink. This wasn't the London he had known, not the hustle and bustle of Spitalfields. This elegant Piccadilly with its display of wealth and opulence was no part of his life, any more than the fashionable world of Paris had been. But he had come to terms with it, learned its strengths as well as its weaknesses and could tolerate it. Yet all the same, he always breathed a sigh of relief when the time came to return to Kent.

Today, however, there was more than usual to tolerate. Robert Bellowes and Harry Clairville Jones were celebrating with a magnum of champagne the performance of their latest machine, a triplane, at the Club trials. Cursing that they had noticed him, and were beckoning him over, he walked slowly across.

'Congratulations. I heard the triplane's a fine machine.'

'Not bad for a first attempt, eh?' said Harry as blandly as if there had been no unfinished business between them. 'Wait till you see the next. Should interest you. So I don't think there's much doubt that Bellowes Clairville is on the way up.'

'I never doubted it,' said Jake drily. 'Not for a moment.'

'And how is dear Rosie? I heard that was your biplane I saw up the other day.'

Jake nodded.

'Not bad.' The stem of Jake's glass snapped suddenly.

'Still, you realise that working with the Potts, you'll never get anywhere. You do know that, don't you, Smith? They don't think in international terms like you – and like us. You could do worse than join us – what do you think?'

'Join you?' He gazed at them blankly. Were they serious? After what Clairville Jones did to him, the two-faced snake. He got a grip on himself. He had to play things cool, much as he'd like to floor them both with his fists.

'I wouldn't join with you, if yours were the last aeroplane left in England,' he drawled. 'Thanks for the drink.'

Clairville Jones's face flushed red, and Robert Bellowes intervened. 'Our little Miss Potts has you in her toils, does she?' he laughed.

'Let's keep Miss Potts out of it.'

'Keep her out of it? She *is* it. She's ambitious, I'll say that for her. Poor Clairville Jones has narrowly escaped, so now she's opening those big eyes of hers at you.'

'That's enough.' Jake began to walk away, but Robert Bellowes's voice stopped him.

'You'd better listen, Smith, or the whole Club is going to hear. You should know, after she schemed her way into flying Pegasus first instead of Harry, and he broke off the engagement, she came to me.'

'*You*?' He wouldn't listen to this fat pompous idiot, but the voice went on. 'She was all too ready to lay herself out for me, if we could just get together and build her an aeroplane. So I sampled the goods, but—' He leered just as Jake's fist caught him, and he staggered back.

'No gentleman, I'm afraid.' Robert Bellowes's plaintive voice followed Jake as he strode out. It didn't sound at all displeased.

There wasn't a word of truth in it. Jake wrestled with himself. Rosie wouldn't go near a chap like Robert Bellowes. Yet a voice inside him pointed out that she was spending a lot of time with Jean-Michel. Certainly she was ambitious, but not for herself. She was an innocent, a virgin, impossible to think that she could offer to trade herself to get onwards in the aviation world. Yet somewhere inside, that voice was saying insidiously: '*But you thought that of Florence!*' Angrily he bade the voice be still and, with a chuckle, it was.

When he saw Rosie again such ridiculous notions were dispelled in the clear light of reality as she jumped up to meet him, eager to discuss the race. And the voice whispered again: *'Remember Florence in the garden?'*

'We've got to get our ideas organised—' she was saying. 'Jake, is anything wrong? You look strange.'

'Rosie,' he said abruptly, 'has Robert Bellowes any reason to dislike you?'

Immediately her eyes fell away. 'You know the Bellowes have always disliked us,' she said lightly, artificially, avoiding looking at him. 'Sir Lawrence still has an official feud with Father—'

'More than that.'

'Why do you want to know?' she demanded fiercely.

'They want me to work for them.'

Her eyes opened wide as she gasped, 'For Bellowes Clairville? Oh *no*, Jake, you didn't—'

'No, I didn't, but I just wondered why—'

Her head went back proudly. She couldn't tell Jake about Gabriel. Nor about Michael. Nor about herself. The past was buried and must remain so. 'Polly and I quarrelled as children with him,' she said stiffly.

His heart sank. She wasn't telling the truth, he could see that. There *was* something else. What had happened between her and Bellowes? Had she really given herself to him? He couldn't believe it. But why not tell him what had happened? There was guilt in her eyes. As she caught him staring at her, she looked away, and did not see the misery in his face.

'Ah, so that's it,' he said easily.

# Chapter Ten

'I've agreed to a control and refuelling stop at Amesbury.' Jake's deep voice made Rosie jump. She had had no idea that he had come into the shed as she was bent almost double over Astra's lower plane. It was July and Astra and the new monoplane, still as yet unnamed, were standing side by side in a shed in the Royal Aero Club grounds, having been brought in crates from the Sittingbourne factory, ready for the Eastchurch to Exeter race. 'I presume you think Astra is capable of making it there? It's about two and a half hours' flying.'

It might have been a joke, but was not spoken as one. Rosie flushed angrily. 'I've got three hours' endurance, and more to spare; you know that's what I've tested.'

'Ground tested,' Jake reminded her. 'There's a difference.'

'Astra will get there – *and* get there first,' she said firmly. 'How about the Mighty Mono?'

'Almost ready,' he replied laconically. In truth, he had been running into problems with the cable bracing, but he had got them licked now – only just in time, for the Royal Aero Club was keeping an interested eye on his rivals, and had been dubious about allowing his entry. Dear old Daisy Belle would be no substitute for his monoplane – what was he going to call it?

It was a graceful machine, Rosie was forced to admit, totally different to anything they had built before. With its propeller and engine in front of, not behind the pilot, rear elevator and wooden structure supporting the tail, the graceful monoplane was still unusual in British aviation, though not on the Continent. Monsieur Blériot had sparked an interest in monoplanes here, however, and the idea was catching on fast. Vickers were testing one out this very month.

Even in ground trials Jake's monoplane had slipped across the grass elegantly and confidently, though that didn't mean it was going to be stable in the air. 'Not enough plane area,' William had judged, shaking his head dubiously. 'Liable to fold up in the air – there are too many accidents with those monoplanes.'

A sudden fear had struck Rosie then, as sharp as it was unexpected. Suppose Father was right and Jake – no, she mustn't think that way. 'Jake seems convinced that that's where aviation is going,' she had said firmly. Doubts were no part of an aviator's make-up – not when she trusted her colleague's judgement. There were no signs of any resistance or stability problems when the monoplane was tested in the air; it flew, dipped and soared like a swallow in flight.

'Perhaps that's what you should call it – the Swallow,' she said idly to Jake, when congratulating him on the first flight trial.

He had glanced at her. 'Aiming to get rid of me? Swallows come, swallows go.'

She knew he was deliberately provoking her and bit back any retort. Ever since their conversation about Robert Bellowes they had kept their talk strictly impersonal and limited to business. Even that was brief, lest edginess and tenseness creep in. Fix your mind on the race, Rosie told herself. Forget everything else. She knew it only needed a match to set alight the explosive atmosphere, and erupt their fragile peace into flame. What's happening? she wondered in despair. From being an enjoyable adventure between herself and Jake, it had suddenly turned into a duel, as if they were to fight out in the air what could not be resolved on the ground. But why, oh why did it have to flare into life on the morning of the race itself?

A dawn start had been agreed, for then the air was likely to be at its calmest. The hot sun of midday could bring unexpected gusts, which even if slight, could wreak damage or even catastrophe. Rosie shivered in her light overalls, regretting she had not donned heavier clothing;

she was expecting it to be hot and was anxious not to carry more weight than the minimum. Too hot for a flying suit, she was wearing only overalls over a short-sleeved blouse and underclothes, leaving her legs bare under the thin trousers to catch a cooling breeze while flying. Just now though she regretted it and stamped her feet in an effort to warm herself, gratefully accepting the offer of a coat from one of the mechanicians and a hot drink from Mr Fisherbutt.

One by one the Royal Aero Club officials were now arriving to supervise the start and issue them with official time cards, pedantically checking their aviators' certificates, which they themselves had awarded to them only two months ago. As Rosie followed Astra as she was wheeled on to the Royal Aero Club field, she saw Jake, his back to her, staring at another aeroplane being trundled out on to the grass. Her spirits sank. Not other competitors surely? They'd been told they were the only two. And what was worse, this was a triplane, and by its side a familiar figure: Harry.

'Looks like we've got a friend coming with us,' Jake said slowly, as she came to stand beside him.

'Did you know about this?' Rosie flung at him fiercely. 'You've been making all the arrangements. You must have known. Why didn't you tell me?'

'Because I didn't know.'

'You mean you didn't want *me* to know.'

Jake's control broke. All the pent-up tension of the last few weeks boiled to the surface and overflowed.

'If I say I didn't know, that's what I mean. You worried his triplane is going to beat Astra?'

'Of course I'm not. But you know how I feel about Robert Bellowes – do you think I'd willingly go in for any race that he had anything to do with?'

'I could say the same about Clairville Jones. You women sure let personal emotions run away with you. Just because Bellowes told you to push off, you want to ditch our company's chances—'

'*Push off?*' she shouted. 'What do you mean, push off?'

231

'You didn't deny it when I asked you. You—'

'Deny *what*?'

'That you—' he bit back the phrase he'd been going to use '—set your cap at him and—'

'And *what*?' Tears of rage filled her eyes. 'You – you *rotter*,' she yelled, and without thinking twice picked up a pot of boiled sago dope left by their mechanics for last minute checking of the wing fabric, and emptied it over his head, in one swift jerky movement of rage. 'You think I'd have anything, *anything* to do with that slug?'

He dripped white sago, clutching frantically for a handkerchief to wipe his eyes clean; when, with murderous eyes, he could see her clearly he seized her in his arms in a tight bear hug so that a good proportion of the sticky mess transferred itself to her, then holding her by the back of her collar like a recalcitrant puppy he took handfuls of the stuff and pushed it down the neck of her overalls where it sank down her bare skin and slowly slid down between her breasts. She screamed her rage.

Half appalled at their actions, but still driven on by white hot fury, they were oblivious of the interested but wary spectators gathering to watch at a safe distance, and the slanging match continued, as they circled round each other, awaiting an opportunity to strike.

A cough and an apologetic 'if you're ready' drew both to full horrified awareness of their childishness and, overcoming an insane desire to giggle as she took in Jake's sago-besmeared cap, hair and jacket, Rosie assumed a stern, offended expression and marched off to clamber carefully through Astra's wires and struts up to her seat.

It was as well she did not see the smirk on Harry's face as he climbed up into his triplane, or hear the words Jake flung at her as he stormed by to the monoplane. Each of the three pilots hunched themselves over their joystick awaiting the official signal for the start. Rosie did not look at her rivals but she was acutely aware of them. In a way it was symbolic. Harry their chief rival, the man she might have married, and Jake – no, she would not think of that, that cad. She squirmed as a blob of sago slipped further down between her breasts to her waist. Ugh. Ugh!

Impossible that Harry should win. Even more impossible that that *beast* should. The two Pinots started their deep growl and she heard the sound of a Clairville Jones engine with a lurch of familiarity.

Jake was off now. She would follow after him, and Harry last, the times to be allowed for at the Amesbury control point.

The signal for her to go. The mechanics with a deft twist of the propeller stepped aside as she gave the hand signal to them. The Pinot accelerated and filled her ears with its satisfying deep growl, the smell of burnt castor oil began to pervade the air, filling her with the usual excitement, and the pinky sunlight of dawn was obscured by blue oily smoke as she trundled over the grass. The biplane, the monoplane and the triplane. Which would win? *She* would. She saw the monoplane's tail in front, lifting clear of the ground, then the machine lifting, rising into the air, soaring up gracefully. It did look like a swallow, whatever Jake said; she was sure he'd based its configuration on the bird's cantilevered wing.

Now for Astra. 'Come, my beauty,' she exhorted. Gently she pushed the lever forward as she bumped across the grass, feeling Astra's tail clear the ground, then pulled the lever towards her to lift the head. Then the nose was up, the rumbling stopped and the ground was slipping away beneath her, the people on the field suddenly smaller, faces upturned; the lever back to almost normal and she was rising. She glanced at the altimeter, 200 feet, good. The Pinot purred comfortingly, the slight dawn breeze whistled cheerfully through wires and struts singing its own song, as she rose up high into the dawn. In front of her she could still see Jake and glancing over her shoulder, Harry was some way behind her on the port side. Then she lost track of them in her excitement. She glanced at her compass, checking west, but with the sun behind her she hardly needed its assistance. She'd memorised the landmarks she expected to see, the River Medway winding its way through Maidstone, the railway lines and the streams, ahead she could see the Sevenoaks to Guildford Road; the patchwork quilt of England was laid out below her.

'I am monarch of all I survey,' she told herself grandly, as she settled down to a steady thirty-two miles per hour. Jake must be going faster for there was no sign of him in front. The *rat*! Biplanes just had to be more dependable, she had agreed with William, simply because of the irrefutable fact that they had twice the wing area for meeting resistance. Though if that were all there were to it, then the triplane should be sturdier still, she puzzled to herself. That she could not believe, seeing its awkwardness in handling.

Up here in the sky the tension and fury began to die away; they were the pettinesses of earth; the sky belonged to purer emotions. She could even restore her equanimity in thinking of Jake. She would win of course, for Astra was the steadier, even if the monoplane were the faster. Tortoise and hare, she told herself comfortingly. But then that sick feeling suddenly returned. What did Jake mean about her setting her cap at Robert Bellowes? Nothing she'd said could have given such a ridiculous impression. Did the rotter simply make it up? Or did it come from Robert himself? And with that all too likely thought, came another. Had Jake toned down what Robert had actually said?

The day was suddenly clouded. She must take her mind off such thinking and concentrate on flying or she might make a dreadful mistake. There was Jake now, flying perhaps thirty yards ahead, emerging from the morning heat haze. She must be gaining on him now. Good. She increased her speed and the Pinot responded. For a moment she thought she'd made a mistake in her eagerness to catch Jake up and that the Pinot would stall, but it didn't and her heart rate returned to normal.

She was gaining on him for sure now and after ten minutes she was level; he was about twenty yards to starboard. 'Traitor,' she yelled across the gap. He couldn't have heard her over the engine noise but mouthed something back lost in the whistling wind. She could see his expression quite clearly: grim, very grim. She began to see the funny side as he leaned over the controls once more. Deliberately she increased altitude to

234

turn. She'd show him what Astra could do. And Harry too. She'd circle round them and back on course, and still keep up with them. She revelled in the thought of the blistering comments Jake would make at Amesbury. The ailerons responded perfectly and she hoped that Harry appreciated the fact. He'd gone back to wing-warping, the idiot.

In the monoplane, Jake was still seething, driving the machine hard, still aware of the stickiness of the dope where his one handkerchief had been inadequate to clear it from his neck. His cap was ruined and sago still adorned his hair. The girl was crazy; you could never trust women. They'd get you in the long run. He'd kidded himself they had a good working relationship. Ha! Look at it. She'd poured dope all over him for nothing. He was no good with women, he decided, except casually. He didn't understand them and wasn't sure he even wanted to. This morning he didn't even like them. Aeroplanes, now, were different. He'd had some trouble with the monoplane on trials, but today it was doing well. You could trust machines; you designed them well and they performed as you expected. Here it didn't matter about the topsy-turviness of the world below, a world where what had seemed honest and pure turned out to be rotten and false. A world where Rosie . . .

Up here, there was just you and the machine. You understood each other. You were the master of your fate, like that poet said. 'My head is bloody but unbowed.' Only his was not bloody, but sticky, he thought viciously. He wished he'd never come back to England. Out in France men were serious about flying. He told himself it was the challenge of the monoplane that had brought him back, the excitement of having his own firm, opening a flying school, but he did not examine the thought lest it prove untrue. He could have done a lot better in France, opened a flying school as Grahame-White had done at Pau, and now was planning to do at Hendon.

Jake had come back, he reluctantly acknowledged to himself, because he wanted to work with the Potts, more fool that he was, not just with William but with Rosie.

For an image he had once held of a girl with brown curls and blazing eyes of truth and courage, a slender figure and a sense of fun that had brought laughter to his world again. The business with Clairville Jones was past, he had told himself when he came back from France. She had done right according to her own lights, he told himself. Now he knew different. She was a she-wolf, like that queen. The she-wolf of England. A madwoman. He was a better judge of aeroplanes than women, that was for sure. Rosie had only wanted him back because she was ambitious and he could put Potts Aviation on the map. That was the reason. No wonder she was mad when he'd stood firm over running the firm his way. Or, to be strictly accurate, reasonably firm. The Potts could only outvote him if they brought Polly back to vote with them – and – forgetting Rosie – he knew William had too much integrity to vote against him for the sake of it. Thank heavens for that. He seethed with fury anew, blinded with anger and wrenching the controls of the monoplane so that it bucked alarmingly, hit a 'hole in the wind' and dropped.

That sobered him up. What the hell was he doing taking it out on the aeroplane? Lucky it was only a hole, and not the engine stalling. If he had got into a spiral dive . . . He gulped, and patted the monoplane affectionately, muttering a brief thank you to the Pinot. It was no part of flying, as he saw it, to bring anger into the sky.

Now in the crisp air of early morning, he began to see things more clearly. He was going to win this race. He had wanted to before, simply to show the world that a monoplane could beat a biplane, but now he was determined to win, because of the triplane – and Rosie. He wasn't going to let Clairville Jones win and he certainly wasn't going to let the she-wolf win. He looked around and saw her mouthing something at him and he yelled back 'Bitch', secure in the knowledge that she would not hear, though he didn't much care if she did.

* * *

And to think that she'd actually wanted Jake back, Rosie
fumed, teeth clenched in fury. He was useful, but now she
wished it were anyone but him. The man was worse than
Harry. At least you knew where you were with a snake.
He didn't appear like a lamb one moment and a snarling
ape the next. Did apes snarl, she wondered vaguely? This
one did anyway. She turned slightly into wind, feeling a
sudden gust. There was the Guildford road coming up
now surely. She and Jake were neck and neck and there
was no sign of the triplane. Indeed she'd almost forgotten
that Harry was in the race. It seemed a contest between
the two of them.

She was beginning to feel warmer now, thank goodness.
The chill start was giving way to a warm day. Somebody
must have sung for the wind even if she'd forgotten in
the furore of taking off, for there was only a light
breeze. Even so, she'd be glad to reach Amesbury to
have a break. It was further than Astra had ever flown
before, but she was confident now that Astra could do
it barring bad luck. The idea of having to put down in
a field miles from anywhere and tinker with the machine
was not a pleasant one. When this had happened before,
Jake often used to come down to help or vice versa, but
that was hardly likely to happen today. Wouldn't he gloat
if she got into trouble? What pleasure it would be when
she beat him in this race. She'd spend the prize money on
what *she* wanted.

The Hog's Back now, another distinctive landmark.
How was the time going? In the London–Manchester
Race Grahame-White in an effort to catch up lost time
had flown by night, the first time anyone had done so.
She shivered. It would be a wonderful experience, but not
over country she did not know. She fancied just how it
could be, the silence and peace, the twinkling lights, the
silver strands of rivers, only the moon for companion.

Jake was dropping – surely . . . Her heart leapt into her
mouth as she circled round. Then he was gaining altitude
again, thank heavens. Quickly she increased speed, lest

he realise she must have circled to watch, and resolutely ploughed on. She'd been flying for two and a quarter hours now and only had three hours' endurance. A pricking of anxiety gnawed at her. Where was she? Would she make Amesbury in time, or had she, in circling, come off route? The Hog's Back was past now, the green lush hills of Surrey giving place to the farmlands of Hampshire, and ahead she could see the flat Salisbury Plain opening up. She depressed her elevator to descend to keep an eye open for Stonehenge which would tell her she had arrived. Jake was somehow ahead now – was that the glimpse of sun gleaming on white wings ahead? No. He must have put on a lot of speed. And of Harry, no sign. So she and Jake were well in the lead. She and Jake . . .

Rosie and he were in front now. Clairville Jones was way behind in his cumbrous triplane. Where was Stonehenge, their landmark? Two miles from there was a designated field for their landing where the Club officials would be waiting to mark their time cards. In their view it would be a miracle if all three aeroplanes managed the journey safely. But not in Jake's – he knew their aircraft were capable of it, only some chance mishap could rob one or other of them of victory. And it was going to be his.

There below them was the rolling expanse of green, and the stones of Stonehenge standing out clear beneath. Man was flying into the new century, a new era, passing over the relics of pre-history, so it was said. Wasn't it something to do with sun worship? Well, flying was modern man's form of sun worship, and pray God they did not defile their worship with the wars that had ruined the last two thousand years; that their sun should always shine, and that the aeroplane would be a harbinger of peace, not war.

He glanced over and saw Rosie was already beginning her descent, and increased his own speed, the monoplane's reactions were quicker than Astra's and he intended to land first. The monoplane surged forward; glancing down Jake could see the shadow of two aircraft – no, *three* – below on the ground as they passed over the barren green slopes of Stonehenge. He depressed his elevator further, enabling him to reduce height more quickly. It was risky, but quicker; he cut off the engine, bumped, rose and landed again. Rosie came in thirty seconds later, making a perfect landing and climbed out, grinning maliciously.

'You want the next village, Middle Wallop,' she jeered. 'Poor old Mighty Mono.'

Jake glared. 'I was ahead of you,' he pointed out.

'Remember the tortoise,' she answered smugly.

'In that case,' he turned pointedly to look into the distance where the triplane was beginning to make its descent, awkwardly and clumsily. Yet Harry landed gently enough to Rosie's annoyance, and nodded coolly to them after agreeing his time with club officials.

'Remarkable,' the official was saying, 'quite remarkable. All three of you to arrive so near to each other. My word,' he rubbed his hands together in glee. 'I quite wish I were on duty at Exeter. Do you wish to continue now, or will you be waiting till evening?' The air would be stiller again by the evening.

'Continue,' said Harry coolly, not even consulting them. 'Wait,' said Jake simultaneously.

'Scared?' Harry threw at him.

Jake's eyes narrowed. 'Let's go.'

Didn't anyone care about her, Rosie thought wearily. Dismally, she realised not. In fact, she could have done with more than the hour's rest that they took while the machines were checked over and the fuel tanks refilled. She could carry eighteen gallons of petrol and ten of castor oil, yet they were all but exhausted in the long flight. The short break was stilted and difficult, the sun too warm, the ground dusty, getting in her nostrils. They were two-thirds of the way now and this time Harry went off first, she following and Jake after her.

Tired, the smell of the castor oil mixed with smoke cloying her nostrils depressed rather than exhilarated her now. Oh, to *be* there. Once she'd taken off and gained altitude she'd be all right. She could relax then. But somehow that did not happen. She found herself worrying about the least sound out of the ordinary, concentrating with grim determination, her hands sweaty inside the cotton gauntlets. Impatiently she took her cap off to let the air cool her hair, as it blew in the wind, and was horrified to see the cap torn away, turning over and over in gradual descent to the ground.

'Damnation,' she said fiercely. 'Oh damn.' What if it rained? But as yet it showed no sign of raining and the sun beat down fiercely as midday approached.

There was Jake. No sign of Harry though. She'd been up an hour already and was glad she'd had that sandwich at Amesbury. I wish I knew whether Harry was ahead or behind, she thought. Racing would be fun, if only it wasn't against Harry and that beast there. He was deliberately keeping neck and neck with her to taunt her and put her off her stroke. Well, he wouldn't succeed.

She began to enjoy herself again, the wind whistling through the wires forming a tune. She started to sing, making up words to its rhythmic strumming. Then she thought once more of Jake's story about the Indian gods and stopped in mid-bar, determined to do nothing, but nothing, he ordered any more. She glanced across at him, looking like a knight of old riding his steed. A precarious steed, though; looking at Jake's large lean figure it was a wonder he managed to stay on that flimsy seat at all. Perhaps aviators should have some kind of strap to hold them in, to stop these accidents when people simply tumbled out of the machines if they dived steeply. She felt as if she were in a chariot race, urging her steed onwards.

'Come on, Astra,' she shouted. 'We're nearly there.' She was doing thirty-five miles per hour at the moment. Another half an hour and she'd be at Exeter.

She spoke too soon. Suddenly, horribly, she was aware that the ginger beer she'd drunk at Amesbury and the tension she'd been under since had wreaked their natural result. She tried to ignore it, twisting her legs anxiously, shifting restlessly. But it would not be ignored. Darn, she *must* forget it. Yet she could not. She tried to will it away, thinking of something else, but it did not work.

Eventually she groaned. There was no help for it. She'd have to go down. She wept in frustration. To lose the race over something so trivial, so humiliating. And it was her fault, not Astra's. She'd have to tell everyone it was a defect though; never, ever would she admit the truth.

She put Astra at the correct descending angle, and depressed the elevator, rapidly picking out a suitable-looking field. She descended quickly, too quickly and bounced. Astra skidded on the wet ground as she touched down again, was swept sideways by a gust of wind and, lurching to a halt out of control, slewed and tipped over on its nose.

Rosie, caught unawares, was thrown out into a sea of mud – that wasn't.

What the hell's the girl doing now? She's going down. Too quickly. Is she going to spiral? Panic filled Jake and his heart still beat the louder even though he realised she had Astra under control. But something must be badly wrong. It wasn't like Rosie to go down so quickly or so incompetently. He banked and overflew again, then depressed the elevator without a second thought and took the monoplane down, filled with fear at what he might find. Perhaps she was ill, perhaps she'd crashed; all thoughts of the race went out of his mind. He saw Astra bounce in the field, but preoccupied with his own landing he did not see what happened next. He came in and landed in the same field, and climbed out, bewildered. Had he made a mistake? Where was Astra? Then he saw it, tipped forward on its nose. But it was empty; there was no sign of Rosie. Filled with fear, he began to run across the field, scanning the long grass bordering the river for a still, slim body, perhaps now silent in death.

He searched for perhaps three minutes, then stopped in astonishment as he noticed a figure walking stiffly towards Astra, a figure who had not seen him, and was completely black, covered in slime from hair and face to feet, looking like something out of an Edgar Allan Poe horror story. Completely black. Only the walk and the blazing eyes in the mud-covered face when it noticed him told him this monster was Rosie. She wanted to run when she saw him, but there was nowhere to run to.

241

'Go away,' she yelled, a sob in her voice.

He strode quickly towards her, half laughing, half concerned. The stench hit him from fifteen yards away. He groaned. 'You, only you would manage to fall into a sewage dump. Oh Rosie.' He began to yelp with uncontrollable laughter.

'Go away,' she shouted, anguished. 'Go away. *Please.*'

'I'm certainly not coming closer,' he choked. 'You idiot, Rosie. What on earth did you come down for anyway? Are you ill?'

'Engine defect,' she shouted defiantly.

'Rosie, you're lying,' he said sharply. 'Now *tell* me what's the matter. Are you hurt? Ill?'

Goaded beyond endurance, her last ounce of resistance gone and thankful only that she'd had time to alleviate the cause of her plight after crawling out of the sewage, she shouted miserably, 'I had to.'

'Had to?' he repeated blankly.

'I wanted to – oh damn you, Jake. I wanted a Potts Pedestal WC, if you must know.'

His face changed. 'You wanted a – do you mean to say, woman, that I've thrown away the race because—' he almost choked with fury, '—because you wanted to piss?'

'I didn't ask you to follow me down,' she cried, a break in her voice and running off, anywhere, anywhere to get away from her indignity.

'You just wait,' he shouted, stalking after her, his long legs covering the ground quickly after the retreating black figure. 'I've lost the race now, barring mishaps to the triplane. We'd better get you tidied up, you nincompoop.' He looked round. 'Come back here. There's a river over there.'

'No,' she shouted, turning round and glaring. 'Don't come any nearer.'

Ignoring this injunction, he walked up to her trying not to grimace at the stench. 'Follow me, young woman,' put out a hand to grab her and changed his mind. But she followed him nevertheless over to the trees bordering the river bank.

'Now, strip off your clothes, and I'll do the best I can with them while you wash yourself.'

'I can't,' she wailed. 'I haven't anything else to put on.'

He sighed. 'I don't go around carrying spare changes of clothing for stupid females. You can have my jacket, if you like.'

'That's not much use,' she snapped. 'It's covered in sago.'

He was bereft of words. Then he finally managed to splutter, 'So get on with it by yourself. If you don't want me around, suits me. I'll go.'

'No, don't,' she pleaded, not wanting to be alone. 'I – I might need your help with Astra,' she added in rearguard defence of this submission.

'Then get your clothes off,' he roared crossly.

Gingerly she began to strip off the slime-covered overalls, hoping that the sewage had not joined the sago underneath, and turned to run down to the river in her underwear.

'Rosie,' Jake called after her, sighing in exasperation. She turned unwillingly. 'Take them off, don't be so foolish.'

'They'll wash on me.'

'And how do you wash what's underneath? For heaven's sake, grow up; it's a fine time to be modest.'

'All right, all right,' she snapped. Then as he made no move to go, 'You're not going to watch, are you?'

'Why not?' he said through gritted teeth. 'I've nothing better to do with the afternoon now that you've thrown the race away.'

All the same, he went to start the work of cleaning the overalls in the water while she stripped and immersed herself in the river in a semi-crouched position since the water was only three foot deep. Then checking to see that Jake was still occupied, she crawled on to the bank and bent over to wash her hair, thanking heaven it was a fast flowing stream and made a reasonable job of it. By the time she emerged, teeth chattering, Jake was laying the overalls and her underclothes out in the sun to dry. He looked up unexpectedly, and she hastily threw her arms

243

round herself for protection, however inadequate. He took off his shirt and threw it across to her.

'Here,' he grinned, pleased at his triumph. 'You can decide which half you cover. But I don't want it used as a towel. You can let the sun dry you off while I go in.'

'What for?' she asked, teeth still chattering.

He gazed at her. 'In case you'd forgotten, dear sweet-natured Rosie, you threw sago all over my hair.'

'You pushed it down my shirt,' she muttered shamefacedly.

'You deserved more,' he retorted.

She was about to answer again when she realised he was removing his trousers, and hastily sat down on the grass. She lay back, letting her hands fall to her side, secure in the knowledge that Jake was bathing. But time passed quickly as the sun dried her skin, and her eyes closed, opening again to find Jake standing over her, already dressed. She sat up promptly, hunching her knees to her chest, trying to pretend nonchalance.

'You looked like Venus de Milo lying there with that shirt across you,' he said, a curious expression on his face.

'I can't compare you to classical statuary,' she answered crossly, furious that he had crept up on her, 'since apparently it's only *your* modesty you're concerned about. Next time—'

'I see the wash hasn't improved your temper,' he retorted sweetly.

'The next time I go racing,' she said defiantly, 'I won't—'

'And the next time I do,' he interrupted, 'it *won't* be with any damn fool woman.'

She scrambled to her feet, oblivious to all else but her hatred of this man, even of the falling shirt.

'What's my sex got to do with it?' she shouted at him, swinging her arms wildly. '*Nothing*. Your sister was telling me all about women coming into their own. And they need to with men like you. My sex has nothing to do with it.'

'I'd say it had a lot to do with it,' he said grinning, his

244

eyes deliberately, provokingly wandering up and down her body.

She went bright red and hastily bent to pick up the shirt. 'A gentleman wouldn't stare.'

'Goddammit, Rosie,' he said slowly, 'any man would stare. Be reasonable. Stop dancing around like a dervish and look at yourself. You're beautiful.'

She stopped in mid-insult, mouth open in surprise, quickly tying the shirt round her.

'Beautiful,' she asked shyly. 'To you?'

To him? Of course to him. It hit him like a sledgehammer. Had it always been there, hidden from the bright sun by clouds. Only when the clouds had shifted slightly had he even guessed the truth and then the veil had closed again. Through fear. But what was there to fear?

He choked out, 'Rosie.' She stepped back when she saw the look on his face, clasping her hands in front of her breast.

'Take them away, my heart,' he said huskily.

Slowly she did so, stretching them at first uncertainly, then with a blinding certainty out to him. Did he or she move first? Afterwards they could not remember. What did it matter when they were in each other's arms and he was smothering her with kisses, his hands running through her damp hair, her arms round him, muttering words of love and adoration; she remembered later a 'dammit Rosie, you're covered in water again', as his hands travelled down her back where the sun had not dried it.

'I love you, Jake,' she said shakily as his mouth released hers. It did not seem to be her saying it, but some voice that had always been within her demanding to be heard and now at last set free.

'We've always loved each other,' he said, shaking his head in bewilderment. 'Rosie.' He kissed her mouth, her neck, her breasts, exclaiming with wonder and desire. The feel of his body against hers was so natural, so right, that she pressed closer till she felt him react and pull away. 'Rosie, don't let me,' he cried. 'It's not fair to you.'

The words made no sense. She knew as surely as when she had first seen that kite fly on the hillside that this was her future, this her life, and he the only man she would ever want.

She took her arms from around him, stepped back, took off the shirt, cast it aside and came to him again. Then as she clung to him, the world went sideways, as if she was lifting into the air, as if in Astra, and the ground, the world, was slipping away beneath her, topsy-turvy, as he lowered her to the grass and he was lying over her; she willed his hands to stop the ache within her, as he touched her then stopped. 'Rosie, are you sure you love me?' he managed to say anxiously. 'I can't—'

'Yes, oh yes.' Why did he even need to ask it, she was thinking hazily. At least she was aware of his slipping to one side, tearing off his clothes, then he was with her again.

'I can't – I must—' he murmured.

'I don't want you to stop,' she cried clearly, distinctly before his mouth closed over hers.

His eyes were dark with love as he held her.

'Is it always as nice as this?' she murmured hazily, wriggling luxuriously as the bees buzzed in the clover around them.

'Better,' he said, 'better. It gets better and better. You'll see. So that when we're eighty, it will be best of all. Rosie—' he hesitated '—did I hurt you?'

'No. Only just a bit at first. Jake, I never knew this was love,' she informed him in wonder.

'I guess it's like flying. Before you've done it, you think you know what it will be like up there in the heavens, but nothing prepares you for that first time when you fly out of the cloud into the blue sky and sun above. Like that sunburst carving on the Lodge door, Rosie. Remember?'

'I remember.' The wasted time. Four, no five years ago, and all that time Jake had been there. Suppose he'd never returned from France, suppose she'd lost him for ever – and suppose she'd married Harry. She could smile at the very idea now, but it had been a near thing.

'Why did I not know then that I loved you?' she asked in wonder.

'Too busy being impressed with your motorcar friend.'

'And you with Peggy Wilkins's bosom.'

'She has fine intellectual qualities, has Peggy.'

'In that case Harry is another Lewis Waller. Can't you see the women in the gallery fainting with ecstasy if Harry appeared on stage?'

'Not from pleasure, I can't. Anyway, what about me? Don't you think I could qualify for some Waller-worship?'

'Oh yes,' she said, kissing his lips lightly, then his chest, and running her lips down. His skin was warm, responsive.

'Rosie,' he said huskily, 'do you mind being a fallen woman all over again?'

'I suppose,' Jake said reluctantly some time later, 'we'd better continue to Exeter.'

'Are you upset at having lost the race?' she asked lazily.

'Lost it? We won, my heart, we won.'

She scrambled to her feet. 'I'd better have a look at poor Astra.'

'Aren't you forgetting something?' he called after her.

'What?'

'Your clothes. It might occasion some comment at Exeter.'

She ran back, laughing, prancing over the grass, and picked up her overalls. 'They're dry,' she said, pleased, 'and so are my drawers.'

Jake ruefully examined his crumpled shirt, gingerly put it on and went to help her pull Astra out of the mud.

'Do you think you'd better come in the monoplane with me?' he asked suddenly.

She turned in surprise. 'Why? Astra will be all right; it's just a bump on the nose.'

He swallowed, nothing to say. How to explain that he couldn't bear to let her go from him now; suppose Astra was faulty? She'd be risking her life. But he had not the courage to put it into words. She turned to climb into

Astra, hesitated and turned back to kiss him, something of his worry communicating itself to her.

'I'll be all right,' she said, 'and so will both of us – now.'

A flame leapt into his eyes, and he walked quickly away after swinging Astra's propeller.

The monoplane was waiting, looking lonely now with its single seat. Astra accelerated past him, a wave of the hand from Rosie. 'Sunburst,' he said in wonder. 'That's the Mighty Mono's name – of course. *Sunburst*! Out of the clouds and into the blue.'

'Sunburst,' he yelled after her.

'What?'

But his call was lost in the noise and the wind, as he turned back to where Sunburst awaited him. Then he realised. Who the hell was going to swing *his* propeller? But the gods were with him that day, he had sung his song well, for a farmer's boy came whistling along the track in the next field. In a trice he was commandeered into service, hanging on to the monoplane's tail as if his life depended on it, while Jake switched on the engine, leapt out to swing the propeller, and back again. Then a wave and a grin to the boy and he was off, soaring into the sky in Sunburst as if this were the first flight, the first morning of the world.

Without surprise, he realised that Robert Bellowes had been lying; today had been the first time for Rosie. Only the fog of misunderstanding had led him to pay any credence at all to Bellowes. That something had happened between Bellowes and Rosie was clear, but whatever it was it didn't affect Rosie and himself. Nothing that Bellowes or Clairville Jones could do would ever affect them again. Not just a sunburst now, that first moment of joyous recognition was past. And ahead of them the sun was shining *in gloria*.


'What's the matter, Thomas? Will it not come right?'

Polly's quiet voice made Thomas jump as he studied, frowning in anxiety over his painting on the easel, glancing from model to canvas worriedly. The concept was in his mind; it would not come on paper. Perhaps it was because of the noise of the small crowded streets outside, the music drifting in snatches in through the open window from the Moulin de la Galette. But he knew it was not. It was because of the sitter. Polly had inspired the idea, but there was something in the way. A barrier that the artist could not cross because the man dared not.

'May I see?' she asked gently.

A nod and Polly relaxed from the uncomfortable position of the pose, stretching her arms above her head to ease away the aching. He glanced at her calm beautiful face with its haunting eyes. 'The Dream' – the idea that had obsessed him for years, and now seemed attainable with Polly as model. The unattainable, to be captured in paint. The reality, he glanced round, was his untidy studio, large by Montmartre standards, but subject to everyday life and its problems. He wanted to capture the look in Polly's eyes, perhaps it was a dream, perhaps she sought something, her Gabriel perhaps, he thought without envy. Her blue dress rustled, as she came to stand by his side. A silence as she gazed at it.

'It's good,' she said at last, 'but it's not what you wanted, is it?'

'No.'

She did not reply but instead crossed to the far side of the studio where there was a large Chinese screen.

'What are you doing?' His voice was sharp.

She emerged again, her face flushed and her fingers unbuttoning her dress. 'Thomas, we both know you'll never get this canvas right unless you have a nude model.'

'No,' he shouted. 'No, Polly.' His face was torn with anguish.

'But why not?' she asked more tranquilly than she felt.

'No.' His face was angry, as he stood up abruptly, knocking the easel askew as he did so. 'Not you, Polly. I'll get another model.'

'You mean I'm not right for the picture?' she asked, upset.

'No, I do not mean that.'

'But I don't mind—'

'I *do*!' he shouted, his face red.

Her head jerked up, as she saw the expression on his face and looked away, flushing red. 'Thomas?' she asked gently, questioningly. 'Do you love me?'

'*Ja! Ich liebe dich*,' he said heavily. '*Aber ich kanne nicht* – Polly, I want—' He broke off and looked at her in despair.

She laid a finger across his mouth, then slowly, deliberately, with no need of the screen this time, continued the unbuttoning of the blue dress, slipping it off, her pale shoulders glowing in the studio light above, slim hips swathed in the froth of petticoats. Her hands went to loosen them, but he caught her hands in his.

'How can I?' he said fiercely, as much to himself as her. How could he, when fate had already decreed what his life was to be. 'You—'

'You said you loved me, Thomas,' she said simply.

He drew her hands to his lips and kissed them passionately in answer. 'You are and ever will by my life, my living, my meaning, but—'

'Thomas,' she interrupted quietly. 'I waited once before and life cheated me of Gabriel. Now I – think I love you, and I want your arms around me.'

Disbelief changed to hesitance, hesitance to flaring joy, joy added desire, as he moved close to her and took her in his arms. 'You are sure?' he asked once more, but stopped her lips in case she should answer no. Then, lost, he bent down and holding her close against his chest, carried her to the couch, and laid her on it. With his large sensitive fingers he took off her remaining clothes, then his own. Blushing slightly, Polly's hand involuntarily moved to cover herself as he gazed at her beauty, but made no demur when he gently removed it.

'The dream,' he said with a sigh.

Then all was a confusion of sensation, of half-muttered, half-sung it seemed, words of love, and his hands moving from one part of her body to another, arousing sensation after sensation; Thomas, Thomas all around her, and with her, and on her, and finally, when she thought there could be no greater pleasure, in her.

'Thomas,' she said shyly afterwards, 'weren't we right to love? Now I feel I'm really yours.'

'Yes,' he said gratefully, overwhelmingly, 'now you are mine,' and held her as though he dared the world itself to try to tear her from him.

# Chapter Eleven

Behind them the sun glowed golden pink; in front the fading light beckoned mysteriously, cocooning them in a caul of love. Bewitched, Rosie held Astra's controls lightly as if she flew a thoroughbred steed powered by the heavens themselves. They had been away only thirty-six hours, yet in that time an invisible line had drawn itself between the past and an unexpected, bright future, dazzling in its promise. Awed on the threshold, they glanced at each other from time to time as if to ensure that the other were still there, half questioning, half exultant at the gates of their Eden.

'Now I know why Tennyson said "'tis better to have loved and lost than never to have loved at all",' she had said. Sometime. Somewhere. Where? When? She could not remember and it mattered not.

'No,' he replied abruptly, fiercely. 'No,' and his eyes held a sudden fear.

He had come to her in the hotel they had stayed in overnight. She had been fearful that he would not, that whatever dragons of doubt had lain within him would fire up to engulf him, now that the day was done. She was sitting in bed bolt upright, waiting for him, a coverlet draped round her bare shoulders, a slim dark figure in the deepening twilight. Her head turned as he came in, his eyes full of love, yet hesitant as if unsure of his welcome. But no longer. Three strides and he was beside her, sitting on the bed. He took her into his arms.

'We shouldn't—' he had said, but did not release her.

'Why not?'

'It's too risky without—'

A short silence, as she realised what he was trying to say.

'That's all right,' she said encouragingly. 'You can design a Potts Baby flying machine.'

A ripple of laughter ran through him as he held her close to him, slipping off the coverlet from her shoulders. 'Tomorrow,' he said thickly, 'I *will* be good. Rosie, why can't I get this damned blanket off?' he added plaintively.

'I think I'm sitting on it.' She wriggled until it came free. 'Next time I go flying with you,' she added, 'I'll pack a lacy lawn nightdress strapped to the mainplane.'

'Why?' he asked, kissing her breasts, but her answer, if any, was lost in the drumming of his heartbeat and the sweetness of his kiss.

Jake's time in Sunburst back to Eastchurch beat Harry Clairville Jones's to Exeter. It gave him satisfaction, even if it did not qualify for any prizes or officially knock Clairville Jones from his coveted position. Jake made only a brief stop at Amesbury and a quick landing near Guildford to adjust an aileron, where onlookers flocked to help him restart the engine. Otherwise he had an unbroken flight. People stopped their work in the fields to stare up at him. Aeroplanes were a more common sight now, though not common enough for the strange-looking machines not to be vociferously cheered as they chugged their way overhead.

Jake landed and looked round for Astra. It was not in sight, and he conducted the official discussions with the Royal Aero Club officials abstractedly. Surely Rosie couldn't have got so far behind? He told himself firmly that before yesterday he would not have been worried; he would have had confidence in her ability to overcome any problems – but that was before yesterday and now he knew it was different. He swallowed to relieve the sudden dryness in his throat. He'd passed her only a quarter of an hour before and there seemed nothing wrong with Astra then. A sickness welled up inside him, unable to keep back visions of Astra plummeting down, or worse, spiralling down, Rosie inside, helpless, doomed.

'You are tired, *mon ami*,' said Jean-Michel, concerned. He had come to welcome them back to Eastchurch. Jake managed to nod, but his eyes went past Jean-Michel to search the empty skies. Then suddenly out of the evening light emerged the shape of a biplane. He swallowed. Steady. It could be a Short; it could be any number of other aeroplanes coming in to land on the Royal Aero Club grounds.

But it was Astra. Rosie landed with a slight bump, and jumped out happily, if a trifle shamefacedly seeing her bad landing had been observed. 'I followed the wrong railway line,' she explained. 'I found myself over Canterbury. Jake – what's the matter? You weren't really worried, were you?'

'Yes,' he said simply, and to mask his relief he went to help wheel Astra in.

Jean-Michel's face bore an interested expression as he glanced thoughtfully from the one to the other.

'So,' he whispered in Rosie's ear. 'Jake does not like women, *hein*?'

'It appears,' she said, the happiness shining from her face, 'that I was wrong.'

'And it is good this, yes?'

She grinned at him, and laughed when she saw the complacent expression on his face. How did he know, she wondered afterwards, peering at herself in the mirror? Was it written so clearly on her face for all to see? The face looked just the same to her, small, almost-heartshaped, two eyes, a nose and a mouth in the same places they'd always been. How could it look different to anyone else?

'I'm in love,' she told her reflection severely, and with some wonder at the sound of these strange words. 'Also, I am loved,' she added. Such momentous statements she could not yet quite believe; only the almost physical dizziness that seemed to befog her every movement and thought convinced her that this was indeed the case.

\* \* \*

255

'Mr Swithin, you have your eyes shut again,' Rosie shouted in despair over her shoulder to her pupil passenger, over the noise of the Pinot.

Mr Thomas Swithin's eyes were tight shut, his hands clasped firmly round Rosie's waist, as Daisy Belle took two decorous turns of the airfield.

'Mr Swithin, are you sure you wish to continue with lessons?' she had asked before they left the ground. Even on the ground runs, his face had been the colour of chalk.

'I have to,' he had replied dolorously. 'Miss Maud Pettigrew will not marry me,' he explained, 'unless I prove I am a person of daring. I am a bank clerk, you see, Miss Potts,' he added rather pathetically. 'It is difficult to be daring at a desk.'

Rosie hid a smile. 'But surely Miss Pettigrew would not want you to do something you did not enjoy.'

Mr Swithin reflected on Miss Maud Pettigrew. 'Yes,' he had said finally. 'If she considers it for my own good. Perhaps she is right,' he sighed, averting his eyes from Daisy Belle, which he and Rosie had pushed out ready for the big flight ahead, when they would actually leave the ground, to get the feel of being in the air.

'Then,' said Rosie determinedly, 'we will make sure that you learn to fly *quickly*.'

Now, thirty feet up in the air, she could feel his hand trembling as he obediently rested it on hers, to sense her handling of the controls. 'Don't clutch me so hard,' she yelled, alarmed. 'Gently, gently.'

After they had landed she jumped out almost as shaken as he. He sat down on the grass, head in hands.

'Mr Swithin,' said Rosie, standing over him grimly, 'you're my first pupil and I'm not going to give up, so nor can you.'

He groaned feebly.

'In there *now*,' she ordered, ignoring Jake's agonised expression as he wandered by curiously.

'But that's a – that's a—' Mr Swithin's voice rose in a crescendo as his gaze followed her pointing finger.

'A monoplane. I know.'

'They're dangerous,' he yelped.

'Sunburst isn't.' Fortunately for Jake's peace of mind this was not his original Sunburst, but another of the same model that the Sittingbourne factory had manufactured for the school.

School was in fact a rather grandiose name for it at the moment. A hastily erected wooden hut divided into two classrooms, and a tender to ferry pupils to and from the railway station were the only tangible signs of a school.

To his evident enjoyment, William had a major role in the school. He was now Tutor of Aviation Theory, taking his duties both seriously and with verve; he had evolved an intricate teaching method, involving numerous paper models of aeroplanes, which he threw with gusto from his chair, leaving the patient pupils to pick them up. There were in fact only two pupils so far, but William behaved as grandiloquently as though he addressed a score each time he opened his mouth.

Mr Swithin trundled across the grass at a decorous seven miles per hour in Sunburst II, consoled to discover that he was not expected yet awhile to take the monster up into the air and perform figures of eight. Painfully slowly he learned the use of the rudder, and then when at last he increased in speed and gained a fraction of confidence, the tail came up off the ground on the grand day he hurtled across the grass at twenty miles per hour, hand clenching on the controls.

'Do I fly now?' he asked without much hope, after this earth-shattering achievement.

'Fly!' snorted Jake derisively. 'Mr Swithin, for some considerable time you will remain closer to the ground than a warthog hunting for grubs.' Rosie shot him a withering look.

'Yes, Mr Smith,' breathed Thomas Swithin respectfully. He hesitated. 'But would it be in order for me to reassure Miss Maud Pettigrew?'

'By all means do so, Mr Swithin,' replied Rosie gravely.

'Sunburst,' murmured Rosie lovingly, as she traced with delicate fingers the old carving in the wood above the door of the Lodge. They had been back from Exeter for two weeks now and August was here in triumphant golden glory. Rosie seemed to have gone round in a daze ever since, love suspended as if they deliberately paused on its threshold. And always Jake's eyes on her, filling her with a glow both physical and emotional, longing for his arms, yet savouring the waiting. There had been a snatched hour away from the school, wandering over the fields, until he turned to her with a muffled 'Rosie' and she was in his arms. There had been the evenings with long cool walks when he talked of the past, of the gold seekers of the Yukon, of the Leadville silver mines, of the wide open ranches and his times with the cowboys of Wyoming and Texas, and of Wild West shows.

'I can't imagine you as a sharp shooter.'

'Rosie, I've been everything in that darn show,' Jake said feelingly, 'except the fat lady herself.' He talked and talked, but never spoke of Florence. She was banished now, dissolved into a past which had no more power to hurt, he told himself. Only at night would doubts return. Not of Rosie herself, but of fate which could bless and then as swiftly take away. 'Kate's away,' Jake explained now, more casually than he felt, 'on a visit to her aunt.'

'Her aunt,' she noticed he said. Not 'ours'. Did he still not feel part of this land?

She was not sorry Kate was away for relations had not improved between them and apart from a formal politeness, there was little contact between them; a tension existed that was lifted the moment Jake said Kate was absent. The Lodge showed many signs of Kate's neat handiwork, however, the unrelieved bachelor starkness had given place to simple comfort and the kitchen was full of herbs drying for the winter.

They went into the garden and Jake pulled her into his arms. 'I don't know you in this dress,' he said. 'I'm so used to seeing you in those darned overalls of yours – or nothing.'

'Doesn't it suit me?' she asked anxiously, a little hurt, for she had personally designed it for the dressmaker with some care. She'd never thought that overalls *suited* her; they were just practical.

He gravely inspected the dusky pink cotton dress.

'It suits you,' he agreed and kissed her. He meant it to be a gentle kiss of re-establishment – but she responded so sweetly that somehow the kiss become longer and more passionate.

'You remember when Polly and Gabriel were here?' she asked after a few minutes. 'Do you think they left a little of their magic behind in this garden? Some of their laughter?'

'Perhaps, but I guess we've plenty of our own. Come here and we'll make some more.' Then, as she put her arms round him again, he said idly; 'Do you like it in the Lodge? Would you be happy here or shall we find somewhere else?'

She looked at him questioningly. 'Live here, do you mean?'

'When we're married,' he said, surprised.

A flood of happiness swept over her. Married? Ridiculous to say she hadn't thought of it, but there had been so much to think of, that there had seemed time enough.

'Why are you gaping like a goldfish?' Jake enquired, romantically.

'I didn't know – I didn't – yes, I did – but you never said. Oh Jake!' She flung herself into his arms with such force that he staggered back under the onslaught, losing his balance and collapsing with her to the ground.

'Darn it, I forgot—' he said as they sorted themselves out.

'It doesn't matter,' she said, half laughing, half crying.

He promptly leapt to his feet. 'It does though.' He rushed round the garden gathering a bouquet of love-in-a-mist, and returned to her, falling contritely on one knee. 'Dearest Rosie, will you marry me?'

'I feel we should be a little more formal,' she told him severely. 'After all, Mr Swithin does not speak of Miss Pettigrew as dearest Maudie.'

'Miss Rose Potts,' he tried again, meekly, 'will you be mine?'

'Are you a man of daring, Mr Smith?'

'I have aspirations,' he told her loftily, 'to acquire the art of banking.'

'Then I will espouse you,' she said, bestowing her hand in grand fashion, with a wicked smile, '*now.*'

He plucked two flowers from the bouquet and stuck them in the low neck of her gown.

'Now,' he answered gravely, 'would suit me very well.'

The low-ceilinged bedroom was cool after the heat of the garden and the lavender-perfumed sheets cool to their touch, as his warm hands held her.

'Do you think that dearest Maudie is as happy as I am?' she whispered to him afterwards as he lay in her arms, and the kiss that he placed on her lips was answer enough.

'Bless me,' said William irritated, 'it's a big step. I suppose you're sure?' he asked hopefully. This disruption to his establishment was far from welcome. But he was a fair-minded man. He could hardly deny that Rosie was old enough at twenty-three to get married or that Jake was a highly suitable husband from all points of view. Yet he disliked change and with Polly no longer at Brynbourne he had begun to rely more and more on Rosie's cheerful whirlwind presence around the house. He consulted Mildred, half hoping she might provide some practical reason for his doubts. But she did not.

'Anyone but you, William, would have seen it coming long ago.'

'Really?' he said, surprised.

'Besides,' Mildred pointed out, 'it isn't as if he's taking her away. They'll live right on our doorstep and you'll see them every day if you wish.'

'That's very true, my dear.' He brightened up. 'In fact they could live here.'

'That is not a good idea, William.'

William sighed. 'Perhaps not. Perhaps Polly may come home now,' he ventured hopefully.

'I doubt it, William. She seems very happy in Paris,' Mildred said wistfully.

'I can't look, Jake,' cried Rosie, agonised. It was

*her* Astra, since the teaching aircraft, Astra II, was unserviceable at the time, owing to Mr Swithin's unfortunate ministrations with it yesterday. Astra was taking off with Mr Swithin at the controls on his first real solo. True, he had several times previously at a height of ten feet steered an unsteady path to the other side of the field, landed Astra with agonising thumps, turned the aeroplane round and flown back again. But this time heaven itself was to be conquered. A whole circuit was to be undertaken at a more respectable height.

At first Mr Swithin seemed to be making a beeline for the only oak tree at the far end of the field; he managed to avoid this at the last moment, turning to the left to head in equally determined fashion for the instruction shed, apparently intent on taking his instructor's head with him. Jake and Rosie fell flat on their faces as Astra swept over them, Mr Swithin's face clearly visible set in an expression of horror as though a Mr Hyde hidden deep within the soul of Thomas Swithin had suddenly burst forth to take the controls.

Then Astra rose steeply to clear the shed, after yawing wildly.

'I can't watch any more,' said Rosie, anguished, dusting herself down.

'Don't worry,' said Jake cheerfully, picking up his cap. 'Astra II will be back in service tomorrow.'

'It's not the aeroplane I'm worried about,' Rosie said, despite her declaration watching Mr Swithin nobly attempting a right-hand turn and fail, sinking dangerously low over the sea. 'It's the thought of what I'd say to Miss Maud Pettigrew that scares me.'

Kate received Jack's letter telling her of his engagement, reading it without surprise but with no warmer feelings towards Rosie. Robert had been right. The girl had been determined to ensnare Jack after Harry had seen through her, and her act of breathless innocence had worked on Jack (she still could not think of her brother as anything else). He was as gullible now as he had been as a little boy – at least where girls were concerned. He was too gentle for the wiles of someone like Rosie Potts. Jack was the older brother she'd always adored, despite the years of waiting for him to return from the US, the years of looking after Ma while she was ill – and then, just as everything seemed all right and Jack was back, Ma had died. No one had ever thought long about Kate herself. Even Jack thought of her merely as a problem to be solved, she told herself without self-pity. It was the lot of women, that they were seen by their menfolk as a duty. But it would not always be so. She was and always had been able to look after herself, or so she had thought until now. She would have to return for the engagement dance – and to see Robert. Her head went up proudly. This was one further problem she would cope with alone. Only one person could help her with this – Robert.

Astra came in yawing wildly and, against all the rules, landing straight in a side wind.

'Turn *into* the wind, Mr Swithin,' Rosie yelled feebly, conscious that he would not be able to hear, but hoping some sixth sense might yet make her message get through. It did not, but somehow, anyhow, Astra slithered to a stop. No aviator jumped out eagerly, however. Jake's long legs covered the ground more quickly than Rosie. Is he ill – what's happened? Her heart was thudding, hoping that her joke about Maudie would not be put into practice. By the time she reached Astra Jake was grinning. 'He's fainted, that's all,' he said laconically.

Mr Swithin opened an ashen eyelid. He looked at the ground as if unbelieving of its solidity beneath him, then at his mentors. 'I flew,' he said slowly. 'I did it *all*. The turns, the figures of eight – everything. Have I passed?'

Rosie looked at the Club officials who had come to join them. 'Just,' said one grudgingly.

'Oh!' Mr Swithin's face became a mask of joy. 'Now I need never fly again,' he said thankfully. 'Thank heavens.'

'Thank Rosie,' said Jake, more practically.

The Kent Aviation School had now had two pupils, both of whom had their Royal Aero Club certificates. The news travelled speedily round the aviation world, and gave two of its members pause to think: Robert Bellowes and Henry Clairville Jones.

Brynbourne Place was showing its most attractive face once more for the engagement dance to celebrate Rosie and Jake's betrothal. Polly came home from Paris on a visit, looking lovelier and happier than Rosie had seen her since Gabriel's death.

'Do you remember our eighteenth birthday dance, Polly?' Rosie said, adjusting the beaded fringe on the hem of Polly's lavender satin ball gown. Too late she remembered what had happened there.

'Yes,' replied Polly calmly. 'Of course. I met Gabriel.'

'Polly, I'm sorry,' Rosie hugged her, the bead fringes rattling furiously. 'I'm always putting my foot in it.'

'No, it's all right. I can think of Gabriel calmly now that there's Thomas.'

'You love him, Polly?' asked Rosie doubtfully. Much as she liked Thomas, a greater contrast to Gabriel could not be imagined.

'Not in the same way as I did Gabriel. And for that I'm glad. Nothing, *nothing* could ever be as glorious or as bad again. I love Thomas because he's honest and good and kind – I don't feel sick with love and I know that this time that's right for me. I'm going to live with him, Rosie,' she added, half shyly, half proudly.

'Will you not get married?' asked Rosie, shocked, not so much at this bohemian unconventionality, but that it should be Polly for whom she wanted all things straight and pure and good, who was proposing this.

'Some day, but not until Thomas can afford it. It worries him that I have so much money and he so little. He says I must be free until he can afford to keep me in the way to which I am accustomed. Free! How foolish men are,' Polly said fondly.

'But to ask you to live with him, that's not honourable,' Rosie pursued, still faintly worried.

'That was my idea,' said Polly blithely. 'He wanted to remain as we were but if we can't be married, then I said I wanted to be as close as possible. And so many of the students do it,' she added anxiously. 'You won't tell Father, will you? It took a lot to persuade Thomas but now he's agreed. So there you are,' she smiled happily. 'Now we're both happy. You *are*, aren't you?'

'Oh *yes*, said Rosie. 'Just think – all that time and I nearly lost Jake through my own stupidity. I actually thought I'd marry Harry.' She shook her head in wonder at the strange ways of fate.

Jean-Michel wandered into the supper room still strewn with the remains of the buffet. He had danced with every fat matron in the country, as well as every stiffly stayed one, and precious few of their daughters. His duty was done. He was restless. Perhaps it was because Rosie was so happy with Jake that he felt dissatisfied. Perhaps he should have married Rosie himself. No, engines were his work, but he could not bear the thought of aeroplanes monopolising his social life, let alone his private life. *Non*. He wanted a wife *pour m'amuser* as he put it, and that verb did not include aeroplanes. Her sister was a beauty, was she not? But something in her eyes told him she was not for him, even had not Rosie warned him firmly that Polly's heart was bestowed elsewhere. At first that had excited him – it would be fun perhaps. He had an interesting talk about Paris with Polly, but there was no hint of that spark, that animation, that told him a lady was delightfully aware of the overpowering charm of Jean-Michel Pinot.

Picking up a lonely macaroon on a large silver plate, he noticed a handsome, dark-haired girl standing by herself at the French windows, gazing into the garden, and wearing the most unbecoming dress he had ever seen. Here was one person who was not enjoying herself. A difficult one perhaps, but then Jean-Michel liked a challenge; he also had a kind heart.

'You are free for this dance, mademoiselle? Permit me perhaps to introduce myself.'

Kate eyed him frostily and cut in before he could do so, 'Thank you, I do not dance.'

'Ah, but no one does not wish to dance with Jean-Michel Pinot.'

Pinot – wasn't that the engine man that Jack was always talking about? Kate's heart sank. She avoided the factory and Eastchurch and Jack's friends as much as possible, preferring the society of the school and the Workers' Educational classes she was starting.

Unsophisticated, she was unused to men like Jean-Michel and no match for his charm. He took her hand gently and despite her protests led her quickly on to the terrace where people were dancing, so that only by causing a public scene could she have escaped.

'You will regret this rashness, Mr Pinot,' she warned him stiffly. 'I am not a good dancer.'

'Splendid,' he retorted quickly. 'I do not dance well either. So we save ourselves the trouble and we sit together and talk of many things over a glass of champagne.'

'I was not aware that I wished to—'

'Your eyes tell me that you wish it—' he interrupted firmly.

'Do they also tell you that—' she snapped back before he interrupted again.

'They tell me that you are a little lost, I think.'

She rose jerkily to her feet. 'Thank you, but—'

He leapt up contritely. 'Ah, do not desert me, mademoiselle. You must forgive me. It is my French awkwardness.'

She eyed him suspiciously. 'What do you want to talk about?' she asked resignedly as he led her to a secluded seat in the rose garden.

'I want to know everything about you,' he said seriously. It was a request that rarely failed to strike a ready response. 'I want to know the flowers you like, and your views on Descartes. I want to know what fills your dreams, and the name of your favourite doll. I want to know what you live for and whether you are enamoured of *tripes de Caen*.'

A smile lit up her face, one full of an unaccustomed mischief. 'Mr Pinot. I shall answer you. Believe me, I shall tell you all. I shall *bore* you away from me.'

And she began.

Exactly fifty-three minutes later Jean-Michel was in love.

Michael Potts wandered around bitterly at the party. No one took any notice of him, and he hid a broken heart with a thunderous and stern expression. He had discounted any threat from Jake, after his return to Kent, since Rosie showed no sign of having alleviated her previous dislike of him. Michael was fifteen now, and his passion for Rosie had deepened rather than lessened. He convinced himself that he had been betrayed, and that Rosie had been seduced from him.

'What's the matter, Michael?' Rosie suddenly appeared, her apricot satin skirt swirling out behind her. She put an affectionate arm round him. 'You promised me a dance.'

'Nothing's the matter,' he replied stiffly. 'I don't feel like dancing, that's all.'

It was true. The sight of Jake and Rosie dancing together, staring into each other's eyes so rapturously, had quite put him off. His would be a lonely future. He would be a bachelor all his life. He knew that now. A bachelor – with revenge on his mind.

'Kate, this is our dance, isn't it?' Jake appeared by her side, belatedly taking in who she was with. He need not have worried after all. Kate was in good hands.

'Forgive me, Monsieur Pinot,' Kate said swiftly. 'My brother is a very persistent man. And I do enjoy dancing with him so much.'

She rose up with a mocking smile. Jean-Michel had been enraptured to discover Kate's identity. But Kate underestimated him. He was not a whit taken aback at her flagrant insult. He was merely planning his next move, a normal procedure for him but never before had he been so uncertain what it should be. And never before had it mattered so much.

'You seem to be getting on well with Jean-Michel,' Jake said as he whirled her away.

'Him? Oh, but one can't take him seriously,' she answered carelessly.

'How can you be so sure? You know, you worry me, Kate.'

'Do I?' she said flatly, not inviting a response.

'You refuse to have much to do with my work or with the Potts, though they invite you often enough. You refuse Rosie's overtures—' She flushed red, about to retort but he went on, 'and spend all your time with these classes for the villagers. I can appreciate that after what we went through at school, but why *avoid* us?'

She did not answer, but the reason was quite simple. She knew all about the Potts – Robert had told her everything.

'And when shall we marry?' Jake asked her beneath the stars.

'Soon,' Rosie whispered, close to him. 'As soon as we can leave the school for a week or so.'

'I want to wake up and find you there beside me. And not with this scratchy net bodice thing on either.'

'I wriggle a lot,' she pointed out. 'It might not be such fun. And this scratchy net thing is very fashionable.'

'October? We can close the school for a week or two then, and we can be by ourselves. Where shall we go on honeymoon?'

'The Kill Devil Hills?' she murmured wickedly.

'If you want,' he said drily. 'I thought of Venice, but if you prefer dusty old sand dunes, fine. We could throw in a couple of visits to the Dayton factories as well.'

'Perhaps Venice will do.'

In his study at Court Manor Robert Bellowes greeted Kate politely, much as he might any casual visitor. 'I am sorry to hear your news.' The eyes were cold.

Kate gasped. 'Aren't you even interested that I'm to bear your child?'

'I of course regret that our pleasant friendship should end this way for you, but I have no proof that the child is mine,' he pointed out gently.

Kate was uncomprehending, then outraged, a red mist

267

of anger clouding her eyes. 'But you know I'd never – You know, you know that I, had never—'

'My dear Kate, how shall I put this? You showed a most gratifying enthusiasm thereafter, perhaps for myself, perhaps for your newly acquired knowledge. How do I know there have been no further gentlemen, any number of which might have been as honoured as—' He stopped as Kate's hand struck him forcibly on the jaw.

'I'm sorry you should feel that way, dear Kate,' he managed to say, eyes glittering. 'Of course, despite what I say, if money would assist you in any way—' He stopped as Kate, staring at him in disgust, simply turned on her heel and left.

He wondered briefly whether he'd done the right thing in making an enemy of her, then dismissed her from his mind.

How could she have been such a fool? Kate thought, sick with shock. Loneliness? No, ever truthful, she forced herself to acknowledge that she had simply been flattered that someone of Mr Bellowes's standing should have taken notice of her, Kate Smith. How could she have been so stupid as to lap up all his flattery and attention? And why had he pursued her so determinedly? For her own sake? Hardly. Too late, she realised she was simply a pawn in whatever game he was playing.

And what, she thought in despair, could pawns do once they were swept from the board?

Harry Clairville Jones bowed politely to young Mr Michael Potts as – just by chance – he occasioned to meet him in Canterbury, and invited him to partake of a brandy and soda at a nearby hostelry. Flattered by the attention as well as by the brandy, Michael waxed eloquent when asked casually how the Flying School progressed and, as an afterthought, production at the Sittingbourne factory where the first orders for all three aircraft were being processed. Exaggeration might have entered into Michael's replies, though he was torn between pride at Potts's achievements and loathing of the man who had made it all possible.

He had few qualms about talking so. After all, he'd nothing against old Harry, he told himself; it was quite clear to him now that that unpleasantness between Harry and Jake had been engineered by Jake himself. It became increasingly clear to Michael as they talked that poor old Clairville Jones had had a rotten deal. He remembered the many occasions when Harry Clairville Jones had been jolly decent to him, giving him rides in the Clairville, so that he could tell the chaps at school about it. Yes, he had a lot to thank him for. It wasn't Harry's fault that after the Potts had treated him so badly he had been forced to take up with Robert Bellowes. That dark episode was firmly in Michael's past now, but the taste it left behind was not forgotten. Nevertheless, that was between himself and Bellowes – Harry didn't come into it.

'Not too keen on our Mr Smith, are you – not that I blame you,' said Harry casually.

'Common sort of chap,' said Michael grandly. 'A rough diamond. Comes from the East End, you know.'

'I couldn't agree with you more,' said Harry flatteringly. 'I wonder now – the idea's just occurred to me. You know I have a few scores to settle with Mr Smith—' he grinned deprecatingly. 'Wouldn't it be rather a lark to pull him down a peg or two?' Michael's eyes brightened. 'There's some kind of gala day at the school – a flying display to attract new pupils, so I've heard—'

'Yes,' said Michael. 'Next week.' He ought to know. Rosie had been unable to talk about anything else for the last two or three weeks, dragging that fellow's name into the conversation at every opportunity.

'Wouldn't it be a lark,' Harry continued excitedly, 'if when they opened up the shed in the morning they found it scattered with suffragette slogans and banners, pictures of Mrs Pankhurst and—'

'By jove, yes,' breathed Michael. 'Some woman chained to the aeroplanes perhaps—'

'Perhaps not a real woman but you're right, that's a brilliant idea – models of women tied up to the struts – I'm beginning to think the brains of the Potts family lie in you, Mr Potts.'

Michael looked modest at Harry's evident admiration. He drained the last few drops of his brandy and soda.

'That way, you see,' Harry continued, 'Mr Smith would look extremely foolish, because everyone would think his sister had organised it, since her connection with the suffragettes is so well known.'

Michael was overcome with the brilliance of the scheme. Jake could rant and rave as much as he liked – but even Rosie would lay the blame on him. She couldn't stand Kate, he knew that.

'There's just one thing,' said Harry carefully. 'We'd need to get into the shed overnight, of course.'

'No trouble about that,' said Michael in lordly fashion. He smiled thickly. 'I could help you too.'

'Better not, Mr Potts. I wouldn't want any recriminations thrown at you,' Harry said easily.

Rosie tossed and turned restlessly, unable to sleep. Why, she did not know. She got up and prowled round the bedroom uneasily, wondering whether to descend to the kitchen in search of refreshment. It was then she noticed the red glow in the sky. Odd. It was three o'clock. At almost the same moment she heard the ringing of the telephone below, and immediately the red glow over Sheppey made sense – a fear coupled with that insistent bell below. Putting her dressing gown on, she hurried out into the darkness wishing for the umpteenth time that William would have electrical lighting installed. Down below, she could see the dark shape of Wilson the butler standing with a candle by the telephone. He hung up on hearing her footsteps on the stairs and turned towards her. His words did not make sense at first.

'Fire, miss. At the aeroplane shed at Eastchurch.'

The red glow that she had seen. 'Fire,' she repeated. Then the full meaning came home to her. *The shed was alight* and inside were all the aeroplanes they possessed, lined up ready for tomorrow when thirty prospective pupils were arriving at 11 o'clock to see a flying display.

'I'll go,' she said hoarsely. Jake – how to get hold of Jake? The Lodge had no telephone. 'Wilson, can you send down to the Lodge for Mr Smith. I'll get dressed and start now.'

'Briggs, miss?'

'I'll drive myself. It's quicker. The fire people are obviously already there,' she said jerkily. Then she ran upstairs, throwing off her nightgown and seizing her overalls as the quickest, easiest garments. It couldn't really be true. This must be some ghastly nightmare she was having. She drove the new Sunbeam erratically over the one road into Sheppey; never had it seemed so far, and always the flames in the sky glaring redder. People were standing outside their cottages staring. How long had it been burning? Had everything gone already, their ambitions and hopes in ashes?

When she got there were two fire-engines, the old Merryweather horse-drawn chemical engine and the new petrol motor engine but, for all their efforts, a good two-thirds of the shed was alight. One side had gone completely, no shape even to tell where the aircraft had stood. A couple of aircraft had been pulled out, one of which she noted unconsciously was Astra. But her attention was on that pile of burning wood in front . . .

'Back, miss, get back—' one of the firemen cried to her, seeing Rosie rushing towards the shed. She could see that inside the flames had not yet reached Sunburst, Jake's original prototype, *their* Sunburst.

'Over there,' she screeched to a fireman, '— we can save that one.'

'No miss. Put the others out first.'

'But we can save—' No use, he had gone. She stood hesitant for a moment, then decided. She could not let Sunburst burn. Tying a handkerchief soaked in water round her face, she forced herself in – it was so near. Of course she could reach it.

Jake, pulling up and leaping out of his Renault, was in time to see Rosie disappear into the smoke. It was her back view but it could be no one else.

All the fears of his life welled up and exploded into one vast terror at the sight of her slight figure, a figure that vanished – as so many others of his loved ones had done.

'No,' he tried to shout, but panic seized his throat and no sound came out. With leaden legs as if in a nightmare, he rushed towards the burning shed.

They tried to hold him back, but he shook them off impatiently as if they were flies irritating him, and pushed through into the building. Trundling towards him was Sunburst and, behind it, smoke-ridden, coughing, clothes already smouldering, Rosie pushing it.

He fought his way to her; he seemed to be shouting 'Rosie', but still no sound came from him. He reached out for her, pushed her forward, and took over the rear position, and in seconds they were free. Spluttering, coughing, he wiped his eyes from the cinders and ashes already clogging the air. Then he saw her smouldering clothes, grabbed a bucket from a fireman and threw it over her, dousing her in cold water.

'Jake,' she tried to say jokingly, 'please don't say "you're always covered in water",' shaking herself like a terrier.

But he did not laugh.

'We got her out, Jake,' she said tentatively.

'You—' he took refuge in anger. 'You risked your life for *that* – a thing of wood and fabric—'

Her eyes clouded. 'Jake? It's not wood and fabric – it's Sunburst. It means more than that, and we've saved her.'

'I nearly lost you. Rosie, I thought I'd *lost* you. How could you do it?' His voice rose out of control.

She did not understand his anguish. 'But I'm all right.'

He stared at her, impotent to explain what he meant – what it had meant to him when he saw her disappear into the flames. The crazy feeling that life was repeating itself, an unbroken circle.

Michael Potts had seen the fire from his window. He listened to the resulting hubbub in the house. A frozen horror took over when he realised that the fire he could see was at the Eastchurch field. This was the night that Harry was going to decorate it with the suffragette banners. Had there been an accident? Something must have gone wrong, that was clear. He'd go to see Harry. With a feeling of dread, he immediately realised he didn't want to see Harry ever again; he wanted to forget all about this dreadful thing that had happened, pretend it had nothing, but nothing to do with him. It must have been an accident, he convinced himself.

'As you see, there sure isn't much left to show you.' Jake was perched on Sunburst, standing up at the controls as if to proclaim that they weren't out of business yet, and addressing the thirty or so prospective pupils who had had a surprise on their arrival at the field. Offer of temporary accommodation from both Short Brothers and the Royal Aero Club had been gratefully turned down by Jake and Rosie. The day was fine, they would use their own grounds and provide hastily arranged fare from Mrs Fisherbutt. Don't admit defeat.

'But I can tell you,' Jake went on, 'we'll be operational again in two weeks' time, just as soon as the factory can get more models turned out. Now we're going to put Sunburst and Astra through their paces so you'll see what we're capable of here—'

'I'll take Astra up, Jake,' Rosie gaily called to him, goggles on already.

'No, thank you, Miss Potts,' he said abruptly, not looking at her. 'I will take it.'

His tone of voice brooked no argument and, unable to argue it out with him there and then she was forced to give way. Jake must be tired from yesterday, she told herself. She felt haggard and drawn, and Jake looked on the point of collapse for all his fine words.

'What happened, Jake?' she asked him wearily, after everyone had gone. 'What do the firemen think caused the blaze?'

'We don't know. No idea. When they got here the doors were closed, no sign of any break-ins. It's a mystery.'

'It's an odd one,' said Rosie thoughtfully. 'We're always so careful before we lock up.'

'What does it matter?' said Jake. 'We've lost fifteen aeroplanes, uninsured, *and*,' he added grimly, 'I nearly lost you too.'

'Weren't they insured for fire?' asked Rosie, appalled.

'No. Too high a risk.'

'Is that why you're doing your best to insure me?' she asked in a low voice. 'By not letting me fly?'

'I thought I'd better take Astra up,' he said carefully, avoiding her eyes, 'just in case the fire had harmed anything we couldn't see—'

'And why should that make a difference?' she flashed at him. 'We're partners, aren't we? Why are things too dangerous for me, all right for you?'

'Your father—' he began apologetically.

'Father has nothing to do with it,' she said wearily. 'It's you and me, Jake. You know it.'

'Rosie.' He looked at her pleadingly. 'It's last night, I guess, seeing you walking into that fire. I thought – hell, I thought you weren't going to come out again.'

'But I did – you've got to trust me, Jake,' she said quietly.

'My brain tells me that,' he said despairingly. 'But I can't—'

'But we've got to be partners as well as lovers. There's no other way we can achieve what we want to.'

'It's all different now,' he said miserably. 'I can't see you go up in an aeroplane without thinking you'll crash the darn thing. I've got used to seeing you teach the pupils, but only by not thinking about it. By not watching you.'

'Surely you don't just want a little wife to protect and look after?' she cried, horrified. 'I can't do it, Jake. I'd go mad unless I can fly at your side, as well as sleep at it. You'll *have* to get used to it.'

'*How?*' The word burst from him.

'Like I do,' she said angrily. 'Do you think the same thoughts don't occur to me, don't you think my heart's not in my mouth every time you're five minutes overdue. But you have to conquer it.'

'How?' he repeated, angry that she could not understand.

'I don't know,' she said. 'But until you do—'

'Are you going to leave me?' he cut in.

She stared at him. Leave? Was he crazy? 'I can't do that, Jake, even if I wanted to. I'd never, never do that,' she cried in anguish. 'But oh, Jake, I can't marry you, not until you can accept me fully by your side.'

'Rosie—' He caught her in his arms and began to kiss her fiercely; they kissed with an intensity and passion as if what could not be sorted out in words could be smothered in the nirvana of passion.

'It's lovely, Thomas. You've made the apartment so attractive.' Polly danced round the rooms in the pride of ownership.

He watched her anxiously. 'And you will be happy here?'

'Who could not be happy, here in Montmartre, with the quietness of the vineyard on one side, and on the other all the enticements of Montmartre beckoning.' How strange, she thought, the apartment showed her what she had wanted to achieve in her painting. The two windows, one looking one way and one the other, and this apartment the meeting point. An idea for a painting began to grow in her mind, and it seemed as if Gabriel were nodding approval to her.

Outside as she looked down, a brightly dressed *midinette* ran by obviously heading for the Moulin de la Galette. To meet her sweetheart perhaps. All Paris was a meeting place for sweethearts. Polly gave a deep sigh of happiness.

'Who could not be happy, Thomas? With all this—' she swept her arm round the apartment '—and with you.' She went to him and put her arms round him; after a moment his arms enfolded her and he kissed her gently.

'We must be happy here, you and I. We *must*,' he said intensely.

# Chapter Twelve

'And about time too,' Rosie addressed an early daffodil crossly. The winter of 1910/11 had been bleak, in atmosphere as well as weather. A new king was on the throne, but somehow there wasn't the excitement, the promise of a new age as there had been with King Edward the Peacemaker. Far from peace, talk of war was in the air. Nothing definite, but hostility towards Germany seemed to be growing. France, England and Russia were in alliance, it was true, but the feeling was that even that would not deter a power-hungry Kaiser. The German bands which so enlivened the seaside resorts were eyed askance; murmurs grew about German waiters. They must all be tarred with the Kaiser's brush was the general consensus. And unrest and turmoil had been the keynote at home too. Another unsatisfactory election over the House of Lords issue, dissatisfaction in the unions, and the suffragettes becoming more and more strident in their demands for the vote.

Rosie's attitude was ambivalent towards the women's cause, when she thought about them at all. Coloured by her dislike of Kate, she was inclined to think their methods outrageous and their cause extreme. Yet she found William's views, that no woman should ever be allowed to vote, equally dubious. Jake took a more practical view that they should be given the vote on the same terms as men – and that as only about a third of the male population had the vote this problem should be addressed first.

Now at least it looked as if spring was coming. Rosie stuck her hands in her pockets and breathed a sigh of satisfaction. She was waiting for Jake to join her to go to the shed, wandering through the small wood that bordered the track to the Old Lodge. She was tired of unrest and disgruntlement. She wanted spring to come *fast*, so that flying could begin in earnest again, and the flying school enter its first full season.

No one wanted to fly much in the winter; only the real enthusiast was prepared to don thick jackets, trousers and heavy gauntlets to go up when the zephyrs of summer became the biting winds of winter, and hot soup replaced champagne on landing.

The winter had been hard work, nothing but plans, designs, experiments, tests and re-tests. The prospect of designing in effect two new aeroplanes had been daunting, but Daisy Belle II with her 90 horsepower 7-cylinder rotary Pinot and 60-foot span planes had taken to the air as sturdily as her predecessor. Sunburst had been rebuilt for pupils with ash, steel-tubing, plywood and linen, and boasting a forty-foot wing span. Astra, dear Astra, had retained the same box-kite configuration with an upgraded engine. With all this work, this promise for the future, why was she not at least content in her work?

She lay awake at night, restlessly turning in her mind over and over again whether or not she had been right to postpone the wedding, to cause misery for herself and for Jake, on a mere point of principle. All this winter they could have been together, and wasn't life itself more important than a principle? In the daytime working with him, she knew she was right – confined, constricted, not able to fly by his side, she might for love of him be tempted to give up flying. Once married to him, she would not have the willpower to deny him anything, and one look in his eyes that her flying made him unhappy, and she would submit. At least this way she could force herself to ignore it.

But how she hated the infrequent rushed meetings, lying silently in his arms, knowing she must leave and longing to stay. It could not go on. They must be forced together or be torn apart. Meanwhile, overtly at least, they both ignored the problem. Rosie thought about Browning's poem 'The Statue and the Bust' – how the couple had waited, and waited – and waited – and in the end did nothing. Would they too be like that, time driving their love to sterility? Several times she had been on the point of throwing herself into his arms, saying that she would marry him whenever he wanted, yet something had always held her back.

She looked up as she heard him coming towards her, a wave of love sweeping over her. She loved the way he looked in the mornings, bright-eyed, eager for the day, 'the pioneer look', she called it. Today it was absent, however. He looked worried and abstracted.

He didn't kiss her, merely put an arm round her shoulders, as they turned to walk to his old Renault.

'You know I was in London yesterday,' he began abruptly, as he drove the Renault towards the Sheppey road.

'Yes,' she said, surprised. 'To see Colonel Cody, wasn't it?'

'Yes, but I went to the Admiralty too, at their request. I didn't tell you, because I didn't want you getting all upset.' He grinned at her, and her immediate spark of annoyance vanished. 'They wanted to take over our field – run the flying school in fact.'

She looked puzzled. 'What for?'

'To train pilots for the Royal Navy.'

'But—' she stopped. 'You mean military flying.'

'Yup.'

'Jake! That would be the thin end of the wedge. We'd be a military establishment; pretty soon we'd be building aeroplanes for them. Then the army would—' Her voice almost squealed in alarm.

'Hold on to your curls, Rosie,' he said patiently. 'I told them no. I know how you feel about it.'

'Phew,' she breathed in relief.

'All the same,' he glanced at her, 'it's not going to go away, you know, this talk of war. And where there's talk, there's preparation.'

'But we don't have to be part of it,' she pointed out fearfully. Why did the memory of that bird suddenly come back to her? The bird that flew to a freedom only the skies could give. A freedom that might now be threatened. But not by her. Never by her. 'Even if the worst comes to the worst, and there is war, there'll still be need for civilian pilots, perhaps for mail or passenger-carrying aeroplanes, still be—'

'Sure,' he said, smiling at her.

'You're not sure at all, are you?' she said sharply.

'No.' There was silence as he drove on to the field, and she saw Daisy Belle II being wheeled out ready for the day. A lump came to her throat.

'Why not?' she asked fiercely.

'Last time I went over to France and Germany it was like a tinderbox – there's old scores to be settled, and when old scores are around, small issues are likely to provide the spark. Everything will go up, everything will change – including flying. What will you do then, Rosie? Your country or your principles?'

'It won't come.' The words died on her lips. That was no answer. 'The end justifies the means is what you're saying, Jake. I can't accept it. No good comes of compromising with the devil – and that's how I see it would be if we let our achievements be used for war.'

He said nothing.

'Say something, Jake,' she commanded, alarmed. 'Say you haven't changed – that you believe it too.'

Jake had seen men fight and die in far lands, for power, for money and for nothing more than frustration; he'd seen men rise beyond it, seek out new worlds on land, at sea and in the air, always the hope of something better driving them on; but he'd never seen evil licked for ever. So long as there were those who sought out a better world, there'd be those that tried to destroy it; and would do so if they weren't stopped. He saw himself once more, a boy of eighteen, standing in the Leadville bar outhouse whipping May's killer like he was demented. Let there be no war. Dear God, let there be no war.

The winter had been hard for others too. Michael, with the effervescence of the young, had persuaded himself that nothing he had done or said had influenced the events at the aeroplane shed in September, so he dismissed it from his conscience as an accident. He had summoned up his courage to see Harry Clairville Jones, and questioned him indignantly. He had absolutely denied he had anything to do with the fire. When he had turned up, he stated, the aircraft shed was already ablaze. Grasping at this straw, Michael had left, and any lingering doubts were pushed out of his mind by the momentous news that Rosie had postponed her marriage. To his mind, this was tantamount to its abandonment. Obviously, he reasoned, she didn't want to hurt Jake by telling him she didn't want to marry him at all, so she was going to wait for the engagement simply to peter out.

Now he was sixteen, his father kept asking him about going to university. Michael did not want to go to university. He knew precisely what he wanted to do; he wanted to run the Sittingbourne factory – at least, the sanitary ware side of it. He liked organising things, seeing how things were made, and whether they could be made more efficiently. The problem was that Father did not agree. Father was intent on his going to Oxford, and so staying at school for another two years. This was ridiculous and unfair, when Father himself had started in the business when he was fifteen. Parents were strange. They were keen on things themselves, but when you said you were too, they decided they wanted something quite different for you; and never listened to what *you* wanted. Besides, Michael didn't want to leave Brynbourne. It was bad enough being away during the week at school, but to be away for weekends too, just learning or wasting time rowing, was unthinkable.

There had been another major problem for Jake over the winter. In early September Kate had announced that she was leaving the school and her Workers' Educational classes and returning to London to their uncle and aunt. The country stifled and bored her.

'I have a feeling she's been lured back to join the suffragette movement again,' Jake had told Rosie worriedly. 'The idiot. You know what Kate's like.'

Yes. Rosie knew how proud and stubborn Kate could

be, and privately thought the movement suited her down to the ground. But she kept silent, for they had had a bitter row when she accused Jake once of mollycoddling Kate. She was an adult woman with a job and did not need his practical support. He had been furious. It was his duty, he had flashed back, to look after her until she was married. As it would be to look after her, Rosie, she had snapped back, were they to marry. He would want to rule her life. Five minutes later she was struggling between fury and tears, and Jake was white-faced with blistering anger. They had come together again immediately, passionately, both frightened at the depth of the chasm still between them.

Much as she disliked Kate, even Rosie was concerned when Jake's aunt wrote late in September to say that Kate was not staying with them, nor did they have an address for her.

'Why?' Jake asked, bewildered. 'Why would she want to disappear? Were we that unkind to her?'

Rosie's conscience pricked her. She should have tried harder to get to know Kate, and now seeing Jake's stricken face, wished with all her heart that she had.

Just before Christmas they had found out where she was, with the indefatigable help of Jean-Michel. After the party, he had cajoled her into accompanying him to the theatre one evening and invited himself to dinner at the Lodge on two others. He had been in France when Kate left Kent, however, and returned to find her gone with no message left. Jake's news that she had chosen to disappear completely surprised but did not daunt him. 'I will find your sister for you,' he announced to Jake. 'Like my engines, I never give up,' he added optimistically.

It took him over two months. Had it not been for his boast, he would have abandoned the quest in despair. It was clear that Kate did not wish to be found. But he had promised his heart, as well as Jake, that he would not rest until he had found Kate Smith. It meant calling at endless houses, with endless rebuffs. Since the French are a logical-minded people, he had reasoned that if Kate wished to disappear from her family, she would find a teaching job somewhere away, but not too far, from her old home. But all ends he had followed up had led nowhere. She could not be teaching, either at a school or at Workers' Educational classes, or his enquiries must quickly have borne fruit by now.

Ergo, he reasoned, she was somewhere else. So where was she? Being a lady of independent mind, he smiled ruefully, his proud, haughty Kate would undoubtedly go to the suffragettes, an organisation composed, so far as Jean-Michel could determine, entirely of proud, haughty, not to mention extremely fierce, ladies. But not one of them could tell him of a Kate Smith. He sighed. She must have changed her name. Why? This is obvious, he decided. She might go to prison and bring disgrace to her brother. He was not entirely happy with this explanation, but it would serve as a hypothesis. Filled with anxiety after the horrors endured by the women on the suffragettes' Black Friday, he had haunted police courts and newspaper offices, to no avail. The thought of Kate, *his* Kate, being mauled by policemen or hooligans was almost too much to endure, and respect for the ladies who were prepared to undergo these indignities began to grow.

Indefatigable as a terrier with a new scent, he had come at last to Holloway. He drove his sports car slowly along the neat suburban tree-lined avenue in search of No. 33. Doubts were already beginning to enter his mind. This avenue did not spell Kate to him, and the excitement of news of a young Mrs Bourne in the movement (Brynbourne?) began to fade.

He jumped out of the motor car, thoughtfully provided tuppence to two small boys, who were lingering hopefully, to act as guardians, and knocked on the door. It was opened by a tall angular woman whose fierceness left him in no doubt that this was a militant suffragette.

'Mrs Bourne?' he enquired meekly, as befitted a mere man.

She eyed him sternly. 'Upstairs. I'll tell her she has a visitor,' she said firmly, before he could mount the narrow staircase.

He knew by the length of time she was away that this time he must surely have found Kate. His heart beat the faster. The woman returned, eyeing him disdainfully and announced that he could go up. He smiled at her in gratitude, but the smile withered on his lips in the face of her frosty glare. Kate was standing looking out of the window.

'I suppose it was inevitable that you would feel it necessary to track me down,' she said wearily, not turning.

In two strides he was at her side. 'Dearest Kate, why, why, *why*?'

She turned to him in amazement. 'Monsieur Pinot, I – I thought you were Jack.' She was only momentarily disconcerted. 'Our acquaintance has been limited, monsieur. I find it surprising that I am dearest Kate to you. And if you reflected one moment, you would surely see the answer to your question.'

There was an edge to her voice, a brittleness. Reading the defiance, the flush on her face, he dropped his gaze to her dark blue dress. Fashions were slim that year, but Kate's dress was not.

'Kate, I do not understand—'

'It's quite simple, Monsieur Pinot,' she said clearly. 'I am to have a baby in March, and I am not married. Now you have made this interesting discovery, you can return to my brother and tell him, and tell everyone if you like. They can stay away or come here. It makes no difference, for I move next week, and then no one, but no one, will find me, Monsieur Pinot. Do you understand now?'

The blow had rocked him on his feet. When in a split second his emotions cleared themselves, he knew quite surely that no one had ever meant as much to him as this girl, and that whatever had happened to her was not as important as she herself to him. Jean-Michel had had many years of experience in expressing himself to women, and now as never before he called upon that experience.

'I understand, chère Kate, very well,' he said calmly, not betraying by one muscle the thoughts that were racing

284

through his head. 'My English is quite good, I think. And what I understand is that you are very unhappy and need a friend.'

For the first time uncertainty crossed her face.

'Aren't you going to rush from my door now you know of my *disgrace*?' she cried. 'Surely you know I am no fit person for anyone who values their social position to associate with?'

'Who is this man?' he asked quietly. 'He will marry you?'

'*I* would not,' she said proudly. She had come to believe it after the first shock, and now hated Robert Bellowes as she had never hated before. And most, she loathed herself for having been taken in by him.

'I am known as Mrs Bourne, a young widow, who spends her time in the offices of the suffragette movement run by Mr and Mrs Pethick-Lawrence, working on their newspaper *Votes for Women*, for the suffragettes' cause, a cause for which Mrs Bourne has much sympathy, and for which she receives enough money that if she is very, very careful she will not starve, and nor will her baby.' Her voice faltered at the last and then grew strong again. 'So what do you say, monsieur, now you see I *do* have friends?'

He eyed her carefully. 'What I say, dear Kate, is what any Frenchman would say, that I shall take you to the Hotel Savoy to dine on one of Escoffier's exquisite meals, preceded by a visit to the Gaiety Theatre to see the delectable Miss Gertrude Millar.'

Her mouth fell open. '*What?* But, oh, Jean-Michel, that's ridiculous, I can't – I'm—'

'*Enceinte?* And what does that matter? You have stopped eating, perhaps?'

'It's not proper,' she retorted indignantly, then as he began to laugh, the incongruity of what she had said struck her. She bit her lip, and involuntarily a smile came to her lips.

'Rosie.'

'What did you say, Jake?' she yelled back, crawling

out from under Daisy Belle II. Normally she would have stayed there, but there was an urgent note in his voice.

'Look,' he said, pointing to the Royal Aero Club field that adjoined their own.

'What about it?' she asked puzzled. There were six Short aeroplanes there. Nothing unusual about that.

'Look at the airmen – and their transport.'

She looked more closely. 'It's a naval van,' she said slowly. 'The men are uniformed.' She turned to look at Jake. 'Did you know?'

'No, I heard a rumour some months ago that the Navy had been offered part of the Aero Club grounds free of charge for six months, but nothing happened, so I discounted it. And now, it seems, we have the Royal Navy with us.'

'Are they any different to any other novice airmen?' asked Rosie doubtfully. 'They're coming to learn to fly, that's all. We just didn't want to teach them here.'

'I think this is different, Rosie,' Jake said grimly. 'If the Club continues to lease the field to them, it's an ideal place for an airfield station in the event of war.'

'*Here?*' said Rosie, her voice sharpening.

'Naval flying is going to play a big part in any war and the Admiralty is getting ready. Just think – aircraft are to fly off ships, and land on water. They can operate anywhere then, and not be restricted by closeness to a land base.'

'And the army?'

'It's going to happen, Rosie,' he said gently, upset by her obvious distress. 'There is no way of stopping it. Farnborough is increasing in size, the Royal Engineers' Balloon Section is now an Air Battalion for airships *and* aeroplanes; it's only a step from using balloons and kites for observation to using aeroplanes for fighting – perhaps even to drop bombs.'

Rosie stared over at the fragile, graceful aeroplanes now darting around like summer mayflies; in the distance was the sound of William's stentorian voice, laying down the law in the classroom.

'No, no,' she cried fiercely.

'It will come.'

'But not for us. Never our aeroplanes. You feel as I do, don't you Jake? The skies are for peace, for uniting nations, not warring with them.'

'You can't stop something you've invented just because you don't like what others are doing with it. It's a Frankenstein's monster.'

'But I don't have to do anything to make things worse. Nor you. Promise me you won't.'

He turned to her sadly. 'Promise is a word for lovers, Rosie. Lovers can shut out the world. But just now, you and I, we have to think of Daisy Belle, Astra and Sunburst. All the controls in the world wouldn't save one of them if the wind blows hard enough. And soon very soon, I think it will.'

Holding tight to Thomas's arm, Polly almost ran up the steps to the entrance to the Grand Palais des Champs Elysées. She had come to the Spring Salon Vernissage last year to see Thomas's work, but now she was here in her own right. The Vernissage, that great social event of the artists' year in Paris, half social, half work for the artists as they added the final varnish to show their paintings at their very best, was the magnet for the whole of Paris it seemed. Inside, the vast public rooms were swarming with the latest Poiret hobble skirts and elegantly suited men, side by side with the anxious artists carrying ladders, brushes and varnish.

Polly possessed a hobble skirt herself, but mindful that she herself might have to add varnish to her painting had not worn it. Besides, every time she put it on, she laughed at herself, thinking of what Rosie would say if she could see it.

'Thomas, there's yours,' exclaimed Polly in excitement. It was well displayed in the Salon of Honour – as it had an automatic right to be since Thomas had won a medal last year – and a group of top-hatted gentlemen crowded round it.

Thomas, tall as he was, could scarcely see his picture,

and waited patiently till the group cleared, Polly straining her ears in vain to hear their comments.

'It looks good, yes?' Thomas asked her anxiously.

'Very good,' said Polly judiciously, looking at his still-life representation of bread and a jug of wine beneath a tree. He had called it 'Loss', and the effect was sad. She wanted to cry when she saw it. Why loss? Save that the bread and jug did indeed look abandoned in a large empty world, bereft of life.

He would not explain, simply shrugging with a smile. She could not know that he painted out the nightmares of his mind on to his canvas, in the hope they might there be exorcised.

'Now,' he said anxiously, 'we must find yours, *meine Liebe*.'

Polly's was harder to track down, being one of the majority that had been given no number, which meant it could have been placed anywhere.

'They've skyed it,' said Thomas angrily, spotting it at last and pointing upwards to where her painting was hung near the ceiling. 'This is foolish – I will complain—'

'No, Thomas, no,' begged Polly. 'I'm so happy, so lucky it's there at all.'

It was her first picture to be accepted for the Salon – she, an unknown English artist. She almost burst with pride. Perhaps next year she too would be entitled to a better position. She gazed up at it, trying to remember what it was like to have painted it. It no longer seemed to belong to her, but to have been torn from her like a baby. And in a way it was – the achievement of herself and Gabriel. The landscape that she loved, given meaning by man. In this case by one very special man – Thomas. The stones of Fontainebleau, with Thomas standing by them, dreaming into the distance. The thinker looking back into the ages, into the future. In her mind it was a companion piece to Rodin's sculpture, given her own interpretation and her own setting.

'You wish to add varnish?' Thomas asked solicitously. 'I will do it for you,' he added, mindful of her skirts.

'No,' she said, gazing at it. 'It can stand as it is.'

She smiled at him. 'I'm so happy I could burst,' she cried.

'Are you happy with me also, Polly?' he asked wistfully. He gave her all he could but was never convinced.

'Only one thing will make me happier, Thomas,' she said to her own surprise, for she never dwelt on it. 'To be your wife.'

His face was stricken. 'I cannot, I will not, you must understand.'

'Kate, this baby is almost as beautiful as its mama. Dearest Kate, you do not mind to have strange gentlemen calling upon you when you are still confined?'

'I don't see how I can stop you, Jean-Michel,' she said resignedly.

After their evening at the Savoy, he had called upon her again, but found her gone. Undaunted, he had tracked down her new lodgings, and as casually as if a long-standing and welcome guest, walked in and asked her to marry him.

Her surprise he had expected, her refusal he had not.

'I can't,' she said bluntly. 'If you want to keep calling on me, that's your decision, but I can't marry you. It's quite out of the question.'

'Because you think I should not care for this baby as if it were my own? Ah, Kate, we French love children and when we have some of—'

'Because I don't want to marry you,' she said impatiently, cutting across this speech.

He turned pale. 'I understand,' he said with dignity, surprised to find just how greatly he was hurt.

'Jean-Michel—' she stopped, then said incoherently; 'It isn't that I don't . . . but I just couldn't. I like you, but I don't love you, and I want to be independent – make my own decisions.'

'In other words, my ridiculous Kate, you are too proud,' he said matter-of-factly.

'Yes,' she replied, glaring, 'I am too proud. Is that a bad thing?'

'Sometimes,' he answered quietly and took his leave.

But he had returned the following day – for the simple reason that he could not keep away.

The summer of 1911 turned into one of searing heat and drought. There was a curious stillness about it, as if with the crowning of the new king the land was poised in suspension waiting for something to happen. And underneath all, a restlessness and tension pervaded Europe. Not long after the June coronation, the good relations with Germany that had lulled so many into a feeling that the Kaiser had been misjudged disintegrated as Germany dispatched a gunboat to Agadir. Europe's hackles of alarm began to rise once more. The threat was unmistakable. On the slightest pretext that her interests were at risk, Germany would not only flex her muscles but use them. And what better excuse than a clash with France over Morocco?

Rosie determinedly set her thoughts away from warfare and on the Circuit of Britain Race, for which the *Daily Mail* were offering a prize of £10,000.

'With that,' she pointed out excitedly to Jake, 'we could build a real clubhouse and expand the school.'

'I reckon we stand a chance,' agreed Jake. 'But the competition will be fierce,' he warned.

He was right. When they arrived at Brooklands to assemble Sunburst – for Jake had won their toss on which aeroplane to enter – even Rosie's spirits were daunted.

'It's completely different to Reims,' she said nervously. 'It's so—'

'Efficient?' he supplied the word. 'We were all beginners then, Rosie. Not scared, are you?'

'No,' she grinned. 'We can take the lot of them on.' She spoke more bravely than she felt. In the aeroplane sheds French accents outnumbered the English it seemed. Among the English, Handley Page, Robert Blackburn and Alliott Verdon Roe were there of course. And Colonel Cody who immediately came across in his kind-hearted way to talk to her. In the next shed she glimpsed the Bellowes Clairville triplane, though there was no sign of Harry.

The weather was bad and, despite the thirty thousand people gathered to watch the beginning, the race at Brooklands was postponed till late in the day.

'I don't like that wind,' said Jake dubiously. 'I don't think you should test—'

She raised an eyebrow. He shrugged. 'Forget it.' But he worried all the same. He was right to. Her short test circuit of the field passed without incident, but in the race itself, Sunburst, swept by a gust on take-off rose prematurely, bounced and failed to rise again, crashing on to its fuselage. Jake wasn't hurt except in his pride. It was a minor crash, however, compared with two or three others of the English aeroplanes, the pilots of which escaped with their lives but precious little of a recognisable aeroplane. Harry Clairville Jones, flushed with his success in the Gordon Bennett Race at Eastchurch, which Jake had not entered, took off triumphantly to circle Britain, only to land again ignominiously five minutes later with engine trouble. Only Colonel Cody upheld the honour of England by finishing the race – the French aeroplanes swept off all the honours.

It was not the fruitful summer Rosie had anticipated. Now a heat wave was upon them, and a malaise still gripped the country. Parliament battled over the role of the House of Lords, the crisis in Morocco dragged on, and in the heat a series of crippling strikes affected the country and raised tempers.

The temperatures grew higher – well into the nineties even in the shade. Too hot to work, too hot to fly, too hot even to plan for the future; the heat sapped energy, and finally it sapped hope.

On 9th August, the temperature reached 97°. Abandoning work, Jake and Rosie went to the beach where at least the water was somewhat cooler and, in this deserted part of the island, quieter save for the aeroplanes roaring overhead.

'Why don't you whistle for a wind, Jake?' Rosie asked idly, after they emerged from the water hardly cooler than when they entered.

'The Indian gods are too far away – they'd never hear me.'

'It might work.'

'I doubt it. I made it up.'

'You *what*?' she cried, gazing at him in horror. 'You mean you *invented* everything about singing for the wind, and whistling—'

'It's basically true,' he said, hurt. 'I just helped the story out a little. Ouch,' he added, as Rosie thumped him crossly. 'I don't know why you're annoyed. It worked for us, didn't it?' He grabbed at her arms, pinioning them to her sides, and drew her into his embrace, and stopping her comments on his character with a long kiss.

'Why are you always wriggling, Rosie?' Jake asked patiently after a while.

'It's this new sunbathing costume. It itches.'

'Take it off – there's no one around.'

'Mother wouldn't like it,' she said primly.

'But I would.'

She laughed, and since they were sheltered by the trees, followed his suggestion. The warmth, even in the shade of the trees, was pleasant on her body, and she wriggled luxuriously.

'That's a Bristol, isn't it?' she squinted up through the canopy of trees.

He looked. 'Yes. Rumour has it it's being geared for military use.'

She groaned. 'Not back to the Kaiser again. I couldn't bear it. I've heard enough about Agadir and the *Panther* gunboat to last me a good long while. Even if Kaiser Bill does go to war in France, why should we be involved?'

'Alliances,' said Jake succinctly. 'Anyway, if France falls, where will his greedy eyes fall next?'

'And if there's war, will there be no room for flying schools? I don't believe it.'

'They'll turn them into military flying schools.'

A silence. 'You mean *we'd* have to train pilots to fly for killing people. That's not what we wanted to do.'

'Sometimes you have to adapt what you believe to changed circumstances.'

She thought about this, then answered, 'You know about Icarus, who flew too near the sun? Father told me about him the very first day I saw a kite flying. That's what will happen to us. We'll fly too near the sun and crash down. Father told me it would be a privilege if man were allowed to share the skies, and I promised him I'd never abuse it.'

'And how about old Daedalus?' said Jake quietly. 'He flew the same way as Icarus, just more sensibly. And he was successful. Don't you think that's what we have to do? Do what you can to help so that good can come out of it?'

'No,' said Rosie simply.

'Kent Aviation is being left behind in the race, Rosie. You realise that? Everyone else is planning for war, actively seeking orders from the War Ministry, cajoling the Air Battalion into backing their aircraft. That's the way it's going – and what are we doing? Play-acting.' His voice sharpened. 'Joy-riding like children.'

He sat up, and responding to the anger in his voice, so did she, aware of the division between them and powerless to close it. His eyes flicked over her in the still air. The slim body he loved so much; the small breasts he caressed with such tenderness, taut now in tension as they were in love. 'Rosie, come to me. Meet me halfway, before it's too late,' he pleaded.

'I can't,' she cried.

He took her in his arms, pushing her back on the grass under the trees. 'Marry me now, Rosie. Please—'

'Jake, I—'

He lay with her, partly on her, as if by closeness he could make her understand.

'It's nearly a year, Rosie. I *can't* wait longer. Something will happen to tear us apart if we wait.'

She looked up at him fiercely. 'Nothing can, so nothing will.' She put her arms round him, holding him tightly, pulling him to her. 'I love you more and more and more. So nothing can alter that.' The oppressive heat bore down on them, distancing all but themselves, demanding release from tension.

He was hardly listening to her words, his hands demanding, urging, coaxing, swept away by desire in sweet passion till her body arched into his.

'Jake – lover mine,' she cried in pleasure as he entered her and gave herself up to his love.

A few minutes later, Michael Potts in search of Rosie and hearing the sound of voices, came into the copse, and peering round a bush saw his Rosie, naked, clasped in Jake's arms, both oblivious to all but each other and the urgency of their love. He stumbled away stunned, his fantasies in shreds as his illusions exploded into stark truth.

Dinner that evening at Brynbourne Place started as a muted affair. The oppressive heat silenced all but William, who pontificated on the gunboat *Panther* and the German crisis, oblivious to the fact that no one was paying attention. Mildred was concerned as to whether Michael was sickening for something. Rosie and Jake sat abstractedly in a world of their own. Would the weather break tonight, Mildred wondered restlessly and obscurely troubled. It was heavy enough for thunder. Perhaps that was what was troubling Michael.

'We'll all be all right so long as Lloyd George is with us,' William announced in glee. ' "Peace at that price would be a humiliation, almost intolerable for a great country like ours to endure",' he quoted from the Mansion House speech about Morocco, as he had done every night since Lloyd George had uttered his stirring words.

Rosie and her mother withdrew to the drawing room for coffee, glad to escape the rhetoric, and Jake, with William and Michael, remained to take port in the dining room. Michael had been newly elevated to the honour on his sixteenth birthday. Usually excited and proud at his new standing, tonight he was subdued as the women left.

'Mother, Jake's telling Father that we've decided at last,' said Rosie happily. 'We are to marry in late September, just as soon as—'

The sound of raised voices made her break off. Then one, louder, shriller, out of control:

'She's mine. She's mine. *Mine!* '

'Michael,' said Mildred sharply.

There was something wrong. Filled with fear she could not define, Rosie rushed after Mildred as she hurried back to the dining room.

Both Jake and William were still, staring transfixed at a white-faced glazed-eyed Michael, for whom news of Rosie's marriage, coming so soon after the shock of the afternoon, had proved the final straw. He broke out again in an unearthly howl. *'Mine!* ' and he hurled himself at Jake who, bewildered, made no attempt to defend himself, as Michael's wild arms flayed about in all directions.

'I hate you!' And seeing Rosie, in a shriek, 'And *you.*'

'Michael, be quiet, sir.' William was shouting, beside himself with rage. But Michael took no notice, as his assault on Jake continued, catching him in the crotch with one vicious blow.

Sharp memories of a crazed Michael standing over Robert Bellowes, whipping him frenziedly, flooded over her as Rosie rushed to Michael to pull him away from Jake, who was now doubled up in pain; but Michael threw her off with such violence that she was thrown to the ground. Then Jake, recovering slowly, managed to pinion the struggling boy's arms, but it needed all his remaining strength to hold him, even with Mildred's and Rosie's help.

'Are you mad, sir?' William shouted at his son. But Michael was past listening.

'I saw you this afternoon,' he shrieked at Rosie, twisting and struggling in Jake's grasp. 'I saw you with no clothes on – you were horrible, disgusting. Like you and Mr Bellowes—'

'Michael – don't—' she moaned in horror. A look at Jake, a revulsion first that their love, between them alone, had been observed, and then that Robert Bellowes should be mentioned in the same breath.

'He was lying on you and you were *liking* it,' he

shrieked back, as Jake's hand came across his mouth to silence him. But he bit it viciously, and tore free. 'You're mine, *mine*. You *shan't* marry him, you *shan't*.'

He wrenched himself away from Jake with surprising strength, cannoning towards Rosie and seizing her in his arms, forcing her lips on to his, before Mildred and Jake, with William impotently shouting behind them, could pull him away.

'Come here, sir,' William's voice thundered and surprisingly Michael obeyed, standing before the wheel-chair. 'You're a disgrace, sir. A disgrace. And you, Rosie—' His eyes swivelled, just as Michael, flushed and with maniacal stare, burst out: 'I don't care if they did burn it down, Harry's a good sort. I don't care if they di—'

'What the devil are you—' Jake, his arm protectively round Rosie, had heard the word burn.

William was even quicker. 'Michael,' he said ominously quietly, 'did you have anything to do with the fire at the aeroplane shed last year?'

'I don't care, Father.' Michael's eyes were glittering with triumph now he knew he had their full attention. He'd get his own back on all of them. 'I told him how to get in. Burning it down was an accident, but it would have been a lark to make this cowboy here look ridiculous.'

Rosie moaned and Jake's arm tightened round her. Mildred was suddenly alert with alarm for her son. William, eyes bulging, slowly took in the meaning of what Michael was saying; then his reaction was immediate and fierce.

'My son a traitor. *Traitor!* A Peeping Tom and a traitor.'

'I don't care—'

'You burnt my *aeroplanes*.' A howl of animal rage as William tried to urge his useless legs out of the wheelchair to hurl himself at his son. Mildred reached him just too late. With all the strength of his upper body and arms, William catapulted himself forwards, choking with effort. As his heavy body collapsed on the floor there was another cough, and sightless eyes gazing towards the ceiling.

# Chapter Thirteen

A choking pall of grief smothered the household. The benevolent despot who had ruled it had been taken from them, had gone, and staff and family alike were stricken. The staff crept about silently, shocked and bewildered, for not only had the Master been taken from them, but the Mistress, that infallible source of strength, remained closeted in her room. Only Rosie remained to do her best to keep the household running and to cope with funeral arrangements, solicitors and the endless stream of callers. She went about in a daze, the one half of her trying to cope as best she could, the other, the half she dared not face, torn apart at Father's loss. As long as she could now remember, his cheerful spirit had been there to lead her, inspire her and comfort her. He had made her believe that the world had limitless possibilities, with him who had shown her the path she had shared all the joys of those early explorations into flight, he had opened his arms to a six-year-old orphan and given her a home. *His* home. Now, without him, she could not believe it was hers still. Perhaps she still belonged to that other 'home'? She shrank from it, for side by side came back the memory of Uncle Alf, casting old shadows to add to the new. How could it still be there, as though it were still a challenge to be feared? Home was here – with Jake.

Almost greater shock than William's death was her mother's collapse. Suddenly Rosie had to be the organiser, the calm lynchpin on whom the household pivoted. To see Mildred in bed or lying on her chaise longue staring hopelessly into space seemed at times a worse torment than Father's loss. She could not reach her mother. Not even when Polly came did Mildred rouse herself, though Polly's presence at least helped Rosie.

Michael had withdrawn completely into himself after William's death, but here Jake had come to Rosie's rescue. Intuitively realising how ambivalent Rosie might feel, he took Michael to the Lodge, for Michael, locked within himself, was incapable of resisting. There the doctor tended him, but without result. Only to Jake's company did he respond, and then only with a slight turn of his head. When Rosie, summoning her strength and remembering what she owed to Michael in the past, visited him, Michael abruptly turned away from her and she did not try again. He needed Mother more than her, she decided.

Then at last Rosie did rouse Mildred, but in a way that left her feeling more alone than ever, in a world where no one seemed as she had thought them. Mildred listened to Rosie's pleadings that she should rise and look after Michael.

Mildred had looked at her with dulled eyes. 'He killed William,' was her flat chilling response. 'And you—' she cried, 'if you'd married Jake last year, none of this would have happened.'

'Mother,' Rosie cried in anguish.

But Mildred could not be stopped. 'Why didn't you marry him? All this high-falutin' New Woman nonsense. Disgusting. If you'd been wearing his ring, Michael wouldn't have seen – what he did—' She choked. 'None of this would have happened.'

Rosie stood still, ashen-faced, pushing the stabbing words away, trying to tell herself that Mother was not herself. But the sting remained, Mother could not love her as she loved Michael and Polly to say such things. Rosie was an alien, must always have been so. Waves of hurt undulated through her stomach, making her feel physically sick.

But Mildred seemed not to notice the effect of her words – probably was not even conscious of having spoken them, thought Rosie defensively. Mildred reached out a hand to her, clutching Rosie's, pulling her back as she turned away.

'What should I do, Rosie?' she asked pleadingly. 'Tell me. *Tell* me. He's my son.'

Rosie fought against her own present revulsion for Michael. Time after time she'd gone over the past in her mind. Remembered how she and Father had left Michael to his own devices, while they were so absorbed in flight and aeroplanes; how the family had treated his attachment to her as a joke. Why had she not seen the warning signs as it continued year after year?

'Tell me, Rosie,' Mildred pleaded again.

Rosie took a deep breath. 'He needs you, Mother. Father doesn't any longer.'

Mildred flopped back on the bed. Then raising herself and saying no more, she took three strong sniffs at her smelling salts, and swung her legs to the ground. 'I'll go and see him now,' she declared in her normal voice, as though nothing had happened between them.

But for Rosie it had, and could not be erased. One by one the struts of her life were splintering. Only Jake, the kingpost, stood sure.

For Rosie the funeral passed in a blur, as if she were acting in a play; her lines had been learned, her actions memorised, and a performance given. Afterwards, isolated incidents stood out, and none so vivid as Sir Lawrence Bellowes staring down quietly at the grave of his old adversary, and picking up a flower and throwing it on top of the coffin, then walking quickly away. Or Thomas, gravely singing William's favourite, 'Land of Hope and Glory', in the old church, his large frame almost dwarfing Polly's slight black-clad figure. And Jake, his golden hair for once sleeked down, his eyes fixed on the coffin of his benefactor. She loved him so much her heart could not hold it all, yet now they could not marry until at least December. The crush of people in Brynbourne Place had emptied at last, and at the reading of the will, came the surprise that William had left all his shares in the Kent Aviation Company to her. With the Sittingbourne factory left to Mildred.

'Why, Mother, why?' Rosie asked her, troubled

299

afterwards. 'Do you not need the income from the shares – and it is *beginning* to make money?'

'I have the house, and Polly, Michael and I have sufficient income from the factory. He thought—' her voice broke '—you deserved it, you've worked so hard, right from the time you were a little girl. He was so proud of you,' she added, as if in expiation for what lay unmentioned between them.

On a hillside long ago. The kite . . . where it had all begun. How far away that moment, yet an unbroken trail had led them to today. Icarus, the wings of Icarus. 'Father,' she whispered, 'keep me from falling. And I'll carry on what you began.'

Thomas walked through the gardens of Brynbourne Place, admiring their straggling disordered beauty. He felt somehow distanced from Polly, seeing her slide naturally back into her home setting. He compared it with his home in Bavaria, its Germanic tidiness compared with this semi-wilderness. How he craved order – and was drawn to the opposite. His passion for Polly overcame everything else. She was his whole life now. He had dismissed the past. Even his own painting was suffering, because of his interest in hers. To him, his canvasses appeared clumsy beside her carefully composed evocations. Now all he wanted was to paint her, in all her moods, in all lights. He turned his head as she came to join him, the black dress swamping her pale beauty. She looked tired. He took her arm protectively and tenderly in his, and she smiled in gratitude. There was no need for words, just the silent communion of lovers.

Michael returned to Brynbourne Place a week after the funeral, still withdrawn and responding only to his mother. Rosie he now regarded with detached politeness, but his eyes gave no hint of his feelings.

Rosie helped the girl from the village who came in to clean and shop for Jake, then joined Jake in the garden. She sat down beside him on the wooden seat and he took her hand.

300

'What did Michael mean about you and Robert?' he asked her abruptly.

It hurt her to think he had been mulling this over for so long without asking her earlier. Once she would have been defensive, assumed Jake thought the worst; now she merely said, 'I never wanted to tell you, Jake. I couldn't bear even to think about it, but it's time now.' She related the whole story, including her suspicions about Gabriel's death, and Michael's coming to her rescue.

Jake said very little, but she saw his knuckles whiten as he clasped her hand. Then he swore long and hard with picturesque oaths that came from no English source.

'And you've never told anybody? Not Polly, not—' he swallowed, remembering the situation then, '—Clairville Jones?'

'No one. Except Mother – and Robert Bellowes himself.'

'You accused him, Rosie?' Jake was horrified.

'You think I shouldn't have done so?'

'It was brave of you. What I would have expected – but—' Anxiety deepened. Bellowes did not forget easily. He and Clairville Jones had tried to burn them out of existence and failed. What would happen next?

'I didn't lie to you, Jake,' Rosie was saying anxiously. 'I just couldn't tell you, somehow.'

'I wish you had,' he said vehemently.

'You think it might have avoided Father's death?' she asked in a low voice, facing the fear at the back of her mind, that Michael's rages needed special treatment.

'I've talked to the doctor, Rosie. He's sure Michael's outbursts won't continue, now that he's growing up. He thinks this shock will sober him, that he's not a danger, if that's what you're worried about.'

'And what about Robert Bellowes, Jake? Will he always overshadow our lives?'

''Not if I can help it,' he said simply. 'Rosie, there's something I must tell you. I've seen Kate.'

'Oh Jake, I'm so glad. Jean-Michel told you where she was at last?'

'No. He said he'd been sworn to secrecy, so I just followed him—'

* * *

'Kate.' It was nearly a year since he'd seen her. He felt rejected, unable to understand her refusal to see him. Where had he gone wrong? He was her brother, he had a right to know where she was. It had hurt him deeply that she had confided in Jean-Michel and not in him.

Kate whirled round. 'Damn you, Jack,' she said quietly. 'Why couldn't you leave me alone? Jean-Michel told you where I was, I suppose,' she said scornfully.

'Nope. He's loyal to you – and it's more than you deserve, Kate,' he answered forthrightly. She went white. 'You walked out on me, your own brother.'

'And what did you do when you went to America?' she cried, stung. 'You walked out—'

'You know why I went – Pa took me to get rich—'

'And when he died, did you come back?'

He said nothing, stunned at her accusations.

'I'm sorry, Jack,' she said more quietly. 'You shouldn't have provoked me. What I'm trying to say is that everyone has to follow his own star – you did it, and now I'm doing it.'

'But what star *is* it, Kate?' he asked anxiously. 'I just have to know you're all right—'

'You know I'm all right, Jean-Michel would have told you that.'

'Why don't you—'

'Marry him?' Her voice was scornful. 'The panacea for all ills. I'll never marry, Jack. *Never*.'

'You've joined the suffragettes again, haven't you?' he countered. 'They've put these ideas in your head.'

She laughed. 'No, not them. *Men* have put them there.'

'Kate, I don't want to see you in prison—' he said. It had been her brief appearance at a magistrate's court that had led to her losing her teaching job and coming to Kent.

She laughed again, bitterly. 'You won't see me in prison, I can assure you of that, Jack. The organisation always looks after girls like me – with babies to care for.'

'Babies—' he repeated blankly.

An ironic smile twisted her lips. 'I thought Jean-Michel would have told you that, at least. You'd better meet your nephew, Jack.' She took him into the adjoining room, and pointed to the cradle.

'Kate!' he cried in anguish. 'Why didn't you tell me?'

She shrugged. 'What could *you* do?' she said with some amusement.

'I could have looked after you – given you money.'

'Money—' she flashed. 'Yes. He offered *that*.'

'Who?' Jake asked slowly. 'Jean-Michel? The baby is Jean-Michel's?'

'No,' she said impatiently. 'Of course not.'

'Then who—' he countered. 'It must have been when you were still at Brynbourne. Who—'

'Poor Jack.' She regarded him almost compassionately. 'It was Robert Bellowes.'

She saw his horrified reaction. 'Yes, I know. How could I? I wonder, too, now, Jack. How could I have been so taken in? Well,' her voice rising, 'it's not for *you* to wonder how I could. I've paid the price and I'm keeping out of your way. I don't want any moral lectures, Jack.'

'Not you, Kate,' Jake said coolly. 'If you are not in need, and you don't wish to see me, then there is nothing I can do. But,' he said dispassionately, 'there's nothing on earth to stop me paying a visit to Robert Bellowes.'

'So pleasant to see you, Mr Smith. Won't you sit down? I take it this is a business call?' Robert Bellowes sat behind the Chippendale desk at Court Manor, eyeing Jake with great amusement, having guessed just why he was there.

'No. More a social call, Bellowes,' Jake replied coolly. 'I've just seen your son.'

Robert Bellowes's eyes narrowed. 'Ah, I see you've been talking to your sister. How is dear Kate?'

'So you do admit he's your son?'

'My dear Mr Smith, I do not. I don't deny that Kate and I enjoyed a most pleasant and intimate friendship. But there is no proof that it's my child, and indeed she

303

admitted as much when she refused my offer of financial support.'

Jake's stomach churned, as he forced himself to stay in his chair. 'I'd force you to marry her,' said Jake slowly, 'but I wouldn't wish a future like that on Kate. Not to a husband like you.'

'Ah well, there we are in accord, for I cannot see myself offering marriage to someone out of the Nichol East End slums, with someone else's bastard,' commented Bellowes pleasantly.

Part of Jake wanted to haul him out and smash him into pulp the way he'd thrashed May's killer back in Leadville. But the pale blue eyes regarding him so triumphantly were willing him to do just that, to put him in his power.

'I can't say I'd want a murderer in the family,' Jake shot at him.

The shock on Robert Bellowes's face was confirmation enough of what Rosie had suspected.

'Rosie,' Bellowes said flatly. 'Her wild stories—' He stopped, thinking rapidly. There had been a witness, Michael. He'd never been sure quite how much Michael had seen that day at the lake. Wise move to get him on their side over that hangar business that year. Though now, with the old man dead – who knew what might happen? None of his uneasiness showed on his face, as he continued, 'I seem to have made rather an enemy of Rosie – such dreadful stories she concocts. Of course no one sensible would believe them.' His fingers tightened on the arms of his chair.

'If you come near any one of those I love again, Bellowes, you'll wish you'd never been born.'

'You terrify me, Mr Smith. Just what *can* you do to me?' enquired Robert politely.

'I guess I'll think of something,' said Jake lazily, getting up from his chair, his eyes glittering like a cobra coiled ready to strike.

Robert Bellowes sat thinking for some considerable time after Jake had left. Jake Smith was a somewhat unknown quantity. He seemed easy-going and in any case could do nothing so far as that unfortunate business at

304

the lake was concerned. Had it been murder? He'd never been quite sure himself. Had the thought been father to the deed? Had he taken that artist fellow on the lake that day, half hoping an opportunity might arise? Had he leaped up purposely to tip the boat? He did not know, and so no longer thought of it. But what he did recollect was that hand, the hand stuck out in supplication. The hand he had ignored. He'd been so sure Polly would come to him after that artist fellow's death. Instead she'd gone to Paris and disappeared from society. Then at the funeral she'd appeared with some German, and hadn't even spoken to him. Had Rosie ever told her what had happened? Somehow he thought not. There was nothing that Jake Smith could do to him on that score. Nor was there anything Jake could do about Kate. Even so, there was a dangerous quality about him; he wasn't a gentleman, and there was a tang of the wild about him. Robert Bellowes knew there was only one thing you did under those circumstances – when danger approached, you struck first.

'Michael,' said Rosie gently. No response. He sat listlessly in the conservatory, staring out into the garden, withdrawn and white. He still treated Rosie as if she were a stranger, the only people he talked to at all normally were his mother and Polly.

'Michael, talk to me, please.'

He roused himself. 'Nothing to say,' he commented briefly and truthfully. He was dead inside, numb; he tried to tell himself this was Rosie, whom he loved so much, but it meant nothing. He regarded her now dispassionately, not quite as a stranger, but as a bothersome acquaintance.

Hurt, Rosie withdrew once again, relieved at the same time. She had been appalled to discover how extreme Michael's passion had been, far beyond a child's adoration, and still blamed herself for not seeing it earlier, and somehow defusing it. The aftertaste of her mother's outburst still stung.

Michael tried to feel guilt about Father's death but in reality he didn't feel anything. The only emotion he felt had been fear that he might be sent away, but he wasn't. *Father was dead*. He tried telling himself this over and over again, but it meant nothing as yet. Only one thought obsessed him.

One month after William's death, Michael came downstairs and joined his mother, Rosie and Jake for dinner instead of eating alone in his room. In between the soup and the fish, he announced matter-of-factly that he intended to leave school and run the Sittingbourne factory. He listened politely to all their arguments against his plans, abolished them quietly and rationally, and started work the following day.

'Rosie.' Jake's arm stretched round her to help her push shut the shed door on its pulley system. 'Have you finished for the afternoon?'

'No such luck. I've a lesson on equilibrium later on.' She grimaced. Every time she had to give a lesson she appreciated just how much William had contributed. Every time she stood before the eager novices, she had to battle anew with the sharp tearing pain of loss. The sooner they employed a new instructor, and the less she had to plough through Lanchester's *Aerodonetics*, the better.

'Shall we take Daisy Belle up for an hour?'

'We?' she said uncertainly.

'Yes. We.' He said no more, but she understood. They had hardly seen each other since William's death, both trapped in the endless legal problems and discussions on the future, as well as trying to come to terms with a future that did not include William Potts. Jake did not have to tell her that, up there, together, they could escape, if just for an hour, gain strength from being physically and mentally apart from the problems of the world beneath. Perhaps there she could exorcise her fear that Michael's outburst had cast a shadow which could not be eradicated.

'I'll fly,' she said mischievously.

'Very well,' he answered her. She hugged him in gratitude, knowing what it had cost him.

'I don't mind. You take the controls,' she told him magnanimously.

Everywhere now an indefinable sense of the threat of war was growing steadily. Talks were proceeding in Paris and in theory the Moroccan crisis was nearly solved. But why then were there suddenly soldiers everywhere patrolling trains and harbours? Up here there was only peace and silence save for the rushing wind, the throb of the Pinot, and the beating of their hearts in their own small isolated world.

'I feel as if we're on a magic carpet,' she yelled in exhilaration to Jake, digging him in the back.

'I don't have a ticket to drive carpets,' he shouted back.

She put her head back to feel the warmth of the late September sun on her face, greedily revelling in the breeze and cloying smell of the castor oil. They must be at about five hundred feet she reckoned, five hundred feet from sadness and grief.

'I love you, Jake,' she cried, exhilarated.

'What?' he yelled over his shoulder.

'You make rotten right turns but I still love you.'

'Not as bad as your landings.'

'Worse, but I still love you. Are we on a journey to somewhere special, Jake?'

'Heart's delight, over the clouds and far away.' He began to sing.

' "I would love you every day, every day we'd kiss and play . . . " Hold on to your hat, we're going down.'

'Do you love me, Jake?' she yelled.

He landed in a meadow, far from anywhere. Two cows peered at this strange object curiously and then reverted to the more interesting occupation of feeding.

Rosie's eyes were shining bright as Jake took off her cap and ran his hands through her hair, scattering pins in all directions. They did not kiss, merely held hands; for the moment it was enough just to be together.

'Jake, this is an enchanted place. Let's stay here for ever, in our hearts at least.'

He held her close, then at last she said, 'You didn't answer me, Jake, when I asked if you loved me?'

He looked at her in surprise, then seeing she was in earnest, held her close. 'Don't you know,' he said amazed, 'don't you know that every time you move I reach out for you, every time you speak, I sing for you, every time you smile, I'm lost in you? Don't you know that?'

And she did. She touched his lips lightly with her own, hesitating slightly before she said, 'But the photograph?'

He stood there stricken, wrestling with himself. How could he convince her that the past was buried, that only the present and the future mattered? That she had forged a path through the mountains of distrust as surely as Hannibal through the Alps.

He took a deep breath.

'Listen, heart's love, and I'll tell you.' And tell her he did, of the misery of his early years. Words tumbled out of him like a river undammed, as he told her, not just of the Yukon, of Leadville, of the cattle trails, but of Pa, of May and what she had meant to him. And of Florence. Most of all of Florence.

'Do you still love her, Jake?' she asked, troubled, when at last he finished.

'Love?' He stared at her. 'I was sixteen, Rosie. I knew as much of real love as – as – Michael.'

'But her photograph—'

'I kept it as a warning, that's all,' he said sombrely.

But the warning had turned into a cage. A cage whose bars had been burst wide open by Rosie.

It was the calm centre of what was the beginning of the whirlpool. The next day Italy declared war on Turkey. Her eyes on Tripoli, she needed Rhodes and its neighbouring islands, and plucked them as ripe plums from the tree. The Balkan countries took note that no one raised an effective murmur of opposition.

'I don't see why you're so worried about Turkey,' Rosie said to Jake snappily, as she struggled over the accounts for September.

'Well, I guess because it's all so intricate. Turkey is friendly with Germany, but Germany is in alliance with

Italy. So Germany can't move, and the Kaiser won't like that.'

'But so what? It's nothing to do with Great Britain.'

Jake considered. 'It's like the share structure of a company. When things go well, there's no problem. But when there is – all the shareholders get drawn in. And Europe – perhaps the whole world now – is getting to be one big company, each with a stake in the future of the whole.'

Rosie lay down the accounts book. He'd mentioned shares. She raised her head slowly. This had to be faced. 'Jake, after Father left his shares to me, I've got forty-nine per cent and Polly two per cent. That means you've still only got forty-nine per cent, and can't therefore overrule me. Do you mind?'

Jake looked at her steadily. 'At first I minded like hell.' He'd known from the start it was heading for trouble to be in any position where the Potts family as a whole could outvote him, but his soft heart and his trust in the Potts had led him to let William off lightly. 'But then I got to thinking – what does it matter? We can always talk things over. Where there's trust, there's a way.'

'Oh Jake.' She flew at him, throwing her arms round him. 'Always, *always*.'

'They're training for war, aren't they?' said Rosie flatly, gazing at the aeroplanes circling and swooping over the Royal Aero Club field.

'It's become fashionable,' said Jake slowly, standing by her side. 'You heard there's a prize offered to the pilots who can carry a passenger the greatest distance before next March. Not any pilot – Army and Navy pilots.'

She forced a laugh. 'We don't need their prizes, or their approval, do we, Jake?'

But Jake did not answer.

'Jake?' she repeated sharply.

'Not at the moment,' he said reluctantly. 'But Rosie, suppose it came to the point where we had to choose between going military or closing down.'

'It won't,' she snapped.

'There's a creature called an ostrich,' he said gently, and deeply troubled. He could not bring himself to force the issue, reflecting that so far as imitating ostriches was concerned, they were both doing a darn good job.

'You're very serious tonight, Jean-Michel.' He sat in Kate's uncomfortable armchair while she prepared him a revolting mutton chop. He would pretend, as he always did, that he enjoyed it, while privately resolving that when they were married – for he always thought in terms of 'when' – he would never allow her near a kitchen again. But as she refused to leave the baby with anyone else, save on very rare occasions, he was forced to ignore the temptations of London's restaurants and partake of whatever she chose to produce. And since it was apparent that women's suffrage had much higher priority than Jean-Michel's *estomac* in Kate's thoughts, this was indeed a sacrifice.

'Mrs Pankhurst wishes to become more militant,' she was calling from the kitchen. 'Mrs Pethick-Lawrence is against it. And last week I went to a meeting of the Actresses' and Artists' Suffrage Society – and oh, Jean-Michel – I do think we shall soon succeed. Mrs Pankhurst says next year. But only if we intensify our efforts.'

'This militancy will never win you votes,' he observed mildly.

'Reason gets us nowhere,' she said indignantly. 'They take no notice of us.'

'They?'

'Men,' she explained succinctly.

'I am a man,' he pointed out. 'I take notice.'

'You take notice because you—' She stopped.

'Continue, please,' he said gently. 'Because I love you?'

'Yes,' she said, half ashamed.

He sighed. 'You are right, Kate. I do love you. And, dearest Kate, I cannot continue in this way. I want you for my wife. And if you will not marry me, then I have to go, I think. I cannot—' He stopped and tried again to hide the emotion in his voice '—go on this way without, I—'

'Bed,' she finished for him positively. 'Very well, if you wish, but I won't marry you.'

He leapt to his feet, angry for the first time with her. 'You have been unhappy, Kate, but that does not entitle you to treat me so. Do not judge every man the same. Yes, I want to love you, to hold your body with mine, but I want more than that – I want you as my wife, not as my mistress. You insult me to think otherwise.'

'I will not marry you, Jean-Michel,' she said steadily.

'Very well,' he said quietly, after a pause. 'But tell me, do you care for me at all, Kate?'

She was too proud, too obstinate, too blind.

'As a friend, of course,' she answered.

He picked up his hat, a blur covering his eyes as he left.

'Goodbye, Kate,' he said unsteadily. 'I think I will not see you again.'

She followed him out, wanting to call him back, but unable to utter the words. As the door closed behind him, the silence burst in upon her ears. She returned to the kitchen in a daze, looking at the two mutton chops lying ready for their supper. With great care she took one out of the pan, and threw it quickly away into the waste bucket. But, seeing its companion lying solitary in its fat, she sat down at the kitchen table, put her head in her hands and cried uncontrollably.

Late in the year, public alarm over the Moroccan crisis subsided, but that of the War Office did not. Conscious of the years in which it had dragged its feet, it was quickly making up for lost time. At the Royal Aeronautical Society, it was not taken for granted that aviation could have military application. New faces replaced the old on committees, new objectives were set.

At Eastchurch, with the Naval testing grounds next door, it was impossible for Jake to ignore the new attitudes. Rosie almost consciously did, shutting her eyes to its implications, concentrating solely on the immense problems of coordinating factory and field, worrying about decreasing orders and wrongly – blindly – ascribing them to change of management.

Just before Christmas two things happened simultaneously. They meant crisis for the company, and this time there would be no keeping it from Rosie. Even she must face what lay before them . . . And face it before they married in January.

'I've called this meeting,' Jake began slowly, in the study at Brynbourne Place, 'because as shareholders we have to make decisions about the future.'

Rosie briefly wondered why he had not discussed them earlier with her, but dismissed the thought.

Mildred sat protectively by Michael's side, but there seemed little need. Throwing himself into running the newly re-named Potts Sanitary Ware and aircraft production, he had little contact with them all save on business matters, not hesitating to seek advice, but confiding little beyond that.

'The War Office has announced the specifications for aeroplanes to be entered in next summer's military trials,' Jake announced, already sensing Rosie's sudden stillness. He began to read from a list in front of him. 'Live load of three hundred and fifty pounds, with endurance of four and a half hours, and fly-loaded at not less than fifty-five miles per hour. Provision for pilot and observer, with clear view, interchangeable parts.' He continued reading while Rosie tried to take it in, waiting for, dreading, what he might go on to say. And he did. 'I think we can design to these guidelines easily. And I think we should.'

'Why?' The word burst from her like a cry of anguish.

'Because we've no choice. I know you're opposed to it, Rosie—' he could not look at her, his eyes fixed firmly on the papers. He could guess the expression on her face.

'There's *always* choice,' she said, disbelievingly. 'Have you forgotten what we set out to do when we began? What you wanted when you set up Kent Aviation?'

'No. But in order to achieve it, we may have to fight first,' he pointed out steadily. 'If this country is at war with Germany, we shall have to defend it. Every other country is going to have military aeroplanes. Do you think we alone should stand out? Or should we let other

312

companies build military planes, not so good as ours? Do you think that honourable? Do you think we should even be allowed to?'

'The Navy has always defended England.'

'Since Blériot crossed the Channel, we're no longer an island,' Jake pointed out. 'Germany's Zeppelins could bomb England today. What are we going to fight them with?'

'Guns,' she threw at him.

'You want others to do what you haven't the stomach for?' In spite of his resolutions, Jake's voice began to rise in anger.

Michael stirred himself. 'Military aeroplanes?' he said with interest, already foreseeing the factory bulging with orders.

'Is it what Father would have wanted?' said Rosie quietly.

Jake braced himself. He had known this would happen. 'Rosie, he was an idealist. But he was practical too. He was a businessman and—'

'And you think ideals and business don't mix?' she inquired, dangerously quiet. 'Well, I'm a businesswoman too and the Potts family have more shares in this company than you. That's business, isn't it?' She could not look at him, or her heart, her resolve would break.

Then his voice, his dear, beloved voice, distant and cool. 'Very well. I understand. But there's one more problem I have to tell you of. As of quarterday – Christmas – our company will be on paper only.'

'What do you mean, Jake?' Mildred said.

'The factory of course is unaffected, but we will have no more flying school, no more sheds – and no more field. The farmer is not renewing our lease. Nothing on earth will change his mind. It's already re-leased to the Admiralty as part of their flying school and naval station in the event of war.'

Rosie stared at him aghast. 'He can't do that.'

'Apparently he can,' Jake said drily. 'Especially if – as I discovered – his family lives in property owned by Sir Lawrence Bellowes – and managed by Robert.'

Inwardly he seethed, but Bellowes would have to wait. The company was more important for the moment.

'We'll move back here,' Rosie said quickly. 'Or find another field. What about Ramsgate? Frinsted?'

Jake shook his head. 'We'd never get a licence, Rosie. Not now. Don't you realise that if there were war, there's a risk of invasion? And even without that, Kent is the nearest county to the Continent. The War Office would never countenance an airfield here now that was opposed to co-operation in its plans in the event of war.'

'No!' Rosie cried. 'No, no, *no*.'

They stared at each other, appalled.

Jake gave a deep sigh. 'I have forty-nine per cent of the shares. Rosie, forty-nine per cent. You, Mrs Potts, and you, Michael, have no voting powers, but I'd like to know your views.'

Michael looked at Jake calmly. 'I think Father would have wanted his aeroplanes to go on, not disappear. I want to help build them to carry on his work.'

She could not believe it. Michael, to desert her?

'Michael!' Rosie cried, devastated. 'But I thought you wanted what I want!'

'Not on this, Rosie,' said Michael, the businessman. 'You never asked me, did you?'

Michael had recovered his old devotion to Rosie, once he had begun work. But within limits. Now the excitement in his eyes was for the factory – not the aircraft in themselves, for he still had no love of them.

'Mother—' Rosie turned in horror to Mildred for support.

Mildred looked at her like a stranger. 'Your place is by Jake's side, Rosie. It's a woman's duty to support her future husband. Isn't that what I've always done?' It could have been an appeal, but Rosie saw it as a rejection.

Jake could not look at her, so alone, so betrayed. If he pleaded with her now, she'd come round to his viewpoint – but he could not do it. She had to come of her own free will.

'We have forty-nine per cent in favour, forty-nine against,' he announced dispassionately. 'Rosie, do you wish to change your mind?' Let her say yes, his whole being was crying out.

'No.'

'And nor do I.' He paused, some of his wretchedness beginning to show on his face. 'We have only one course of action. We must ask Polly to return for her decisive vote.'

'Let's promise that we'll help each other get what we want if we can,' Rosie heard a twelve-year-old Polly saying eagerly once more. 'Let's promise—'

'Oh, what it must have been like dancing here in the old days,' mourned Polly, her eyes sparkling as she whirled round with Thomas to the music of the accordion player at the Moulin de la Galette. 'Just think of all the famous painters who came here.'

'And now there's just me,' teased Thomas, steering her round a waiter rushing by, a tray of drinks on his upheld hand. 'The Merry Widow would not have been merry very long if she danced that every day,' he observed as they sank down exhausted at a table. 'At least I feel warmer now.' He glanced at the bleak December day outside.

'Gabriel used to say that every time a human danced an angel laughed,' she said casually.

'Do you miss him?' said Thomas abruptly.

'Miss him?' she repeated, startled he could know so little of her. 'No, Thomas, I don't miss him. I feel him near urging me on,' she said gently. 'He was so enthusiastic. I love you, you should know that.'

'Do you, Polly? I would do anything, anything for you—'

'Then let us marry,' said Polly beseechingly, 'and forget about this money problem.'

He went quite white. He had been living in a fool's paradise, and now he must leave it.

'Thomas, oh Thomas, I'm happier than ever I thought I could be,' she was saying. 'Thomas, I am to have our baby. So now we can be married, and we can give all my money to our baby, and make us all happy.'

He stared at her in distress and shock. And he'd been

so careful. Not careful enough, and now his paradise, so lovingly erected, crumbled in ruins about him. He saw Polly draw back, conscious of his lack of enthusiasm.

'Thomas?' she asked questioningly. '*Thomas*?'

'I can't,' he cried, 'I can't—'

'But money is so—'

'It isn't money, *meine Liebe*. I'm already married. I can't – don't you understand? I *can't* marry you.'

'Married?' she repeated blankly. 'Married?' The music was suddenly raucous, grating, their surroundings tawdry. 'You'd better tell me,' she said, without emotion.

'My family wanted me to marry Hilde for it joined our two estates. I lied about the money too, you see. She does not even like me very much. I came to Paris to escape. But divorce is not possible.'

'Do you have any children?' Polly asked politely, in a voice she did not recognise as her own.

He shook his head. 'She refused to – she would not even sleep with me. She does not understand what love between a man and woman is. Or if she does, it is not with me.'

She flinched as he reached out to take her hand.

'You know,' she said brightly, 'it always puzzled me that when I tried to paint my "Honesty" picture, with you as my model, I could never get the eyes right, I do see now.'

'Need it make any difference?' he said heavily and without hope.

'Difference?' she asked in genuine surprise. 'Why, of course. I shall leave. We have lived a lie, so what else do you expect?'

'But the baby? My baby. You will need—'

'I will need a house built on rock, not shifting sand. And I will build it myself.'

Polly sat dazed at the study table in Brynbourne Place. She still could not take in what all this was about. Bitterness consumed her entirely. She had loved and lost, loved and now been betrayed. If only he had told her . . . but he had not. The whole basis of their love was based on a lie.

She had remained cold, dead inside, all his arguments and persuasion in vain until at last he gave up trying, hopeless despair in his eyes. He helped her pack, he saw her to the train, one last appeal in his eyes that was not put into words, for he could see his cause was lost.

'The baby,' he muttered, 'you will tell me?'

Polly thought about his request somewhere within the misery that consumed her whole being. She inclined her head. 'Perhaps,' she said in a cold clear voice. She did not intend to do so.

Since her return no one had asked her of Thomas, for which she was grateful. She almost welcomed this incessant talk of aeroplanes. She did not understand it, she knew Rosie wanted something of her, that she talked endlessly to her, but her mind was full of Thomas and could not absorb what Rosie was asking. Then she managed to fasten on one fact when Jake was talking.

'War?' repeated Polly. 'War with Germany?' Bitterness took over. Her whole self concentrated on that issue.

'Polly darling,' Rosie pleaded, worried by Polly's lack of reaction. 'Father wanted to make a better world by flight, not a worse one.'

A better world! Polly smiled cynically. Impossible. Rosie was a dreamer, like Father, who knew nothing of the machinations of men.

Jake abstained from any attempt at persuasion. He had little hope of Polly's support, but he had to prove to Rosie how serious the problem was. Polly, for all his brave words, was in love with a German – a kind good man. How could she vote to support a war against his country? What would he do next? He could not face that question 'next'.

'I vote with Jake,' said Polly deliberately, breaking across Rosie's passionate outpourings.

Rosie stared at her, unbelievingly. 'Polly, do you understand what—'

'I understand quite clearly, Rosie, thank you.' There was a bright smile on Polly's face. Rosie took it as animosity towards her, but it was not. It was a smile of revenge, and only Thomas was in her thoughts.

'But, Polly, don't you remember what we promised each other when we were children?' she cried, anguished. 'It was *your* idea.'

Polly looked at her blankly and slowly she remembered that summer day. That too had ended in disaster. Was that all life was? Tragedy and disaster?

'We were only children,' she said in a high remote voice. 'We didn't understand.'

Rosie, defeated, slowly looked round the table. Mother, Michael, Polly – and Jake, all ranged against her. Four strangers. Four enemies. She read the pity, the struggle in Jake's eyes, and hurt the more. What could she do?

'I can't change what I believe in, Jake, just because you have. I'm no Vicar of Bray. So I can't stay. You see that?' A question that did not require an answer. 'You can do what you like with my shares.'

A scraping of a chair as Jake leapt to his feet, coming to her, and seizing her by her shoulders.

'Mother, you said it was my duty to stay by Jake's side if I married him. So if I can't work with him, I can't marry him either—'

'Rosie, stop.' He was shaking her now.

She pulled herself free. She was quite calm, for she knew there was no other course. 'We don't see things the same way you and I, Jake. So I must be the one to leave. You're needed here. I'm not. You can find other mechanics, other flyers—'

'Leave?' Mildred cried. 'But Rosie—'

'It's no use, Mother, you have all – even Polly – made your views quite plain. Now I've made mine plain.'

'Rosie,' Jake's anguished voice broke through to her at last.

'Don't, Jake,' she cried. 'Please don't. I must, don't you see? We can't plaster ourselves together just with love. I'll always love you, *always*, but you can't hold me just by that.' The tears running down her cheeks, she ran to the door.

'But where will you go? Rosie, don't be foolish. This is your home,' cried Mildred, her voice sharp with anxiety as Jake rushed across.

The answer was clear. The dark place was all around her now. 'Where I should have gone a long time ago,' she said quietly, and the door closed behind her.

Jake did not follow her. He was incapable of it. His past rose up sickeningly, overwhelming him, choking him into remembrance. It wasn't dead, as he'd thought, only dormant, and now the cage had closed upon him again. He'd thrown his life, his love, at Rosie's feet in one glorious misguided outpouring of trust, and she disregarded them. He had thought that however wide a gulf their opposing views might open up between them, their love could span it. But this bridge had to be built from both sides, and it seemed to him that he alone reached out. Slowly he walked across to the windows and stared up into the winter sky. There alone was truth, there alone could be his salvation.

# Chapter Fourteen

'The King's decided not to go to Goodwood,' Rosie called out gaily. 'What have you been up to now, Kate? Threatened to force-feed him?'

Kate came through from the kitchen, drying her hands on a towel, and laughed. 'I plead "Not Guilty" this time, your honour.' She leaned over Rosie's shoulder to glance at the headlines. 'War in Ireland?' she said. 'After all they've tried to do to avert it, with even the King stepping in as peacemaker?'

'No,' said Rosie, soberly reading on. 'It's not Ireland. It's because of what's happening in Europe.' She read on: ' "Mobilisation on the Continent. Great Activity in Home Diplomatic Circles." Kate—' Rosie laid down the newspaper, 'even if there is a war, and England gets involved, will it affect us? I mean, what we *do*?'

Kate sat down opposite her at the small table, staring through the lace curtains on to the placid suburban street below. Impossible on this hot late-July day in 1914 to believe that any war hovered near, let alone war with Germany. 'I think it will affect us here in England, at least so far as everyday living is concerned. I don't see how it can fail to, with the Kaiser's navy so powerful now. He can blockade us, starve us into submission.'

'There have been wars before – but it hasn't affected the civilians.'

'But no Kaiser before. And Jack used to—' Kate broke off in confusion. 'I'm sorry Rosie.'

'Don't be,' said Rosie, as matter-of-factly as she could. 'I can't blot Jake out altogether, and he is your brother.' She had tried to forget him, told herself that the future was what was important, not the past. Yet the merest casual mention and without warning the edifice she had built round her heart disintegrated, and let the pain through once more. Her life too – the life she had so carefully erected for herself brick by brick – was now under threat. What if these bricks were but mere playing cards and on a toss of a dice in hands other than hers, they collapsed around her, two and a half years of empty struggle whistling down the wind . . .

Dazed with shock and convinced that Brynbourne held nothing for her, Rosie had booked in at the Hotel Cecil in London to give herself time to think. Next week was Christmas, a Christmas she should spend at Brynbourne surrounded by all those she loved most. But she would not be there. She felt as if she was being sucked nearer and nearer to the centre of a whirlpool, and the centre was the dark place. A dark place that now had to be faced. With pain, she remembered Jake saying that he'd rather a bear tackled him from the front than from the back. Wasn't that what she had been doing all these years – burying the dark place, assuming it would die without air. She had been wrong; it had merely festered. All the insecurities that stemmed from her childhood took her over: Jake's love had been swept away, Father was dead, and the world of flight closed to her for ever. And she had thought herself secure.

'*You'll come to me, Rosie, you'll come to me . . .* '

Very well, she would. But not in defeat as he had expected; she would storm in to challenge this thing that had begun the infection so long ago. In Bethnal Green as a child she had learnt that she had to fight to survive, otherwise she'd land up like countless other children there, in one of the small coffins that passed by so often; or in the match factory; or on the streets; or a seamstress – one of the swarming hordes that existed to underpin London society. She had fought many battles then and since; but still the dark place had lingered. There was one more battle to fight, and it could be delayed no longer.

'*You'll come to me, Rosie . . .* ' So be it. But it would be on her terms, not his.

Did she still fear Uncle Alf, or was it the life he represented? Although he had always lived in Hoxton, to her he had always epitomised the Nichol, that pit of seething humanity where all the vicious scum of London used to gather and fight for mere existence. 'Never go near the Nichol' she'd been told as a child. Never turn off the Bethnal Green Road into one of the dark alleyways that led to the heart of the Nichol. And so she would run past dark alleyways – counting them one by one until at last she was past and could climb the stairs of their own home. The Nichol and Uncle Alf were one. The Nichol had been pulled down now, but there were other places around here just as bad she'd heard. Even now in Hoxton there were still families crowded in one room, no water, no privacy, but for the most part the people were clean, proud and hostile to strangers.

'But I'm one of you,' she wanted to shout as she climbed down from the omnibus in Shoreditch High Street and saw ironical faces sizing up the quality of her clothes, even though she was dressed simply, and hurried on her way to Drysdale Street.

There were places she half recognised from her childhood. Mr Pollock's Toy Shop. With a lurch of the heart she recalled peering in the windows as a child, to admire the paper cut-out princes and princesses and the delicate toy theatres with their fairytale backdrops, a world that had nothing to do with her daily life, and having heard her parents refer to 'Up West' she imagined the West End of London peopled with these wonderful beings. But the staircase to the third floor building in Drysdale Street held no such magic, the smell of damp, mingled with that of boiled fish-heads, almost made her resolution fail, but she pressed on. She knocked on the door, remembering how she had stretched up to the knocker as a child, trying to still the trembling in her knees. Fear struck her, hoping her aunt would open it, not Alf. What if he were there alone? But, after a few minutes the door was opened and she saw her aunt, red-rimmed eyes, rubbing them against the unexpected extra light from the open door. Then the shock of recognition. 'You're Rosie,' she said then, without much surprise and without interest. 'You'd best come in. I'm working, mind.'

Rosie could see that. The pile of cut-out blouses by the side, and a small one of Brussels lace to be sewn on to the finished article contrasted incongruously with the shabby furniture and few decorations. These same blouses would be on sale for perhaps 19s 6d and her aunt would receive a meagre 1s 6d.

Her aunt sat down to talk to her, but Rosie noticed that her eyes strayed to the blouses, as if she resented the loss of the pennies that these precious minutes were losing for her.

'Your uncle ain't here,' she said, tacitly assuming that no one came to see her. No curiosity, no wonder as to what Rosie was doing here. She accepted her presence, as she accepted the lot that was hers in life.

'I wanted to see you – and Hoxton – again. I remember coming here when I was small—' Rosie chattered nervously. Yes, she remembered. She recalled Uncle Alf looming above her in coarse avuncularity, bending to kiss her, leering at her as though at some secret they shared. She remembered beer-sodden breath and the huge smoke rings that he blew, that had both fascinated and repelled her, his terrifying rages. It was all she could do to continue to sit there talking normally to her aunt.

A loud laugh on the threshold, and Uncle Alf stood there. Involuntarily she rose to her feet. She was twenty-four now, Rosie told herself firmly, and a public figure thanks to her flying. She had no need to fear this man. Yet all the old feelings of panic were swelling up unbidden.

'Well,' he said, lounging against the doorpost, blowing his nose on the ends of his gaudy neckscarf. 'If it ain't little Rosie, come to pay a visit to her loving aunt and uncle. I've read about yer, up in aeroplanes and all.' His eyes held an appraising curiosity, running over her critically. 'In trousers—' he leered, making the word sound indecent.

'I've given up flying,' Rosie blurted out almost defensively, and then cursed herself for having parted with this information.

' 'Ave yer now? 'Ow about joining your aunt in the family business? Or you could go cleaning steps for a penny an hour.'

She flushed as he suddenly strode forward, thrusting his face under hers. 'Nice to see yer back in the nest, Rosie,' he whispered. 'I said you'd come.' He was staring at her triumphantly, thinking he had won this battle of wills, but she summoned up her last ounce of resistance. Never, never would she give in now to the dark place that had lain hidden so long. Now it was open at last and she had the power to conquer it.

'Why are you so hostile to me?' she flung at him. 'I've never done you harm?'

' 'Ostile? 'Ostile, is it?' he mocked, but less certainly now. 'What's that when it's at 'ome?' His eyes gleamed maliciously. 'And what are you 'ere for – something cooking in the oven, 'ave you?'

'No!' she cried, outraged, when she realised what he meant. 'I'm here because – because—' as she saw his mocking face it became harder to continue '—because I want to find out about my family.'

'What family might that be?' he jeered, but to her surprise her aunt took a stand.

'Be quiet, Alf,' she intervened sharply. 'The girl's right. What is it you want to know, Rosie?' There was little warmth in her eyes, however. The past was an emotion she could not afford to indulge in. The present took all her strength.

'My family – do I have any left?' Rosie blurted out. 'Father – Mr Potts told me my sisters and brothers were killed, but I thought perhaps I might have other aunts or uncles.' She averted her eyes from Alf. 'And what happened to the house? I mean, everything in it?'

A loud cackle from Alf, hastily shushed, then her aunt said kindly enough, 'Yes, yer Ma 'ad a load of brothers and sisters. Don't know what happened to them. One went in the war, that I recall. Saw 'is name in the lists. None left round 'ere that I know of. Yer Dad – well, there was only Alf and 'im left. And the 'ouse – well, there weren't nothing there much, and what there was old

Tooks from the pub took – yer dad owed 'im yer see.' She broke off apologetically. ' 'Ouse were only rented, Rosie.'

So it was gone. An overpowering relief. No need to see it. It was swept away; no dragons remained to be fought there at any rate. She felt curiously empty.

Alf eyed her, and suddenly said, ' 'Ow about it, Doris? Have a night at the old Pav, shall we? Bit of a celebration, seein' as 'ow it's almost Christmas?'

Her aunt's mouth fell open. It was clear that it had been a long time since the last night out.

'No, I'll—' Rosie stopped. If she refused, she would seem to be retreating. 'That would be very nice,' she said quietly.

He grinned as if discerning her feelings quite well.

The Pavilion Music Hall was a far cry from the Alhambra in Leicester Square, the only other hall she had visited. The Pav was overcrowded with hot sweaty bodies, chiefly men, and she was thankful that her uncle had paid 1s 6d for chairs so they were not part of the steamy mass below. Alf kept calling out to the regulars and his voice, together with the smoke rising to the small balcony, made her feel faint. Yet she was determined not to display weakness before him. He plonked a greasy baked potato, oozing with butter, before her, and surreptitiously she pushed it towards her aunt whose eyes brightened at the unexpected treat. Rosie sipped beer, which was harsh and strong, unlike the soft Kentish beer she sometimes drank. But if she could see this challenge out, she could walk away into a clean, if bleak, future.

The artistes were a far cry from Marie Lloyd. A few, such as the *lion comique*, were old and tried favourites but many were newcomers, their futures dictated solely by the reactions of the mob. One young girl, half-way through 'There's no place like home', was booed off the stage in tears. A comic achieved his first laugh when he ran off the stage followed by the jeers of the audience. The mood could change in an instant, from insults to adulation.

Rosie felt trapped in this humourless bearpit of a place. Her aunt was clearly enjoying every minute of it, and so there was no escape. Possessively, Alf called for more beer and laid his hand on Rosie's thigh. She reacted instantly, feeling contaminated even through the thick material of her dress. The noise around her, the stifling atmosphere, were no dream. This was what home had been like, this what she longed to escape. But she had been trapped by Uncle Alf with his furtive whisperings, his conspiratorial arm around her. 'You need a barf, Rosie. I'll barf yer.' Shivering in the sink, waiting, waiting. 'Not nah, Rosie, but you'll come to me, you'll come to me . . . ' One day she'd seen the bird, and knew that somewhere up there was a place without Uncle Alf, when if only she could get there, she'd never have to come home again.

'You'll come to me . . . '

She looked down at Alf's hand on her thigh, a podgy, possessive hand in which all the nightmares of her childhood concentrated. The hand of a man who had known no other kind of life than this, no other form of love between man and woman, and who never would. A man whose power over those weaker than he was his cry of rage against his world. A man who had lost his power over her.

Unemotionally, deliberately she removed Alf's hand from its hold, pushing it aside without rancour, as he laughed coarsely. But this time it sent no shivers down her spine. Everything slipped into focus for her. There was nothing for her here, now that the dragons of fear were slain.

If Kent held nothing for her, neither did London. The hopper's child at last was free.

She fell asleep that night in the comforting warm cocoon of the Hotel Cecil, content for the first time since she had left Brynbourne Place. The future lay ahead. A bleak, painful one, but her own. Untethered, she could fly free. Of the other chains that bound her, the chains of love, she could not, would not, think.

The next morning, however, she woke to the realisation that it was but a day or two to Christmas, and that she had nowhere to go, either forward or back. Back meant Jake – and the never-ending heart-searching as to whether she had been right to leave, with Mother's words ringing in her ears on the duty of women. She longed even now to return, to throw herself into his arms. When she walked out into the Strand packed with shoppers and workers, all belonging somewhere, her desolation increased. What should she do? Where should she go? Perhaps to Gamages or to sit in St Paul's. There she could reflect quietly and try to work out a plan of action.

The Strand was bewilderingly busy with horse traffic still mingling haphazardly with motor traffic, and the fumes and the smell of horses filled her nostrils. Then into the maelstrom of bustling activity marched a small band of women carrying a banner protesting against forced feeding and imprisonment. They were doing nothing but walking peacefully, yet Rosie noticed that several of them had been hit by vegetables thrown by onlookers – mostly women, Rosie observed. Then to her amazement she saw a familiar face amongst the small group. Sheer surprise made her call out:

'Kate!'

The tall serious-looking girl turned her head, hesitated for a moment, then came across to greet her. She bowed formally. 'Good morning, Miss Potts.'

'Kate – oh, Kate, can I talk to you?'

Kate had clearly intended to walk away again, once the dictates of good manners had been satisfied, but looking at Rosie more closely and hearing the distress in her voice, she nodded reluctantly and accompanied Rosie back into the hotel lounge. She listened completely amazed to Rosie's story as, to Rosie's own surprise, everything came pouring out.

'You've left Jack – Jake – for good?'

Rosie nodded miserably. 'How could I go on? We want different things. The only way I could marry him would be to abandon flying, give up aviation, give up everything except being his wife. I'd even do that if I thought we'd be happy, but I don't. This must sound very foolish to you—' she broke off disparagingly.

'No,' answered Kate slowly, thinking hard. 'No, it doesn't. I can understand.' Isn't that what Jack had done to her? She too had felt she had to escape from his loving protectiveness. 'I never liked you, Rosie,' Kate went on matter-of-factly. 'I know now that I was prejudiced, but even so I thought you had nothing else in your head than to fly aeroplanes.'

'You were so stand-offish,' began Rosie hotly.

'Perhaps,' Kate acknowledged. 'Now,' she frowned, 'there are more important issues than personalities. I wonder if you'd be interested in the Cause?'

'The Cause?' repeated Rosie blankly.

'Women's Suffrage,' said Kate impatiently.

'The suffragettes – oh, I—'

'I know – you think we just chain ourselves to railings, set fire to pillar boxes, and enjoy going to prison,' said Kate, resigned. 'But they are only the means – the end is recognition that we have a right to be treated as equals to men. For centuries we've been regarded as adjuncts to them, the vote is just one sign of it. We pay taxes but have no representation—'

'Nor have a lot of adult men,' pointed out Rosie.

Kate waved this aside. 'Yet there are whole areas of life we cannot participate in just because of our sex. The only way they will listen is for us to use their own weapon: fighting. Oh, I'm so useless at explaining—' she broke off impatiently. 'You should come along and hear Mrs Pankhurst – she's in America now, but you could talk to Mr and Mrs Pethick-Lawrence, who are her deputies and run the newspaper I help with, *Votes for Women*.' Kate went on to talk excitedly about the Pethick-Lawrences, their kindness and their rational approach to the Cause, the prison sentences and the forced feeding, and the way the women prisoners were treated. She talked, it seemed endlessly, to Rosie of politics, of bills that failed to become law, of disappointment after disappointment, about growing support in Parliament and the opposition of the Prime Minister, about Lloyd George and his views, until in the end Rosie's head was spinning.

'All right, all right,' she cried, laughing. 'I surrender. I'll come. But—' she hesitated '—no militancy for me.'

And so she had come to the small house in Holloway, rented cheaply by Kate from one of the richer suffragettes.

'We live very simply,' said Kate, somewhat embarrassed, as she opened the door. 'I don't get paid very much at the headquarters, and I can't go back to teaching, of course. There's a girl comes in every day, but—'

'We?'

'Paul and I.'

Paul? Was Kate married then, thought Rosie startled, already regretting she was here. Kate led the way to the upper part of the house which she rented and opened a door. Immediately Rosie liked the cool ordered atmosphere of the room; it spoke of Kate, reserved and calm. A girl rose to her feet and bobbed, then disappeared into the adjoining room. Kate went straight to a simple cot by the window.

Rosie's first thought was that this was the girl's child but the devoted care with which Kate picked her baby up and the loving words she murmured to it demolished that idea. Kate glanced round and saw Rosie's look of amazement. 'You did know, didn't you?' she asked uncertainly. 'Jack must surely have told you?'

'No,' said Rosie, trying to hide her shock. 'He didn't. I hadn't realised you'd married. Who—' Too late she saw the flush on Kate's face. 'I'm sorry,' she said quickly, warmly, realising now the reason for Kate's disappearance. How could Jake not have told her – and how like him to keep his family's affairs to himself.

'How stupid of me,' she went on lightly, 'and what a lovely baby.'

'There's no need to be sorry,' said Kate proudly. 'I've a wonderful son. I'm very lucky.' She laid him gently back in the cradle cot. 'You'll need to know whose it is,' she added as a statement of fact, not a question.

'No, I—' Rosie began to say awkwardly, but Kate impatiently waved this aside.

'Paul's father is Robert Bellowes,' she said quietly.

They celebrated Christmas quietly together and then Rosie hurled herself into her new tasks on *Votes for Women*, working in the Clement's Inn HQ of the Women's Social and Political Union. She had taken at once to Mrs

Pethick-Lawrence, whom she found a warm, reasonable woman with gentle calm eyes – except when in action. With a famous aviator on her staff, she had immediately suggested a series of interviews with all the women who had flown as pilots or as passengers, especially the handful that had gained their aviator's certificates.

'The root of the franchise problem lies in sex domination,' she explained to Rosie. 'So we must do all we can to show that women are capable of anything that men can achieve.'

But Rosie adamantly refused. The door to the world of aviation had closed behind her and she would not open it despite the temptation. Apart from this she obediently covered suffrage meetings, criticised and reported on parliamentary sessions, and studied and absorbed the doctrines of women's suffrage.

When Mrs Pankhurst returned like a whirlwind from America in February, Rosie listened enthralled to the strong forthright speeches coming with such vehemence from this delicate-looking woman. She listened with admiration, tinged with doubt. A doubt that was to be given substance later that month when Kate came rushing home one day with shining eyes.

'Mrs Pankhurst is organising a huge demonstration. We're window-breaking in Oxford and Regent Streets – we're all going to hide hammers under our coats and strike exactly at the same moment, smashing the shop windows nearest to us. My station is Swan and Edgars. And Mrs Pankhurst will be in Downing Street.'

'Kate!' Rosie was appalled. 'But you promised. No militancy because of Paul – what happens if you go to jail?'

'There's no risk of that,' said Kate happily. 'Not this time. There'll be too many of us, they can't arrest us all.'

'It won't get you anywhere,' said Rosie despairingly. 'We've had this argument so many times. People will just get exasperated.'

'We aren't getting anywhere without it,' Kate pointed out. She had a point. Huge meetings in the Albert Hall in the last four weeks, even with Lloyd George speaking ostensibly in their favour but in the event proving a paper tiger, had achieved nothing. Indeed with the number of women anti-suffragists ranged now against them, the cause was regressing rather than striding forward.

'Kate, don't go! *Please!*'

But she did. Even had she not been forcefully opposed to militancy, Rosie would have stayed behind. Someone had to look after Paul – just in case.

At eight o'clock Kate had returned ashen-faced. She had narrowly escaped arrest, but over two hundred had not been so fortunate. Yet Kate was unrepentant. 'We've made them take notice,' she kept saying in response to all Rosie's arguments. Even when four days later the police came to Clement's Inn to arrest the Pethick-Lawrences for conspiracy, she still maintained she was right. Militancy got the government worried, was her argument.

Rosie was not convinced, and as the summer continued she sided more and more with the Pethick-Lawrences and not with Mrs Pankhurst and her daughters, who spurred their followers on to more and more acts of militancy. By the middle of the summer there was tension in the Clement's Inn headquarters, and October saw a huge meeting in the Albert Hall where a split in the movement between the Pethick-Lawrences and the militants was announced by Mrs Pankhurst. The Pethick-Lawrences were withdrawing, taking *Votes for Women* with them.

Stunned, Rosie and Kate walked to the omnibus stop, realising that this could be the parting of the ways for more than Mrs Pankhurst and the Pethick-Lawrences.

'What shall you do, Kate?' Rosie asked slowly.

'I don't have any choice,' Kate replied forthrightly. 'I follow Mrs Pankhurst. Perhaps I can get work on the new newspaper, *The Suffragette,* unless Christabel Pankhurst intends to run it solely from Paris. What will you do?' she asked carefully, not displaying for a moment how much she had come to depend on Rosie's companionship.

'I can't follow you, Kate,' said Rosie, sadly. 'You know how I feel about militancy. I'll continue working for *Votes for Women* if the Pethick-Lawrences still want me. We can still live together, can't we?' she asked anxiously.

For the small house in Holloway was coming to mean a lot to her and so was the baby. Kate seemed to hesitate, and Rosie feared what she would say. But it was relief on Kate's part, nothing else.

'Of course,' she said warmly.

Yet Rosie saw less and less of Kate as time went on. Paul spent much of his time with Mrs Hoskins, their landlady, whose 'marching days were over' she informed them, but considered looking after Paul as part of her work for the Cause. As first the Franchise Reform Bill was withdrawn and then the Women's Suffrage Bill defeated, militancy grew in strength. As public opinion tended to soften towards militants because of their stoicism under forced feeding, the Cat and Mouse Act was passed in 1913, discharging awkward prisoners but with the powers of re-arrest at any time. Kate, sentenced for window breaking at the Garrick Club, was released but defiant and Rosie lived in fear that, reckless as Kate was, she would once more vanish inside Holloway Prison at any moment.

Rosie found herself dissatisfied with just working on *Votes for Women* now that there was no organisation to work with, for the Pethick-Lawrences had been too loyal to split the suffragette cause by taking their own followers away from Mrs Pankhurst. But Rosie's life took another new turn. The Actresses' Franchise League had been advertising their suffragette propaganda plays in *Votes for Women* for some time, and in May 1913 they decided to set up an Independent Women's Theatre Company, to be run entirely by women. An announcement inserted in the newspaper proclaimed that they were looking for new writers.

Scribbling a short play out in her spare time, Rosie found to her pleasure that it was accepted; she wrote another and that too was accepted. A complete season of the plays was to be given during the winter of 1913/14 with everything run by women, the acting, stage management, producing and financing and, drawn into the circle, she found a new kind of escape from the never-ending ache that meant Brynbourne.

It had been two years since she left, two years since

she'd seen Jake. She wrote to Mildred regularly, never revealing her address or clues as to where she could be found, and received letters back through her bank. Never a word about the company. And never a word of Jake. Only of home. It was just as well. She had to blot him out of her life completely.

Rosie was so busy and so tired at the theatre, she hardly noticed Kate's comings and goings, but could not ignore the growing militancy as 1914 began, with wanton attacks on paintings and the Rokeby Venus, and the first death last June as Emily Davison flung herself under the King's horse at the Derby. Where would it end? Not in the vote, she despaired, if they continued this way.

There was another deeper reason for her dissatisfaction. Even Rosie was unable to ignore the excitement over the Schneider Trophy in April, when for the first time an English pilot in an English aircraft, a Sopwith Tabloid, won the Schneider Trophy, and Europe woke up to the fact that British aviators were not a collection of Keystone Cops in the air, but in danger of seizing the laurels from the Continent. And she was not part of this triumph for which she had worked so long and so hard. And neither, apparently, was Jake. She searched every report diligently, but there was no mention of his name. Why not? Where was he? Had he gone abroad? The agony of not knowing grew worse, and she threw herself into work to exhaust herself physically in order to dull the pain of uncertainty.

It had been that same day that Kate had told her, 'There's a very special operation being planned, Rosie. Do come. You'd enjoy this one.' She laughed when she saw Rosie's face.

'Enjoy?' asked Rosie indulgently. 'What's on the programme this time? Knocking down Stonehenge?'

'Burning Robert Bellowes's aeroplane sheds,' replied Kate succinctly.

'*What?*' In a trice mingled emotions seized her, transporting her back to Kent and all it had meant, the remembered smell of burning aeroplanes – hers – coming to her once more. No, she could not do that, even to Robert Bellowes. Devoted as she was now to Kate, she still found it hard to imagine what attraction that slug had ever had for her, and now his treatment of Kate was added to her own score against him. Side by side with her immediate revulsion at Kate's news was the sickening thought that this would be a just revenge on him especially when, according to an article she had seen in *The Times*, Bellowes Clairville Ltd was ready for final trials with its new seaplane. Robert Bellowes – still the thought of him had the power to make her giddy with revulsion. Never could she accustom herself to the thought that he was Paul's father, and she had marvelled that Kate could maintain such a detached approach to him. Now seeing Kate's face exultant, she wondered if she had been wrong about the detachment.

'It wasn't my idea,' Kate was saying. 'But imagine the pleasure. Poor Robert's pocket hurt. You knew he married?' she went on casually. 'He married a sweet little heiress called Poppy, daughter of some lord or other. Trust him,' she snorted. 'Poppy!' she repeated derisively. 'Oh, Rosie, *how* I'll enjoy it.'

For a moment Rosie was tempted anew by the sweetness of revenge. She struggled with herself, then said regretfully, 'I can't, Kate. You know how I feel. Not even for Robert Bellowes can I change that. If I couldn't change for Jake, then I won't for Robert Bellowes.'

She sat up all night waiting for Kate to return on the evening of the raid, but no Kate came. The next day she had a telephone call from Mrs Pankhurst's office to go to Victoria Railway Station. There under police escort she was horrified to see Kate and about twenty others swathed in blankets, being watched by a scornful, sniggering crowd.

'They were ready for us,' said Kate bitterly, after Rosie had bundled her into a cab. 'Oh, Rosie, it was terrible. They stripped off our dresses, even the older women, and left us in our petticoats.' She did not elaborate, but Rosie guessed the mauling and lewdness that had gone on. How like Robert Bellowes. She shivered in disgust.

'The police didn't even arrest us,' said Kate, 'once

they'd had their fun. Just escorted us back. Now I know what close arrest means,' she added bitterly.

'Oh, Kate, will you not stop now?' asked Rosie wearily.

'Stop? Good heavens, no.' A small smile appeared on Kate's lips. 'There's one good thing. Robert Bellowes's wife was so horrified when she saw what was happening, she's decided to join us.' She threw back her head and laughed and laughed.

To the frenetic tempo of ragtime, the London season danced on, skimming like a dragonfly over the troubles that seethed beneath. London lazed in sunshine, worried about civil war in Ireland distanced by the heat, a grasshopper oblivious of winter to come.

Carson's menacing threats in Ireland, and the crisis meeting at the Palace to avoid civil war, filled the newspapers. Gun-running and shootings by the army centred attention on Ireland and away from the distant Balkans, as London looked forward to the prospect of a holiday weekend. Then the price of flour shot up, headlines spoke of Europe as an armed camp, on the 30th of July the British Fleet put to sea, on the 31st, bewildered, the man in the street read that the Stock Exchange was closing, that the gold sovereign was being withdrawn, and that the whole of Europe was drifting to disaster, as Austria's ultimatum to Serbia expired.

Then at last awareness focused. How? Why? No one could answer. Why should Austria's quarrel with the hot-headed troublesome Serbia affect England so far away? Then a new element, and reason was provided: Belgium. Gallant little Belgium was invaded by Germany. Seizing thankfully on this one issue, the Government acted. An ultimatum was issued.

The scene on the bank holiday at Hampstead Heath where Kate and Rosie had taken Paul, clutching his balloon, was a festive one of bright dresses, large hats and parasols. Nothing suggested that this bank holiday was different to others. Not until the latest edition of the newspaper was delivered to the bands and they turned from ragtime to play the National Anthem, and the audience rose. Here and there small groups of people huddled in knots to discuss the situation. In Parliament John Redmond stood up to pledge Ireland's support for England in the event of war, Catholics would fight with Protestants in the common cause. With his speech, the Kaiser's last chance of a neutral Britain vanished. And at 11 o'clock on Tuesday, 4th August, England was at war.

Three of the four squadrons that composed the new Royal Flying Corps set off with gallant optimism across the Channel to Amiens under the command of Brigadier-General Sir David Henderson. Since June the Naval Wing had come under the aegis of the Admiralty, and was now termed the Royal Navy Air Service, leaving the Royal Flying Corps under the control of the Army, and operating from Netheravon. Their role: scouting and reconnaissance, and raids on airship bases. It was a new and fragile force, fighting in a new element, but their fledgling wings flew confidently to meet the challenge.

'War, Jean-Michel.'

July had been wet and oppressive in Paris, the newspapers full not of war but of the Caillaux trial – it was not every day that the wife of the prime minister was arraigned for the murder of the editor of France's best-known newspaper. It served Paris well as a debating point far easier and of more immediate impact than the trifling affair between Austria and Serbia, which was irrelevant to France. Now Polly eyed her husband in some alarm.

'You really think the murder of this archduke will mean that France will be drawn in – that Germany may be at war with France and England?'

Jean-Michel watched his lovely wife sadly. 'I think it most likely that this will be the spark that lights that tinder box – yes.'

Polly stared out of the windows of the apartment in the Avenue Montaigne, which she and Jean-Michel had bought in Paris after their marriage. Waves of the past rose up sickeningly before her. Instead of war, she thought only of Thomas, a past she had thought forgotten or at least carefully put away. Even when she looked at her son she did not think of Thomas now. Jean-Michel had insisted the boy be called Thomas after his father; time enough, he had said carelessly, for children of their own. And now there was Rosemarie sleeping peacefully in her cot.

She had not told Thomas of the birth of his son. The past should be buried deep where it could never return.

She owed that to Jean-Michel. Her thoughts went back to New Year of 1912, when she had wondered in despair what the future was going to hold. Should she stay at Brynbourne Place, with the fiction that she was a widow, as Mother had urged? But Jean-Michel had understood how much she needed to get away.

'Miss Potts,' he had said at the New Year gathering, a strange affair without Rosie, and without Jake, who since Rosie had gone had rarely visited Brynbourne. 'I think, Miss Potts, that this year will be a hard one for us all – and for you in particular. You are very sad, I think.'

'I'm surprised you think that,' said Polly bitterly.

'And bitter too.'

'Perhaps,' she acknowledged.

'Do not judge my sex too harshly, Miss Potts.'

She gasped. 'Who – I do not think I wish to discuss this with you.'

'But I on the other hand wish to discuss it with you,' he had replied swiftly and gravely. 'Come, Miss Potts,' and, taking her hand, he took her into the conservatory. There as she stood stiffly, 'Miss Potts, please be seated. I cannot sit until you do so, and I have something most important to say.' Something in his eyes made her acquiesce. 'I think you have been unhappy in love, Miss Potts—'

'I don't—'

'Please answer me.'

She bit her lip. There was something about his kind eyes that made her nod her head stiffly.

'And it is hopeless, this love?'

'Yes.' The word fell bitterly from her lips.

'I too,' he said. 'So you see we have much in common, Miss Potts. And because of this, I would like you to become my wife.'

She gaped at him, speechless, and he continued calmly, perfectly in command. 'You think I jest. I do not. We do not know each other well, but we know enough. It is amazing what marriage can achieve without love.'

'I could not.' She rose. 'You are—'

'Practical, Miss Potts. All we French are. I need a wife, and—' he hesitated, 'excuse me, you need a husband. You are gentle, gracious and loving. There is no need of grand passion, I – perhaps, forgive me for being practical, I expect faithfulness, but I do not expect you to share my bed until you wish it.'

A red flush swept over her face. 'I'm afraid it is impossible, Monsieur Pinot, much as I am honoured. You see, I am expecting a baby.'

'This I suspected,' he said calmly; he had thought out his feelings on the subject. 'So all the more need for you to marry me – you are not a—' He caught himself from mentioning Kate's name. From now on, there was no Kate. 'If we have children together, this child will be as important to me as our own.'

Polly looked at him, her eyes swam. 'It is ridiculous, it is foolish,' she was saying, but every instinct in her was telling her to accept his offer.

'Very well,' she said dully at last. 'Very well.'

She went through the wedding in a daze and when at the end of June Thomas was born, Jean-Michel was as proud as if it were indeed their own. It was six months later that he came to her one night, appearing as calm as always. 'Dearest Polly,' he whispered, 'I think it is time. Yes?'

In gratitude and affection she put her arms round him and led him to their bed. Now in 1914, their daughter was a year old, and Polly was accustomed now to living in the centre of Paris, putting from her mind that other Paris she had known. The Avenue Montaigne had little in common with Montmartre and, busy with motherhood, she kept her thoughts from straying there. It was as if there were a different city altogether from the one she had lived in as a student.

Now, sharply and unexpectedly, with the threat, perhaps imminence, of war, Polly was caught by the old love. While Thomas was in Paris she was to some extent in control – she knew where he was. But now – Thomas came from an army family. He was mature, but still a reservist. He must in any case surely return to Germany. The newspapers were full of the chaos at the railway stations of foreign nationals desperate to get home to escape possible internment. He would go back to Germany and she would never see him again. She could not sleep that night, and Jean-Michel watched her in concern but said nothing.

What had made her come? Now the cab had left her here, Polly's courage evaporated, the half-crazy urge that had sent her helter-skelter to Montmartre; this compulsion and over-riding need to see Thomas again, to show him his son, was fading as reality set in. But she would not leave now. Her love for Thomas welled to the surface, overflowing in a tide that could not be stemmed. Hesitating, clutching their son by the hand, she stood on the steps to the house where their apartment had been, every detail springing into loving life in her memory. She approached the bell, but once there her courage deserted her.

'Polly.' The voice, so deep, so familiar. So loved.

She turned, and Thomas was there behind her, somewhat thinner and greyer, less vibrant. She could not move. His eyes on the child, he opened the door pushing them in. Then with a gasp she was in his arms.

'Polly.' He had no other words to say. 'Polly.'

'I must go,' she said ridiculously. 'I must go.'

'I too. To Germany.' So little to say. So much.

'I wanted to see you – to tell you—' Mutely she pushed the child forward and he stared bright-eyed and inquisitively up at the stranger.

'Why, why did you not tell me, Polly?' he cried in anguish.

'I'm married, Thomas.'

'I am glad for you, Polly.' It was an effort for him to speak. He hugged the boy, and set him down.

Tears blinded her eyes. 'I must go.' Foolish unmeant words. Go, when they belonged together? She could not look at him, but hurried down the steps again, dragging her son with her.

'Polly.' The word shot through her. 'Do you still—'

She turned. 'Yes,' she said, hardly daring to raise her eyes to him lest her resolve fade.

'I too, *meine Liebe. Auf Wiedersehen.*'

He had made it easy for her. Two words to give her the strength to leave.

Jean-Michel was waiting for her when she returned. He rose as she came into the room, his face serious. 'Go to Marie, *mon fils,*' he said quietly to Thomas, then turned to Polly. 'You have seen him?'

'Yes.' Then, 'How did you know?'

He shrugged. 'I can read your face, Polly. And why else take Thomas out on a day like this? Did you go to bed with him?' he enquired in polite tones.

Polly gasped. 'No!' she cried, outraged.

He smiled slightly, as if it no longer mattered very much. Seeing this, Polly broke out, 'He is his son, Jean-Michel. Thomas will return to Germany and will never see him again. He had a right.'

'And I – do I not have rights also?' he inquired. 'You did not feel you could discuss this with me before you left? You preferred to leave me not knowing whether you would return or not?'

'You thought I would not return?' she cried, astounded.

'I believed it possible.'

'But I—' She stepped forward, amazed that he could think she might not have come back, then realising with a great wonder that there had been no choice for her. She had *wanted* to return here. Here was home – and her husband.

'Yesterday has gone,' she said quietly. 'And tomorrow is still to come. Of course I would return – if you still want me.'

'Tomorrow—' he picked up *Le Figaro*, 'France mobilises. It has just been announced. Yes, I want you, Polly.' She came to him, and he put his arm round her. 'Neither of us knows what tomorrow may bring, and it is better with two, is it not?' He gave her a tired smile.

Three months of war. 'Over by Christmas, indeed,' Rosie thought grimly, wrenching the van doors open to begin unloading the props. Over here in France there was almost a festive atmosphere compared with anxious, worried England, a gay optimism even when Paris itself had been most under threat. Even now the forces were bogged down in the mud on the Aisne after the retreat from Mons. Had they not turned the Germans back from the very gates of Paris? Without a doubt victory would soon be theirs, reasoned the French; then the British Expeditionary Force could go home and leave France to its rejoicings.

At least she was better suited to this than working as a VAD in a hospital, Rosie thought. She had battled with her conscience on the outbreak of war, appalled at the fervour with which Kate had flung herself into supporting the war effort with the same energy as she had supported women's suffrage. Immediately on the outbreak of war the suffragettes had pledged support for the war effort, and suspended militancy. All suffragette prisoners were released and recruiting took the place of arson. It was war, war, war. Everyone spoke of patriotism, yet it was because of war and what it would mean that she had left Brynbourne. What should she do? Should she follow her conscience and have nothing to do with the war at all? The first dismal sight of the hordes of Belgian refugees arriving convinced her this was impossible. War was here, and the Kaiser had to be defeated. But the jingoism appalled her.

At the beginning of September she quarrelled with Kate. Women were actively recruiting everywhere, and Kate had flung herself into it with enthusiasm, even casting aside her usual severe dark dresses for those like today's bright blue and white cotton, full of feminine flounces.

'How can you, Kate? They're boys, mere boys you are encouraging to join up,' she raged.

'You're a pacifist, Rosie,' Kate taunted her. 'Do you want to be overrun by the Hun like Belgium?'

'No, but I don't want to be the cause of sending boys to their deaths.'

'That's merely shifting responsibility,' blazed Kate. 'Someone had to tell them their duty.'

'Not if the cause is good enough,' flashed Rosie. Then, sadly: 'It's no use, Kate, I'd better leave. We'll never agree over this.'

'No,' said Kate sadly. 'But what will you do?'

'The Actresses' Franchise League have started a Women's Emergency Corps – I'll join them. There's talk of organising concert parties to tour troop bases, perhaps even in France; they'll need drivers to go with them. I'm better at driving than nursing or handing out cups of tea to refugees. I'll offer my services.'

'I'll miss you.'

'And I you, Kate.' Rosie hugged her.

'Rosie, can't you change your mind?' Kate pleaded. 'Why don't you go back to aviation? Flying and designing is what you do best. If you're going to help the war effort in one way, why not the way you can do most good? You can't feel so strongly about not using aircraft for military purposes now, can you?'

'Oh yes,' said Rosie quietly. 'I haven't changed my mind at all.'

How could she sort out her mixed emotions? How explain the difference between helping the men caught up in this catastrophe and compromising her ideals for flight? Yet the pain, the temptation was not so much to fly again, or to work with military aircraft, but that to enter the world of aviation again was a sure path to Jake.

'Don't worry, Kate, I'll find my own answer,' was all she could manage to say as she hugged her goodbye.

# Chapter Fifteen

Rosie grimaced at the dreary landscape as the railway train chugged interminably slowly through Normandy and nearer to Paris. In France, clad in her mantle of war, the usual February bleakness seemed intensified. Here there was nothing but grey, and grey-greens, unrelieved even by the red brick that gave variety to the English scenery, though occasionally wooden-beamed houses gave interest to the outlook. The train was full of French *poilus* on leave, still apparently confident and managing to laugh after a bitterly cold and wet winter spent in trenches on the Aisne River, the war now a stalemate with neither the Allies nor the enemy making any advance. Paris was saved for the moment, but Rouen was threatened and who was to say what the spring might bring? Meanwhile, both sides hid in their trenches, where they might escape the attention of the enemy's scouting aeroplanes. The artillery men camouflaged their positions, for all too quickly observation aircraft could report their findings to provide the accurate range for renewed shelling.

The fledgling Royal Flying Corps, which had accompanied the Expeditionary Force to war, had expanded together with its role. With the coming of spring 1915, it was clear their job would no longer be confined to observation; their guns could maim and kill, observers could drop bombs on both stray and selected targets, and increasingly the little aeroplanes were fighting the enemy's in aerial duels. Such was the fear of the Zeppelin airship that little attention had hitherto been paid to the increasing numbers of German aeroplanes seen in the air. The Zeppelin menace itself was still as great. The raid on the Zeppelin sheds at Düsseldorf in the autumn, gallant as it had been, had done little to wipe out the threat, as the devastating air raids over England had proved in the New Year, as well as the bombardment by German ships of the East Coast towns, in the worst of which there had been over 700 casualties just before Christmas. This was a new kind of war, in which England herself was no longer inviolate, and women and children were in the front line. The greatest menace was that of the new army fighting from the air, an army that had to be combated.

As early as September a German Taube monoplane had bombed Paris. Rosie had feared for Polly then, reading of the loss of life caused by the raid, and feared even more when her letter went unanswered. It had taken six weeks for Polly to reply and then not from Paris. She was staying at their Normandy country house, she explained vaguely, with the children. Those that could had left Paris because of the nearness of the Germans, she explained. Those that were left talked in hushed tones, black clothes were conspiciously in evidence as casualty lists grew longer, all public buildings were closed, omnibuses were few and far between, and the price of meat and fuel had shot up. Gay Paris was carefree no longer; she had put away her pretty frocks and was preparing to fight in her own way. Rosie read and re-read Polly's letter; now she knew a lot more about what was going on in France, but little more of Jean-Michel. She had been delighted, but puzzled, when Mildred had written to tell her of Polly's marriage to Jean-Michel, and had immediately written to Polly, overcoming the bitterness that she felt at Polly's betrayal. Polly's reply had explained much and what it left unsaid Rosie could guess. Poor Polly, first Gabriel, now Thomas. But with Jean-Michel, Polly would be happy, Rosie thought. So the absence of references to him in Polly's letters now puzzled her.

With the coming of 1915 and the knowledge that there was going to be no speedy end to the war, Rosie realised that she could no longer blind herself to the inevitable: the aeroplane would become a major factor in warfare. She tortured herself by going over and over the stand she had taken on that fateful day. Who had been right? She or Jake? Jake had correctly seen war as inevitable; and therefore his duty was to help in the best way he could.

Seeing the wounded men being brought to Le Havre to the rear hospitals, and the slightly puzzled look on their faces as though this were not what war was supposed to be about, Rosie wished Kate were here to see the results of her passionate recruiting. Rosie would listen to the stories told by the endless streams of Belgian and French refugees, a scene that could so easily be repeated in England if the Channel ports were not defended, by soldiers such as these. And if soldiers, should not the Kent Aviation Company also play its part?

Then she heard that two days ago a new squadron had arrived – a squadron with KA3as on its strength – and she knew then that Jake was still designing. The KA3a (Kent Aviation 3a) had been the third of the single-seat fighters to be designed by the factory, she had gathered from newspaper reports. But there was no mention of Jake himself, which was odd. Still, he was at least safe, not risking his life daily going up against enemy fire, but she would not think of him further.

She had blinded herself to war's inevitability and now, proved wrong, was faced with the question: could she help? Yes, but what was the best way? With aeroplanes? She thought again of the hillside, of her pledge to Father never to abuse the privilege they had. She had not and she would not. Yet the thought continually tore at her that perhaps she chose this way because to acknowledge otherwise would be to acknowledge that the years she had spent away from Jake had been unnecessary. Tears of frustration pricked at her eyes. What was the use of abstract argument out here in France where survival from day to day was what counted?

The first concert party to come to France had now returned to England, after giving thirty-nine concerts in two weeks. She and one or two others had remained in Le Havre to help with the organisation of the next, due to arrive in two or three weeks. But there had proved little to do and she eagerly took the opportunity to go to see Polly in her country home about forty miles from Paris.

The concert party had developed a routine of hospital concerts followed by the actors and actresses touring the wards and giving solo performances for the more seriously wounded. Rosie had followed them round all the concerts, performing as driver, dresser, scenery shifter, even pianist – whatever was needed. The strain had been great, but she knew it was nothing compared with what would happen when the next concert party arrived. This would coincide with the new spring offensive, and makeshift hospitals were already being prepared in case the regular hospitals were not sufficient.

When this war was over, she would seek Jake out . . . She pushed away the temptation to think of him. Probably by now he had forgotten her, already found someone else, was even perhaps married. That must be why Mildred never mentioned him in her letters – and Rosie had always been too proud to ask after him.

At last the railway train chugged to a halt at Gisors and Rosie jumped down to the platform, carrying her suitcase – no porters nowadays.

'Polly!' She was thinner surely than she used to be, even gaunt. Perhaps it was the light, perhaps the particularly long slim dark coat that she wore. Rosie dropped the suitcase and ran forward, catching Polly in her arms. 'Oh Polly, how wonderful to see you again.' The pent-up affection inside her burst forth and the two girls were half laughing, half crying together. 'Polly, you're slimmer than ever, how do you—' Then she noticed the lines of unhappiness etched under Polly's eyes and broke off. 'How stupid of me,' she said quietly.

Polly smiled sadly. 'That's all right. It's so lovely to see you again, Rosie; that's all that's important at the moment. Come along.' She tucked Rosie's arm in hers and led her outside. 'No motor car, I'm afraid. Just the pony and trap. But we do have a chauffeur. Of sorts,' she added in a whisper. Rosie smiled. He was very ancient and had clearly been in the family for generations, and drove at a sedate pace.

There were no signs of war in Gisors, no soldiers, no signs of shelling, no ravages of passing troops or refugees. So far the war had not travelled this far, but it was perilously close. Only the absence of young men revealed that France was at war, otherwise the town appeared to slumber peacefully on with its wooden-framed houses. The Pinot château was grey stone, set in a large park some kilometres outside the town, but its gardens were unkempt and ill cared for.

'The gardeners downed tools and set off to war last August,' said Polly wrily. 'I can't blame them with their country to defend, but it doesn't make life easy. Some of the local women come in to help in the house, but they can't do the heavy work.'

By English standards the château and its furnishings were simple, almost primitive, but with a stark beauty of their own. Polly had at least installed a bathroom. 'I had to,' she explained, laughing. 'I could never look Potts Sanitary Ware in the face again. Our friends think it most amusing.' A shadow passed over her face, but she said no more.

Later, when the children had been swept off to bed by their nanny, and she and Polly had finished a huge meal in which it was evident that food at least was not yet a problem in France, Rosie asked quietly, 'How often does Jean-Michel come to see you?'

Polly flushed. 'Not often.' She looked at Rosie piteously. 'Not that I expected it. He's been so busy of course, with all the extra engine production—' She caught Rosie's eye and broke off. 'He hasn't come at all,' she admitted. 'And I don't think he will,' she said flatly. 'He tried hard, but he can't get it out of his head that I was disloyal to him in going to see Thomas. It's not even as if I had been unfaithful to him. He says he can't understand it himself, but he thinks it would be better – for the children, he said – to be away from Paris now that the Germans have started to bomb it.' Polly laughed weakly. 'A tiny bomb on the Opéra last autumn and two tiny bombs on Notre Dame in January, which could hardly tear a hole in the roof.'

'Weren't some people killed at the Gare du Nord?'

'Yes, but all the same it's a ridiculous exaggeration to say Paris isn't safe. The Germans haven't even tried again. It would take them years to subdue Paris that way. It's just an excuse on Jean-Michel's part,' Polly said bitterly, 'because he can no longer stand the sight of me. How can he be so unfair, when I know he still loves that Kate—'

'*Kate*?' asked Rosie startled. 'Are you sure?'

'Of course I am,' Polly said impatiently. 'He told me about her before we married. I thought then that it was to make me feel better about Thomas, but I know now it was to assuage his own conscience. He'll never get over her, never.'

'But he can't have seen her for years,' Rosie said incautiously.

Polly looked at her ironically. 'And you've forgotten Jake?'

Rosie cried out, appalled at the sudden jab of pain.

'Oh Rosie, I shouldn't have said that,' Polly said penitently. 'Please forgive me. I just seem to go round and round in circles here on my own, I get things out of proportion.'

Rosie reached out a hand and touched Polly's across the table in forgiveness.

'Do you love him?' she asked. 'Jean-Michel, I mean.'

'Love?' repeated Polly bitterly. 'I just don't know. He's my husband. I loved Gabriel and I lost him. I loved Thomas and I lost him. The word has ceased to mean anything. I don't know and I don't care whether I love Jean-Michel or not. I just want to be with him.'

'Perhaps—'

'When this war is over,' Polly finished for her, and they laughed.

'Do you not paint any more?' asked Rosie.

'Not now. I did when I got back to England after I left Thomas. I painted then,' Polly replied after a moment. 'Angry, savage, horrible, *horrible* pictures, and then when I got over my immediate anger I looked at them and I was ashamed. To think I should use my gift for revenge, for something other than trying to create something beautiful – it was like you and aeroplanes, do you understand?'

'Yes,' said Rosie in a low voice. 'Oh yes, I understand.'

'And I haven't painted since. I've been too busy with the children. Jean-Michel tried to encourage me, but somehow I didn't have the inspiration – I hadn't the courage to go back to that world, in case I should meet Thomas again. That won't happen now. He's returned to Germany and is probably in the trenches. He could be back in France for all I know, or Russia or Africa. Isn't that where there's a lot of action taking place now?' She threw back a strand of her bright hair. 'Oh, Rosie, where is the world going? And we used to find it such a beautiful place.'

'It will be again.' But her words rang hollow, even to Rosie's own ears.

She stayed at the château for two weeks, seeing Polly cheered visibly by her visit. She enjoyed Polly's company and their long walks in the February cold, even seeing a bleak beauty in the countryside and enjoying the huge log fires and food of the château after the bleakness of hostel life in Le Havre.

On her last morning she came down early, grimacing at the usual French offering of stale bread and coffee in place of her substantial English breakfast and wondering why the French lay so little store by this vital start to the day – as necessary as castor oil to the engine. Polly was reading a letter in a handwriting Rosie recognised. It was from Mother.

'What's Mother got to say?' asked Rosie lightly, trying to disguise how much she wanted to hear.

'She's going to turn Brynbourne into a convalescent home for wounded soldiers.'

'*What?*' Rosie's amazement surprised even her because, as she thought about it, it seemed a logical step for Mother.

'She'd been sheltering Belgian refugees, and now that they're gone,' explained Polly, as she read on, 'she feels the house is empty. Now that more and more wounded are being looked after in Margate and Canterbury hospitals she thought she'd do this.'

'But she's not a nurse – does she plan to stay there?'

'Oh yes, and apparently she *is* a nurse. Or at least she's a VAD. They organised before the war, knowing Kent would be busy with casualties if war broke out. She joined Sittingbourne VAD, and that's how she got into this. She's already got the first houseful. Michael didn't approve of course, especially having to move to the Lodge with Mother now that Jake's no longer—' she stopped. 'Oh heavens, there I go again.'

'That's all right.' A pause. 'Where is he?'

'I don't know,' said Polly quickly.

And if she did, thought Rosie, she wouldn't say. Everyone seemed to be in a conspiracy to tell her nothing lest she be hurt. Her heart leapt painfully – he must be married, that was the explanation.

Somehow Brynbourne being turned into a convalescent home seemed the last straw. Every haven of warmth and security was vanishing.

The journey back to Le Havre seemed twice as long and her visit to Polly, enjoyable as it had been, seemed merely now to serve to show what she had lost – perhaps through her own obstinacy and stupidity. War made one realise that one had to take every chance of happiness before it was snatched away, never to return. At least Polly had had those years of happiness with Thomas. Yet what had she, Rosie, done? Postponed her marriage to Jake too long. And for what? For principle. Then she had left him for the same reason. How unnecessary, how arrogant, seen with hindsight. And yet perhaps she had been right, she thought tiredly. Suppose they had married? Suppose they had then quarrelled bitterly over the future of the company? Or over her own desires to fly? She rubbed her eyes to remove a piece of soot as the railway train steamed into Le Havre, and convinced herself that the smarting that ensued was solely due to the inconvenience of coal-fired boilers.

Rosie found she had been right to leave while she could for talk of an early spring offensive had intensified. Once the wounded started arriving at the rear hospitals, the concert parties would be busy again. When the girls had first arrived, they had begun with serious songs and drama, but found that comedy music-hall songs were more appreciated. It was a far cry from women's suffrage and equality of woman with man, but Rosie suspected that the mere sight of a prettily dressed woman did more for the soldiers' spirits than a soliloquy from *Hamlet*.

'Neuve Chapelle' – the words on everyone's lips. Sir John French had begun the spring offensive three days ago on 15th March, and the wounded were beginning to arrive from the front-line field hospitals. Neuve Chapelle – the village had awoken that morning, its apple orchards beginning to show signs of buds with the approach of spring; the manor house, mill and farmhouses slumbered peacefully as they had done for hundreds of years; in the centre of the village were the church and churchyard dominated by a huge crucifix. By the evening only the crucifix remained standing amidst the ruins of what had been Neuve Chapelle. Even the gravestones had been blasted to rubble, their contents scattered. For Neuve Chapelle had stood on a German salient jutting into the British front lines, vulnerable and tempting. The fierce bombardment that began the offensive, and the ground attained in the first hour of fighting, should have carried the British far forward. But reserves were held back and other mistakes made, so rumour went, giving the Germans time to re-group. The enemy could not drive the British back, but they did not retreat themselves. The blow to German morale was great, however, and for the first time for many months, the British Tommies rejoiced.

The soldiers were full, too, of the part that the new unit was playing. The Royal Flying Corps had flown behind the enemy lines and dropped bombs on to the railway station at Don and the railway bridge at Menin to slow up reinforcements reaching the German lines. It was a new concept in warfare, and one the corps was proud of, and would not forget. Suddenly airships, the Royal Naval Air Service and the Royal Flying Corps became an accepted part of warfare with a dangerous and increasingly important part to play.

The RFC had done sterling work in tactical observation and reconnaissance in spotting General von Kluck's swerve away from Paris in the autumn of 1914 and they were coming to be relied upon as the eyes of the army, who were hidden deep in their trenches. But aerial combat between scouts was becoming a familiar sight. Bitter fights took place as each side sought to conceal its positions from prying eyes, and they usually ended with one or the other aircraft falling from the skies to its end.

Despite her resolution to play no part in military flying, Rosie found herself drawn like a magnet by all she heard about the Royal Flying Corps in France. After all, she argued, there was no harm in *looking*. She might see a KA3a. It would be interesting technically, she convinced herself, even necessary for that dreamed-of time when the war should end. On the rare occasions that a Sopwith or Bristol Scout flew over, she craned her neck to see, to the non-amusement of her passengers in the old Halley van, if she happened to be driving. What were they like to fly? What was the KA3a like to fly? She'd seen pictures of it – a biplane of course, since the development of monoplanes had been discouraged by the War Office. It was a pusher, but sleek and slim compared with Astra. Yet looks weren't everything. How did it handle? she wondered wistfully. Its speed? Its – no, she must not think about it any longer. All the same, when the group organiser asked her to drive to RFC HQ further north, she did not refuse. The wounded of Neuve Chapelle were filling the hospitals at Boulogne and Wimereux now; soon they would be at Le Havre too. If ever she was to see aircraft in action she must seize it now for the days to come would be busy.

'St Omer again?' she inquired.

'No.' The organiser frowned. 'Advanced HQ at Hazebrouck; they moved there for the push, and should still be there. I oughtn't to send you really, but it's urgent that—'

'Oh no, do please.'

'Straight there and back then. Apart from you, we can't risk the van getting caught up in the action. It might get commandeered and it's the only one we've got, bless it. I wonder though—'

Rosie escaped quickly before she could change her mind. It was a long drive, involving an overnight stop at Abbeville to the great pleasure of the Army Tour Major there, who was not often called upon to find billets for attractive young Englishwomen. As she drove further north, she could hear the distant boom of sporadic shelling and her pulses quickened. The very smell of war seemed to intensify. It took her some time to track down the HQ owing to the fact that few people knew that they were there, quartered temporarily in the HQ of the Second Wing, in an English-looking moated house. When at last she located them, she ran into more trouble trying to find someone to pay attention to her. Everyone was still talking excitedly about the push, the part the RFC had played in it, and the great part it would play in other offensives.

'I'm sorry.' The second lieutenant was young and charming. 'We're just being frightfully proud of ourselves. The chaps did a good job, you see, co-operating with the Army and all that. We really showed them. Reporting on enemy positions and so on. Bombing. They'll think twice before they set us down as amateurs in future. Why,' he smiled kindly at her, 'before we know where we are you women might be flying too. What would you think of that?'

'It sounds very scary,' said Rosie meekly. 'If I might have this list approved please.'

'What? Oh yes. I don't expect you've ever seen an aeroplane close to have you?' he continued pompously.

'One or two,' murmured Rosie.

'Would you like to?' He disregarded her comment. 'I'm going to the aerodrome now. I could—'

'Yes,' she breathed. 'Oh yes, *please*.' She fluttered her eyelashes at him. 'Is the new squadron with the KA3as based there?'

He looked startled, then clearly put this down as a display of gratuitous erudition for his benefit and recovered his composure. In the Crossley staff car she was hard put to it to answer his questions about the girls' concert parties, and his enthusiastic discussion of the London theatre scene past and present in which Gaiety Girls seemed to play a rather larger part than the works of Mr Bernard Shaw.

The aerodrome proved to be nothing more than a large field, with the squadron personnel living in tented accommodation next to it. Though spring was on the way there were few signs of it yet, and though a pale sun was shining, the blue-overalled mechanics in their distinguishing forage caps looked half frozen as they went about their work. One of them noticed her, and whistled, until his fellow nudged him, having observed the General HQ markings on the motorcar.

'I shouldn't have brought you,' muttered her escort ruefully. Rosie wasn't listening. Her eyes were fixed entranced on two KA3as among the half-dozen aircraft lined up on the field. She was about to jump down from the Crossley when her companion stopped her.

'Stay here,' the lieutenant sternly commanded her. 'Do not move or I'll be on a charge, and you,' he added, 'will be SBB.'

'SBB?'

'Sent back to Blighty.'

She grinned and did not remonstrate; she folded her hands meekly in her lap, and looked the picture of innocence. As soon as his immaculately uniformed back had disappeared into the command tent, she leapt out and ran over to the KA3as, putting her finger on her lips to silence the vocal enthusiasm of the mechanics. Not only a woman, but a woman in tweed trousers and jacket!

Rosie caught her breath. The KA3a was even more beautiful close to than seen from a distance. The smell of the castor oil in her nostrils overwhelmed her, the familiar blue fumes above the last aircraft in the line, whose engine was being tested, made her choke as much from emotion as from the smoke, as she swept back into the past. But it was the aircraft itself that mesmerised her. No need to ask if this was indeed the single-seater KA3a. Its lines spoke of Jake's touch, as surely as if she saw the designs before her. There was something of Daisy Belle's solidity coupled with Sunburst's sleekness in its bleached-linen fabric covering and its ash and spruce frame. She ran her hands over the polished wooden propeller. Mahogany, of course, like Daisy Belle's.

'What's her maximum speed?' she shot at the mechanic.

'Fast, ma'am, very fast,' he replied politely.

She sighed, took a closer look at the eight-cylinder rotary engine. 'Seventy – eighty? Eighty probably.'

The mechanic shot her a look of surprise and some respect. 'Eighty-one, ma'am. And very manoeuvrable – it's the ailerons do that, we reckon. Nice little job.' He paused curiously. 'You like aeroplanes, miss?'

She nodded mutely. Then unable to stand it any longer, turned her back on the aeroplanes, and went back to the Crossley. Her guide was just emerging from the tent looking so satisfied with this mission that he failed to appreciate the significance of Rosie leaping quickly in before him.

'Done it,' he announced. 'The CO wasn't there, and the second-in-command isn't such a terror. Even the general's a shade nervous of the CO. I didn't fancy telling him he was to be posted.'

He cranked the engine and leapt in beside Rosie as it roared into life with a cloud of smoke, and he began to hum in high glee, 'A poor aviator lay dying . . . '

As their Crossley turned out of the aerodrome gate, another turned into the entrance. It was open-topped, like theirs and drove in at speed; its khaki-clad passenger was half-turned from them, uninterested.

'There's the CO now,' remarked her companion smugly, happy at having escaped in time.

Rosie did not answer, could not answer. In those few seconds pain had torn her heart wide open. It was Jake.

Half-glimpsed, dismissed, then doubted, he turned quickly round to look behind him. The General HQ Crossley was already vanishing into the distance, carrying its phantom from years past, a ghost from a youth that was over, a youth when happiness could be plucked from the bough of life like a ripe apple – an apple that had fallen before its time to lie rotting on the earth.

Major Jack Smith, MC, did not recognise that youth. The years when he was Jake Smith vanished the day he had signed on for the Royal Flying Corps. Jake? An incredulous stare, and it was amended to Jack, the name he had not answered to, save to Kate, since he was fourteen years old. Now Jack seemed a name to symbolise a new beginning, a name to sweep away the traumas of youth, the exhilarations and triumphs of peacetime flying and leave him free to fight a war – where he had a part to play. Here the enemy was tangible; it could not steal under your guard, tear away at you from inside, could not thrust the past before you and call it Rosie. A trick of the light, or his overtired imagination? The winter had been long, and spring was slow in coming.

'Sir?' His driver broke into his thoughts. 'We're here.'

Jake grunted, ashamed of having been caught in some daydream of his own. He jumped down from the Crossley and strode into the Command Hut. His second-in-command sprang to attention.

'Sir.'

'Who's been visiting us, Mitchell?'

'General HQ, sir. New orders.'

Jake's eyes flickered to the table. 'Who from HQ precisely?'

'Second Lieutenant Hastings, sir.'

'And?' The word seemed to echo in his head interminably.

His No. 2 stared. 'No one else, sir.'

'No one else?' Was he going mad that he saw her everywhere, even on a bleak March day in some barren waste of a foreign country? After all that had happened, was Rosie so much in him still?

He stared outside at the mechanics taking advantage of the pale sunlight to service the squadron aircraft. They were working on the KA3as now. He hardly ever thought

358

of the KA3a's origins now. It had become merely a tool to fight with. Odd to think it was his design, that it was all-important at one time as it was only the KA3a and its predecessors that had saved him from complete despair in those dark days after Rosie had left. The disbelief, then growing realisation that she was not coming back; the incomprehension – and then the bitterness. Could she not see that war was inevitable and, if England were to remain free, that she couldn't fight with one hand tied behind her back? Everyone and everything had to play its part.

The savageness, the bitterness, invaded him as he worked far into the night on designs. Then came the blow when the War Office ruled against monoplane designs for the military trials, and the KA1 and 2 had had to be scrapped. He had taken Daisy Belle and Astra, blended the best of each, to produce the KA1 scout; and then redesigned Daisy Belle to be a two–seater military plane with the idea of its being able to drop bombs. That had been born out of bitterness. He hadn't been able to build either in time for the trials, and the awards had gone to French designers. Three months later he produced the KA3. The War Office had immediately recognised its potential and ordered six in 1913. In 1914 the improved KA3a had come into service, just in time to fly out to France with the RFC, but by then everything had changed for Jake.

'What the hell do you mean, Michael?'

Jake, gaunt as a rake, had faced the cool eighteen-year-old. It was hard enough to come back to Brynbourne early in 1913, to see the factory again for the first time in a year, but he had not expected this.

'Now you're in the Royal Flying Corps you've neither the time nor the interest in keeping things running here, and so I propose to sell Kent Aviation,' said Michael steadily.

'You can't,' Jake shot out. But he knew only too well that Michael could sell, if he wanted. Now that Rosie had given her shares to the family – for Jake had refused to take any – and with Polly away, Michael could in effect make what decisions he liked. Mildred would do what

Michael wanted in the end. Jake with his forty-nine per cent was still the minority shareholder. What a fool he'd ever been to agree to William's cock-eyed split of shares. What a trusting fool he'd been all round . . . Until Michael had sprung this blow on him, Jake had not realised he cared so deeply about the company. It was part of his life, his achievement, something to hold fast to.

He had to keep cool. 'What have you to sell?' he inquired gently. 'A defunct school taken over by the Admiralty, a lease on a few fields near Ramsgate, one or two orders for poor old Daisy Belle – what else, without me?' He laid some emphasis but not too much on the last two words. If Michael were one tenth the businessman he obviously considered himself to be, he'd understand. Kent Aviation *was* Jake. Jake was the designer, and without a new design there was no company.

'There's the KA3,' said Michael matter-of-factly.

'But the Army—'

'The patent is in the company's name, not yours, Jake. Nor the Army's.' There was no hint of triumph or smugness in Michael's voice. Jake swallowed. The room was swimming round him, but he retained his temper, even though he itched to lash out.

'What happens when the Army needs to update it?'

'We've thought of that,' countered Michael.

'We?' asked Jake sharply.

'The new owners and I.' He spoke as though it were already a *fait accompli*, Jake noted.

'Who?' Jake asked abruptly. There was something here he did not understand.

'The Bellowes Clairville Company.'

Jake let out a cry of such anger that even Michael flinched. '*No.*' Inarticulate, a red mist before his eyes, blind fury seized him as it had not done since the death of May. It seemed to him that before him was not Michael whom he'd known since a boy, but a hobo, covered with the dirt of the mines, evil written all over the face. And he acted as he had done then. With two strides, he had seized Michael by the collar and was shaking him, sturdy though he was, like a puppy. More in surprise than physical pain and terrified by the look on Jake's face Michael yelled out and, disturbed by the noise, the lady clerk rushed in, appalled at the spectacle before her. Only her faint cry, 'Mr Smith!' recalled Jake from the saloons of Leadville to the Kent of 1913. With an exclamation of disgust, he flung Michael from him, sending him crashing against the wall, turned round and walked out of the factory.

Three days later Michael received a packet through the Post Office containing Jake's shares in Kent Aviation, together with a quit claim for any payment.

He stared at it for a while, wondering if he were pleased or not. To get rid of Jake Smith yes – but it would make the sale of Kent Aviation a foregone conclusion now. He'd never liked aeroplanes – always, always, he'd had them forced upon him and he had borne with them for Rosie's sake and for Father's. But now there was no Father and no Rosie. With the sale of Kent Aviation he would have the money to develop the sanitary ware side the way he wanted – eventually. Yet he was canny enough to see that with the War Office requisitioning more and more factories for war matériel production, Kent Aviation would be the only way that Potts Sanitary Ware could continue to operate. Without it, the whole factory might be turned over to shell-making. So he had worked out a good deal with Bellowes, who had problems of his own at Ramsgate. Michael would continue to manage Kent Aviation from Sittingbourne, until the war ended, and in return he passed over the lease on the Ramsgate airfields to Bellowes.

He told himself that Father would approve, for he was taking care of Mother, doing the best he could in the circumstances. He told himself that Rosie too would approve, when she returned. And one day she *would* return – now that he had got rid of Jake Smith. What he had more difficulty in explaining even to himself, was how he could reconcile his new working partnership with his old vow of vengeance on Robert Bellowes. Being Michael, he gave up trying.

Rosie could be once and for all banished from his life, Jake told himself as he had left Michael. In some indefinable way, this was yet some further betrayal of hers, but at least his dreams would be the less troubled, and the future, whatever it held, would be untainted because she and Kent Aviation formed no part of it. She had gone, like Florence. Like May, like Ma, like Kate. But most of all like Florence. In his nightmares Florence's face, smiling down in mockery from that swing, was replaced by Rosie's till he woke and cried out. Or those worse dreams to bear, where Rosie came to him laughing, smiling, wholeheartedly, with such trust, such love on her face that the waking dawn was cold.

When the War Office asked him to join the newly formed Royal Flying Corps in 1912 he had eagerly snatched at the opportunity, dividing his time between instructing at the newly established Central Flying School and, with their agreement, at the Army Aircraft Establishment at Farnborough where he designed and worked on the KA3 for Kent Aviation. Now he would be free to design just for the army – and test-fly for them. For he had made it clear that flying was always to be part of his life. He had been given the job of test-flying the Bellowes Clairville BC2 and gave an adverse report, asking for a second opinion in case he was prejudiced. But he had not been. The second test pilot had killed himself in it. The aircraft was pronounced unstable and unmanoeuverable, a hard verdict on Clairville Jones who prided himself on his aircraft's inherent stability. And so now the Bellowes Clairville Company would be thrown back on the KA3 – and the need for an improved model if they were to have any aircraft in the Army line-up.

The specification for the improved model submitted by Clairville Jones proved unacceptable to the War Office and Michael was forced to come to Jake cap in hand. He got nowhere. It took Mildred to persuade him, or rather her presence to remind him of what she did not put into words – that she and Michael needed the income from the continuing production of the KA3. Grimly appreciating the irony, Jake had agreed on one condition: the patent in the KA3 should pass to him, while the production remained at the Sittingbourne factory.

With the coming of war, Jake was determined to fly again. Anything to be in action, and so still the constant thoughts of Rosie that beset him night and day. Reluctantly the War Office had agreed.

This wasn't the France he had known in pre-war days, Jake reflected, when he had travelled round with the Wright brothers from air show to air show, when enthusiasm and optimism for the future had lit up the sunlit plains, as little aircraft had bravely buzzed around the sky like dragonflies.

This was a bleak, dull, France, where villagers tried to hide their fear and carry on as usual, but where the long columns of refugees pointed the way to their probable future; where the local *estaminets* rang to the sounds of soldiers' songs of marching or bawdiness, not the French folk songs of yesteryear; where drinks were swallowed quickly, almost furtively, not for communal pleasure. It had not been like that at first. Then there had been a proud tilt to the French *poilus*' bearing, a confident optimism that the Boche would be driven back by Christmas. But the long winter and the war of attrition that was beginning to develop had put paid to that. With the coming of spring and the talk of the new push at Neuve Chapelle, flagging spirits had revived, but the fiercely fought contest and the small amount of ground won in the offensive, ensured that optimism was replaced by apprehension. How long would those trenches be occupied? And how much ground would the next advance cover, if this one had accomplished so little?

He had flown out to France with his squadron at the beginning of the war, as flight commander Captain Jack Smith; many of the men were among those he had trained at the Central Flying School. No one expected much of them now; they were thought to be a band of adventurers, perhaps useful for a spot of scouting. Just how useful had been quickly evident when they had reported the enemy turning from Paris, and won General Joffre's commendation. Bombing raids, observation – fighting. It had been simple in those early days with barely a hundred aircraft and the Germans in much the same state. Now expansion was evident everywhere, more and more officers flying in with their biplanes, more and more German aircraft to be seen. This was going to continue for a long time yet.

After a few weeks, with the onset of winter, he'd been posted back home as an instructor, as had many of the older, experienced pilots. They were needed to train new recruits in England. But the need for leadership again became paramount with the coming of 1915, and he was back in January, promoted to Major and given command of a squadron. The new pilots were arriving all the time. Those of them who had been civilian pilots would have had some military flying training – there was a big difference. Constant flying at 6,000 feet for one thing. This morning – early in March – he had to show a new flight commander the ropes.

There was the fellow now, climbing out of a Sopwith Scout. Jake strolled towards him, then stopped in amazement. He'd been expecting a Captain Jones. What he had not been expecting was that it would turn out to be Harry Clairville Jones.

Why should he have been surprised? He hadn't reckoned on the fellow having so much guts, he supposed. He imagined Clairville Jones would be more interested in his safe job at the factory, producing and designing engines – since foreign engines were so hard to get now, there was a premium on English designs and he rather gathered that, after the failure of the BC2, Clairville Jones had gone back to his original speciality.

An ironic smile on Clairville Jones's face mirrored Jake's own astonishment.

'I was told the CO was Jack Smith – I hardly expected you.'

'Jack was my baptismal name,' replied Jake shortly. 'Rather unusual to have a flight commander with no military experience. I'd better get you started right now.'

'I had training in England,' said Clairville Jones easily. 'And I flew with a Home Defence Squadron for a few weeks.'

'England isn't France. There aren't many Huns around in the sky there.'

'There are such things as Zeps, you know,' replied Clairville Jones shortly. 'Let's get on with it, shall we?'

Jake hesitated. 'Look,' he said impulsively, 'the past is – long past. We've a war to fight, and in the corps we need all the flying experience there is. I guess it isn't my place to quibble about where it comes from.'

Harry raised an elegant eyebrow.

Jake shrugged. 'If you're going to push me the whole way – I was going to add I admire you for coming here. It can't be easy when you don't have to. With a job like yours, it must have been tempting to stay put.'

'You don't have the monopoly in patriotism, Smith,' Harry replied coolly, 'but I appreciate your remarks. As you say, France isn't England. And this is rather different to our last meeting.'

How this devil managed to get under his skin. Jake felt a sudden stab of pain that still meant Rosie – then he realised this was exactly what Harry had intended. He drew on his gauntlets. 'Let's get going. We'll take "A" and "C" up – the two KA3as. At least I don't have to tell you how to fly it,' said Jake, as they walked across to the aircraft. He meant it lightly, but Harry's glance was inimical. 'Stick with me, and I'll give you a Cook's tour of the area; then I'll make a mock attack on you, to see how you cope. I'll wave when we begin the fireworks and rock my wings when I reckon it's time to make for home. Clear?'

'Clear,' said Harry calmly, as he climbed into the KA3a.

Jake ran across to his own aircraft and the mechanics swung the propellers. The two aircraft began to bump across the grass field gathering speed before gently lifting into the air. Jake headed for the nearby town of Béthune, well away from the front, circled it and flew towards the canal that led to the coast. In the far distance could be seen the grey scar of the front line trenches, to which he was giving a wide berth.

So much for orientation, Jake thought. Now for the test. He was curious to see how Clairville Jones handled an aeroplane, involuntarily remembering Rosie's opinion of his flying in the past – remembering and hurting. I'll climb to 10,000, he thought, then turn and slide behind him to see if he can shake me off his tail. But as they reached 9,000, Harry unexpectedly seized the initiative, rolling over, and completing the roll on Jake's tail.

'What the devil—?' Jake exploded, automatic reflexes making him put the KA3a into a swift steep turn; he glanced back at Harry. The face was masked by goggles, but something about the arrogant tilt of his head told Jake this manoeuvre was no accident. If that's the way you want to play it, pal, he thought grimly, so be it. He regained the initiative, sitting himself once more on Harry's tail, and this time staying right there. If I were a Hun you'd be a gone 'coon, Clairville Jones.

But he wasn't, and there was no Lewis gun to halt Harry in his dive – a dive that was heading due east, straight for the front lines.

'Idiot,' breathed Jake savagely. 'Can't he read his own compass?' And swift upon that thought came another. Harry could fly all right, he wasn't an airman in the sense that Jake understood it, but he knew how to handle an aeroplane – and he knew exactly where he was heading. Why?

Swift upon that came the answer. Harry hadn't forgotten the past. He hadn't forgotten that he had been rejected by William Potts in favour of an upstart from the East End, an upstart who had consistently and rightly kept the reins of power in his own hands, who had later – as Clairville Jones must know full well – been responsible for the adverse report on his BC2. He hadn't forgotten – and he hadn't forgiven.

Jake rocked his wings, but without hope that Harry would take the slightest notice. He didn't. The lines were only a mile or so ahead now, and the altimeter was reading only 5,000 feet. What the hell was he to do? This was no novice pilot. But he'd have to stick with him and ensure he got back. The RFC needed pilots, even damned fools like Clairville Jones.

There were bursts of AA fire to the south of them, and now at last Harry was pulling round. But they were white bursts, not black, so it was British gunfire – a German aircraft must be over the lines, and Harry was clearly going to try to bag it. Jake groaned. The fool, the bloody fool. Where there was one . . .

There it was now, an LVG, wasn't it? It was about 12,000 feet and climbing to regain the lines, with Harry steadily climbing in pursuit to close height and distance. Harry would never make it, Jake decided. There was only one thing he could do: he headed due east for the lines, making what height he could to head off the LVG. Then he spotted what Harry hadn't – another LVG also coming in from the west, on its home run from whatever devilry they'd been up to. Harry was the meat in their sandwich. About 1,000 feet below his intended victim, he was a sitting target as he continued his climbing pursuit of LVG number one, now directly over the lines, while the second headed right for him, unseen by its intended victim.

There seemed to Jake to be no choice. Harry had ceased to be Harry, his old enemy; he was simply a British pilot who was needed alive and well. No time for warning flares, all Jake could do was to fly to head off the second German two-seater. Too far away to fire an effective burst, he turned and side-slipped, hoping that the mere sight of him would deter the LVG.

The occupant of the rear cockpit saw him, grabbing at the rear-firing machine gun and attracting the pilot's attention. Jake was almost in range but the German, at a disadvantage, deciding discretion was the better part of valour, stuck his nose down and scooted across the lines, running the gauntlet of the fire. The exploding shells forced Harry from his target, and the two LVGs flew to the safety of their own lines.

Jake headed west, not even caring if Harry was following or not. The damned fool had nearly killed both of them by his childish rivalry, more important

367

obviously to him than keeping a careful watch on the skies.

The two KA3as landed almost together. Jake took off his helmet and gloves, determined not to speak first. What had he expected? Curt thanks? Gratitude? All he got was a careless:

'Sorry you frightened the fellow off. I was about to give him a burst.'

Jake stared at him, speechless. Didn't the fellow realise he'd saved his life? Then he saw that the patronising smile on Harry's face did not reach his eyes. Harry *did* realise it – and would not lightly forgive it.

Jake's mind was taken off Clairville Jones by the Neuve Chapelle offensive, in which he and his squadron were flying almost continuously. When the offensive paused for breath, he heard that Captain Clairville Jones was doing well, but by then he had no energy for old feuds. What strength was left over from his day filled his sleep in nightmares of flying – and Rosie. Today he had promised to go over to Boulogne on a hospital visit, still with Rosie on his mind. Damn the woman, would she never leave his dreams?

The visit was dispiriting, but the injured pilot, one of his men, had been pleased by the visit. The drive back through village after village of decrepit houses and fearful villagers, was cheerless too. Jake began to long for the offensive to begin again, for the impetus started at Neuve Chapelle to carry the British forward. He longed for something to happen – anything to banish the thought of the past from his mind, a past that Clairville Jones's visit had resurrected.

As his driver turned in at the old farm-gate that served as entrance to the aerodrome, another Crossley tender drove by. Almost involuntarily, he turned his head, and saw Rosie.

But it was too late. She was a ghost to be dismissed with other phantoms of his long night.

# Chapter Sixteen

For once the cheerful companionship of the actors and actresses failed to enmesh Rosie in its charm. Never more alone than in a crowd, she thought wrily. Who was it who had been desolate and sick of an old passion? Whoever it was, she knew just how he felt. Sometimes she was certain, sometimes less so that Jake had seen her. As soon as her wits returned to her, she had demanded of her companion the CO's name.

'Major Smith, Jack Smith,' he replied in surprise, as though everybody would have heard of Major Smith.

She tried to get her chaotic thoughts into order. Jack – that was how Kate always referred to him. Somehow it distanced him even further from her, to know that he'd reverted to using Jack. Everything in her longed to be able to seize the wheel, drive back, demand to see him, demand – demand what? Nothing had changed since they parted. Not on her side – and if on his, he could have easily communicated with her through Mother. She looked at the lieutenant's blithe, youthful face and wondered if he too had known the torments of love. No sign of it, as he whistled cheerfully all the way back to Hazebrouck.

'You said he was being posted,' she inquired stiltedly. 'Where to?' Her heart was pounding so loudly he must surely hear it.

'No idea,' he replied gaily. 'Personal letter from the general. Not done to steam it open.'

'Could you find out?' Rosie plunged on recklessly.

He turned to look at her in surprise. 'I could try,' he said. 'Know him, do you?'

'I used to work with him,' she managed to say casually.

That it was not casual enough was made evident by his next remark.

'I'll do what I can. Lucky chap,' he added, and she managed to grin.

He did find out. Major Smith had been posted to instruct at a new flying school set up in Le Crotoy, so his hastily scrawled note that reached her a few days later recorded. But what to do? She could not travel to see him. She must write. But what to write? After agonising for some time, she bought a picture postcard, wrote her address on it and drew a sun emerging from the clouds. No need even to write Sunburst across it, no need to sign her name.

She received no reply.

She stared out at the bleak town of Le Havre. Their hostel was in the town's workers' quarters built on reclaimed marshy land, with row after row of houses, only enlivened by the beginnings of some gardens being cultivated by the Tommies who lived there now. After seeing the aerodrome, she longed for the sky once again, felt chained by the earth and cursed her own stupidity. She was impatient with her way of life, rebelling against the war that imposed such limits, a longing for a past when all seemed possible and within her grasp. Now aeroplanes were used for dealing out death – never, never could she ally herself with that. Yet there must be something she could do more than she was to help the war effort. There was in any case nothing else left for her.

It seemed somehow symbolic to have seen Jake driving off into the blue; the end of her story, she thought bleakly. It had been over three years now, and still he had as much power to hurt as he had the first day she had left. She lay awake most of the night and only when dawn came did she fall into a fitful sleep. When she awoke, she was thinking of Polly and of Brynbourne. But even Brynbourne was changed now that Mother had handed it over for a convalescent home.

It took the concert that evening to make her see her way clearly. It was held in the Harfleur valley, muddy and marshy from the wet winter. The army base's new cinema hut was packed to overflowing with troops, waiting their turn to go to the Front, and was lit by candles which added to the heat in the hall generated by the numbers of smoking, laughing troops. The atmosphere was stifling, almost tense, as a handsome young actor called Ivor Novello began to sing a new song he had just composed: 'Keep the Home Fires Burning'. An almost visible wave of emotion swept through the hall as softly the men began to join in the choruses. Rosie knew then that was where she should go. Home. Not the East End, but Brynbourne. Brynbourne and its family had always been home. And now it offered, as well, the answer to her problem.

A Kentish spring. Rosie marvelled that the countryside could still look so peaceful, so quiet and optimistically green, and the birds sing so cheerfully when hardly fifty miles away across the Channel the land lay war-torn.

'Pleased to see you, Miss Rosie,' the station-master greeted her.

Miss Rosie – how that took her aback. Here she was a woman of twenty-seven and being greeted by Mr Jobbins as if she were a child again. She had not been here for over three years, but everything seemed just the same. Only the recruiting posters adorning the walls of the waiting room proclaimed a difference from that former peaceful England. Would Brynbourne, too, seem as solid and welcoming now as it had been to her during years past. She was glad now that she had not told Mother she was coming. How much nicer to walk to Brynbourne, to give herself time to get her thoughts in order.

The smell of the April shower had left the lane crisp and fresh. Somewhere a song thrush sang as she walked along the lane and turned on to the footpath through the orchards and meadows. The banks were bright with primroses now, and the orchards about to bud. And here was the tree where she and Jake had stopped to shelter from the rain all those years ago. She walked on quickly. Jake was no longer here, the past was the past. Yet, even so, a bird of hope sang somewhere inside her. Today everything seemed possible, even entering the Lodge, no longer Jake's domain, but Mother's and Michael's now that Brynbourne was a convalescent home.

Involuntarily she ran her hand once more over the wood carving of Sunburst just as the door was opened, not by a maid now but by Mother herself, older, greyer, still obviously in working clothes of grey wrap-round skirt and bibbed apron. The eyes flashed in shock, then warmth, and then with a cry Rosie was gathered into her arms in a way that would have astonished her a few years ago.

'Silly child, silly child, why did you stay away so long?' Mildred cried, half laughing, half hiccuping with tears, as she hugged her to her. Rosie could not answer and Mildred did not seem to expect a reply for she continued, 'What have you been doing? Where are you going, silly child? Have you seen Polly?' All in the same breath.

'Steady, Mother,' laughed Rosie, disengaging herself with difficulty and following her into the small parlour, the warmth of the welcome making her entry in this frighteningly familiar territory easier.

'How long will you stay?'

Rosie hesitated, grinning. 'I'm staying for quite a while. As long as I'm needed. I'm working here. I persuaded the Emergency Corps to get me a job at a convalescent home. This one. The matron jumped at it.'

Mildred's face slowly changed from disbelief to happiness as she hugged Rosie again.

'I never thought of you as a nurse,' she said forthrightly, 'but you can train, I suppose. You'll have to learn to make a bed better.'

'I don't think you'll have a great success rate with your patients if you let me loose on them, replied Rosie cheerfully. 'I'm going to drive an ambulance. For you, and as extra help for the local hospitals. I could cook if the matron prefers it.'

'Driving,' said Mildred hastily. 'I remember your attempts at cooking. There's one of your old vans stored in the workshop. I suppose we could convert that into our *own* ambulance. that would give us priority for your services. We'll get petrol for emergency allowances and it

will save being at the beck and call of the hospitals. Yes—'
She beamed happily. 'Matron must be delighted. And we
can collect patients that come straight from the railway
trains from Dover.'

'Why aren't you the matron?' asked Rosie curiously.

'I'm a humble VAD,' said Mildred seriously. 'No more.
I just happen to own Brynbourne and I was already
trained as a VAD – I joined the Sittingbourne detachment
before the war and got my certificate. It's worked out very
well,' Mildred said with pride.

'I know you're a wonderful nurse, Mother,' said Rosie
warmly.

'We're so busy,' said Mildred, 'I don't have time to
think whether I'm good or not. The Kent and Canterbury
Hospital have forty beds for military use: there's only
one doctor left as from this month – the rest are in the
services. And he's from Belgium! And with the offensive
beginning in earnest they want us to take more of their
patients here, and more quickly. If you're not careful
you'll end up driving only for them and not us at all.'

Rosie laughed. 'How many beds do you have here?'

'Fifty.'

'What? Where on earth do you put them all?'

'We – or I should say Matron – turned the ballroom
into one large dormitory.' How odd to think that the
room which she'd helped decorate so often, and danced
in, was now a convalescent dormitory. 'They send a
message from Dover or the hospitals as to how many
wounded men are being despatched, and we meet them
from the railway trains. And it would be such a help
to have our own driver.' Mildred put down her cup in
enthusiasm. 'Are you really going to do it?'

'Yes,' said Rosie quickly, gladly. 'There's plenty of
people to do my touring job now the routine is
organised. And I'm a voluntary worker anyway. When
the government lets women join the Services and doesn't
leave us to form ourselves into voluntary organisations it
may be different, but now I can please myself.'

'You sound as militant as dear Kate used to be.'

Mildred had been the only person to have a soft spot

for Kate when she lived here, Rosie remembered in some surprise. How long ago that was. And how much Rosie missed her. She'd go to visit her as soon as she could.

'Have you heard from her?' asked Rosie wistfully – she had received only a couple of short, scrappy letters in a year.

'She's cooking for Belgian refugees in London, I gather.'

His name hovered between them. One short second and she would be asking about Jake – but then the door opened and Michael came in.

Michael Potts, now nearly twenty, prided himself on his business acumen and on his handling of situations and staff. He steeled himself to think of nothing but his efficiency in running Potts Sanitary Ware and the Kent Aviation factory. He told himself that all that was important was business. He continued in the grooves he had carved for himself, as though they were tramlines with regulated stops; he was driven by an engine of his own creation. Of medium height and serious-looking, he had fined his intelligence strictly to the task in hand, at which he had succeeded. Having told himself that to sell Kent Aviation to Bellowes Clairville Co. was the logical and indeed only course open to him after Jake's defection – as he chose to see it – it was clearly up to him to make the amalgamation a success. His mother's remonstrances that the Bellowes had been his father's enemies were met by patient logic; he had no time to spare for such side-issues – this was business. And a business that by his hard work and dogged single-mindedness was still successful. He chose not to demand more of himself lest he was pitchforked back into the horrors of the past.

Undecided as the War Office was as to whether sanitary ware was an essential occupation, he convinced them it was, especially as it was subsidiary to Kent Aviation, which was producing the KA3a with which some of their squadrons were to be equipped and which was popular with the pilots, for its manoeuvrability and reliability, two qualities which were not often seen together. He knew he should be grateful to Jake for having continued to improve the KA3, but he begrudged him his triumph over taking the patent away and the fact that there was no gratitude in him. He was dependent on him so far as the KA3 was concerned, and this he did not like. Robert Bellowes didn't like it either, but he, having his own factory and the seaplanes, was at one step removed.

Apart from manufacture of the KA3a, Kent Aviation had little to do now. It had no designer and it was Bellowes's intention, thwarted so far by Michael Potts, to absorb the manufacture of the KA3 into his own aircraft works and close down Kent Aviation altogether. Michael had resisted this move. He told himself that it was solely because he needed it to keep the sanitary ware factory open. He would not acknowledge that he owed it to his father. Nor would he acknowledge that emotions played any part in his present life. Devoted as Mildred was to him, she could not break the wall of silence around him. He thought himself impregnable, for he had ceased to care.

Or so he had thought until he opened the door that spring afternoon and saw Rosie, neat in her dark green travelling dress, sitting there.

'Michael!' She sprang up and came to him, kissing him on the cheek, sensing his retreat. The shock written all over his face was quickly replaced by impassivity.

'Rosie's come back, Michael. Isn't it wonderful?' Mildred watched him closely. He was a grown man now and surely over his calf love.

'Splendid,' he said cordially, coming forward to kiss her.

'There's no room here,' said Mildred carefully. 'I told her the old chauffeur's flat is free above the stables.'

Did she imagine it, or was that relief which flitted across his face?

'Would you prefer me to move there?' Michael asked.

'No, I don't want to upset anything,' said Rosie firmly. 'The stables will suit me well. I'll be all the closer in case there's an emergency.'

'Emergency?'

'Rosie's going to drive an ambulance for us.'

Again an unreadable look crossed his face. But it must have been her imagination that her presence disquieted him, for he offered to help her move her luggage in and to make the chauffeur's quarters more habitable.

'Would you like to see the factory?' he asked casually.

'Yes,' Rosie said, steeling herself for the ghosts that might still lurk there. The factory looked much as it had done previously, and it was with a familiar sense of homecoming that she saw Potts pedestals lined up after their final glazing. No painting now, of course, but still intricate workmanship on the chain handles, the word 'Potts' proudly embossed on each cistern. As they entered the aviation factory sheds, the familiar enveloped her. The sawdust flying about, the smell of freshly cut wood, oil and dope, the engines waiting ready for installation, the trestle scaffolding, the canvas being stretched and sized. She had been a part of it, and was no more. She had thrown it away and others had taken it up. Aviation had moved on and left her behind.

'I can't get used to the idea of you and *that man*—' she burst out vehemently.

'Things change,' Michael said casually as though expecting her reaction. 'I don't meet socially with him.'

'You can never do business with a snake,' she said sharply.

Michael laughed. 'You can if you're a snake too.'

'And is that what you are?'

He gave her an amused glance. 'One of my coats, Rosie. Only one.'

She felt uneasy, that there was something she did not recognise about this new Michael. He seemed to have got over his infatuation for her; perhaps the shock of Father's death had done that; the naked look of devotion in his eyes had gone, to her relief.

She glanced up at the ceiling where one or two of Father's old kites still adorned the rafters, bringing back the past more vividly than any aeroplane could do. One or two of his inventions were still in evidence; the speaking tube that had connected him with all parts of the factory; the shredder that worked by the turn of a handle.

'I'm surprised you or Robert haven't cleared the kites out,' she said.

'There was no need,' Michael said coolly. 'And I'm left pretty much to myself, so long as I'm successful.' He stared through the window out to the flat marshes beyond. 'It's not like it was in Jake's time. They trust me.'

The name dropped so casually jolted her. The first mention since she'd been here. She had realised he had little to do with the company now, but when had he gone? She longed to ask, yet pride and sense held her back. The last thing she wanted to do was to spoil her homecoming to Kent by lingering on the past. If a new life was there, it had to be new. And yet and yet . . .

'I thought I saw him in France just before I left—' she managed to say '—in uniform.'

'Did you?' He turned and his gaze ranged casually over her.

Goaded at his indifference, she rushed on; 'I was surprised to see him in the Royal Flying Corps – I thought – I suppose I thought he'd still be designing aeroplanes here – or at Farnborough perhaps.'

'Yes,' he said, a small smile playing at the corners of his mouth.

He knew, he *must* know, how much she wanted to hear of him; he must speak, he *must* – but he did not.

Finally she burst out, 'What happened? When did he leave?'

Michael's eyes went blank, but he seemed cool and she did not notice the trembling hands gripped white on the back of the chair, could not sense the blind panic, the unreasoning emotion that swept over him at her talking of Jake. Was it past or present emotion? Either way it made no difference. Michael was past reason.

'He left here – oh, it must have been about a year before the war broke out. Soon after he met Helen.'

A strike of fear. A blow in the stomach. 'Who?' she whispered.

'I never knew exactly who she was,' he said. 'Shall we go?' He started to walk from the factory, Rosie behind him. 'Someone he met in London. Anyway, it wasn't long after that he left – I heard he was in Farnborough near where she lived. After they got married, that is. Anyway, apart from the updating of the KA3—'

She could not hear his last words, as he crashed open the factory door. She was deaf to all but her own heart crying out in pain, as he continued, 'He may be in France. He may be raising a family of little Smiths and little aeroplanes in England. I don't know.'

Each word plunging upon her like a stiletto of sharp steel.

'Shall we go to luncheon? There's still a reasonable one at the Swan Hotel,' Michael said casually. 'Or the best they can manage with food shortages the way they are.'

Mutely she accompanied him, her legs and arms apparently obeying some instruction her conscious mind was incapable of giving.

The Lodge was now deserted of ghosts. Jake had gone and for ever. He had left Rosie behind, love obliterated by what he might even have seen as a betrayal, she forced herself to think. Had he even recognised her in France as he had driven past, shrugging his shoulders at the past? She remembered that old photograph of Florence; he had not forgotten her so quickly. Now she too was part of his past. And it was her own fault. It was she had chosen her own path, not Jake. And he had chosen his – Helen.

For me it's tomorrow to fresh woods and pastures new, she thought ironically. But where did they lie, and what could they hold – if not Jake?

It seemed strange to be living at Brynbourne, now it was so changed. The matron, Miss Wilson, once she had got over her initial distrust of Rosie's presence, suspicious that she might claim privileges, became cordial, and Rosie became so involved in the home that it deadened her own unhappiness. It was strange, too, to see Mother cooking and caring for others, and Rosie wondered at her adaptability but, if Mother could take it, then so could she.

The work was hard. Besides driving, Rosie often found herself acting as orderly, general cleaner and handyman. The Neuve Chapelle battles had led to what was being talked of as a second Battle of Ypres, and vicious fighting was raging over terrain that was first lost then won. Advance or retreat was measured in yards, and by the beginning of May the Allies were once again back to the original Neuve Chapelle line. In the meantime they fought successfully to hold Ypres, the key to the Channel ports, despite the new weapon introduced by the Germans – gas. Not many cases had yet reached England for as yet no one knew how to treat its consequences. Rosie had seen two in the hospital when she came to collect convalescent patients, and that was enough. The haunted eyes, the blue tinge to the face and the rasping for breath remained with her day and night.

Desperate to help in any way she could, Rosie managed to persuade the matron to hold musical evenings in the library in preference to turning it into another ward. She had already seen in France the effects music could have on sick men, and was convinced that it would prove as useful here. The evenings were a great success, ranging from sing-songs with herself playing at the piano, to professional musicians visiting from London or Canterbury playing classical music.

It was through such an evening that she first became aware of Second Lieutenant Peter Favell, a fresh-faced young soldier with an engaging smile and a good baritone voice. He was not quite twenty-three. He had been gassed and wounded, with a shattered leg, but was apparently recovering well from both. By now 'Keep the Home Fires Burning' was the song of the moment, and with her playing the piano he was constantly called upon to sing it. Sometimes he could not, for the effects of the gas were still making him cough and vomit.

'Just bad luck,' he announced cheerily when she inquired what had happened. 'Hadn't even poked my nose over the top of the trench and one of those German aeroplane Johnnies came along and dropped a bomb on me.'

Rosie shuddered. Dropped from an aeroplane. Was it

for this that William and she had flown that kite all those years ago? Was it this for which the Wright brothers had striven? To have the ability to drop bombs and to maim and kill?

'Made rather a mess of my leg.' A shadow flitted over his face, soon banished. He never mentioned the gas. 'They think they've saved it though.'

From sentimental songs of home, he progressed daringly to those of love and the room resounded to 'You are my honeysuckle' and 'If you were the only girl in the world'. Rosie never noticed that his eyes were fixed upon her as he sang. She took to walking in the conservatory with him as he practised hobbling on his crutches; he not infrequently fell over, sometimes pulling her with him, and he laughed so hard that it took some time before she realised the anguish underneath.

'I'm going to write a poem for you,' he announced cheerfully, as she struggled to get him up after one spill. 'It will begin, "Rosie, I give you a posy—" '

'That's very original. Look, do help, Peter – I can't manage alone with you sitting on the ground waving that crutch in the air.'

'I'm inspired,' he said, hurt. 'The muse is with me. I can't think about mundane things like crutches. Wait a minute – it will come, I'm sure.

> A posy
> Of violets for you.
> All I need is a tiny seed
> Of love that is yours and true.

'There, what do you think of that?' His eyes were fixed on her anxiously, only a slight hint of laughter.

'Quite wonderful. You will clearly be the next Rupert Brooke.'

'Do you think so? Breathless we flung us on the windy hill and all that. I wonder if I'll ever do *that* again?'

'Of course you will,' she said gently. 'It's a leg you've broken, not life itself.'

'Not yet,' he sighed. 'But you're right. So was George

Borrow: "Sun, moon and stars, brother, all sweet things".'

'If you think I'm your brother, then I'm really sorry for you,' she laughed.

'I don't,' he replied gravely. 'Not for one moment do I mistake you for my brother, Rosie.'

Hauptmann Thomas Dietrich was lying in the ruins of an old Flemish manor house near the Menin Road at Ypres. All day their gunners and infantry had been trying to blast the British 3rd Dragoons from their trenches. The trenches had been shot to pieces, but the Dragoons still hung on with the same determination that they had shown all day.

The ruins of this manor house reminded him in some way of Polly's painting of Fontainebleau – the shape of that stone perhaps. But then everything reminded him of Polly. She haunted him. If only she hadn't come – he could have managed then, to go back to the Bavarian estate, to face Hilde again, his family, to join the army to do his duty by the Fatherland and the Kaiser, to become just one more cog in this pointless war, instead of painting. Perhaps he should have continued painting in Paris, been interned, but there was no point. No point to anything without Polly. But now there was a son. He wanted to live now that he had a son. He wanted to see him again. Why, oh, why had she come? He could have borne every ugliness and pain this war thrust upon him, if only she had not come again to remind him of what life could be like.

'Halt!'

Shapes in the darkness, noise. *Himmel!* They were coming, the Dragoons, the idiots were charging the ruins; they could be mown down.

The machine-guns of the German front lines opened up but the Dragoons kept on coming in with bayonets. His small German unit in the manor house was overwhelmed, only a few of them escaping. One of them was Thomas Dietrich.

Why him, why him? Why, when so many good men

were dead, should he live to fight another day? And fight he did. For all the next day the German howitzers pounded the nearby village of Hooge into rubble, but as if that manor house were some prized possession of war, orders came that it had to be retaken. Thomas got his men there, but found it a death-trap, machine guns opening up on them every step they took. There seemed no escape from the ruins this time. He knew now what it was like to be a fox, turning, twisting to escape the hounds. He'd always detested hunting. When this was over, he'd ban it on his estates. Then he was running, running, through the ruins, gathering what was left of his men, who were falling one by one. With an effort he heaved a wounded man on to his shoulders and ran blindly every moment expecting the sharp spurt of pain and oblivion that would send him to joint the rest. Of his fifty men, only five managed to escape. Once more Thomas was one of them.

They would pin another medal on his chest for this, he was told. The Iron Cross, first class. He stared at his superior officer blankly. Another medal? For losing forty-five men? This was a crazy world. And one he did not wish to know.

Kate hurried along the Strand that October night as the second winter of the war approached. Her mind was preoccupied as to how the food cards could be stretched to last the rest of the week for her refugees. She was so tired of scrimping and saving, of the constant trips to the East End markets to see what she could scrounge. She was still well enough known there for the occasional treat to come her way. Paul came first in line for these, tucked up at home now with her neighbour looking after him. Next came the refugees; last came Kate herself.

She must be the only one worrying about food rations, she thought grimly as she walked along the dark Strand. The windows of the hotels and restaurants might be curtained to allow no light to escape, but behind there were the sounds of champagne corks popping, of dancing, of people laughing and having a good time. Eat drink and be merry for tomorrow we die, she thought. How could you blame these young men? Tomorrow they might be back at Loos or somewhere equally dreadful. It was their escape for an evening to go to a show. Full House signs were displayed outside all the theatres, and those with the lightest entertainment were those that were full soonest. The Gaiety was playing *Tonight's the Night*, and although daytime fashions were now subdued, in the evenings women emerged from their chrysalises to don their gayest dresses and jewels. The Strand was crowded for all the gloom demanded by the law. Dim oil lamps picked out a late news vendor, as khaki uniforms crowded everywhere.

She glanced up as a sudden streak of light flashed over the street; the searchlight beams were criss-crossing the sky. Suddenly fearful, she began to hurry. Sometimes there were raids on London. Those searchlights . . . She passed a couple of youths who had stopped to light a cigarette and caught a few words: 'The Zepps are on their way, the swine'. A few people stopped to stare up into the sky, curiosity still overriding caution, but most like Kate quickened their step.

A barrel organ was playing 'Keep the Home Fires Burning'. It was the last thing she heard save the wail of the bomb. It exploded only a few yards from her.

In the roadway, glass and bricks fell on to her already dead body. She was one of the last to be found, but it made no difference for she had been torn apart by shrapnel.

Jean-Michel raised his head wearily from a desk full of orders. Engines and still more engines. Engines for Morane-Saulniers, engines for Farmans, engines for the aircraft desperately needed for the expanding French air forces. Gone were the days when Jake Smith was one of his few customers; now, even had it been War Office policy, he would not have the time to supply to England; all his capacity was needed here. Suddenly the French armament business had woken up to the excellence of his engines. With the coming of war, Jean-Michel Pinot had become a prominent, rich and honoured industrialist, showered with awards. He would rather have been at the Front.

He suffered from *ennui* – a world-weariness that he could not understand himself. He thought he still loved Polly, yet he did not wish to see her. That German stood in the way, and he had not the energy to push him from his sight. One of his children was fathered by another man, a man his wife still loved. He did not blame her, how could he? He still loved Kate after all. But he could not fight it either. So much for the rational Frenchman, he thought bitterly. Perhaps when this war was over they would sort something out . . . Meanwhile . . .

He stared blankly at the tall man in khaki uniform coming through the door, then recognised him.

'*Mon ami*, Jake.' At once more animated than he had been for months, he leapt up to seize him in his arms. Then his eyes narrowed. 'You are not happy, Jake. What is wrong? I hear you are in the Royal Flying Corps—'

Jake shrugged. 'At Farnborough again now,' he said. 'They wanted to make me an instructor at Le Crotoy. I – I wasn't having that.' No, one thing to be in action, quite another to instruct where you had time to think, to think about what you saw, whether that was Rosie or not. 'Luckily they called me back to Farnborough – they needed me to develop a scout with the new interrupter gear – I thought I'd adapt the KA3a, but I've started a new design.' Talk for the sake of talking. 'The KA4. A single-seater – good fighter—' He broke off wearily. 'What the hell am I talking about?'

'You have not come to tell me of aeroplanes, I think,' said Jean-Michel coolly. Why did a pulse beat so hard? Why did he fear to know why Jake had come? 'It's Kate, isn't it, *mon ami*? That is the reason.'

'Yes.' Relief that Jean-Michel had made it easy – for him.

'Ill?' A wild hope.

'She's dead, Jean-Michel.'

'So.' A long drawn-out sigh. The waste, oh, the waste. And now it was too late. 'Her pride, *my* pride,' he burst out. 'I would not plead, she would not yield. Jake—'

he crashed his fist down on the table at the hopeless futility of life. Polly, the children, Thomas, everything was blotted out, everything save the pain of loving Kate, the tearing reality it still had, the only woman who had torn aside that civilised, charming facade to bring Jean-Michel into life. It had been painful, it had hurt, but he had been alive. As he had not been since he last saw her. With Polly, the pain had been dulled, and he had been content.

'Tell me,' he commanded dully.

'She was one of the victims of the Zeppelin that bombed London three weeks ago.'

Three weeks. How had his heart not told him Kate had died?

'She was working in the Aldwych and was on her way back there.' Jake spoke with difficulty. 'Outside the Strand Theatre. It was pure chance.'

Pain crossed Jean-Michel's face. He would not ask. *He* did not need to. He knew what bombs can do.

'And the child?'

'He is being well looked after.'

'There is a home—' Jean-Michel paused. How could he say that? He *had* no home at the moment. 'I'm sure Polly would—' Something in his voice made Jake look up from his own grief and realise something was amiss.

He came to perch on the side of the desk and took Jean-Michel's hand. 'Damn this war, damn this war.'

'*Ah, mon ami*, it is not the war,' said Jean-Michel sadly. 'It is ourselves that we are so foolish. What use is pride if it parts two lovers? Jake, I do not know what parted you and Rosie, but I tell you this,' he half choked, 'go to her if you love her still, and tell her, force her to be yours, for this is a poor world without love.'

See Rosie again? Plead with her? The words came back to him, and he pushed them away. She had left him. Now Kate, too, was gone. There was no room for emotion in a war like this. He would return to France.

'Miss Potts?'

385

Rosie struggled out from under the ambulance, where she had been working, to see a pair of elegant, booted, female feet. She rolled over on to her knees and stood up. Facing her was a pretty, well-dressed girl she did not know, so well dressed in fact that Rosie was immediately conscious of the dirt on her overalls and the grease on her hands. She looked at them, and the girl smiled slightly, making Rosie instantly take to her.

'Miss Potts, I'm Philippa Cardon – you would know of me also as Poppy Bellowes.'

Robert Bellowes's wife? This pretty, warm-hearted-looking girl married to the slug? Poppy saw the look of distaste cross Rosie's face and said hurriedly, 'Is there somewhere we can talk?'

Silently, warily, Rosie led the way to her rooms over the stables and Poppy, looking round appreciatively at the bright attractive room, took off her coat and sat down, her simple black dress falling in graceful folds around her.

Black? Rosie wondered. Why black? A brother perhaps . . .

'You know, Miss Potts, that I worked in London for women's suffrage during the summer of 1914.'

'Yes,' said Rosie stiltedly. 'I – I admired you for that.'

'What you may not know is that I moved in with Kate Smith after you left.'

Rosie gasped. 'But she never told me.'

'I think,' Poppy regarded her hands, twisting them in her lap nervously, 'she might have wished to spare your feelings. She knew you had no more love for my husband than had she. Not knowing me, you might have wondered—'

'I know Kate, though,' said Rosie warmly. 'I would have been pleased. How is she?' she asked anxiously.

The look on Poppy's face, and Rosie's own sudden realisation: Poppy had used the word *knew*. 'She's dead, isn't she?' she blurted out in a high voice she did not recognise. 'That's why you've come.'

Poppy crossed to her, sitting beside her and putting her arm round her. 'I could not find you. It's taken time – it was three weeks ago in the Zeppelin raid on London. Oh,

Rosie, I'm so sorry. I know how fond you were of her. And I too,' she said with a break in her voice. 'She taught me so much.'

Blindly Rosie turned to her. 'How—?' then broke off. She didn't want to know. 'What about Paul?' she asked as steadily as she could. Time enough to try to absorb the stark fact that Kate was dead.

'He's with me at the moment. His uncle thought that best, until we know what the future holds.'

Poppy Bellowes knew quite well what Captain Smith had meant – that Paul should stay with her until her work in London came to an end with the war and she made the decision of whether or not to return to Robert. But to Rosie, it meant something quite different. Until this war was over, and he could take him home – to Helen.

When Poppy Bellowes had left, Rosie carefully, numbly gathered up every magazine and newspaper she could still find to read what had happened on October 13th.

Five Zeppelins, bombing many towns, not only London, had come in all, but it was L-15 that had caused the destruction in the Strand and Aldwych. Seventy-one people had been killed, 128 injured that night, and one of them Kate. A page-boy from the Gaiety Theatre had been blown to pieces; a home for Belgian refugees – where Kate had worked – was also hit; nineteen bombs altogether had fallen in the Strand. All the theatres had been transformed into emergency first-aid centres, Leslie Henson had forestalled an incipient panic in the Gaiety audience, a public house had been hit . . .

When she had gathered all the facts, she told herself that now she knew it would be easier to mourn Kate's loss. But it wasn't. Instead of grief, came first a hatred of the dreaded Zeppelins; of the Kaiser who had sent them; of an unknown German people; and then came a hatred of war, fiercer than anything she had known before.

The next day she visited the Sittingbourne factory and, refusing Michael's offer to accompany her, went into the shed where the KA3as were being assembled. She stood in silence so long looking at them that the mechanics, tired of asking her if she needed anything, went back to their work. After an hour, she nodded to herself, tiredly. No passion now, no emotion, just a rational acknowledgement that Jake had been right all along – and she wrong. It was not enough just to do *something* to help win this war. To win through to peace, she had to be prepared to do what she could do best. Even if it meant building and flying aeroplanes intended for fighting, even for bombing. Even if it meant breaking the commitment she'd made never to abuse the skies. At the moment there was no place for her here, but if the opportunity arose, she would take it – and take it eagerly, in remembrance of Kate.

Once decided, she turned away from the KA3a, lest its sleek lines sent her delving deeper into the past; into a past that held Astra, held Sunburst – and most of all had held Jake. Jake, whom it seemed to her now as her grief for Kate flooded over her, she had tossed away as foolishly and uncaringly as a leaf to the wind. And sing though she would, neither he nor Kate would come again.

# Chapter Seventeen

By the new year of 1916 Rosie was used to being at Brynbourne again, even bringing herself to walk, often with Peter Favell, to the places where she and Jake had laughed and loved. She knew she was doing valuable work driving the ambulance, cheering up her patients and soothing their fears, and had even taken her VAD certificate. She told herself that she could cope with anything, but sometimes the past came back unexpectedly.

'Mother! You can't mean it?' She gaped at Mildred as though she had taken leave of her senses. What would she think, Mildred had asked, if she were to marry Sir Lawrence? She'd known her mother had taken pity on Sir Lawrence when he was confined to bed for several months with liver disease, but to *marry* him?

'Why not?' said Mildred tranquilly. 'I've grown fond of him, and I don't want to spend the rest of my life alone.'

Rosie couldn't believe her ears. Mother? To speak like that of Sir Lawrence when he and Father had hated each other so much?

'I could never quite believe in the famous feud, you know,' Mildred said. 'It seemed to me it was forty per cent of one and sixty per cent of the other – and at times I was never sure which way round it was.'

Rosie regarded her mother with dismay. 'But—'

'You think I'm being disloyal to William?' broke in Mildred briskly. 'Of course I'm not, but there's no gainsaying Lawrence has been very quiet since William's death. It wasn't his wife's death upset him – it was William's. I think he misses him.'

Rosie managed to laugh.

'Robert's another kettle of fish though,' added

Mildred. 'The sooner that wife of his comes back the better.'

'I suppose he'll be there tonight,' sighed Rosie. 'At this jolly dinner party we've been invited to.'

'He's Michael's business partner, after all.'

Rosie said no more, for she was curious to enter Court Manor after all these years, even if it meant meeting Robert again. She took care to look her best – one needed to feel fully armoured against the foe – and put on her glacé silk skirt made from a dress she'd had years before the war. The year that – no, she would *not* think of him.

Sir Lawrence had been a widower now for three years and the house had a bleak austerity that a housekeeper could never alleviate. Sir Lawrence's eyes brightened at the sight of Mildred and it dawned upon Rosie that perhaps the match was not so incongruous after all, though they made an odd couple, she tall and stately, he only just over five foot with his bristly hair, now dimmed from red to grey. How quickly war changed the tempo of life, Rosie thought, in so many ways. How unthinkable two years before, in peace, to have contemplated such a union. But now everything was changing. The unthinkable became the possible, the possible became fact.

Prosperity had thickened Robert Bellowes. He still looked like a slug, but a fatter one, Rosie decided, gorged on his prey.

'How is your dear wife?' she asked him demurely.

'She works in London, as you know. Well, thank you, however.' Robert's tones were off-hand, but his eyes were cold.

'And Mr Smith?' he enquired politely.

Her eyes flashed with anger, but she had brought it on herself.

'I'm afraid I don't know. Michael mentioned he was married now, so I would hardly expect him to visit Brynbourne often. You will know about his work for the factory, of course.'

Had she not been so concerned with keeping her tone cool, she might have observed the flash of surprise in Robert's eyes, replaced by curiosity.

'Ah, yes, married,' he said slowly, glancing at Michael speculatively. 'And in the Royal Flying Corps with dear Harry.'

She gritted her teeth. 'I wonder you have not considered it yourself, Mr Bellowes.'

His eyes narrowed. 'Like dear Michael here,' he said softly, 'my presence is needed here in the country's interests. I must say, Miss Potts,' he added, apparently changing the subject, 'it's an odd thought to think we may become siblings – when I had quite set my heart on marrying Miss Polly once and even—' He stopped and his eyes wandered deliberately over the bosom of her white tussore blouse. She did not notice, too occupied in absorbing the horrible thoughts of seeing the long line of family occasions stretching ahead, with herself consigned to the company of Robert Bellowes. Herself – and Michael. She looked across to where he was animatedly chatting to Sir Lawrence. How, oh how, could he have forgotten the past so completely? Forgive if one could, but always remember. For Robert himself would surely do so.

De Havilland 2s. He'd have preferred the KA3a, but then maybe he was biased! Jake grinned to himself, looking at the squadron's scout aircraft lined up on the airfield. It was May now and the squadron, a new one, had already been out in France a month when he arrived yesterday evening to replace the former CO who'd been injured in a flying accident. So far he liked the looks of the squadron. New, but keen as mustard. There was only one flaw in the set-up. Another squadron shared the field with them, flying FE8s, and Harry Clairville Jones was in command. Either the Germans had taken a year off, thought Jake uncharitably, or he had the luck of the devil. He had survived *and* been promoted.

It didn't take long before the two men met. Clairville Jones's manners were nothing if not impeccable. He wasted no time in coming to welcome Jake, the newly arrived CO.

'Good to see you again, Jack,' he said pleasantly, shaking hands. No Jake. So this was strictly business.

'Heard you preferred a desk – you know how rumours fly.'

Jake kept his temper.

'Want to get your bearings?' Harry continued laconically. 'I'll take you up if you like. Not much doing at the moment.' Jake nodded reluctantly – this was beginning to sound familiar. But be darned if he was going to say no.

When they met a few hours later, Jake realised he'd misjudged Clairville Jones. This was going to be a regular patrol with three other FE8s flying behind Harry, and Jake tucked safely in the rear in his DH2, as they climbed steadily, heading for the front line trenches. There was some high cloud and a watery sun, but otherwise it was a fine day and Jake felt his spirits rise with the excitement of active flying once more, even if he were tucked safely out of danger. Except of course that with the DH2, a pusher plane with the engine behind him, it cut down his rear view, which was usually where the danger came from. But that was a small risk on a patrol such as this.

He began to think about the new machine-gun interrupter gear, whereby a forward firing gun could be fired through the whirling blades of a propeller on tractor type aircraft, and his designs for a new aircraft, the KA4. Why the hell give it to Kent Aviation though? It would be a Farnborough product, not an improved model of the KA3, but totally different. He had no cause to grant Kent Aviation any favours, not with Bellowes in control. Yet even so, he owed a lot to William. What would he have thought about it?

Jake wrestled with the problem as, at 12,000 feet, the aeroplanes levelled off, heading over the lines. A few bursts of 'archie' from the German AA guns, nothing serious, all routine so far. Harry was turning to the north to begin the patrol, watching for hostile aircraft. The sky seemed totally empty, as they headed back along the patrol line some fifteen miles inside the German lines. Then he saw trouble ahead. One of the FEs was waggling its wings, dropping out of the formation. Engine problems obviously, and he was making for home.

Almost immediately Jake spotted them. Three aircraft, Fokkers, flying out of a watery sun. Surely Harry had seen them? Ahead he could see his aircraft, two coloured streamers fluttering back from the interplane struts, but he was giving no sign to them that he was aware of enemy presence.

How could Harry not have noticed them? Jake fumed. The idiot was turning – if he wasn't careful he'd bring the four of them right under the enemy machines, giving the Fokkers height advantage. One of the other FEs waggled his wings, trying to draw Harry's attention to the danger, but Harry still flew on, seemingly oblivious.

To hell with it, he wasn't going to just sit here, following a madman. Jake began to pull round but instantly checked. The Fokkers had winged over and were beginning their dive, a curving dive to bring them right behind the four British scouts – and guess who, thought Jake grimly, is going to be sitting target Number 1 at the rear. Fool that he was ever to come up with Clairville Jones again. But surely even Harry wouldn't go so far as deliberately to lead them all into this trap – or would he? With Jake at the rear, and with three other aircraft, he still had a sporting chance, if – when – Jake was blasted out of the sky.

The pilot who had first waggled his wings, fired off a red Very light which even Harry could not ignore, and then turned, with Jake following him. Just before his wings obscured Harry's machine he saw it begin to half roll – away from the action. So now he knew. Harry was taunting him: get out of this if you can.

He and the FE8 with him were the target for two of the Fokkers, the last going for the other FE8 engaged in a slow turn. Only now did the latter see the danger – too late, for the Fokker was firing and it was forced to dive away.

No time to watch the antics of others. Jake had his own skin to save. The leading Fokker of the two was behind him now. He heard a couple of pluk pluk sounds as bullets went through his rudder, then a clang as one hit the engine. Well, it had happened before. One bullet wasn't the end of the world. Then other bullets hit it. The motor coughed, spluttered, then seemed to pick up.

Time to get going. Jake turned the DH2 upside down and pulled back hard on the stick. The aircraft nosed down and dived. Head for the lines, my friend, he told himself, and quick. The engine was beginning to make ominous spluttering sounds and there was no sign of the other FEs now, certainly not one with the patrol leader's streamers. The Fokker was still after him, and no wonder, for Jake was losing speed fast. The Fokker closed in; Jake kicked the rudders to make himself as difficult a target as possible. More bullets zipped through the upper and lower wings. A louder clang on the engine behind him.

The lines were coming up fast, but the Fokker was coming faster. The sound of bullets was beginning to sound almost musical. Then the firing stopped, suddenly, completely. He looked back to see the Fokker hit by a burst of fire from a swooping FE8. There was no mistaking the coloured streamers. Unbelievably, against all the odds, Harry had come back to help him out. The Fokker flicked into a vicious spin and went down.

And that was thanks to Major Harry Clairville Jones. A debt repaid, thought Jake gratefully, and he would tell him so. No sign of the other Fokkers and FE8s. Jake's engine was spluttering more now. He wasn't going to make it much further. He and Harry were on their own as they went back over the lines, and now that the Fokkers had gone, the German archie was starting up. At below 2,000 feet and Jake unable to climb now, they were both in trouble. Shells were bursting all round them.

'Leave me,' Jake yelled, pointing upwards to Harry, the sign making his intentions clear. No point in both of them going down. There was nothing Harry could do for him now. He should at least get himself out of danger. Yet he could see Harry grinning, apparently not the least worried by shells exploding all round him, as if this were just another stage in the battle between them. He took no notice of Jake's gesture.

He's some strange fellow, Jake thought, glancing across – just as the FE8 was hit. In a flash it was on its back, diving, wreathed in smoke, shedding pieces of wood and fabric. Jake could only watch horrorstruck for a moment, then his own engine stopped. He had to land. And quickly.

Nothing but shell holes, old trench works, shattered tree stumps and rusting barbed wire below. He was inside the British lines, but only just. Nothing for it but to crash and hope for the best. The sound of gunfire ceased, as he hit the ground. The left hand wings caught what remained of a tree trunk and were ripped away, the rest of the top plane smashing down, just missing Jake's head. Then the wheels dug into a shell hole, the cockpit crunched into the ground and Jake was flung out, landing heavily on his left side and arm. A sharp pain, and then nothing.

He came to on a stretcher, being taken into a tent.

'Where am I?' he asked.

'Forward CCS, mate,' said a disembodied voice behind him. 'You've got your essentials, but you've banged your arm up a bit.'

Casualty Clearing Station. He'd come through it, he thought – just as he became aware of the pain. But what—? Then he remembered. 'What about the other FE that crashed?'

'Came down in the front lines – sir,' his informant added belatedly, noticing the crowns on Jake's cuff.

'The pilot?' Jake asked sharply.

'Dunno.'

Jake walked slowly along the ward, his arm in a sling. Now his head had cleared he remembered everything that had taken place. He came to the bed he sought, with the still figure in it. The head turned slightly at his approach.

'Never liked you,' whispered Harry Clairville Jones. 'All my fault this business. Wanted you to go down.'

'I know. But you saved me instead. Why?' Jake asked abruptly. He had to understand.

'Damned if I know,' Harry managed to say; he tried one of his old careless grins but it was too much for him. He coughed – bringing up blood. 'The dog it was that died, eh?' he cracked, but his eyes were frightened.

'You're not going to die—' Jake began to say, but those eyes on him made him stop. He knew, Jake knew, it was only a matter of time, and not much time at that.

'Waste though,' whispered the croaking voice. 'Never get that engine right now. Give my love to – to—' he frowned in surprise. 'Do you know, I can't remember her name.' He gave up with the effort.

'Rosie,' said Jake to the unconscious man. 'Give your love to Rosie.'

The next time he passed, the bed was occupied by someone else. No need even to ask.

Rosie slammed the ambulance doors shut. Another patient, another year of this endless war of stalemate. Faces, always new faces. New casualties arriving by the shipload at Dover, and on these occasions she would be called in as an emergency driver to collect them from the railway station and drive them to hospitals. She was used now to helping to heave stretcher after stretcher into the already crowded wards. It was only when she realised that a smile on her face was positive help to the wounded, usually no more than boys, that she began to conquer her dread of this duty. They said she'd get used to it in time, but she never had. It was a relief to return to Brynbourne where some at least of the patients were near to release – though to what future? Either back to the carnage they had left, or to a life impaired by disability.

'Have you heard the news?'

She spun round, started at the unexpected voice, then smiled when she saw Peter Favell. 'You still here?' she joked. 'We should have got rid of you long ago.' A shadow passed over his face, which puzzled her, even as she continued blithely, 'And what news would this be?' Every day Peter seemed to have some new item of gossip, generally tall stories to make her laugh.

'You've got me all wrong,' he said hurt. 'This is real local news. I got it from Judy. Kaiser Bill's awarded the Iron Cross to our cook here.'

'If Judy says so it must be right,' laughed Rosie. Judy was a VAD night nurse and well known as gossip and flirt. Rosie had noticed with pleasure that Peter seemed to be a favourite of hers, though he never seemed to notice. But then he was everyone's favourite.

Peter lingered as she locked the van up. His wounded leg had healed long since, though he still limped. But he had never regained full health since the gassing and his family had successfully pleaded – and paid – for him to stay on. He'd been here nearly a year now.

'Do you have time for a walk?' he asked hopefully.

She hadn't, but had not the heart to tell him so. The gardens at Brynbourne were neglected by pre-war standards, but the late tulips were making a bright show and everywhere other signs of spring were evident.

'What's the matter, Peter?' she asked, concerned at his unnatural quiet. 'Your leg isn't playing up, is it?'

He shook his head. 'No. In fact, they're getting rid of me. Good news for you, eh?' He forced a laugh. 'They've at last got to the bottom of why I'm still coughing so much. It isn't gas, it's consumption.'

Peter, with his robust cheerfulness and good looks? Rosie was still with shock, then: 'How bad?' she asked bluntly.

'Quite. Enough to wipe me off the active list. Enough,' he paused, 'for the folks at home not to want me back with them.'

'Not want you back?' Rosie was horrified. Peter came from an old county family and somehow she had gained the impression without being told so, that the effort of living up to his family's expectations was sometimes more than he could cope with. It had been his father who insisted on his son's following him into the Army, whereas Peter's own inclination had been for the Navy.

'I've got a young sister and brother, you see,' said Peter anxiously, as if reading her thoughts.

'But it's not catching, if you're careful,' she cried.

He shrugged. 'They still don't want me. Can't blame them. They're looking for a sanatorium but it's difficult with so many converted to general hospitals or convalescent homes.'

He looked so forlorn that she put her arms around him

397

as she would a child to comfort him. His grip tightened round her. 'You'll come and see me, won't you, Rosie?' he asked thickly.

'Of course,' she said absently, dropping her arms and staring round the neglected rose garden, as if somehow it might provide an answer to all his suffering. How ridiculous for Peter to be sent away from Brynbourne when there could be nowhere better for consumptive patients. The air of the North Downs was just as good as Switzerland. Suddenly her mind was made up.

'You shan't go,' she said quickly.

'But—'

'You can share my rooms over the stables,' she said decidedly. 'There's plenty of space.' There wasn't, but she was already rearranging and planning in her mind.

His face lit up, then fell again. 'I can't do that, Rosie,' he said awkwardly. 'There's your reputation to think about.'

Reputation? She began to laugh. War took little account of reputations. Then she saw his hurt face, and though she did not understand it, said gently; 'Peter, I'm years older than you. I'm nearly twenty-nine, and I'm a qualified VAD. I shall simply be your nurse, that's all. We'll soon have you better. Of course if you don't want to come—' she added offhandedly.

'You know I do.' He seized her round the waist and danced her round. But not for long. The tiredness swept over his face again, and quietly she suggested they return.

'A Zep came down in the sea off Westgate last night,' he told her on the way back. 'They tried to tow it in but it sank. Lost too much gas. They got the crew off, but that L-15 won't be flying any more jolly bombing raids against London. I say, are you all right?' he asked concerned, seeing her face suddenly pale.

L-15 had been the Zeppelin that had bombed the Strand, dropped the bomb that had killed Kate. Suddenly Kate was vividly before her again. Kate with her brave outlook on life, her stubborn refusal to consider anything but her own way, Kate with her annoying pride – and Kate the loyal and trusted friend, Kate the counsellor, Kate the carer. She was transported back to the little household, their family of three – Kate, herself and the baby. The baby – Paul – would be five now, soon perhaps to be cared for by Jake's wife. Helen – what a name! She had a vision of a tall, stately fair-haired girl, supercilious and cold, and Jake in her thrall. She told herself that she was being irrational, but could not shake the illusion from her mind.

'Are you all right, Rosie?' Peter repeated.

'A friend of mine was killed by that Zep in the October raid.'

He squeezed her hand and she smiled at him gratefully. How could that mean much to him when on the Western Front he had seen men mown down by gunfire all around him; men fresh from England one day, only to be dead on the morrow. What could the death of one woman mean to him? But to Rosie she had been Kate and irreplaceable.

Rosie was travelling to Canterbury, on loan to the Kent and Canterbury Hospital for a few days, while another convoy of ships unloaded casualties at Dover after the opening of the Somme offensive. Up till now the warmth of the summer and Peter's companionship had seemed to help her skim over her own problems like a dragonfly over water. Now the Somme offensive, the mighty blow that was designed to overwhelm the enemy and hasten the end of this long war, had opened on 1st July. It had been preceded by a tremendous barrage to blast the enemy trenches and barbed wire, but the attempt failed and the British launched their men against long stretches of uncut wire and, once the barrage was lifted, the Germans, far from being pulverised, had emerged from their underground bunkers to man their deadly machine-guns. At the end of the first day, some ground had been won, but at the price of over 57,000 casualties. Many were dead, the rest filled field and rear hospitals, and then the hospital ships to England.

This morning Rosie had been detailed with the other ambulance drivers to pick up patients from Canterbury East railway station. They had parked the ambulances and were waiting on the platform. The Dover train steamed in with a belch of grey smoke. She had been here often before. Railway stations were places of such sadness now. Even the reunions were sad when leaves were short and the shadow of the trenches hung over every day. Everywhere khaki-clad soldiers milled around, some waiting to return to France, some returning on leave, leaping from the train before it had even drawn to a halt, their loved ones surging forward, surrounding her with their laughter and warm tears. She was used to the procedure; she knew whereabouts the wounded men would be carried down on to the platform. Now the doors were opening and the medical orderly in charge jumped out, lists in hand. Then there was hubbub as names were called and the stretchers brought down one by one for this last stage of their journey. Some patients could walk, but most were still on stretchers.

'Here,' Rosie answered at the announcement of the Kent and Canterbury's name, still moved at the sight of the men on the stretchers; some figures were still, others making an effort to absorb their surroundings, trying to enjoy this first real glimpse of England. The railway train belched smoke as it prepared to depart, enveloping them unexpectedly, so that Rosie coughed and spluttered as she pointed out the exit to the stretcher-bearers. Then out of one carriage jumped a group of Royal Flying Corps officers.

The grey smoke swirled around her, as the khaki-clad officers hurried past her along the platform. What made her turn just then as another, last to leave, hurried past her to join them, his figure clouded in smoke? Even as he walked towards her the smoke cleared and as in a dream she called out, 'Jake!'

Then he was face to face with her, still with shock. His arm was in a sling, his face hard and bitter.

She opened her mouth, but no words came. In the distance she heard someone shout 'Rosie'.

'Coming,' she managed to call, her attention momentarily diverted, then looked back. She saw the muscles on his face move as he swallowed. Was it in embarrassment, in shock? Was he as paralysed as she? Then she remembered that he was no longer hers, but Helen's. He had married, he wanted her no more – and who could blame him after what she had done? Blindly she turned away as another belch of smoke engulfed them both just as he stepped towards her. Unable to resist, she turned again to find him gone, leaving only the empty impersonal platform.

He had wanted to run to her, seize her, never let her go again. What the hell was she doing in Canterbury? Then the thought: She could have stayed, but she didn't. She had chosen to turn away, to leave him once more.

Jake climbed up into the Lanchester and said curtly to the driver, 'Let's go.' As they drove the few miles to Bekesbourne, he regarded the countryside objectively. He thought he knew Kent so well. But that was a different world. Now it seemed to be sprouting huts and sheds in as fertile a fashion as once it had sprouted cherry trees. Airfields and emergency landing grounds replaced meadows and downland. Field sheds sheltered aircraft, not cattle.

His own B Squadron was stationed at Dover, at Swingate, but kept some of its aircraft at Bekesbourne for home defence. Swingate was used as a transit airfield as well, which didn't make life easier to bear for Jake – seeing aircraft flying out to France where he longed to be himself was hard to take.

He had arrived from France due for recuperation leave, but he had chosen not to take it. Why should he? You didn't need two arms to run a squadron from the ground. And there was to be no more active flying for him, that had been made quite clear by Farnborough. Squadron commanders – and designers – were too important, they pointed out reasonably, to be risked on active operations. In any case, there was no home for him to return to, only the depressing lodgings at Farnborough; there was no place to escape, for the pain was within. Farnborough had wanted him back there permanently but he had refused, knowing his worth. He needed to be working with aeroplanes, not just sitting at a designing board. They had been forced to reach a compromise. He would spend as much time at Farnborough as was necessary for the design of their new two-seat bomber, the British Army Aviation I. Meanwhile he was to take up the position of B Squadron commander at Dover Swingate RFC aerodrome. There, he would be near enough to the Kent Aviation factory, he had pointed out to Farnborough, to do most of the work on site. He had no intention of doing so. He banished Kent Aviation, Michael Potts and Robert Bellowes from his mind as often as he could. It had been sheer weakness on his part that once again he had pleaded with Farnborough that the KA4 should be so named, and that production should consequently remain at Sittingbourne. Heaven knows, he owed Michael Potts nothing, and with this last gesture he considered his debt to William Potts paid in full. Now that Harry was dead, this seemed easier, as though the past had then collectively taken one step back in his thinking. The only reality was the fighting taking place all over the world; even home defence, B Squadron's main task, was actively involved in the fight against the Zeppelin airships as they made their deadly way to London. And there was a threat of twin-engined bombers from Germany too.

There was going to be plenty to occupy his mind. He might be back in Kent, but his Kent now had nothing to do with Rosie Potts. He could forget her, forget the sharp jab of agony when he saw her turn away from him today. Their love was long past. Why then did the remembrance of a spring day under an apple tree long ago make his mouth twist in pain? Why did it seem not six years ago but yesterday and Rosie his once more?

'Raining, sir. Shall I put the top up?'

'What?'

His driver repeated the question and Jake nodded. So it was rain, that dampness on his face. For a moment he had wondered.

# Chapter Eighteen

'Feel like a walk?' Peter asked suddenly, laying aside his *Morning Post*.

'Why not?' Rosie replied quickly, despite her surprise. Peter did not often feel up to walking nowadays, preferring to spend his time in a deckchair looking at the gardens, or at their window overlooking the walled vegetable garden. He tired very easily.

'I thought I'd like to see the poppy fields again. Just once.'

There was a note in his voice that alarmed her. 'They're not abolishing poppies, so far as I know,' she replied lightly, to give him an opening.

'No,' he said, grateful for this. 'It's me. Doc Hargreaves tells me the old chest has stepped up its action. What they call the last stage is rattling right down the road faster than Wells Fargo.' The joke fell flat.

'Oh Peter.' She put her hands in his. The brightness of the August day made it incongruous to think of death as a reality. Just as incongruous as the thought of the battles raging on the Somme, while they looked out on tranquil gardens. 'Are they sure?'

'Quite,' he said. 'It seems the air of the North Downs can't quite achieve miracles. Six months if I'm lucky, he said. Luck!' He gave a mirthless laugh.

'What can I do?' The hopelessness of a question to which there was no answer.

'I wish to God I'd pegged out over there,' he burst out violently. 'That would have been something. But this way – it's like cheating. I feel I'm letting the chaps down by going this way.'

'That's nonsense,' she said forcefully. 'Look at the tower of strength you've been to the patients here.'

'Till I had to hide myself away,' he said bitterly.

She was silent.

'I'm being pretty selfish aren't I?' he said wrily. 'Here's you taking pity on a dying man, taking me into your home, pampering me, so that I'm as happy as a sandboy. But I'm still a sandboy under a death sentence.'

'I understand,' she said. 'I do. And you must go on staying here – if you want to—'

Somehow she'd manage, she was thinking. Extra hygienic precautions would be needed now, extra nursing, but with Mother's help she'd manage. She'd have to try to lessen her driving duties if they'd let her.

'Want to?' he was saying. 'Rosie, you don't know how much it means – it feels like home now. And you—' he broke off, and then said quickly, 'Rosie, there *is* something you could do. Would you marry me?'

'*Marry* you?' She stared at him, completely taken aback.

'You know I'm crazy about you. It isn't fair to ask you, I know. But it needn't make any difference to you, and it wouldn't be for long,' he added bitterly.

'Oh Peter,' her heart was crying out within her. 'I can't.'

'No, no, I quite see.' He started to walk more quickly. 'That's all right. It was just a thought.'

'No, you don't see,' said Rosie quickly. 'I love – I've always loved someone else.'

'I've always thought there must be someone,' he said, hurt showing on his face. 'Why don't you marry him? Is he in France?'

'No,' she said bleakly. 'And I can't. He's married to someone else.'

'Then why not marry me, Rosie?' Peter seized her hands. 'I know it's not fair to ask you, but the thought that time's running out makes a chap selfish. And,' he paused, 'I wouldn't expect, I *couldn't* expect – old Doc Hargreaves wouldn't allow it – us to share the same bedroom. Nor,' he emphasised in case this were not clear, 'would we really be man and wife except in name. Too dangerous for you.' He smiled brightly.

To marry Peter, to find a refuge however temporary from the constant agony. Jake was tearing her apart, ever since she had seen him at the railway station, a ghost that could rise up at any moment to remind her of the past. Perhaps if she could bring some kind of happiness to someone else, it might alleviate it. Replace one pain by another's suffering.

She smiled at him. 'Very well, Peter, I'll marry you.'

They were married quietly in Bredhill church, with only Mildred and Michael present. Peter had chosen not to tell his parents till after the event. He was adamant about it. Rosie found the wedding easier than she expected; the words that she had dreaded hearing lest they remind her of the wedding she should have shared with Jake, seemed to acquire a new meaning with Peter at her side. She promised silently to him that her loving companionship would be his. Mrs Favell. How strange the words sounded. A new name for a new life.

Michael Potts watched his Rosie marrying Lieutenant Peter Favell dispassionately. Somewhat to his surprise he discovered he did not mind in the least. His passion for Rosie still existed, but it had changed since his father's death, as if it were a remembered passion, frozen in time, a sense of some kind of irrevocable commitment that had if anything strengthened. Provided she were not marrying Jake Smith, however, he had no objections to the marriage. And he had – he realised sometimes in surprise – put a stop to that for good, with his lie about Jake being married to a mythical Helen. Only it didn't seem like a lie. It was so long ago he had almost come to believe in it himself. It was over and done with, and Rosie now would remain at Brynbourne with Peter. Things changed too much and he didn't like that. He liked things to remain as they were. He hadn't liked moving to the Lodge – and he hadn't liked it when Clairville Jones enlisted. Odd that Harry had decided to go to war. What made men volunteer to risk their lives, when they had every reason not to do so? Harry was doing a much more important job for his country here than he ever could flying about in aeroplanes on the Western Front, and yet he had chosen to go. And died as a result. Very strange. He, Michael, took the rational view that there were dozens of soldiers, but only one Michael Potts. And Michael Potts was needed to run the Potts Sanitary Ware factory, not to mention the projected KA4.

'Papa?' There was a note of doubt in Thomas's voice. It had been a long while, yet something in the stranger's face gave the boy confidence and he rushed towards Jean-Michel, and was caught up in his arms. At four he was already showing signs of his father's physique, unlike the delicate Rosemarie who had inherited Jean-Michel's and Polly's slim neatness.

At the noise in the garden Polly glanced out of the window, and her heart suddenly began to beat more loudly. Surely that was – she flew to the door of the château and ran outside, pausing on the front steps just a moment, as if uncertain just what her welcome might be if she ran to him as little Thomas had done. But Jean-Michel was making the decision for her. Seeing her on the steps, he put the child down and began to walk quickly towards her. He wanted to run, but restrained himself. Too much had happened. Those last thirty metres seemed endless, but now Polly was running towards him, and was there, holding out both hands to her husband.

Jean-Michel kissed them, first the left, and then the right. Then he put his arm round her and led her into the house.

'It is not warm, my love. You are not dressed for autumn.' He glanced at her thin voile dress.

She did not feel the cold, could only wonder that he spoke of it, full of fear that this visit might not mean what she had assumed. It was only when he had led her into the small library and closed the door behind them that he spoke. Or rather started to speak. Then he put out his arms, and with a small choke she was in them,

406

and they were embracing with a fervour that surprised them both.

'Jean-Michel,' she was sobbing. 'Jean-Michel—'

'Forgive me, Polly,' he whispered. 'Ah, forgive me.'

'No reason – oh, no reason.'

'It seems so foolish now, but I could not come. There was a large plain, an empty desert within me that I had to cross with no map. But, you see, I have found my way.'

She was thankful only that he had come, and enquired no further, for which he was grateful. How could he explain that it was 13th October, that Kate had been dead exactly one year, and that morning he had arisen quite certain, but unexpectedly, that it was time to begin again. Enough of mourning. The love he had for Kate would continue, would always be there, but it could be gently buried while the business of life was transacted and a new kind of loving learned. A loving of tolerance, acceptance, and a joint understanding.

Perhaps it was something to do with the watershed offensive that was just about to begin again on the French Front at Verdun, the sense that after the emotional and draining stalemate of 1915 and most of 1916, the terrifying speed with which Paris had once again so nearly fallen had sharpened everyone's nerves. Verdun had remained French and, despite the onslaughts, despite the appalling casualties, had been held. And once again it was imperilled, but the Somme offensive by the British had taken the sting out of the German onslaught on the Verdun front. The weary French had breathed again, but only for the moment. *Ils ne passeront pas*,' was the cry, and his countrymen were rallying themselves for a winter offensive to drive the enemy back to the Meuse. But how long could this savagery continue, where to be found the men to replace the appalling losses in front of Verdun and on the Somme? Suppose it were to continue for years to come, till even Thomas were old enough to fight? Sometimes it seemed this war would last for ever. And so he had come, not one day, not at Christmas, but that very morning.

Rosemarie thrust open the door. 'Papa,' she cried, 'Thomas is horrid.'

'*Non,*' the boy exploded through the door after her. 'It is not fair. Because she is a girl she thinks she can have everything—'

'*Mon fils,*' said Jean-Michel firmly, 'you must learn that it is for men to solve such problems each for themselves. It is not for me to teach you. Out.' And he pushed them both out again.

'I'm afraid,' sighed Polly, 'that Rosemarie is just a little spoilt.'

'Then we must make sure,' said Jean-Michel, taking her hand, 'that she shares the limelight. Perhaps with a little brother, or better still a sister.'

Polly stared at him, half outraged that after these years away he should assume that her bed awaited him so quickly, that she wanted more children; then she sensed the uncertainty behind the smile, behind the charm that shone from eyes that watched her so carefully.

It seemed to her that the rest of her life might be affected by her next words; that Gabriel was urging her on – to choose life, not regret.

'You are right,' she said softly. 'And they need a father's hand.'

'Then, dearest Polly,' said Jean-Michel, happiness flooding his face, 'shall we make the necessary preparations?' He took her hand, but seeing she did not understand, cursed himself for his inability to speak openly, knowing he must speak heart to heart if he were truly to win Polly back to him. So he took her in his arms. 'Come to love me, Polly. Now. And forever.'

Michael stared unbelievingly at the official letter in his hand. He had known, of course, that universal conscription had now come in, but surely he was exempt? They must know he was needed here. It must be a mistake. The letter was a total surprise; conscription had not even entered his thoughts. If he had been called up, so perhaps had Robert Bellowes. What would happen to the factory if so? Now that he was in danger of losing it, he realised how much he cared about it. Both the sanitary ware – and the aircraft factory. It had been his, a legacy handed down to him by his father so that he might carry on the traditions. If he were not there, then . . . His train of thought led to a bleak future. The factory would be ruined or pass out of their hands, which was just as bad. He summoned the company's Wolseley and told the driver to take him to the Bellowes factory just outside Ramsgate. Now that Harry was dead, Robert had wasted no time in buying his shares and dropping the Clairville from the name.

'Michael?' Robert looked up from his desk in surprise. He disliked seeing Michael Potts here for this was his own domain, the domain of the seaplanes that he understood. It made him forget that the KA3 made most money. Seeing Michael Potts was a constant reminder that he could never entirely rid himself of the shade of Jake Smith, that Jake Smith held the patent on the KA3 which subsidised his beloved seaplanes, and now the KA4 too.

Without a word Michael held out the letter and Robert took it. 'Report to Fovant Camp, 3 pm 4 November 1916.' Robert laughed to himself. Poor Michael. He hadn't even had the benefit of training as had Robert so he was going to be one of those poor bloody infantry, as they called themselves. Another of Kipling's Tommies. Cannon fodder.

'What about you, Bellowes?' asked Michael anxiously, taking the letter back after Robert's casual examination. 'You'll support my application to be exempt?'

'I'm exempt myself,' said Robert offhandedly. It was untrue. He *had* been called up, but had been discharged as unfit for military service. Exempt sounded better. 'And Michael, I feel that the War Office would never sanction both of us as exempt. They would point out that the production of the KA3 and KA4 can be moved here, and that you can appoint a manager for the chamber pots,' he added disparagingly.

'No,' declared Michael decidedly. He appeared cool, he was thinking furiously. So much for Bellowes's loyalty. He'd been a fool, but he'd win yet.

Robert raised an eyebrow. 'You have no choice, Michael. I own the Kent Aviation Company and you're leaving. You have no one to run it.'

Robert had underestimated Michael Potts. He had assumed that by the constant humiliations he heaped on the boy who had once thrashed him into a slavering whimpering animal he held the upper hand. Suddenly however that boy reappeared. Not with a physical whip in his hand this time, but something far more dangerous.

Michael stared at him unblinkingly. 'You own the company, Bellowes, but Mr Smith owns the patent, and choice of manufacturer.'

Michael did not overplay his hand. He made no suggestion that he would be in touch with Jake Smith pleading for him to demand that production remained at the Sittingbourne factory as the price of Bellowes's company continuing to produce the aircraft. He did not need to. Robert Bellowes would know that faced with the possibility of his new KA4 being produced at Ramsgate by Bellowes or at Sittingbourne, that while Jake Smith might not choose Sittingbourne, he would under no circumstances choose Ramsgate. Not with Robert Bellowes in charge.

Robert Bellowes's eyes narrowed. 'Very well, Michael,' he said smoothly as though it were of no great moment to him. 'Then you must find a manager for your whole factory – acceptable to me of course. It won't be easy.'

There he was wrong, thought Michael, though he merely bowed his head in agreement and said, 'Very well.' For his plans were already made.


'No,' Rosie cried aghast. 'Michael, how can I—'

'You must, Rosie. There's no one else,' Michael said matter-of-factly at the small dining table at the Lodge.

'But my job here and Peter—'

'There are a lot of people who can drive,' said Michael steadily. 'Not many are competent to run a factory, and even less know about building aeroplanes. Peter will understand. Help you perhaps.' He did not know of Peter's condition.

Rosie stiffened. 'Peter's not well enough,' she said.

'I'm sorry,' said Michael sincerely. He didn't want

to see Rosie suffer, especially now she'd got over that ridiculous love of hers for Jake Smith. 'But you don't want the factory under other hands, do you? Father's work gone—' He broke off as she cried out, and realised he had gone too far.

'I don't know,' she said wearily. 'What do you think, Mother?'

She turned to Mildred, who looked at her compassionately. Mildred, now married to Sir Lawrence, had moved to Manor Court, but paid frequent visits to the Lodge on her way home from her work at Brynbourne. 'Peter needs you, Rosie – but so do we.' What more could she have expected from sensible, straightforward Mother, who saw everything in uncomplicated lines?

'I'll talk it over with Peter,' Rosie said, defeated.

But as she climbed the stairs to their home she was utterly confused by conflicting emotions. There was Peter, there was the chance to be among aeroplanes again, there was the terrible thought that she would be working at least partly for Robert Bellowes, and an even worse spectre – that she might come into contact again with Jake Smith. Michael had not, it was true. Farnborough had dealt with everything, but she knew now that Jake was back in Kent. What if he decided to come to the factory?

She tried to pull herself together. Surely, if he came, they could behave like adults? He was married. So was she. Why need she fear seeing him so much? As if she would forget everything, his wife, her husband who needed her, everything to be with him again. It was obvious that he no longer felt anything for her. He was married and happily. If he came – no, she could not think about it. She would think about the important thing: aeroplanes. A throb of excitement seized her at the thought of the challenge. She might even test-fly the aircraft herself. She remembered again what she had vowed after Kate's death – to take any opportunity to do the work for which she was best qualified. Now the chance had come.

She checked herself: Peter must come first. He looked

up from the chesterfield as she entered, laying aside the book he had only been pretending to read. He held out his arms and she ran to him.

'I'm sorry I was so long, darling.'

'How was tea at the Lodge?'

'Not half so good as the one I'm going to get you,' she told him gaily. She left it some while before she broached the subject, and then told him of Michael's offer, making as light of it as she could, hiding, as she thought, her excitement. His face clouded for a moment, then he said; 'You must do it,' in tones of surprise that she should ever think anything else.

'But—'

'Do you think if they suddenly said I should go back to the Front, I'd refuse?'

'No, but—'

'It's the same thing, Rosie. We all have to do what we can at the moment. What I can do is convince you that's where you should be.'

'Oh, Peter.' She flung her arms round him. 'If only things had been different.'

'Yes,' he said wistfully. 'If only.'

Robert Bellowes viewed Rosie's appointment with mixed feelings. Part of him longed to veto it in a quick triumph over her. On the other hand the temptation of having Rosie in his power – subordinate to him – was not to be resisted. Always, always Rosie Potts had come between him and his plans, standing just beyond his power to hurt. So, yes, he'd give Michael his petty victory. It would give him great pleasure knowing how much Rosie would dislike living with the knowledge that he was the ultimate voice in the company, and how he could revel in his knowledge that her marriage had been in vain. He knew now for certain that Jake Smith had not married – curious, he had made enquiries to make sure. It had been an invention by Michael, which amused him greatly. That husband of Rosie's didn't look too well. He toyed with the idea of making Rosie his mistress, the ultimate revenge for his humiliation. And it would humiliate that so-called wife of his, Poppy, wherever she was, to have as her husband's mistress one of her own friends, for Poppy had lost no time in telling him of the friendship developing between the two of them, whenever on rare occasions Rosie managed to visit London.

Time enough, he decided eventually, for that master-stroke. Slowly, slowly at first.

The Potts factory had advanced under Michael's direction. Keen to exploit new trends, he had taken advantage of the wartime surge in factory production to diversify into multiple unit automatic slop water closets. With women coming into factories, more sanitary accommodation was required and particularly in the North multiple units were much in demand. Trade was slower in Kent, however, and with the difficulties of transport north, the programme was now running into difficulties.

'I suggest we slow down on the multiples,' Rosie told Michael after going through the orders. 'It doesn't seem to me the way for us to go at present. I prefer to stick with southern trade on the old pedestals. Perhaps I'll launch a patriotic model with a discreet Union Jack – on the outside of course.' She remembered Polly's delicate flower paintings, how she would laugh to see today's garish cheaper models. Night after night, Rosie ploughed through all the local government legislation to learn her trade. Demand was falling, however, even for pedestals, though Rosie failed to see why people should need less water closets in wartime than any other time. However, it was obvious that their income depended as much on their running of Kent Aviation as on the sanitary ware. Perhaps more.

She dreaded going into the factory for the first time to see the new KA4 now beginning to be assembled. How far removed it was from the aircraft she and Jake had flown, yet this tractor scout plane with its planned streamlined fuselage was as much his handiwork as Sunburst. Before them on the production line however was not yet the KA4 but KA3bs, an improved version of the KA3a, their RFC roundels in the process of being painted on.

'Of course, unlike these, the KA4 will have the new forward firing guns,' Michael pointed out to her.

Rosie's interest quickened. She remembered hearing in France about the new synchronising interrupter gear that was being developed in order to synchronise the firing of the gun straight ahead through the turning blades of the propeller.

'Did you say it's still going to use a Clairville engine?'

'Yes.' Michael hesitated. 'Harry designed a new one specially for it before he died, but I gather that Farnborough aren't too happy with Clairvilles at the moment. They've been asking for them to develop a new engine for the KA4, and with Harry dead the new man isn't up to it.' He shot her a glance. 'I shouldn't say that of course, but it's true.'

'I have to know,' said Rosie firmly, 'if I'm to run this factory properly.'

'Farnborough are investigating now. If they come up with something we – or rather Bellowes – is in trouble. Bellowes is opposing any change of course, but Farnborough are adamant. So is he, claiming it's specified in the contract. It's a question of who gives way first.'

Her heart sank. To walk into a problem like that straightaway was more than she'd bargained for. But she refused to show her dismay. 'Very well,' she said coolly. 'Now let's do that stock and spares inventory.'

As they methodically worked their way through, she asked the question that had been puzzling her. 'Michael, if you have to join the forces, why not ask for the RFC – with your knowledge of aircraft you'd be invaluable on the ground, even if you didn't want to fly.'

'No,' he said dispassionately. 'No more aircraft.'

'I don't understand,' she said, puzzled.

'It's quite simple – I don't like them. I like running factories. Not making aircraft.'

'But you always spent so much time with Father and me,' she said bewildered, without thinking.

'With you,' he said briefly. And the matter was closed. Even for the sake of escaping the trenches he was not prepared to go to Farnborough to work on aircraft – for there he would probably be sent. And there he would meet Jake Smith.

Jake fumed at being summoned to Farnborough before he was due. The colonel was apologetic. 'It won't take long, Major. You can fly back this evening. The rest of the work will wait. Sit down.'

'Thank you, sir,' Jake said resignedly, easing his long legs in front of him.

'It's this problem with the engines. Bellowes is still holding out for the Clairville and he's every legal right to do so. Produced by Kent Aviation with Clairville providing engines. We didn't foresee then the problem the Clairville would have dovetailing with the interrupter gear. Bellowes says they can be overcome. Up to now we've had Michael Potts on our side, and didn't need to call you in. Now, with the new management an unknown quantity—'

'New management? What new management?' Jake asked sharply.

'Potts has been called up. A Mrs Favell is taking over.'

'Who?' asked Jake blankly. He'd never heard of her, and if she had had any experience in the aviation world, surely he would have done?

'Apparently she's very experienced in aircraft,' said the colonel doubtfully.

'Not in this country,' said Jake decidedly. 'Nor any other that I know anything of.'

'Mrs Rose Favell—'

Rose. Rosie. A wave of sick horror swept over him. Too big a coincidence to be anyone other than Rosie. Who else would Michael have handed over to? Only to Rosie. He knew how Michael's mind worked. Deviously.

Aeroplanes were far from his mind. She had married. For a moment such a black cloud swept through him, he was back to the dark shadow of Florence on his return to Leadville. He heard May saying, troubled: 'You mean to say she didn't tell you, Jake? . . . She married 'bout a year after you left.' All the while Rosie was there, he realised he'd had some faint hope that sooner or later

415

their separation would end, as surely as one day would the war. Now he knew he had been deluding himself, just as surely as all those years before with Florence. Rosie had passed from his life, as surely, as unheedingly as the schoolmaster's daughter had done. His mouth twisted in disbelief that this could happen. Rosie, married to someone else. It didn't make sense. She was his, *his*. But she wasn't. That had been why she had walked away from him at Canterbury. Because she was married and could not face him in her betrayal. Yet, a small part of his mind was saying, did that not suggest she still felt something for him, or why walk away? Why not walk up to him and say, Hello Jake. How are you? No, he must stop fooling himself. It was her guilt had made Rosie walk away. She *wasn't* a Florence, she would know she had betrayed him. And could he blame her if he still carried this illusion that they were meant for each other. She was twenty-nine now – no longer the girl he had loved, he told himself. No longer the Rosie he knew, triumphant and laughing in the sky, the Rosie he had laid down with in the green grass, the Rosie he had loved. She preferred the arms of another man. She had gone. As had his reason for living.

Michael Potts sat, still disbelieving, in the railway train, on his way to basic training camp. He still could not understand why fate had done this to him, or why shortly these clothes would be taken from him in exchange for ill-fitting khaki. Soon he would be caught up in the machine of war, as surely as all the thousands of other khaki-clad men he saw around. The railway train was full of them, but he had chosen to travel in a first-class compartment as if to underline all he was leaving behind. He had it all to himself. But a girl climbed aboard at the last moment to his annoyance. True, she did not even glance at him, even when he got up to put her luggage on the rack.

'Thank you,' she said composedly, sitting down and reading a Baroness Orczy novel.

Michael eyed her curiously; she was about his age, perhaps a little younger, and as sure of herself as he knew he was.

He found himself continuing to stare at her, over the top of *The Times*, liking the way her nose turned up and her fair hair was pushed higgledy-piggledy under the uniform hat. What uniform? Not WAACs for sure, or Navy. He'd seen it before . . . Women's Legion of course. Like Rosie's. He looked away blushing when she suddenly looked up at him.

'Do I have a smut on my face?' she inquired sweetly.

'No.' he blushed in a way that amazed him. Usually he didn't even notice women.

'Good.' She went back to her book. He tried hard to look anywhere but at her. Then as the train went into a tunnel it stopped, with no lighting. He could hear her breathing, and it seemed to him her breathing had quickened slightly.

'You needn't be afraid,' he said quickly. 'I'm not going to jump at you. I'm far too nervous.' What on earth had made him say that? It wasn't like him at all.

'Of me?' she inquired, her voice coming hollowly out of the blackness.

'No. I'm on my way to join up.'

'Oh.' A pause. 'Which camp?'

'Fovant on Salisbury Plain.'

'That's where I work.'

'Really? You're not—'

'I work in the canteen. I think I'd like to join the Navy though,' she said wistfully.

'So would I at the moment,' he said fervently.

She laughed, and he wondered at himself again. He didn't normally make jokes. By the time the train started again he knew her name was Sally Thompson, and she was the daughter of an army brigadier – that explained the first class and the self-confidence he thought. By the time they reached their destination, he was chatting happily, and it was Sally Thompson's presence enabled him to survive the next few weeks.

Another squadron taking off for France, leaving him behind. Jake stood on the field watching the last of the biplanes soar out over the Channel. Once more his application for active service had been turned down, on grounds of age, rank and his wound. His wound, he thought wrily. Only a faint scar and an ache reminded him of his shattered arm. He knew the reason for his being kept in England was only the KA4. So the War Office pacified him by keeping him here at Dover as a compromise. He'd be busy enough if the predictions for 1917 came true and the Germans revived the Zeppelin menace, not to mention the threat of those new Gotha bombers if they ever entered service. Home defence – essential, but how he longed to be in France, away from England, away from *her*. He felt ashamed to be sending these new untried boys into battle and be cowering here himself.

Jake walked moodily back to his office and tried hard to get interested in engines and forget the KA4. Ten minutes later he was on his feet again, as an aircraft roared in to land. Before his horrified eyes, a Sopwith came in, bounced, went up again, bounced again, skewed sideways, and finally lurched to a stop. Jake closed his eyes, counted to three, then hurtled outside. The pilot was climbing down from the aircraft as Jake strode over to him.

'What the blazes do you think you're doing?' he thundered. 'No one lands like that on my field. Ever been in an aeroplane before . . . you—'

'Yessir,' said the pilot meekly.

Jake stared at him. 'Don't I know you?'

'Yessir. You taught me to fly. Second Lieutenant Swithin, sir.'

'*I* taught you to fly? repeated Jake grimly.

'Well, Miss Potts, sir.'

'And what, Lieutenant Swithin,' said Jake stiffly, ignoring this, 'are you doing on my field?'

'I've been in France, sir. Back here for rest and recuperation. They've posted me to your squadron, sir. Want me to fly KA3b, I gather.'

'You in France? You must have terrified the Germans. You certainly terrify me, lieutenant.' Jake paused, gripped by an old yearning. 'Feeling like a spin now?'

Swithin visibly blenched. 'Er, yessir,' he said weakly.

'Good,' said Jake cordially.

An hour later Lieutenant Swithin was as conversant with the workings of the KA3b as it was possible to be on the ground.

'Remember, Swithin,' shouted Jake, leaping into his own KA3b. 'Throttle lever quarter open for contact. Petrol lever half open. And bring that aircraft *back*.'

He could almost imagine himself at Eastchurch again, as his KA3b soared into the air, after Lieutenant Swithin's lurching rise. He kept him up for fifteen minutes, long enough for a first attempt. Up here, the years seemed to roll away as he heard again Rosie's excited laugh. 'Go on, Mr Swithin. Go *on*.' He forgot the pain and anguish, forgot the war, in the sheer excitement of flight.

Jake landed, watching Swithin come in after him, watching him ignore his instructions to flatten out and come in level, and once again pancaking. Jake closed his eyes and when he opened them again his pupil was safely down.

'I did all right, didn't I, sir?' Swithin asked anxiously, but clearly preening himself in pride.

'Not bad, Swithin, not bad. We'll work on those landings though. Go along and see the Adj now. By the way,' he called after him light-heartedly, 'how is Miss Maud Pettigrew?'

Lieutenant Swithin beamed. 'Now Mrs Swithin, sir. Or Pettigrew-Swithin as she likes to be known.' His face lost some of its cheerfulness as he considered this. 'And Miss Potts?'

The sun lost its brightness and all the quicker since it had been his own doing.

'Well, I believe, thank you,' Jake managed to say, and Swithin, slightly puzzled, went on his way.

Jake stood still. The past could not be resurrected, the bright day was done, and now had come the dark.

# Chapter Nineteen

Peter lay by the window looking out over the Brynbourne vegetable gardens, still covered with a thin sprinkling of white frost in this cold January of 1917. In the last few weeks, smiles did not come to his face so easily. 'I wish I could have seen another spring here,' he said abruptly.

Rosie looked up sharply from her paperwork. 'Let's just pretend it's spring, shall we?' she said steadily. How easy to lie and say, 'But you will.' There was little chance, the doctors had told them. 'Come on.' She came to kneel on the chesterfield at his side. 'Look,' she said. 'Try hard. Don't you see all those daffodils, yellow and trumpeting like mad at you? And the trees – they're already beginning to bud. The almond trees are in full bloom – if you look hard you can see them, Peter.'

'Only through your eyes, Rosie. If you weren't here, I couldn't see them. Not one.' He fell back against the cushions; even the slightest effort made him tired now.

She jumped down from the sofa and drew up her chair to sit closer by his side.

'Perhaps a miracle will happen,' she said. 'They do, sometimes.'

'Not at this stage,' he said thickly. 'We both know that.'

She was silent.

'I just hope – I don't like your being so close to me. You shouldn't – just in case. Not now.'

'This is where I choose to be,' she said steadily. 'And we take enough precautions.'

'Only because I made you,' he pointed out. 'Listen, Rosie,' making an effort at brightness, 'when I'm – when you're on your own, you must be happy. I want you to be happy enough for both of us. You say that chap of yours is married, so I can't say go off and marry him with my blessing.' His mouth twisted as though saying even that cost him some pain. 'I want you to go back to aeroplanes again. Not just building them, but flying them. Like you used to. Like—'

'I don't think I could, Peter,' she said wretchedly. 'You don't know what—'

'He's something to do with it then?'

'Yes.'

'After this war's over,' he said after a moment, 'and it will be sooner or later, too many fellows will have died for those that are left not to do the best they can to set the world to rights. And you can fly - use it somehow to bring back some sanity. That's where you belong, not driving ambulances and lugging wounded soldiers around. Nor running factories for the benefit of Robert Bellowes.'

'I don't do it for him,' she interrupted crossly. 'I do it for Father's sake.'

'So start a flying school,' he said urgently. 'Build aeroplanes yourself after the war, give flying displays. I've a fair bit of money of my own and I want you to use it like that.'

'Peter, I can't—'

'Yes, you can,' he said firmly. 'You're fond of me, aren't you - I know you are, so do it for my sake. It wasn't so bad being married, was it?'

'No,' she said, choking, laying her hand against his cheek, 'it wasn't so bad at all.'

Winter on Salisbury Plain coupled with basic soldier's training was a nightmare for Michael, alleviated only by those bright patches of sunlight when he was with Sally. Sally was in the Women's Legion, working in the camp canteen, and he lived in fear that one day this idyll would end and that she would be moved elsewhere. That he himself would be going overseas receded almost to the back of his mind. His fear now was at leaving her, not at going to the Front. That would be a minor inconvenience, until he could get back to her again.

Meanwhile he stolidly endured the twenty-mile marches, carrying full pack and weapons, the endless drill on the camp square, the torturous physical training and even the bomb-throwing practice.

That other world when he had been a businessman running a factory seemed a million years away; aeroplanes now were faraway objects up in the sky. Only with Sally did he feel a human being again, and not an automaton being moulded into cannon fodder. Only with Sally did he become Michael Potts again. But the winter was coming to an end, and so was his training. Embarkation was the word on everyone's lips. Talk too of a spring offensive. But first there was leave; he paid a speedy visit to Brynbourne to see Mildred and Rosie, and then met Sally in London. He felt almost shy of her as he saw her in her smart hat and coat waiting for him at Victoria railway station.

She did not notice him at first and he pecked her on the cheek, making her jump. Her grey eyes lit up as she put her hands in his. 'Let me look at you.'

'Why?'

'I've forgotten what you look like. It's been three days.'

'You'll know me again by the time we go back,' he said softly.

The grey eyes met his steadily. 'Yes,' she said.

He took her to *Chu Chin Chow* at His Majesty's. He'd never bothered very much with the theatre before he met Sally, and was amazed by the experience. He'd been taken to pantomimes when he was young, and, with Sally's presence and the need to forget the axe that would now so shortly fall on their friendship, the musical play seemed to have the same effect as those pantomimes had done, propelling him into another world of magic and enchantment.

They hummed the 'Robbers March' in the cab which took them to the Strand. They had taken supper earlier since even this hotel restaurant was bound by the wartime restrictions of closing at 10.30, though the bar was open at their hotel. Once there, they looked at each other uncertain what to say.

'Rosie used to stay here,' Michael managed jerkily, handing her her drink.

'You talk a lot about her,' said Sally, somewhat curious.

'Do I?' Michael said absently. 'She's my sister. Adopted,' he added after a pause. 'You must meet her.' Rosie – it had been like meeting a stranger, seeing her again at Brynbourne. Now that he knew Sally, he realised he thought less and less about what Rosie might be doing. 'Yes,' he said, 'I'd like you to meet her. On my next leave.' He caught his breath and she reached for his hand.

'Are you scared, Michael?'

'Only of losing you,' he said abruptly, staring into his glass.

'It's only for a while.'

'Will you wait for me?'

'Yes.'

'I can't believe,' he said in a low voice, 'I can't believe—'

'What?'

'That there's you.'

'Shall I – shall I make you believe it?'

He looked at her, and at the two room keys in his hand. 'You don't have to—' he said anxiously. 'I'm going abroad. I might be killed.' Words, but words. They meant nothing besides this moment, this answer.

Jake still fumed at Dover. He was stagnating in Kent. Too full of memories, too full of pain. Yet how could he leave? Now was the very time that the enemy would start to launch a new bombing campaign against England. It could start any day. The huge dark shapes of Zeppelins threatening their skies once more, to rain down death upon helpless civilians. And the new Gotha bombers they'd heard about. What had the enemy in mind for those?

But all the same – he wanted to see what was happening at the Front again. To take action to the enemy. Action, anything for action. Day after day he saw squadrons leaving for France. The average survival time for pilots was only a few weeks now; they needed all the experienced pilots they could get. Yet every time he applied he was told he was more valuable here. He knew he was – to them. But to himself? Sometimes when his squadron flew patrols from Bekesbourne he went up with them, but when the station commander found out, he was given such a dressing down that even he dared not do it again. Yet if they were risking their lives, why couldn't he? What use was a CO who led from the ground? Orders may be orders in England. In France, however, no eye would be on him.

In France the spring offensive had just been launched. The poor bloody infantry would bear the brunt at Arras but the RFC now had a crucial role beforehand. No one doubted by now the usefulness of the air arm in winning mastery of the air space, necessary for the success of the offensive. But the losses were heavy, particularly for the new German scouts. Reinforcements were necessary and the swift manoeuvrable KA3b was what was needed. B Squadron would be flying over on the morrow.

And he was damn well going with them. The idea was that they would get a new CO out there; he was supposed to remain at Dover and wait for a newly formed squadron to come along, train them in home defence and in the use of the KA3b – while all the offensive action was elsewhere. But the embryo squadron would not be flying in for ten days and he had his own plans for those ten days. The perfect reason to go to France – and if a detour was made to Arras in squadron interests, no one would be the wiser for it here in England.

Directly he was over the Channel, he throttled down to 950 rpm and began to relax. It was safe here to fly straight, no need to wheel and turn, for though the new German Albatros scouts were good, they could not yet threaten the Channel.

When the squadron landed to check in at the RFC depot at St Omer, he kept out of the way, simply refuelling and flying straight on to Vert Galant, the front line aerodrome, which they were to share with the famous 56 Squadron and two others. The mud, the smell of castor oil, the uninviting tents and huts – how it all came back. But in one way it was different now. A grim professionalism had set in, a need to win the war, no matter what the cost. That suited him down to the ground. A new breed of pilots was coming to the fore, Albert Ball, James McCudden, no laughing cavaliers these. Just dedicated, determined pilots. He held back from the temptation of flying – for the moment. He had a duty to get the KA4's problems solved. That was more important than the life of Major Jack Smith.

The Pinot factory on the outskirts of Paris had moved some of its production away, just in case Paris should once again fall into jeopardy, and it was at the Orleans factory that Jake tracked down Jean-Michel – a Jean-Michel who looked much happier than on his last visit, Jake noted immediately.

'Country air suits you, Jean-Michel.'

'I cannot say the same for you, *mon ami*,' replied Jean-Michel forthrightly, looking at Jake's set, drawn face, the lines of unhappiness that were beginning to etch themselves deep on his face. 'I tell you, my friend, that if you do not relax, you will have a face as lined as those boots so beloved by Mr Van Gogh – or else you will be dead,' he added.

Jake shrugged and said nothing.

'So,' said Jean-Michel, thoughtfully. 'And you bring me news of Rosie?'

'No,' said Jake shortly.

'I thought now that she was at the factory you would see her.'

'I don't visit the factory,' Jake said sharply.

'You must forgive an old friend, Jake, but I find this curious.'

'I can do my work through Farnborough.'

'Then why,' asked Jean-Michel, 'have you come to see me?'

Jake grinned suddenly, the years rolling off him. He flung himself down in the chair by Jean-Michel's desk. 'I've got a serious problem with the KA4.'

'Ah. *Mon ami*, I think this problem calls for a little luncheon first, does it not?'

There was no sign of food rationing in the meal that

426

followed in a small local restaurant. Four courses and five glasses of wine later, Jake sat back with a sigh. 'You're right,' he said. 'I feel better.'

'Food is a wonderful solver of problems,' said Jean-Michel complacently. 'Now tell me,' wiping his lips with his napkin in renunciation of the pleasant things of life.

'I've got to change the Clairville engine. It doesn't work effectively with the interrupter gear I'm using. And I think it's the engine at fault.'

'So? You want Pinots,' asked Jean-Michel practically. 'What problem?'

'Bellowes – and Rosie, Mrs Favell,' said Jake bluntly.

'Ah yes, I heard she had married, but—'

'That aside,' Jake interrupted him, making clear this was forbidden territory, 'Bellowes naturally is sticking out for the Clairville, and though Mrs Favell—' he spoke with an effort '—runs Kent Aviation she is naturally subordinate to Bellowes.'

'But can you not talk to Rosie – get her on your side?'

'No,' said Jake simply. 'I won't do that, there's no point. You see, I need support for my view.'

'I can perhaps assist,' said Jean-Michel thoughtfully. 'I have felt for some time that the rotary engine is not the way to the future. It is good, yes, but we must pass on. I have developed a water-cooled V-8 engine like the Hispano-Suiza in the Spads. I think it would suit your KA4 very well. Let me tell you – ah, I always forget. You are not an engine man, are you?'

Jake shook his head mutely, remembering Rosie's indignation when he bluffed her over his knowledge of engines, and passed a hand over his face. Jean-Michel watched him in concern.

'What ails you, my friend?'

Jake shook his head impatiently. 'Can you come up with me to the Front – talk over the problems with some of the COs?' That would look after the KA4, he thought to himself. Now he could do as *he* wished.

'I come,' said Jean-Michel simply. 'But no flying for me. Me, I am not brave, and Polly needs me.'

'Everything is well with you?' Jake asked.

Jean-Michel smiled. 'Everything. Polly is soon to have our baby. It is not generally a good time to bring children into the world, but for us it will be. You too should have children. No matter what—' but he broke off as he saw the misery on Jake's face.

The weather was poor at the Front, and at Vert Galant Jake fretted and fumed, impatient at being unable to fly, while Jean-Michel was engrossed in discussions about engines. The first aircraft with the new interrupter gear were in production now, and Jean-Michel had every intention of making up for lost time. The CO of 56 Squadron politely hinted it was time Jake found his way back to England, having 'delivered' his squadron, and was stiffly reminded by Jake firstly that he was officially on leave, and secondly that he had a role as designer which necessitated his being here with Monsieur Pinot. But the exchange did not improve his temper as the weather obstinately refused to improve.

At last it did and he seized the opportunity to take his KA3b up on a dawn patrol. He was led by the young captain he'd heard so much about, Albert Ball, who seemed a man after his own heart. Ball obstinately clung to his Nieuport, despite the fact that the squadron now flew SE5 scouts. And in view of his record, the authorities wisely decided to turn a blind eye for once.

Ball took the lead, blithely ignoring Jake's rank, and, amused, Jake did not argue the point. Ball had sense on his side, for he was the expert here. The two aircraft crossed the trenches unobserved in cloud at 12,000 feet, escaping the usual cacophony of German 'archie'. Jake immediately appreciated Ball's artistry; he never flew straight for long, he continually twisted, turned, watched, searched, every inch of the sky. No Clairville Jones here. This man was a professional.

Ball had obviously noticed something – he was waggling his wings and pointing off to the north. Then Jake saw them too. Six German scouts about 5,000 feet below them, their black and white crosses clearly marked on their green and mauve coloured wings. Ball was diving fast now, leaving the KA3b behind. The Nieuport was the faster machine Jake noted, deciding to have a word with Jean-Michel on his return. *If* he returned. He caught himself sharply. No thinking that way. The fight was all, indifference to one's fate a weapon. But the expectation of victory was a greater one.

Ball was easing up behind the Albatros scouts, and they were scattering. Ball turned on one, firing. Jake picked his own target, but it turned quickly and he'd no chance of a shot. First the Albatros, then he was enveloped in cloud, and when he emerged he was alone. All signs of Ball and the Germans had vanished.

Jake headed south, exhilarated now, all the old emotions flooding back; the duel between one's vulnerability on the one side and the thrill of the hunt on the other. War and death stalked the skies, but beauty too, moments that should be captured, appreciated to the full, lest death were the victor first. That way one cocked a snook at fate.

A glimpse of movement below alerted him. Jake checked again – it was an Albatros heading north, it would soon be right underneath him, about 3,000 feet below the KA3b, and he obviously was unaware of Jake's presence. Jake rolled over and down, all his old expertise automatically coming back to him. He straightened out to come down behind the Albatros, glancing back to ensure his own tail was clear. It wasn't. Swooping down from high cloud came three or four more Albatros scouts, closing in on him fast.

He cursed his blind complacency. He'd fallen for the oldest trick in the book. A trap. Even Clairville Jones wouldn't have fallen for that one. Swiftly, he calculated his chances. He might get in one quick burst at his target ahead – but now it had seen him, going into a right climbing turn to take itself and its pursuer deeper into German-held territory if Jake were fool enough to follow. He was. Nothing to lose now. Within range, Jake pulled the trigger of his Lewis, firing a long burst. Bullets hit the Albatros's tail, then crept up the fuselage. He could even see the terror on the goggled face of the pilot as he turned back to look. Then the pilot's head jerked back as the whole aircraft shuddered, and went spinning into an uncontrollable dive.

But where were the others? Jake continued turning, to avoid the scouts now diving towards their prey. The leader was coming in for the kill; Jake side-slipped the KA3b, catching the Albatros pilot off guard; the Albatros tried to reverse its turn, but lost speed and the nose dropped, allowing Jake to gain several yards on the enemy machine. This was his only chance. Jake pulled the stick forward and dived for the lines. He began to breathe again. The Albatros was outmanoeuvred and he was safe unless the AA fire got him. But luck was with him, as he zipped back across the lines. As he came in to land he noticed Ball's Nieuport on the ground. So he had got back safely. Good. The RFC couldn't afford to lose men like Ball. Or even damn fools like Jake Smith.

Jean-Michel came out on to the airfield to meet him. His face was grim. He had seen the battle over the lines.

'Jake, this you must stop. You will kill yourself. This is not for you. You call me here to talk of aeroplanes, not to attend your funeral. You are like a little boy, *mon ami*. Nobody loves me, so I shall run from home, then they'll be sorry.'

Jake's eyes blazed, about to make a blistering retort. Then he saw the concern in his friend's eyes and said, forcing a grin, 'Perhaps you're right.'

'Of course I am right. This is not what you learned to fly for all those years ago. Do you see Orville Wright flying here? No. He will wait till the world is sane again and he has something to teach.'

Jake's face sagged, unwilling to acknowledge the sense of his friend's argument. 'Let's look at this engine, Jean-Michel,' he said uncommunicatively.

A week later, back in England, he heard of Ball's death – he was being put up for a posthumous Victoria Cross. War took the best, and left the tired warriors to fight on.

Hauptmann Thomas Dietrich stood in a trench on the German positions on the Messines Ridge. The British were uncannily quiet. What were they planning? Did he care very much? How he had remained alive so long, he did not know. Fate was so unfair. Hans, his sergeant, had died; he was two months married. And Frederick with his four small children, and Gerhard on his first offensive action. Gerhard had been sixteen. And here was he, an old man of nearly forty still alive, action after action. They pinned medals on his chest for it. They didn't realise it wasn't bravery, but cowardice at not wanting to face life that sent him racing forwards.

It was early June, and somewhere he could hear a nightingale, singing as sweetly and surely as ever it did in days of peace. With a sharp twist of pain, he remembered the birds singing in the trees at Brynbourne. Did the nightingale not know that there was a war on that it sang so loud? Foolish bird. It must be some way away, for there were no trees left here now, no grass, just the endless wasteland of battle. And yet it was so important to hold on to this expanse of mud. How the British would love to take this ridge. But the German positions were impregnable; it would have to be a big offensive to take it. And did it matter if they did? The Germans would soon win it back once more. It wasn't just a ridge. If the British captured it, the ports might fall to them and the ports were crucial to the submarine blockade which would starve the British into submission by preventing food ships from reaching them. Already it was effective. And for that he was standing here in a deep trench, sheltering in a muddy hole propped up with wood, drinking coloured water that his batman called coffee. When would something happen?

He did not have long to wait. On 7th June the offensive began. It opened with a huge explosion from mines planted deep under the ridge along a ten-mile front. Thomas Dietrich was tossed thirty yards by the force of the explosion, a crazy form of art as bright shapes and severed limbs flashed past his eyes or his mind – he never knew which. Then all was oblivion, as the spinning world inside his head came to a stop.

Eight hours later a stretcher party found him, amongst the pieces of his troops.

'*Er lebt noch immer!*'

Impossible.

'*Nein.*' The orderly bent over him and found a feeble pulse. '*Ja! Kommen Sie hier,*' barking at the stretcher bearers.

When Thomas Dietrich eventually woke, he was in a field tent with two men bent over him. Someone seemed to be screaming. Was it him? Then a golden-haired girl came to his side. 'Polly?' he asked.

The girl shook her head.

He did not hear what she said. 'I am alive,' he croaked.

'*Jawohl.* Be cheerful, my friend, you have had a lucky escape.'

Tears formed in Thomas Dietrich's eyes. The nurse thought they were tears of relief but they were not.

They said the village was called Passchendaele and for some reason they eventually had to take it. Michael Potts didn't know why. He just accepted it, just as he accepted having to lie in this trench with a dozen other men whose accents he couldn't understand, and even when he did the words meant little to him. Passchendaele was only five miles away from Ypres – it didn't sound very far. Apparently it was, however, for the 11th Battalion, Queen's Own Royal West Kents were detailed to take the village of Hollebeke which was only a few hundred yards away, as their first objective.

Instead, Michael thought about Sally and about their nights together. He hadn't persuaded her into staying with him that night; he'd made sure she didn't do it out of pity because he was going overseas. No, she had stayed because she loved him. And the wonder of it. That had been the loveliest thing of all, better even than holding her in his arms. It had been the first time for both of them, clumsy, inexpert, but a promise for the future. Even in this trench he could think of that as something beautiful.

Michael had plenty of time to think here in this trench while they were waiting, for they had been here six days now. He thought about sex, about how he'd thought of it as something disgusting and degrading until he met Sally.

Ever since he'd seen Rosie and Jake that day. Had they felt as he did with Sally? He thought now it was possible they had done, and the thought made him uneasy.

And then he remembered. He had told Rosie that Jake was married, because he didn't want her to marry anyone else. There hadn't been a Sally then. Now that there was he was ashamed. He wanted everyone to be as happy as he and Sally were. Rosie had married – was it his fault? Had he perhaps affected Rosie and Jake's lives? Perhaps Jake wasn't so bad. He'd liked Jake until Rosie had loved him. Should he write and tell her the truth now she was a widow, or would she be upset? No, he'd write and tell her, put the record straight. He remembered tomorrow was her birthday, 31st July. She had had a hard year with Peter dying, and the factory giving such problems. This might be the best birthday present she'd ever had. Full of excitement, he pulled paper and pen from his pack, scribbled a short letter and gave it to the runner to take back to the adjutant for censorship.

The offensive began early next morning; a German shell in retaliation to the opening bombardment scored a direct hit on the command tent, and everything was destroyed, including the post for home. Just after 3 am the 11th Battalion went over the top, and with it Michael Potts. But the advance was quickly pinned down by machine-gun fire, for Hollebeke was surrounded by pill-boxes. Two companies were sent in to clear them, and Michael's was one of them. At the end of the action Hollebeke was in British hands, but Michael lay in agony in a shell-hole on the outskirts of the village. In fits of consciousness, he muttered, 'Sally' or 'Rosie' alternately as though the two names were a magic talisman. But they were not, for when at last the stretcher bearers reached him he was dead. His last thought was of pleasure that he'd had the courage to write that letter. He never knew that the letter was now only a charred fragment buried in a pile of debris.

Rosie's face paled as she read the revised specifications from Farnborough for the new KA4. So that was the reason for the new Pinot engine. And she'd sent it back.

But she'd been right. This was too radical a change for the production lines – the factory could never make the changes in time. To alter an already tried formula for this new experiment? Impossible in the time. The old KA3as and bs were pushers, with rotary engines. Now Farnborough were demanding tractor water-cooled V engines. For Farnborough read Jake. On paper it might work – never in practice with the specification Jake – Farnborough – had given for the aircraft. Not in the time anyway. Two hundred by Christmas? For once Robert Bellowes had been right, much as it went against the grain to admit it. Jake's name had never even been mentioned between them on the rare occasions they met, each skirting courteously round the other as if awaiting an opportunity to pounce. For Robert was as dependent on her as she on him, she realised. That was the only thing that prevented open warfare.

How could she cope with this new problem after the previous disasters of the year? Peter, who had died in February and left her unhappier than she would have believed possible. Now Michael had been killed three weeks ago near Ypres.

Mildred was silent and withdrawn from shock, wrapped up in her own grief, and, busy at the factory, Rosie could not spare time to be with her for more than snatched moments. It had taken a girl called Sally to do that. Sally who had appeared for the memorial service and never left, offering her services as driver for the convalescent home. It had taken several days before she told Mildred who she was, and Mildred simply opened her arms to her. Sally had cried for two days, then dried her eyes and begun her duties, moving in to the Lodge, and spending much of her time at Court Manor.

Now she had to cope with this problem with the KA4. What would Jake say when he discovered what had happened? What would *Jake* say? How could she even care what he thought or said about the KA4? What did it matter? *People* mattered, people whose lives had been shattered by the loss of their loved ones. Everyone seemed to be in black now, she thought wearily, looking down at her own thin black dress. Women wore black dresses, men black armbands, black crepe hatbands. The memory of Peter's patient face at the end – she raised a hand across her eyes, as if she could blot it out that easily.

Despite her protests, as Peter had grown steadily worse in February, the doctor had insisted that he needed more expert care than she could give; indeed she was only permitted to keep Peter at home if she allowed the nurses to tend him, and if she herself wore a mask when she went near him. Peter joked about it and said she'd make a wonderful highwayman, but her eyes, over the white mask, shone with unshed tears.

Unshed till that last morning when, very early, Rosie was called in by the night nurse. Peter reached out his hand to her. His grin was almost as cheerful as ever. But only with difficulty did she identify the song he painfully tried to croak: ' "Goodbyee," ' she took up the words in a whisper as his hand had slipped from hers.

And Michael. Now he was gone too. Too late to make up to him now for the years in which, in her all-absorbing quest after flight, she'd so blithely disregarded his devotion to her, too late to tell him that she needed a brother as well as a sister, especially now. Sally had told her how often Michael had talked about her. Michael would never come home to Brynbourne, or to Sally, for it seemed to Rosie that he had at last found himself in finding her.

Waste! War was only waste. Yet the day's work still had to be done, endlessly, without respite.

Let Jake rant and rave. She knew she was right about the new engines. She waited for an explosion of wrath from Farnborough but none came.

It came from Jake himself.

White-faced with fury, he stormed through the door two days later. She was in the middle of a hasty lunch-time sandwich, caught mid-bite as he loomed before her in the small office.

She thought her heart would stop. Why could she think

of nothing more to say than, 'You've shaved off your moustache again.'

It was as if she had not spoken. 'What's all this about returning the test Pinot VIII?'

She swallowed, to her horror feeling tears hovering near. She stood up, keeping her hands on the desk to support her trembling legs. 'It wouldn't work.' Was that weak shrill voice her own?

'Don't you think I might know best? That I might have been consulted?' The words blistered out as though all his bitterness stored over the years was finding expression in one engine.

'Jake—'

Could this be Jake? This was a stranger, not the man she had known. She pulled herself together, suddenly feeling stronger. She began again. 'Major Smith, I don't think you realise the difficulty of changing the production lines so drastically.'

'And I don't think you realise,' he said witheringly, 'that pilots out there have a life expectancy of three weeks – because they're sitting mostly in vulnerable pusher planes with outdated rotary engines. Or hadn't it occurred to you that men are actually getting killed out there?'

She blenched, shrinking back, and belatedly he took in her black dress. 'I'm sorry,' he said stiffly. 'Who—'

'Michael was killed at Ypres three weeks ago, and my husband died last February,' she told him tonelessly.

He stiffened slightly. Michael dead and Rosie a widow? Somewhere at the back of his mind he registered that Rosie's husband had died, that she would be free. But anger was his first reaction. Anger against war, for Michael's lost life – the small boy who had been so self-important, whom he'd taught to use a whip, taught to fish, taught to stalk game. Anger at the death of this unknown husband of Rosie's, rage at the futility of this slaughter made him clumsy.

'My sympathies,' he said awkwardly.

'Unnecessary,' she replied curtly. 'You're here on business. Let's discuss it.'

'Quite,' he snapped back, riled by her attitude, her

436

remoteness. Now he was beginning to react. Rosie's husband had died. Yet anger was obliterating everything else but this battle between them. Anyway, she wanted none of him, that was obvious. 'I've told Monsieur Pinot to re-deliver that engine, and follow it with two hundred more. As soon as the prototype arrives, I want it tested and a full report the same day.'

'Just who do you think runs this factory?' she blazed at him. 'They'll be ordered when I sign the authorisation.'

'When Bellowes approves the order,' he reminded her sardonically.

She flushed red. 'I run this factory and—'

'Good,' he cut in coolly. 'I hope you'll have something left to run when I withdraw the production.'

'You can't,' she came back quickly. 'The agreement with Farnborough was to use Clairvilles.'

'My specifications demand something the Clairville can't produce. That invalidates the agreement.'

'Jake,' she made a despairing appeal. 'Can't we talk this over sensibly, like – like we used to?'

His eyes became hard as glass. 'Like we used to?' There was nothing to stop his meeting her halfway by saying yes. But this self-contained woman was not the Rosie he had known. Or thought he had known. Perhaps she had never existed save in his imagination. The Rosie he thought he knew would never have betrayed him as this woman had done, would never have married another man – the betrayal was with him yet.

'There's nothing to discuss,' he said abruptly. 'Either you take those engines and work to my specifications or the contract is void. And don't be afraid of telling Mr Bellowes – I'll have great pleasure in telling him myself.'

Rosie stared at him unbelievingly. How right she'd been all along. His wife was welcome to him. How doubly glad she was to have heard from Poppy that Paul was to stay with her, for good now, as she was not returning to Court Manor. How impossible it would have been to be married to him. He simply wanted a doormat, not a wife. As a girl she had sensed it, feared it, and now as a woman she knew it.

437

'Very well. If Mr Bellowes agrees, I'll produce the prototype and test-fly it and then report to Farn—'

'Just a minute,' he interrupted sharply. 'Test-fly it? Who?'

'Me,' she said coolly.

The years fell away and he was faced with the turbulent Rosie of yesteryear, all his old irrational fears sweeping back.

'You won't go near it,' he shouted.

'You can't stop me,' she cried in triumph. 'I'm in charge of production.'

'No—'

'Why not? Don't you trust your own designs?'

Whitefaced with fury, Jake opened his mouth to speak, thought better of it, turned on his heel and went out slamming the door behind him; workers scattered to both sides as he stalked through the factory. Rosie sank down, covering her face with her hands. What had she done? Dear God, what had she done?

Thomas came rushing up to Polly, ungainly and eager, and as always kind. 'What is it, *Maman*?' he asked anxiously, seeing her abstraction.

'I'm all right, darling.' She was.

Polly looked round at the bustling market. Paris markets always filled her with excitement, even in wartime. It was a long time since she'd been here, and she sauntered through the small market, feeling as she had when she was a student. She had brought Thomas out for the day to see the sights of Paris, since she was staying in their Paris apartment for the first time since 1914. Thomas was entranced, running around everywhere.

'When shall we go to England, *Maman*? Is England like this? Shall we go soon? Shall we go on the big train?'

'Yes, Papa has to go on business and we go tomorrow to stay with Grandmama, and Auntie Rosie.'

'I should like that.'

Soon this war must surely be over and life could be as before, full of normal peaceful things. The scene in the

438

market caught her attention; the vegetables, the fruit, and people swarming everywhere. She stared and stared, holding the scene in her mind's eye, until at last Thomas said again, 'What is it, *Maman*?'

'Nothing,' she replied absently.

When Polly got home late that afternoon she kissed the baby, handed the children over to their nanny and went upstairs to her old studio. It was dusty, for the maids were forbidden to enter, and she herself had not been there for years. She went straight to the desk to get out pad and pencil, and began quickly sketching in the scene that had emblazoned itself on her mind's eye, before she forgot it. The work absorbed her for many hours. Jean-Michel, returning to find the house apparently empty of Polly, came eventually to the studio, pausing outside, then opening the door. He saw Polly with canvas already in front of her, frowning in concentration over her sketching, and quietly went away again.

'*Ja, Herr Doktor*, I understand.'

Understand? Of course Thomas understood. He understood that now he had only one leg, and a hand that would never work properly again. Why could he not be dead?

'At least it's not your right hand,' said the doctor consolingly, unable to understand this man; he should be thankful that he was still alive, that he would not have to return to the trenches of France. Instead he lay silent, pale, and living somewhere else, it seemed, not here.

All night Thomas tossed in misery between sleep and wakefulness as in his nightmares bodies floated through space, and arms and legs performed *danses macabres*; only now it was *his* leg, *his* arm floating away from him . . . Then he would cry out, his face sweating and a night nurse weary from long hours of tending dying patients, came to calm him down.

He stared at Polly wide-eyed. it was her, it *was*. 'Tell me, Polly, tell me—'

'Tell you what, *Herr Hauptmann*?' asked the nurse puzzled.

'Tell me—' He could not make any further effort and sank back into troubled sleep.

He woke up with the words still on his lips: 'Tell me. Tell me what? Tell me how I am to live when I chose death!'

He glanced around him. The bed next to his was empty. 'He is dead,' the nurse told him. No point being too retiring with bad news. Thomas felt ashamed: how could he cry for death. When death came so willingly to others, no need to summon it hither. But what of the empty years ahead of him? There was no purpose any more in the world.

Eventually he was bundled into a van to be taken to the rear hospital for transfer back to Germany. As they left, they passed stretchers being brought in from the battle-torn territory that was still being fought over. They had been fighting for Ypres since 1914. When he first arrived in France they were battling for Ypres, and now three years later they were all still here.

War was crazy. He wanted to shout aloud, to say, look at this stump I called a leg – war is cruel, not noble. But who would listen to such a wreck of a man? Then the answer came to him like a triumphant song: there was no more Polly, he might never see his son again, he could not fight again, he must go back to his estates, to Hilde, take up the struggle where he had left it long ago, but there was *something* he could do. He could cry war aloud in his painting. Suddenly he was sure now that he would get well. His blood began to throb; if this crazy war still continued then he would go back to the battle-front and paint, show people back home what war was really like, not the troops of gallant Uhlans riding into battle with clean flags and immaculate uniforms, but men scrabbling over a cup of coloured water, for rats to eat in the trenches, men who you worked side by side with reduced to animals. This was what war was like. The jagged tree stump standing stark in a sea of mud that once had been a forest, the hand sticking up in mute appeal from the

440

debris of battle, the women left alone to weep . . . Yes, that was what he could do – and that was what he was going to do.

'Air raid warning, sir,' shouted his driver, seeing a van going by displaying the warning signs. 'Want to turn back?'

'No, they won't make for Ramsgate again,' said Jake shortly. His visit to Bellowes would be made now, while he was in the mood, still smarting from his encounter with Rosie. The towns of Thanet had suffered enough from the Gothas; they wouldn't be the target yet again. The black Gothas would be making for London this time.

Robert Bellowes kept him waiting, kicking his heels in the ante-room. Part of his method no doubt, thought Jake. Well, it wouldn't throw him off his stroke. When at last he appeared he was expansively cordial as he ushered Jake in. Rosie's warned him, thought Jake instantly, seeing this as another betrayal. Rosie and Robert Bellowes in alliance he thought bitterly. Another of life's little ironies.

'I've told Mrs Favell,' he began without ado, 'that the KA4 is to be tractor design with the Pinot engine, not the Clairville.'

'There's a water-cooled V8 engine produced by Clairville that would prove better for your needs than the Pinot,' said Bellowes smoothly. 'And cheaper.'

So that was it. Expense – he would put the costs up so high if the Pinot were used that Farnborough would turn down the specification.

'Leopards don't change their spots, I see,' Jake said evenly. 'If Farnborough can't get the specification it wants, it will get it produced elsewhere.'

'In the time?' Robert raised his eyebrows.

Jake hesitated, and seeing him lose ground Robert relaxed smugly.

'That won't be your problem,' Jake pointed out coming back at him. 'You'll have lost the KA4 – and Kent Aviation. Or is that your plan,' he shot out, 'to put it into liquidation to take revenge on the Potts?'

441

Robert looked astonished. 'Do you know, Mr – um – Major Smith, that hadn't occurred to me. What an idea. Dear Rosie. She told me of your little encounter. Do you find her changed?

'Shall we leave the personal side out, Bellowes?' said Jake abruptly.

'How can we? Why, we're almost related. Now my father and Mrs Potts are joined in union, you so nearly once wedded dear Rosie – not to mention, as you know, your own little nephew—'

Jake pushed the chair back violently. This was the man who had ruined Kate's life, almost ruined Polly, perhaps murdered Gabriel. What the hell was making him so smug?

He took a deep breath. 'I'm calling your bluff, Bellowes.'

Robert's eyes narrowed.

'I told Mrs Favell I was sending back the prototype engine for testing. You can also tell her I'll be testing it myself and if it comes up to Pinot's quoted performance, I'll be needing two hundred. I'll discuss price with Pinots. And if you don't countersign the order – you *and* Mrs Favell – the KA4 will be transferred to Farnborough for production and you can get all the lawyers you like on it. It won't do you any good with an empty factory.'

Robert nodded, too good a businessman not to know when the cards were against him. But there was a flush on his cheeks. To be worsted by Jake Smith, of all people. Yet to himself he hugged the sweet thought that he alone knew why Rosie Potts had married, why there were barriers between them that Jake Smith could never tear down.

'I'm sure you would, for old times' sake, not wish this fate on Rosie. She'll be wanting to know what you've decided. I hate to give her bad news. I'm very fond of Rosie—' Jake grew tense '—in fact were it not for Poppy, my errant wife,' Robert smiled deprecatingly, 'we would probably – but there, you're not interested in my private life—'

He was lying – he must be – Rosie would never touch

this snake. Or would she? He didn't know this new Rosie. The thought of Rosie in this man's arms . . . With an effort he pulled himself together, remembering how Bellowes had lied before.

Jake stood up, towering over his enemy, suddenly trembling in suppressed passion. 'I'd like to get out that old bullwhip, Bellowes, and— What the hell's happening?' He turned as a man burst in the door.

'Air raid, sir, Gothas!'

Outside, people were running for cover as the sky was suddenly full of black shapes roaring overhead. There was the crash of a bomb landing in the yard and a whimper from the desk as another landed on the petrol store which went up with a whoosh. All round them was black smoke, gushing in the door, as Jake rushed to it, turning to look at Bellowes. But Robert was fleeing into the factory, not out.

'No, out this way,' Jake yelled, 'safer.'

'My seaplanes,' yelled Bellowes, as bombs fell on the main factory, bringing debris and the roof crashing down on the production lines, separating him from Jake who was momentarily blinded by the smoke in his eyes.

Then someone – his driver – was pulling at Jake, dragging him from the office. 'Leave him, sir, there's nothing you can do. The whole place is going up.'

Jake was immobile, staring into the dust and smoke and flames. All he could see was Robert Bellowes's agonised eyes staring at him, trapped by a fallen beam, crying weakly. All the bitterness in him welled to the surface. He should leave him. He would risk his own life too if he stayed – and why should he stay when Robert Bellowes had ruined the lives of so many dear to him. As the hatred seethed through him, the same madness gripped him as after May's death, he wanted to whip the fellow to death, see him choking, die before his eyes. The smoke was billowing round him now, the flames licking at the walls and he saw that man, half-dead, lying at his feet. What good had it done? May had still died.

With a groan, Jake rushed forward, without reason, without thought now save that he had nothing to live for.

The smoke pushed him back and, wrapping a handkerchief round his nose and chin, he tried again, crawling now under debris already alight. He began the task of freeing Robert Bellowes, burning his hands, wrapping his jacket round them and trying again. Almost free now, it had become a battle, a choking, searing battle, as more plaster came down, burying them both.

At last he pushed aside the last of the debris. Robert was unable to help himself and with a last spurt of energy, Jake staggered to his feet, slinging the inert man over his shoulders, and in one last mad rush hurled himself towards the door and air. Then he was through, into more smoke, but now he could fight through and drop his bundle on the ground, collapsing on top of him. He rolled off Bellowes, struggling to regain his breath, as people rushed to their aid, throwing water over them. Bellowes opened his eyes, tried to sit up and lay back again as if bewildered, brushing off helpers impatiently, as he stared up at Jake, now shakily on his feet, coughing and spluttering.

'Why?' he whispered. 'Why?'

Jake stared at him, turned to vomit from the smoke, and turned back. But there were no words to say, so he walked away down the pathway back to find his driver, back out of this hell, to find the clean air, and still that plaintive sound in his ears: Why? He did not know why. Clairville Jones had had no reason when he came back to save him. Why did you need reasons?

Robert Bellowes staggered unsteadily to his feet, brushing off helpers like flies, his eyes fixed on one figure: Jake Smith walking away. 'Why?' he hurled after him yet again, but could not find the answer. In Jake's place he'd have abandoned him, like he did Gabriel Marriner, like Kate. So why had not Jake Smith acted in the same way? He'd be beholden to him for the rest of his life. He had to get even – somehow. Even if it meant his last secret, his last hold over both of them. No, he couldn't. Jake was almost gone. It would pass. Be forgotten. How tempting it was to let it pass.

Then Robert felt again the smoke in his throat, felt the

444

heat on his leg, the scorch of the flames as they had drawn nearer. They were trying to get him on a stretcher now. With his last ounce of strength, he pushed them aside, stumbled a few paces forward and shouted out with all his remaining strength to the man he hated.

'She thinks you're married, Smith . . . she thinks you're married.'

Jake stopped, his head went back, he did not turn, but with something that might have been a lift of the hand in acknowledgement, walked swiftly on to where his driver waited.

# Chapter Twenty

This was where it had all begun, on this hillside long ago. Long ago, in the last century, before the clouds of war had gathered across their blue horizons, long before misunderstandings had forged their snakelike way between herself and Jake, a hillside bathed now not with the brilliant demands of spring, but in mellow gold sunlight. Although it was only mid-September, the trees tired of their summer green were beginning to yellow, and the cobnuts were ripening on the hillside where so long ago she'd looked up through a haze of trees beginning to spark their buds of green.

'Run, Thomas, run,' Rosie shouted absent-mindedly, as she noticed the kite obstinately refusing to rise. It was an old one of William's she'd lovingly preserved. 'There's not much wind today, you'll have to run.'

*Run, Rosie, let's run –*

*Shan't . . .*

But little Thomas stood still, perplexed, with Rosemarie by his side, clutching her own smaller kite; he did not say anything, as befitted a man, but his eyes were pleading for his aunt to come to help. Rosie ran down to him, taking the cord from his hand and winding it round her own, then she took his hand in hers so that he could feel the cord communicate with this wondrous being of the air.

'Come,' she said, filled with a sudden inexplicable lurch of excitement, 'let's run together, Thomas, let's run—'

'Yes, yes,' he squealed, suddenly fired into action.

They began to run downhill, Rosemarie scampering along behind. Rosie began to laugh in pleasure, feeling the resistance of the air blowing against the full skirts of her grey silk dress and gently tugging her hair, calling her with its siren song. She laughed outright in delight as the kite began to respond, catching a current as they played out the string, though Thomas was clutching so hard that it was difficult.

'Make it go up,' he cried. 'Look. It's going, *it's going*!'

'Up,' she cried involuntarily, transported back twenty years as she saw the kite spiralling upwards into the sky; she halted on the gentle slope of the hill, staring skywards. 'Up, up, up,' she cried again, perhaps to Thomas, perhaps to the kite, perhaps to William. They watched as it soared and danced and jumped on its path to the sun, until at last it lost the current and spiralled, spinning, to earth.

She cried out in dismay, remembering her own terror as a child, believing that the thing of beauty was dead, would never rise again.

'Don't cry, Auntie Rosie,' said Rosemarie coming up beside her. 'I don't think it's deaded.'

'I think it will go up again,' said Thomas confidently.

'You're right,' she said, smiling at them. 'Let's go and try again, shall we?'

She picked up the kite from the grass, warm from the September sunshine, and they ran back up the hill. *Icarus*, she remembered out of the blue. Icarus. William was so vividly in her memory now, he seemed almost to be walking beside her; she owed to him her home, her love of flying, everything. Father, she thought, have I let you down? I don't fly any more. I'm building military aeroplanes. Would you have done the same? Would you? Had she turned from all that that hillside had once offered her, spurned William's heritage? She ran the factory, but she no longer flew except the occasional test-flight. Perhaps when the war was over . . .

They reached the crest of the hill and she turned to the children. 'Now,' she cried. 'Ready?'

Ready? The sun as she looked up streamed into her eyes, dazzling her, and it seemed that there etched against it was a figure, walking towards her up the hill far away, but known to her. Known out of her deepest heart. A trick of the sunlight. It must be one of the men come with a message. No . . . She was back in the old shed, working on Pegasus, working so hard she did not notice the arrival of a stranger. The most unusual man she had ever seen.

'Ready,' repeated Thomas impatiently.

'No,' she whispered, 'not yet.'

This was some hallucination, this was not the man she had so bitterly quarrelled with only three weeks ago, the man with lines of bitterness etched on his face, the khaki-clad professional soldier who went about life so coldly, so impersonally. This was a man dressed in an old buckskin jacket and trousers, striding towards her with a light of laughter on his face.

'Jake,' she whispered, powerless to move, but her body seduced her into life.

He broke into a run, an inane grin on his face. She could not bear it. Eleven years went whistling down the wind to make her that confident, eager, headstrong girl again, to enslave her in his web of love . . . No, she would be lost, *lost*.

'Stop,' she cried out. He halted in surprise. She could never have found the strength to call again. Then seeing across the ten yards or so that separated them the uncertainty on her face, he relaxed, folding his arms nonchalantly, challengingly, across his chest, legs apart, supremely confident.

'Go away,' she cried weakly. 'Don't come any closer.' If he did, she would forget his wife, forget Thomas and Rosemarie, forget everything save her overpowering need to throw herself into his arms.

He cleared his throat deliberately. 'I was aiming to come a whole lot closer,' he drawled slowly, to taunt her so it seemed to Rosie. Why, why didn't he know how much she wanted him? Then she was angry. How could he mock her so?

'Go away!' she yelled stridently, so that again he paused, seemed to consider, and came on.

'Nope.'

She licked her lips nervously, watching the yards diminish, wondering why she did not turn and run. Leave temptation behind. Leave him to his wife. The ground beneath her seemed to sway, so that she was glad of Thomas's hand, aware of his, 'Who is he, Auntie Rosie? Is he a cowboy like Mr Buffalo Bill?'

But she could not answer him, any more than she could stop the slow tread of Jake's boots as they covered the ground arrogantly, till he was face to face with her. She quivered in anger that he could do this to her, but she would not turn away. She lifted her head proudly and looked him in the face.

The lines on it seemed to be turning upwards from the eyes now, in laughter. Surely it was the Jake she'd known that stood here now, looking at her with such tender love that she was dizzy and furious at the same time. She opened her mouth to speak, but he forestalled her. And it was not her he addressed.

'Run along,' he said to Thomas, 'your mother wants you. She sent me to fetch you both.'

So that was why – irrational disappointment flooded over her. It had been her imagination – that look of his. How dared he? He was gloating over her, that he was married, safe from her, Rosie. He was merely underlining her powerlessness to hurt him further. Jake took Thomas and Rosemarie by the hand, and swung them round. 'Look,' he said, and pointed to the foot of the hill, where Polly was waving from the gateway into the meadow leading back to the Brynbourne gardens.

'Think you can find your way to her? Here, take this,' and he put the smaller kite in Rosemarie's hand. Without a backward glance they ran off down the hill, leaving Rosie and Jake face to face.

'Not you,' he said softly, putting out his hand to stop her as she cast him a withering look and went to follow them. The touch of his hand on her arm seemed to leave a searing mark.

He was so close she could see where his moustache had been, she could have put out her hand and touched his golden hair, but she seemed impotent to move, suspended in space between the old world and some new world she did not understand. Then she told herself that he had come to discuss the KA4, how the loss of Bellowes's Ramsgate factory would affect the KA4 at Sittingbourne, to quarrel once again about the test-flying, the prototype KA4. Why – she'd done all he asked. Even bowing to the inevitable when Farnborough sent their own pilot down to test the prototype for themselves.

'If it's about the KA4—' she began belligerently.

'It's not about the KA4 – we can argue about that later.'

'There's no argument. We just differ about the engine. But I've done everything—' She was talking nervously, giving herself time to re-erect her defences.

'It's about us. I love you, Rosie. More now than ever.'

She cried out in distress and shock, looking round for escape. How could he torture her so? She turned and ran blindly till she ran up against the thicket of bushes that bordered the copse, and there was no way for her to go. No way that couldn't be blocked by Jake. He was coming after her, still with that grin on his face, the buckskin looking as incongruous on that Kent hillside as ever it did in the aeroplane shed.

'Go away,' she shouted fearfully. 'Go back to your wife.'

That stopped him. A look of surprise crossed his face as if he had forgotten this still remained between them.

'Go away,' she repeated, and when he did not move, turned herself and began to force her way through the bushes.

'Rosie, stop, come back,' he cried. 'Rosie, *I'm not married.*'

She was aware of the spider's web beside her, the smell of the blackberries, large and black around her, the green leaves with the dew still on them and the yellowing leaves above her. Slowly she came out on to the crest of the hill again, not saying anything, trying to understand. Below lay the world she knew, and had learned to live with. With her was Jake and a sudden hope, a glimmer of sunlight opening up.

'And Helen,' she asked slowly. 'Where is she? Is she dead?'

'Rosie, I don't know who this Helen is. But I'm *not* married, I never have been. I've never wanted to be, except to you,' he said patiently. 'I don't know how you got the idea I was.'

She stared at him – then she remembered. It was Michael who had told her. Michael had lied. Why, why oh why had he done it? Poor Michael. How tortured he must have been. She was filled with sadness for the days they could not change, the years they could not relive. She and Jake. The grief and agony she had been through. She looked up at him, grinning at her, so sure, beginning to walk towards her. She was filled with panic that she would just fall into his sway again – nothing resolved, nothing learned – only to find out too late. She ran towards him intending to pass him and escape down the hill, but he held open his arms, catching her as she fled. 'Rosie – I—'

'You can't just come bursting into my life,' she said angrily, 'saying everything's going to be all right – and looking so like you did when you first arrived—' she added weakly, as she tore herself free.

'Rosie – I—' Jake stepped back puzzled. 'What's the matter? We've lost time, but we're still the same people. We've both been through a lot but why not start again?'

He made a move towards her, but she said sharply, 'Don't touch me.'

'Rosie,' he said quietly swallowing hard. 'I don't understand. Everything's all right. Don't you love me any more? I thought—'

'How can it be all right?' she cried, backing away from the almost physical aura he was throwing over her like a net. Oh, how she needed time to think. 'You didn't want me as a . . . partner, you couldn't accept that. You were scared. I couldn't give you what you wanted. I was wrong about using aeroplanes for war – I know that now and I'm sorry, but the gap is still there between us. And it's widened – we don't know if we can cross it.'

'Don't you think a war's done that for us?' he broke in angrily, looking at the slim figure standing so near, so far from him, knowing that at any moment she could slip away from him again, and once gone would never be recaptured. 'This is our only chance, Rosie,' he said desperately. 'With war all round us, and such suffering, do you think you have the *right* to turn down happiness?'

'You're so conceited,' she yelled back ridiculously. 'How do you know you'd make me happy?'

'I don't,' he said humbly, 'but I'd try.'

She caught her breath. Only a few steps across the grass and she'd be in his arms. But the first step was too immense.

'I'm not coming all the way to you, Rosie,' he said impatiently. 'You can damn well come to meet me halfway.'

'Why should I?' she said, childishly pitting her will against his.

'What the hell do I have to do?' he inquired politely. 'Lassoo you?'

'Isn't that you all over?' she cried vehemently. 'You think the answer to everything is just physical action, taking advantage of mere physical inferiority to try to prove your case. The domination of the male over the female.' She was talking for the sake of it, talking rubbish, anything to put off the moment which must inevitably come – decision. 'I learned that from the suffrage movement. Just like when we first met. I should have known then, when you just picked me up and threw me in a horse trough. Well, you can't—'

'Now that,' Jake said, exasperated, 'is one helluva good idea.'

Ignoring her shriek, he strode over to her, and picked her up in his arms, swinging her round against him.

'Now where,' he said thoughtfully, grappling with her flailing legs, and pinioning them against him firmly, 'will I find a horse trough?'

He marched round the copse, managing to keep one hand over her mouth to stop her indignant shouts.

'Don't see no horse trough, ma'am. Of course,' he added cheerfully, 'there's a decent-sized thorn bush here.'

He held her above it, then lowered her. 'Now, are you going to be reasonable?' he panted. The grunts under his hand indicated not.

He lowered her further so that her thin dress was

catching on the long spikes, then lower still so that she was in the midst of it and beginning to squeal in pain.

'Well, do I drop you?' he said menacingly, taking his hand away from her mouth, but did not wait for her answer before setting her on her feet again.

'I think you,' she said glaring at him, 'are—'

'Rosie,' he said sharply, 'only one thing matters. Do you still love me?'

She caught her breath. 'How can—'

'Answer me,' he commanded.

'Yes,' she shouted defiantly. 'But—'

That was all she had time to say before she was in his arms and all the kingdoms of the earth were hers, as she felt his lips on hers again. Six years, six long years of shadow and war, since they had last kissed, and it seemed yesterday, as she opened her mouth to his and a flame of joy swept through her body. His arms were gripping her so tightly they were hurting her, his hands hard against her ribs, but she could hardly speak for the gentleness of his kiss.

'Do you love me as you used to, Rosie?' he said, as he finally lowered his hold.

'I never stopped.'

She felt his surprise as he said awkwardly, 'But your husband—'

Rosie sat down on the grass, pulling him down with her. 'You don't understand – how could you?' she began steadily, looking down into the valley, anywhere but at him. 'Peter knew he was dying when he asked me to marry him. He told me. He had consumption, you see. I had a loving tenderness for him. No more. I – because of his illness, there was no question of our—' she stumbled, and he reached for her hand.

'Loving together?'

'Yes.' She looked at him then, gratefully. 'I thought since he needed me and I had no one – you were married—' Her voice broke.

'What happened, Rosie?' asked Jake angrily. 'Did Bellowes lie to you about my being married?'

454

'No,' she said. 'It was poor Michael.' Strange, she felt no bitterness, only a great sadness.

'Of course,' said Jake slowly. 'Of course.'

'How he must have hated me. And I never knew.'

'He loved you, Rosie. Love gone wrong. But we've come through it, both of us. And despite all this war, there'll be peace again. We can fly again as we used to, for sheer pleasure. Remember? That's if you still want to fly. Do you?' he asked casually.

She was unable to believe that he knew so little of her. 'What else do you think I want to do with my life except fly?' she said indignantly.

'I'm sorry – I thought you might have left it behind – along with me,' he said wrily. 'You don't fly now anyway. I doubt if you could. Modern machines are rather different.'

'What on earth do you mean, *couldn't* fly?' Rosie was outraged. 'I can still outfly you any day. I take up aircraft whenever I can. Even the prototype KA4—'

'You've *what*?' Jake's face was a study. 'I told you not to. Farnborough would do it. Those machines are dangerous, Rosie. You've no idea. Especially the prototype.'

'I read the handling notes and I took it up,' she said belligerently. 'It handled very well—' Her voice wavered at his thunderous look, but she plunged on. 'I found the tractor arrangement worked well. More secure,' she added brightly, hoping to placate him. It did not work.

He might have known that she wouldn't be able to resist temptation in the few weeks since their meeting. As soon as she got that prototype engine through, he might have guessed she'd disobey and take it up. Why, oh why, had Farnborough called him back at that very moment to discuss the KA4 problem yet once more? Why had his own confusion made him decide to wait before coming to claim her, to give the bitterness of their last encounter time to fade? The idiot, she was as headstrong and wilful as ever.

'You haven't been trained to military aircraft. You could have killed yourself,' he yelled at her.

'Don't be silly,' she said forthrightly. 'I can fly anything.'

'I forbid you to take the KA4 up again.'

'Forbid. Who are you to forbid me?' she flared, leaping to her feet.

'When we're married, I—' He scrambled to his feet after her.

'Married? Who said anything about being married?' she inquired dangerously, hands on hips.

'But I assumed—' he broke off. 'Damn it, Rosie,' he said angrily, 'here we go again.'

'When – if – we married you'd forbid me to fly, would you?' she inquired sweetly.

'If I thought it was too dangerous for you, yes,' he snapped blindly, unthinkingly. 'Of course.'

'Of course,' she repeated sarcastically. 'And what about what I feel? I'm as good a judge of what's safe in an aeroplane as you are.'

'No, you're not.'

'I am—'

'You don't fly as well as me. You never have,' he retorted, goaded.

She gasped in outrage. 'How dare you! Of course I do. I have less practice than you, but I'm every bit as good. I'll prove it.'

'How?' he said impatiently.

'I'll – I'll—' Impassioned, she cast around wildly for some way to prove to Jake once and for all that she was a person in her own right, that she should be taken seriously. There, at the foot of the hill, was the far end of the old flying field and in the distance the workshed. She clutched Jake's arm. 'There,' she said triumphantly. 'Right now. The old shed. Mr Fisherbutt keeps Astra and Sunburst in there in flying condition. He says he's going to start a museum with them. We'll test it now. I'll race you, you in Sunburst, me in Astra.' Her eyes were shining, alive, determined.

'Don't be stupid, Rosie,' Jake shouted, 'we can't—'

'You're scared. That's why you didn't want me to test-fly your rotten old aeroplane,' she hurled at him.

'I'm *not* scared. And you're not up to flying it.'

'Then we'll race and I'll prove I still am.'

His anger boiled over. He'd given half his life, so it seemed, to loving this woman with her damnfool ideas; what was she getting them into now? All right, he'd race her, then she'd see sense. If they didn't both break their necks.

How could he tell her he had indeed been scared at the thought of her test-flying the damn KA4? Suppose he'd got it wrong? Suppose she'd been killed?

'All right, all right,' he shouted at her. 'I'll wager you I win.'

She stopped still from her headlong flight down the hill.

'What's the stake?' she asked, glaring up at him.

'If I win, you marry me,' he shouted down, 'on *my* terms—'

'And if I win?'

'You can decide whether you want to marry me – and we *discuss* terms.'

'No. On *my* terms,' she answered shortly.

A tense second quivered.

'All right.' He glared at her.

Then he was running down the hill after her, buckskin fringes flying in the breeze, long legs swiftly catching her up as she ran hampered by full skirts, jumping over hassocks of grass, over rabbit holes, catching at brambles, brushing past autumn-coloured ferns. She was breathless by the time she neared the shed; Jake was well ahead of her now, already bursting through the doors and standing transfixed at the site of Sunburst and Astra, standing side by side as if untouched by the years.

When she reached him, he was almost crying. 'Why didn't you tell me? Why didn't you tell me?'

The age of innocence in flying was recreated before his eyes. The shed with all its old familiar untidiness and smells seemed suspended in time. Mr Fisherbutt in the midst of his usual afternoon hour of loving dusting and polishing, turned in surprise, his old face breaking into a pleased smile of recognition.

'Why, Mr Jake—'

Jake walked up to him and clasped his hands in his. 'Are they ready to take up, Mr Fisherbutt?' he asked, as if he'd last called in but yesterday.

No doubting what he meant. 'Always ready to fly, sir,' was the reply, as though he was asked this question every day. Then: 'You mean you *really* want to take them up?' Mr Fisherbutt's face brightened.

'Miss Rosie does—' said Jake scathingly.

'Just need fuelling, sir,' Mr Fisherbutt said eagerly. 'Won't take long,' and promptly bustled off to collect fuel from the garages where it was stored.

Unable to trust themselves to speak to each other, Rosie and Jake wheeled Sunburst and Astra out on to the field, their tempers giving them added strength. Rosie cursed impatiently at her skirts flapping round her legs, then gave an exasperated sigh of horror. 'Jake, I can't fly yet.' Jake cast her a scathing look of triumph as she continued, 'I can't fly in *this*.' She looked down at her grey Liberty silk dress; the dress was flimsy as the day was warm for September.

'You're not backing out now,' Jake said grimly, 'unless you concede the race to me. My terms!'

'I'm not backing out, but it's dangerous to fly in these skirts. And—' she was rummaging round the shed, 'I can't find any old trousers here. I'll have to go back to the house—'

'Oh no. I'm not letting you out of my sight. You'll find some excuse not to come back.'

'I won't! I want to race you, you stupid man, because I'm going to win, but—'

Jake looked rapidly round the shed. 'All right,' he said decisively, 'I'll *make* you some trousers. Take that dress off—'

'No,' she cried outraged. 'What are you—'

'Then come here. I'll soon give you trousers.' He pushed her none too gently into a chair, snatched up a pair of wing fabric shears, found the sewing twine and needle, pushed Rosie back in the chair from which she was already rising, straddled her legs with his back to her, and heaved her legs up, forcing them apart.

'Keep still,' he ordered curtly, in answer to her protests.

'Jake, what are you doing?' Her voice rose in a squeak.

'I'm making you trousers, so you can't wriggle out of your wager, madam. Sit still or I'll cut you and not the dress—'

'Jake, don't—'

But it was too late. The shears were cutting a large triangular piece out of the dress and petticoats between her legs; then he was threading one of the huge needles she used to use on Pegasus.

'What's Mr Fisherbutt going to say if he comes back?' inquired Rosie behind him, torn between indignation and a desire to giggle.

'He thinks we're both mad anyway.' He bent over the mutilated remains of her dress, dexterously stitching along the line of the leg. 'If you don't stop wriggling, Rosie,' he said, suddenly all too conscious of how close his hands were to her, of the tops of her black stockings, and the few inches of soft flesh between them and her thin lawn French knickers, 'I'm going to have to sit on you to keep you still.'

Perhaps she was aware too, for her answer was slow in coming and unusually meek: 'Very well, Jake.'

'There,' he said at last, swinging free of her. 'Finished. You said you wanted trousers and you've got them.'

'Thank you,' she said sweetly, looking down to inspect the odd-shaped garment in disgust. 'Sure you wouldn't like to dope them to my legs?'

'Sago, it was sago you tipped over my head,' he reminded her gently.

'You deserved it,' she said scathingly, stalking out of the shed.

Mr Fisherbutt had already fuelled the aircraft by now and was beginning to turn the propellers. Seeing it, they both raced to their respective aircraft to start the engines. The mere act of climbing up into Astra again made Rosie laugh across to Jake in pleasant anticipation. 'Where shall we go?' she shouted.

'Fly west – just in case the Germans decide to send over the Gothas. How about Scotney Castle area, Bayham

Abbey and back? About two hours' flight at the most there and back. That's fair, isn't it?'

'Enough for three hours you've got there,' said Mr Fisherbutt with pride. 'Eighteen gallons each. Shall I be here with a stop watch?' he asked hopefully.

'No need, Mr Fisherbutt,' said Jake lazily. 'I'll be back at least half an hour before Miss Rosie.'

'We'll see about that,' she shouted grimly as she lovingly went through her cockpit drill.

How strange to be back in Sunburst, Jake thought. It took some time to accustom himself to the simple controls, to feeling naked and exposed compared with the newest military planes. How odd to see aeroplanes without a Lewis gun. Suddenly he was looking forward to the race. It was worth it. Could he still remember how to operate her – a moment's anxiety after the KA3b? Only an oil-pulsating gauge instead of the KA3b's air pressure gauge, air speed indicator compass, inclinometer, altometer and rev counter.

Rosie found no such difficulty. She was back home where she belonged.

'I'll give you a handicap,' shouted Jake.

'I don't need one,' she yelled, revelling in the familiar sound of the old engine. It might have only half the power of the KA4, but those first Pinots were solid and sure, however flimsy the structure that supported them. She wriggled tensely in the cockpit, feeling the slight breeze ruffling up her 'trouser' legs, and between the gaps in Jake's stitching. She grinned to herself. How stupid, how ridiculously, gloriously stupid. Then she remembered that Jake was the enemy – and how much depended on this race. She was going to win. She had to.

Mr Fisherbutt stood aside and then she was off, conscious that thirty yards to her right Jake was taking off once more in Sunburst, the years of separation slipping away as though they had never been.

Hold the tail up, she told herself, or we'll be off the ground too soon. Up into the currents like Thomas's kite earlier. Had that only been hours ago? It seemed another age. Now the nose was up and Astra rising, flying west away from war; she was conscious only of the golden sun of September, of the wind singing through Astra's wires and Jake in Sunburst slightly behind her. If only he knew, she laughed to herself, how perilous had been her flight in the prototype KA4. Totally unfamiliar with a tractor water-cooled engine, she had nearly stalled several times, once going into a dive she had been lucky to get out of. The mechanics' faces had been grey by the time she landed and strolled up to them more nonchalantly than she had felt. But she'd tried again and got the hang of it before she let the Farnborough man test it.

Yet the experience had been nothing compared with this. This, this was what flying was; it had nothing to do with the demands of war. She had been right all along, yet wrong as well. Aeroplanes did have to play their part in war, but that wasn't what they were meant for, any more than ships were solely pieces of war matériel, or soldiers not also human beings.

She looked around her, exulting. She was ahead of Jake, and already they were flying over Leeds Castle. She would win. She would make him pay. She would finally – after he had pleaded with her – agree to marry him, but what terms she would set! She began to think lovingly what these might be . . .

Jake watched Rosie pulling ahead in dismay. If only he could get the hang of these controls again. Surely he couldn't have forgotten so quickly how alarmingly Sunburst used to bank if you applied just a shade too much rudder. He breathed again. If the angle had been steeper . . . but he was fine now, and could concentrate on catching up Rosie.

For the first time the possibility that he might not win occurred to him. During the time he had spent at Farnborough, gradually emerging from the chrysalis of shock that had followed Bellowes's words, Rosie was never far from his thoughts. He had had nearly four weeks to come to terms with the past, to realise how Florence had coloured his actions and to banish her firmly from his life for ever. How ironic that it had taken Robert

Bellowes to teach him. Instead of revelling in his power over his enemy, he had chosen to speak. It couldn't have been easy. Just as it hadn't been easy for Jake to tear away the protective layers the years had built over his heart. Only Rosie could strip away the last veils, however.

And so he had come – and it had resulted in this stupid wager. Suppose he lost – and she walked away from him once again? He set himself grimly to gain on her. Sunburst was capable of more than 40 mph if he put his mind to it; it could outstrip Astra. By the time they were flying over Boughton Monchelsea they were level. A startled glance from Rosie, then she hunched over the joystick again. But Sunburst was piling on speed now, and he was drawing ahead. At the halfway point, having circled round Bayham Abbey, he rocked his wings as he began the homeward lap and passed Rosie still flying towards the abbey. He laughed at her grim set face; she'd lost her flying hat and her curls were blowing about in the wind. He began to cheer to himself, singing a song of victory to the wind. He relaxed, glorying in his triumph.

But he relaxed too much for, in a burst of speed, as Rosie fully regained her expertise, she gained on him again, drawing level. She waved cockily as she drew slightly ahead mouthing something he could not hear. Panic began to seize him. Suppose he could not overtake her again? Suppose he lost . . . An idea came to him. He glanced down and saw Cranbrook Mill beneath him. He began to whistle softly . . .

Rosie took a swift look behind her. She was way ahead now, he was dropping back – *No*, her heart leapt – he was dropping *down*. Not out of control, not spinning, thank heavens, but down, and down fast. She would win now for Jake couldn't keep up. Yet she was uneasy. Why was he dropping? To fly lower or – suddenly worried, she circled in a tight turn. Too tight, and for a moment she thought she'd lose control. Then she levelled out, breathed again, and saw where Jake was. He had landed on some flat ground by a small river. Was he ill? In trouble? She couldn't leave him . . . All thoughts of the

462

race fled as she concentrated on her descent. If he could land, then so could she. Her fears flooded back in force as she saw Sunburst stationary, but no pilot clambering out. In her anxiety she almost switched off too soon, but pulled her hand back in time. Concentrate she told herself, despite her pounding heart. It wouldn't be easy on this stubble. She hit an air bump, and Astra banked perilously, rose again and on her next attempt came in smoothly.

She switched off, leapt down from Astra and rushed towards Sunburst. She found Jake calmly lounging back in the wicker seat.

Seeing her, he commented, 'Not too good a landing, Rosie. Always your weak point.'

She was speechless. 'Just what are you doing, Jake?' she managed to splutter at last.

He looked at her, tossed his goggles aside, and leapt down from Sunburst. Ignoring her rigid, unwelcoming expression, he took her in his arms: 'Now I know you love me, Rosie,' he said triumphantly. 'You turned back although it means you'll lose the race.'

'You cheated me,' she yelled furiously, tearing herself free.

'Why not? I had a good teacher,' he pointed out.

She opened her mouth to protest, had second thoughts, then third thoughts. 'That was different,' she hurled at him. 'I *had* to land then.'

'Not that different,' he said gently. 'It had the same effect on me. Come, Rosie, admit it.' He put his arms round her and enfolded her unprotestingly in them, holding her tight against him. 'I'm not going to let you go now, Rosie, for all your fighting,' he said firmly. 'Once upon a time I let stiff-necked pride save me from rushing right after you and dragging you back by the scruff of your neck.'

'Isn't that you all over.'

'*All* over,' he repeated, pulling her even closer.

'We're not at a sewage farm this time,' she pointed out.

'No,' he said, releasing her, 'and this isn't the time. Nor the place,' glancing at the stubble. So he felt the same as she did. It was too quick, too much to absorb. She squeezed his hand affectionately.

'Here, sit down. We can at least admire the scenery.' He took off his jacket and threw it on the ground. 'There, you won't feel the stubble through your – er – trousers now. How are they by the way?'

She giggled. 'Look at them! I particularly like the baggy look; the gusset's nearly down to my knees.'

'I wasn't too sure what effect a more tailored approach might have on me.'

She took his hand. 'It's all been so quick, Jake. I can't believe it's all true; the hill, you, me, Astra—'

'It's days like today that carry us through the black ones. You want to slow them down, say stop – I want to enjoy every second, have time to remember every detail.'

'Oh, but I shall, Jake. I shall remember that grasshopper there, bouncing his way over the stubble, the poppy blooming all on its own over there, that butterfly on those Michaelmas daisies in the hedge, the blackberries. I shall remember this patch of earth, Sunburst and Astra waiting for us on the corn with the sunlight on them, and you—'

'You won't have to remember me, Rosie. I'm going to be there.'

'Are you, Jake? The war's still on. You've a dangerous job.'

'Not now. I'll stay where I'm needed. I'll stay at Dover. I've been promoted to colonel, I'll be lucky if I even get to *see* an aeroplane, let alone fly one.'

'Perhaps you feel you're not so good at flying as you used to be,' she said wickedly.

'Now you know you don't mean that, Rosie,' he said indulgently. 'It took me time to get used to Sunburst again; otherwise I'd have been ahead. Look at the way I pulled ahead—'

'And then I overtook again,' she interrupted.

'Because I didn't want the race to go on,' he said firmly. 'I want to marry you. Let's forget about that stupid wager. Why do we need terms?'

Oh, the temptation, with the light in his eyes and the

smile on his lips. She must talk to overcome it. 'Kate taught me all about suffrage and sex domination. Don't forget I'm a New Woman.'

'Is the old one still around too?' he inquired lazily, his hand on her thigh.

She laughed, putting her hand on his. 'She is, but she'll keep.' She hesitated. 'Are you really saying you don't think I fly well? What should we do if we married? Would you try to stop me flying?'

'No, of course not, but—' He broke off, unwilling to face it again, that he didn't trust her to fly as well as he could, irrational though it was; that he feared for her. He was appalled that after so many years it was still there, dormant in him.

'Right,' she said decidedly after a moment. 'Then the wager's still on. And so is the race.' She sprang to her feet and raced to Astra, he racing after her.

'Rosie – no, don't be—'

'I'm not arguing with you, Jake. I'm going and I'll win.'

'And who?' he inquired dangerously, 'is going to swing your propeller?'

She bit her lip. 'You, Jake, if you've any honour in you. I'll give you five minutes' race-time. Or shall we toss for who goes first?'

Jake pretended to consider. 'I'll do it,' he said airily.

She watched him suspiciously. Why had there been no argument? Then she dismissed the niggle of doubt and checked her watch, switching on.

'Right,' yelled Jake, leaping aside from the propeller as Astra's Pinot roared into full life and trundled off over the corn. Relaxed with relief, he watched as the nose lifted and she took off, admiring her style. She was right; she was good. He continued watching critically, unperturbed by the five minute deadline, as she gained height, just as he would any of his students.

Trust Rosie, he thought, as she disappeared from sight. She hadn't thought the problem through; only how it affected herself. *Who was going to swing his propeller?* She had played right into his hands. It took him a leisurely

465

ten minutes to find a farmer's boy on a tractor and pay him to come to his aid.

The boy nervously swung the propeller, and was so entranced that he almost forgot to get out of Sunburst's way, but then Sunburst was up, soaring into the air in pursuit of Astra. It was only when he reached cruising speed at 300 feet that he reflected fully that for the first time he had watched Rosie detachedly. Not as the woman he loved, lost, then found again, but as a pupil like Mr Swithin, or any of his novice pilots. He began to wonder at himself, hope rising in him. It was all right, he thought jubilantly; he had conquered his fears. Florence was now truly dead to him for he knew the way to lose was to fear too much. He gained speed, not through any thought of the race but to see Rosie, to tell her.

When he came in to land he could see Rosie, white-faced with relief, standing on the field, and Mr Fisherbutt gripping her hand. As he came to a stop, Mr Fisherbutt tactfully disappeared, as she threw herself at him.

'Where were you? Oh, Jake, I thought you'd crashed. You idiot!'

'No, I was fine. I made good time,' he said carelessly.

'Nonsense. You're twelve minutes late. And I've won,' she cried triumphantly.

'No,' he pointed out. 'You haven't. I have. I was *fifteen* minutes behind you taking off because, young woman, I had to find someone to swing *my* propeller for me. You didn't think of that when you so blithely soared into the blue, did you?'

'No,' she said doubtfully, then rallying. 'But how do I know it was fifteen minutes, and not five?'

'You don't,' he said blithely. 'You have to trust me – oh Rosie, who cares?' He took her hand, and they walked towards the hill.

But she was still in shock. 'I can't Jake,' she said soberly. 'I don't think I can marry you on your terms.'

'But I—' He started to tell her that those terms were outdated now, that there was no need, but she was still speaking.

'We've been behaving this afternoon as though all those

years didn't matter, as though we're the same people that stormed and fought all those years ago, but we're not. I've worked for women's suffrage, in war work, I've been married, and now we meet again and still we've had misunderstandings, quarrelled – it's not just the past. We didn't see the same way then and we don't now. We've been pretending all this lovely day that we could go back. You're thirty-four, I'm thirty – We were children then. Today's been a lovely dream, Jake, but we'd wake up.'

He stared at her blankly, finding himself holding both her hands as they stood on the hillside, and a dark shadow of evening began to creep towards them. Not now, just as he'd torn away the last barrier within himself. Wasn't that just what she'd done before? Walked out at the last moment when he'd thought her his? The golden promise was slipping away, but he would not let it this time. He'd try once more, one last time.

'Don't walk backwards, Rosie, walk forwards. Look,' he swung her round to where the sun was beginning to sink in the west, 'it's bright there. The war will end, and we will win. Now that the Americans are coming in, it's only a matter of time. They're bright and full of youth. They believe in victory and that's what will count. And so must we. Think to the future. After this war's over we can fly together again, open a school, give flying displays, people will flock to them for the excitement. It will be flying just as we knew it, but with all the extra experience that flying in war will have given us. Civilian flying is going to expand. Someone soon will fly the Atlantic – we might even do it ourselves, you never know. Don't you want us to be part of it? Just as we were together at flight's beginning?'

'Maybe,' she said dully, 'but I'm scared, Jake. I knew it wouldn't work when you didn't arrive just now. I'm scared of marrying you only to lose you, by losing myself. Help me, Jake.' She held her hands out to him. But he did not take them. The air was suddenly cold.

'I can't help you, Rosie. Only you can. If you're too damn stupid to take the chances of the road to happiness,

there's nothing I can do to change your mind. Not now.'
He shivered, looking at the setting sun. 'Maybe you're right,' he went on. 'Maybe it is too late for us. Six, no seven, years too late. The first time you said, "Let's wait" I should have known.' Blindly he turned and began slowly to walk back down the hill.

Rosie watched him, unable to move, cold horror sweeping over her. Minutes, no, seconds to decide her life. Which to choose? Who was right?

*Icarus, oh Icarus . . . that thing on the ground so still, so dead. Was that the magic that had soared above?*

William had comforted her and picked up the kite. It seemed to her now that William was here again. Blinded with tears as she was, she could not see. He was placing the kite in her unwilling hands. She threw it from her and he placed it there again.

*Fly it, he ordered sternly. Fly . . .*

And Icarus on the third time of trying lifted hesitantly in the breeze, almost fell, then caught a current again, and soared triumphantly upwards.

'*My kite went up again,*' she'd cried.

'So it can, Rosie, so it can,' William said kindly to her now. It had exploded into being on a hillside long ago . . . And the hillside, and William, were here again.

'Jake,' she cried, 'Jake—'

He turned slowly as if without hope; then, as he saw her running towards him his face brightened. But he did not move. He could not. Then as she came up to him she put out her arms hesitantly, then more confidently, cannoning into him.

'Jake,' she cried, clutching at the fringe on the jacket, 'take me with you.'

He detached her hands from the jacket and held them tight. 'Airbumps and prangs included?' he asked gravely.

'There won't be any, not if we fly straight,' she whispered uncertainly, then repeated it confidently as she saw an answering light in his eyes.

'Not the way we flew just now?' he said uncertainly, gaining time, gaining hope, gaining Rosie.

'The worst bumps are just above the landing ground,'

she laughed unsteadily. 'Anyway, how could anyone fly straight in these ridiculous trousers?'

'In that case,' he retorted slowly, 'I'd better take you home to change. There's no—' He stopped as a flame of love began to choke him, and started again, '—there's no stream nearby. Not this time.' At the tone of his voice as much as his words, she looked up at him and what she read in his face brought a catch to her voice. But he still held her hands as if needing some extra reassurance.

It exploded into being on a hillside long ago and in a field beside a stream, but how to find the words to bridge the years?

'It doesn't matter, Jake.' A hint of a laugh in her voice. 'I'll make do with your shirt—'

'Not for long you won't,' he muttered, taking her into his arms.